IN OUR BONES

IN OUR BONES

Jade River

Nine Pentacles Press

Nine Pentacles Press
PO Box 6677
Madison, WI 53716
USA

For the women who know this truth...

"There will be a story of a time when women were strong and men were kind. It will live in our bones. And, when we return we will find each other again and recreate whatever we can of this truth. This knowledge will reappear to open our hearts and show a way for people to live."

The walls surround me, large oppressive blocks of stone in a windowless catacomb. This, they tell me, is my purpose, to sit day after day in this place looking into the future, looking for answers, looking for a connection to the Mother to share with the people. I can't believe this is what they want of me. I fail to understand why one would be called to such a life. But, the Wise Ones around me seem to accept, even savor, these times in darkness. They tell me to embrace the darkness, to become one with it. I know somewhere deep inside me a resonance with the darkness exists, but I cannot still myself, or my thoughts, long enough to embrace the experience. Each day they ask more of me, expect me to step into this existence, but I cannot find my way there. I only want to be with "*Them.*"

Three cycles ago, when I was fourteen, they found me. They came as a band of five riders and a Soft One. My father fished each day while I was kept company by the dolphins and sea birds that flourished near our home. My mother had been gone so long I barely remembered her. She was carried off by one of the big waves that sometimes overtakes the island when the Earth Mother shakes. It seemed only by chance I was not washed away with her. The wave did pick me up, but it deposited me in a tree. Its branches clutched me and would not let go no matter how hard the water tore around me. When my father found me where the wave had left me, they freed me easily into his hands.

I *felt Them* coming, but I was too shy to greet *Them*. I ran into our lodge and peered through a crack in the open door. My father called to *Them*, smiling as they rode into the yard. He shocked me by dropping to one knee. A Soft One swung off her mount, her clothing billowing around her like waves in the sea. She placed her hand on his head. He rose, reverent in a way I had seldom seen. But, it was not the Soft One who called to me. It was *Them*, the five of *Them* still sitting astride their tall horses, soft leathers cut close to their bodies, bows stowed in their saddles, knives in their belts and short swords strapped across their backs. I could not help but move closer to get a better look. What happened next I have no words to convey. It was like when one jumps into the cold sea and it takes your breath away. However, in this *surge*, there was no shock. Instead, a kind of pleasure passed over me. In that same moment, all five of *them* looked up at the lodge.

The Soft One spoke to my father, "Fisher, have you a daughter?"

My father answered that indeed he had a daughter and that he had recently taken her to the nearby Palace to celebrate her womanhood. The Soft One smiled and asked if he would fetch me.

My father gently called to me, "Giada, come. "

I only dimly heard him as I was drawn out the door toward *Them*. It occurred to me that perhaps I should be scared. In fact, I thought they would frighten many girls, but I had no fear. I stepped closer until I was standing beside one of the women on her horse. The smell of leather, animal, and woman mingled together to make an oddly pleasant fragrance. I found my hand reaching out to touch her boot before I realized what I was doing. She caught her breath, but looked away. At the same moment, I heard a quick intake of breath from the other four, and they too dropped their eyes. The Soft One walked to the woman I had touched and asked, "Is it She?"

"Yes," the mounted woman answered, a little breathless. The Soft One then looked to the other four of *Them* who all nodded their heads as she asked the same question of each.

"So be it," said the Soft One.

"Fisher," she continued, "your daughter is chosen. When would you have us return for her?"

My father looked shocked, proud, and a little wistful. "Could you come for her in the Blooming Moon?" he asked.

"Certainly," the Soft One agreed. And, although my father offered them fish for dinner and a bed for the night, they said this news was too important and could not wait.

From that moment on, I was never alone. It was not that any of *Them* physically stayed, it was that they never left. I could *feel Them.* I could *hear Them.* Although I didn't understand how I knew, I was conscious there were more of *Them* and that they were coming for me.

All I had ever known was my father and my village. It had never occurred to me I would leave. Life here was pleasant and predictable. The people fished, harvested oysters, wove nets, patched boats and worked among the trees. We traded for cloth, baskets, metalwork, and, of course, honey. On holy days we walked to Phaistos, the closest Palace, to celebrate. Our community was not large and I knew everyone.

My father was respected and well liked among our people. Despite that, I was concerned about leaving him alone. We lived by the sea, a little distance from the village and I worried he would be lonely. I had always assumed that when I was older I would join him fishing. Now it appeared he would continue to make these outings alone. He, however, did not seem worried. My father assured me he could come where I was going whenever I wished. He told me to be chosen was an honor. I planned to ask several villagers to check on him and make sure he did not become reclusive. Recently, I had noticed the village weaver's eyes lingered long on him whenever they bartered for fish. He, in turn, met her gaze with an attentive smile. I hoped my absence might encourage what I perceived to be a possible romance.

Although it was only a few moons away, the Blooming Moon seemed long in coming. I breathed in the *scent* of *Them* on the breeze, and sent a soft *touch* of anticipation toward *Them* each day. Even when the Blooming Moon began, they did not come right away. It was not until the moon was full that someone arrived. I cannot express my disappointment at the women who came for me. There was not one of *Them* in the entourage. It was the Soft One and three who looked very much like her. They stayed in my father's lodge one night, then sat me on a horse and carried me off to my new life.

*****

I learned the Soft One's name was Reya and that we were traveling to Malia, one of the four Palaces on the island. Reya said it would take several days, but she was glad because in that time she hoped we would become friends. Her hazel eyes were watchful as she engaged me in conversation. Reya shared, if it was acceptable to me, the Queen had asked her to be my mentor. Because I had no sister, and my mother had been only briefly in my life, the idea of having someone as a friend and confidant pleased me. I warmed to her increasingly as the journey continued.

I think what amazed me most about Reya was she never seemed to get dirty. At the end of the day I would be covered in dust from the road and sweat from the horse. Reya, however, would look pristine. Her thick brown hair stayed in its long braid and her pretty face was as clean as when we started. Even after a full day's, ride she still smelled like sweet spring herbs. I never saw her do anything extraordinary to accomplish this feat. It was like dirt did not cling to her. I decided this was definitely a skill I wished to emulate.

Reya was pleasant, and as we traveled she shared interesting and helpful information about Malia. I guessed her to be about fifteen cycles older than me. She seemed very wise in the ways of the Palace. When I said as much to her, she explained. "I was raised in a Palace, not Malia where we are going, but at Zakros. I came to Malia from there. I have never known life outside a Palace. I'm sure if I were coming to live in your village, you would have much to share with me that I needed to know."

I had wondered about so many things since Reya and the others appeared at my father's lodge. Reya said she would try and answer my questions. So, I began with one which I had often pondered.

"What does it mean to be chosen?"

6

"Well," Reya replied, "once every few cycles, one of the Palace Hearth Queens appoints a group of Guardians to travel the island and see if a Young Queen is among the girls coming of age. There is no way to know when a Queen is born unless she is born into a Palace. There, Young Queens are most often recognized. But, many Young Queens also come from other places. Periodically surveying the island is how we discover if there is a new Queen living outside a Palace. A Hearth Queen selects one of her women to travel with the Guardians and they make a circuit of the island. Usually the party returns with nothing to report. But, occasionally, the Guardians recognize a new Queen. The Guards identified you, Giada, as the Young Queen of Malia."

My attention was diverted from our conversation. I had not known a name for *Them*, but I surmised Reya was calling *Them* "Guardians." I let that information seep into my consciousness. Of course, they are Guardians, I thought. The name fits them well.

"Giada?" Reya inquired quizzically. I realized she had been talking, but I had not been paying attention. Rather than ask her to repeat herself, I returned to my questions.

"What does it mean to be a 'Young Queen'?" I asked.

"That is a complex question," Reya replied. A Young Queen is the..."

I was too impatient to wait for what I anticipated would be a tedious explanation. How did the Guards *know* me?" I interrupted.

Watching me closely, Reya asked, "When they came did you *feel* them coming?"

"Yes, I believe so," I answered.

"Did you *hear* them?" She asked again.

"Yes" I answered. "I can still *hear* them, not out loud, but with a voice in my head."

"They can *hear* and *feel* you also. That is how they *knew*."

I had been wondering about something else in the intervening time. "Why wouldn't they look at me?"

"You will discover the answer to that yourself in time," Reya replied with a smile in her voice.

"How will I find that answer?" I asked, feeling disappointed by her response.

"You will know," she responded. "Trust me, you will know."

*****

Thus began my new life. I had known there were four Palaces scattered about the island. It was at the Palaces that people gathered to celebrate the holy days and hear the wisdom of the Goddesses. They were where grain was stored, healing took place and edicts were issued. The people of the countryside turned to the Palaces for the needs a village could not supply. I had celebrated the coming of my womanhood at the Palace near my home, but I had never been to Malia.

I found Malia full of activity. Nearby, people farmed olives and raised goats and other livestock. A little closer to the city center, I caught site of woodworkers making bows, and potters crafting giant vases. But, my first site of Malia obscured all that. It rose, huge and sprawling, on the crest of a small hill that overlooked a red fertile valley and the sea below. I was captivated.

And well I should have been, for the Palace was truly a wonder. Corridors joined room after room. Amazing frescos adorned the walls, and people moved in what looked to me like constant motion. They carried food, clay tablets, clothing, bedding, and many other things I could not identify. I expected so many people gathered together would have an unpleasant smell, but instead the odors of wood smoke, spice, and clean laundry were carried on the breeze.

Around me were so many exceptional things, I know I gawked. Conversations swirled. People smiled as Reya and the other Queen's women passed. Bantering in friendly camaraderie, they called, "Welcome home" and other warm greetings to the women. In retrospect, I realize I must have been a sight in my worn shift, staring at all the wonders that surrounded me. Everyone pretended not to be watching, but I was conscious of their eyes following me with curiosity and interest.

But I did not see any of the Guardians in the crowd. I could *feel* they were close, and it was like a hunger. I wanted to go to them. I wondered what would happen when I saw one of them. Would I *feel* the surge that had flooded through me in my father's lodge? I wanted to experience it again. It made me feel alive, excited, and aroused a feeling in me that I only later came to understand.

Reya and her women took me to my room. I had never seen anything like it. A fresco of a young woman stood alone, the most outstanding feature of the main space. Room was a misnomer. It was not actually a room. It was a suite. There was a bedroom, its bed surrounded by supple, white curtains and lifted high off the floor. There was a room just to sit in, a balcony that overlooked a Courtyard, and in the final space was an amazing thing, an indoor bath. The bath was deep enough that when I stood in it, the water came to my waist. Soft towels were piled on a bench nearby, and Reya sent women to bring me clothing. They had worked to make things for me since I had been found. Reya had estimated my size, and I learned garments were waiting.

Reya stripped off her clothing and slipped into the bath, inviting me to do the same. I found myself shy. Although I had been swimming naked in the sea for as long as I could remember, suddenly taking off my clothes in front of Reya felt awkward. So, I turned by back, slipped off my sandals, and pulled my shift over my head. Cautiously, I backed toward the water. Reya giggled good-naturedly.

"Giada," she said with a smile, "there is nothing you have which all of us here in the Spring Hall do not have. Please come in and see what you can do about finding yourself under all that dirt." Feeling more at ease, I moved down the steps which led to the water and began scrubbing.

The women returned with clothing: a skirt which softly cascaded toward the floor, and a shirt that hung loosely around my shoulders. The women excitedly showed me each of these. One of them helped me with my hair and even convinced me to try a little of the eye makeup they wore. I could see some of my reflection in the dark surface of the bath, and the woman who looked back at me was transformed from the scruffy child who had entered Malia. As I dressed, the excitement in the air increased. From twitters of conversation, I began to understand I was to be taken to the Queen. I did not know if this was common for newcomers to the Palace or if a visit with the Queen was an exceptional event.

I did not have to ponder this question long, as I was shortly escorted through a maze of rooms and halls to the Queen's chamber. I knew in that moment, it was an exceptional experience. I did not realize it would continue to be extraordinary each time it happened. The women did not pause at her door but moved into the Queen's room as if they were accustomed to being welcome there.

The Queen was sitting on a small padded bench with her back to us as we approached. Thick dark hair cascaded down her back in waves, with occasional currents of silver. It appeared she was studying a piece of clay. She turned toward us as she heard us enter, her face full of delight for Reya, and then her eyes rested on me. I could not guess the Queen's age, but judged her to be as old as some of the grandmothers from my village. She was a small woman, but something about her made her seem much taller. I found her to be almost beautiful. A dynamic *energy* shone from her in a stunning way that overshadowed her actual appearance. She seemed wise, kind, insightful, fierce, and proud all at the same time.

Reya said, "This is Giada, the Chosen of the Guard."

The Queen did not respond immediately. In fact, it appeared to me as if she might be about to cry.

That passed quickly, and she motioned me to her side. "Come child. I have stood in your place, and I do not remember it being comfortable, so let us get the formalities over quickly." As I moved toward her I caught the scent of flowers and an undefined sweetness which I believed was the woman herself.

She gazed at me for a moment and then continued. "There are questions I must ask of you." After a short pause, she began,

"Do you wish to be called by the name you were given? That is Giada, correct?"

I was simply confused. I said, "I beg your pardon? What other name might I be called?"

She replied, "For some of the chosen, their birth names are not what they wish to be called when they are queen. If you have another name, you would know it. It would have come to you in your dreams or you would have *heard* it being called on the wind."

"Hum," I answered ineloquently. "I have only known my name to be Giada."

"Then, we will call you Giada. And, my next question... when the Guards came for you, did you *hear* them?" she asked.

"Yes, I *heard* them clearly. I *heard* them coming before they arrived and louder as they drew near," I said excitedly because she was suddenly speaking to me about something I wanted to understand.

"And do you *hear* them still?" she questioned.

"Yes, I *hear* them now. Where are they?" I glanced around, and replied so quickly I almost interrupted her.

The Queen smiled. "You will see them soon enough. And, can you *feel* them?"

"I *feel* them strongly." I answered. "I *feel* you, too. What does that mean?"

"A Queen can always *hear* her Guardians. That is what makes them her Guards. And a Queen can *hear* another queen. It is one of the ways we communicate." She smiled, and I felt our *contact* rise to another level, as if she had been holding her *energy* in check until she hoped I would not be frightened by its intensity.

"I have someone I would like you to meet," she said and nodded to one of her women standing by a door to her left. The woman disappeared momentarily and reappeared with someone following her. I could *feel* her before I could see her... her presence so powerful it *felt* like a strong wind on a cliff above the sea.

Then she was in the room. She was dressed like the Others in soft leathers that did not restrict her movement. Her knife was at her side, and she carried a sword casually across her back. Her hair was bright gold and her eyes a smoky blue, the color of the ocean on a cloudless day. Her leathers creaked as she moved and carried with them their pleasant smell. I was taken aback with how different she looked from anyone I had ever known. She was older and taller than the Guards I had seen before. But, to me in that moment, she appeared ageless.

I could not breathe. I could not think. I was totally overcome by the woman entering the room. Our eyes met and I felt I was falling, falling into her eyes, falling into her. I could no longer find the space where I ended and she began. In the *current* that ran between us, I felt a sense of completion. As Reya had predicted, I knew in that moment why the Guards had not looked at me. The intensity of this connection was not something which would be wise to experience accidentally.

Suddenly I could smell the sea. The chamber faded. I was standing on the shore watching a younger version of the woman before me. She faced away from me, concentrating on a large boat under construction. Her hand held something I could not see that moved rhythmically over a portion of the stern. A voice called from nearby and she turned toward a man with the same distinctive hair. Her face brightened and her affection for him could be seen clearly. As they moved closer, I could see sadness in the man's eyes as he looked at her. The young woman seemed reluctant to acknowledge this emotion, and instead began taking the things he carried from his hands.

The distant voice of the Queen said, "Giada, this is Petra."

Petra moved toward me. She tapped her left shoulder over her heart with her closed right fist and inclined her head. She then reached out her hand. I could not move.

She dropped to one knee before me, her hand still extended, and said, "I greet you, Young Queen. What is it you would have me call you?"

"I...um...I'm...," I stuttered.

"Be at peace, Young Queen. I am for you as all Guardians are for a Hearth Queen." And then, she took my hand.

My emotions swirled, and I could not make any coherent thought rise to the surface. I wanted to lie in her arms. I wanted to stand beside her should she ever be in need. I wanted to hold her if she was in pain. And, I really wanted to kiss her. That thought made me blush, the warm feeling spreading over my face and making it even more difficult to gather my thoughts.

Rising from her seat, the Queen moved the few steps toward us. Petra rose and greeted her with a warm smile, circling the Queen's waist with a strong arm. The smell of flowers and leather blended together in a heady combination.

Smiling genuinely back and indicating me with an inclusive wave, the Queen said, "Petra, this is Giada." Then, gazing directly at the Guard she questioned, "Is it She?"

Looking seriously into the Queen's eyes, Petra responded. "Yes, Sacra, it is She."

And thus, I was confirmed as the Young Queen of Malia.

*****

"Sacra is the Hearth Queen. Petra is Peer of the Guards," Reya answered one of the several questions I had been firing at her after my time with the Queen.

Reya and I sat in my chamber, sipping tea and eating bread and oil from the kitchens down the hall.

"What does that mean?" I continued to query.

With a smile she said, "If you will stop asking questions long enough for me to answer, I will explain."

"All right," I muttered. I much preferred a conversation in which I could break in, but Reya appeared set on uninterrupted talk. I shoved a large piece of bread into my mouth hoping it would help keep me from speaking.

She began, "Like you, each Hearth Queen is found by the Guards. Sacra was found in the Palace of Zakros. She and I both were born there. Because she grew up in a Palace, the Guards recognized her at an early age. But, as you know, Queens do not always come from the Palaces. The Guards *know* a Queen because of the connection between a Queen and the Guardians. The connection spans time and space. It is a link of mind, body, and spirit that can be immediately *felt* by both the Guards and a

Hearth Queen. This *link* allows a Hearth Queen to contact the Guards if...

I nodded, swallowing and breaking in again, "Yes, I know what you're talking about."

Reya leveled a glance at me that clearly implied I should not interrupt again. I gazed back at her without remorse, but schooled myself to be quiet.

"Sometimes the Guards discover more than one Young Hearth Queen. When an additional Queen is found, we hive. Just like bees, the coming of an extra Queen signals the need to create a new Palace. There are four Palaces now. If a fifth queen is found in your time, we will build yet another. Each of these Palaces has a Hearth Queen." She paused to give me time to consider her words, and then continued.

"Everyone on the island has training in movement and protection. We all need to know what to do if an animal attacks or if Sea Raiders come to shore. With the exception of one of the old Warders, I am one of the best shots with a sling of anyone in the Palace." She shared this conversationally, with no hint of bragging. "But, some women excel in these skills. It is as if they were born to the work of a Guard. Guardians have other skills too. Diplomacy, mediation, weapon-making, communicating with strangers, and even healing are among them. Many are gifted in additional areas as well."

I smiled and nodded, but kept the silence.

"A Hearth Queen can tell which women are called to the Guard. In the same way the Guardians recognize a Hearth Queen, a Hearth Queen can identify a Guardian. Adonia, who was Hearth Queen at Malia before Sacra, found Petra when she was about fifteen delivering a boat she and her father had made. When they ride out, Guards sometimes find women not raised in a Palace, but whom they suspect are born to the Guard. If the Guards find someone they think may be a Guardian, they bring her to one of the Palaces and present her to its Hearth Queen. She can confirm in an instant if a foundling is a Guardian. Sometimes, a Hearth Queen *knows* one of them is a Guardian, but not for her. When this happens, they are taken to other Palaces until a Hearth Queen recognizes them as one of her own."

"When a Guardian is confirmed, her training begins soon after. Sometimes they come as young as eleven, although the most common age for them to arrive is around fourteen. Most of those identified as one of the Guard choose to pledge themselves for a lifetime to a Hearth Queen and the Guard... in that order. Although other things or people may become important to one of the Queen's Guard, nothing can supersede their commitment to the Queen." I noticed that Reya said these last words wistfully and I wondered what lay beneath her tone.

"Reya," I confided, "I feel an excitement when I think of *Them*."

"Of course you do," she said matter-of-factly.

"Although a Hearth Queen may choose anyone she wishes, many Queens choose a Guardian to share their bed. This is true with Petra and Sacra. They have been pledged for the last thirty-two cycles."

At the mention of Petra, my emotions swirled. I felt disappointment, possessiveness, and jealousy. Petra was pledged to Sacra? That could not be. I had never stopped to estimate her age. With a shock I realized she must be near thirty cycles older than me. That didn't matter. My connection with her was too deep, too strong. My feelings toward her were too profound to accept she was pledged to another. Struggling, I got up and walked to an archway, my back toward Reya. I wasn't sure it would do any good, as it appeared the Queen's women had some facility with understanding the undercurrent in conversation and behavior. But, I could not face her eyes at this moment.

My connection with Petra had been so profound I felt certain it meant there was a unique affinity between us. I could not form the question I wanted to ask. But, confirming my conjecture, Reya began. "There is an energy which runs between all Guards and a Queen. In a Peer of the Guard, the connection is often amplified. You will know many Guards soon. It is likely you will be better able to assess your reaction when you have met more of them."

I could not decide if I was relieved or distressed by Reya's explanation. I considered if my contact with all Guards would be similar to the one I shared with Petra. If I was going to be speechless every time I encountered a Guardian, I thought perhaps I should stay in my room. However, if something similar to the energy between Petra and me was present with each of them, I couldn't wait.

2

Every morning the Wise Ones come for me. They come in groups of two or three, making almost no sound as they drift into my room. I do believe their feet touch the ground, but at times I wonder because their long white robes float to the floor, obscuring their bodies so they seem to hover a few inches above the ground. I find them ethereal and different from other people I have known. I have no problem *connecting* with Reya, the women in my chamber, the Guardians, or even the Queen. But, the Wise Ones intimidate me.

It's not that I can't *hear* and *feel* their *touch* in my mind. In fact, I *hear* them too well. Unlike the Guardians, *contact* with the Wise Ones makes me uneasy. The Guard's *touch* is strong, fierce and confident and, for me, a pleasure to take in. To me, the Wise One's *touch feels* intrusive. It is as if they move through my consciousness to places I consider private. Their *touch* feels probing and at times disapproving. When I communicate in this way with most people, I pull them toward me, and take into myself what I choose. But, the Wise Ones' *touch* is in my mind if I choose it or not. I find it penetrating and uncomfortable. They do not allow me to reach toward them and invite them in. Instead, their *energy* overtakes me, and I have little control over how it happens or where it goes.

I mentioned my discomfort to Reya and she looked at me uncomprehendingly.

"You are concerned because the Wise Ones *find* you in your own space?" she inquired, still looking uncertain.

"Yes," I said. And I described the way their *touch felt* to me.

"But, they are trained to *see* into you," Reya replied. "If a Wise One could not make *contact* with you, she would not be accepted into the Sisterhood. They train for many cycles to perfect their ability to *find* the interior self of others."

"Ugh," I replied. "Regardless of their intention, it still *feels* uncomfortable to me." With further thought I added, "Is that what I am supposed to be learning?"

17

"Well, yes," Reya answered. "The Hearth Queen is always one of the Wise Ones. How could one be Queen without being able to *see* into the hearts of the people?"

For once, I was surprised and silent. It had not occurred to me that to be Queen, one must also be successful at the skills of a Wise One. My confidence in my ability to eventually be effective as Queen plummeted.

"The Wise Ones are the oracles of Malia. They are advisors to the Queen, the Peer of the Guard and the community." Reya continued, "Their proficiencies are multifaceted and complex. Most of them can sit with someone who is troubled and give counsel or insight. They work to heal those with grief or loss. When a person is mind sick, it is the Wise Ones who tell us how to comfort them. Some of them work with those sick in body or dying. A number of them are gifted with future seeing while others watch the stars for understanding of their influence. All of them have some form of divination at which they excel."

"What is divination?" I asked, interested in spite of my misgivings.

"Divination is a way for the Goddess to communicate with a Wise One. This happens in many different ways. Some can read the embers of a fire. Others can interpret the flight or sounds of birds, or hear the voices of the dead. There are almost as many ways to divine as there are Wise Ones in the temple.

"I do not think I will ever be able to do any of those things," I said.

Reya replied, smiling, "We will see, Young Queen. We will see."

Unlike me, the women of my chamber greet the Wise Ones with the utmost respect, calling them Mother or Sister and backing out of their way. They give me the impression I should be equally deferential, but I cannot find it in me to be happy they have come. They normally hover for a moment and then one of them *calls* to me. Their call comes in both spoken and unspoken language. I can *hear* both, although I often pretend to be doing something else and do not answer. One of them will then drift near me and put a tingling hand on my shoulder. At this moment, I wonder why I did not answer them in the first place, as this *touch* sends a shudder down my arm. Even though I know it is coming, I still jump.

"*Young Queen,*" she will say, an echo of her internal voice accompanying her statement, "*It is time for the Mysteries.*"

"All right, all right," I declare impatiently, as if my breakfast is the most important thing I can think of.

The truth is, I do not like the Mysteries. The Mysteries, I have learned, are the skills of foreseeing, silent communication, manifestation, ritual, divination, and meditation. The precincts of the Wise Ones are deep within the Palace. In fact, it is their realm that primarily constitutes the temple regions of Malia. My journey with them each day is the same. We go down the stairs that lead from my chamber, through fresco-filled hallways, and continue down several more flights of steps until we arrive at a place the sun does not easily reach. Several of their rooms are not dark but lit with light wells from above and lamps from within. It is in these rooms they congregate, at work with the duties of the spiritual life of the temple. They busy themselves with reading, writing and other duties I cannot decipher.

When everyone arrives they stop and gather in one of the central chambers. They circle together, some sitting, some standing, and begin to chant. Their chants vary from melodious tunes celebrating the earth, the Great Mother and the turning of the seasons, to wordless intonations.

I find the latter disturbing. These songs move around the room gaining strength and intensity as they build. Their vibrations bounce off me, the walls, and engulf the women. Periodically, one or another of them will gaze at me. I feel certain they expect me to be moved by the energy manifested by their chants. Some of the Wise Ones clearly enter an ecstatic state during this singing, but it has not yet happened to me. It's not that I don't try. Each day I enter the chanting determined to let the ecstasy overtake me. But, nothing happens other than my feet start to hurt, and I feel bored by the third repetition of the song. There are times, however, when it feels as if there are more voices singing than there are women in the room. This, I cannot explain.

When the chanting is over, each of them resumes the activities they were doing when we arrived. One of the more patient ones takes me in tow and works with me on learning the meaning of the marks they make on their clay tablets. She will point to one of the marks and say, "This is jar." Then she will ask me to find the other places on the tablet where that word is scribed. She will continue to point out words until the meaning of the whole tablet becomes clear. They appear to be taken aback at how quickly I have learned the basics of this practice, and truthfully, I like the challenge. Although I have only been working on this for a short time, each day my understanding grows. I can now sometimes decipher what a text means on my own.

My favorite time with the Wise Ones does not happen within their rooms, but on the outer walkways or on the grounds of the Palace. Each day a Wise One takes me out into the light and asks me to watch with her for signs and omens. As Reya said, this includes many ways of seeking information. I have been watching birds, letting water flow through my fingers, feeling the wind, listening for sounds in nature, and watching for patterns in sacred salt. Although I am not particularly interested or gifted in any of these practices, I do enjoy them far more than darkness. Like everything else, the Wise Ones seem certain in time I will find something for which I have an affinity and will be able to use it for direction and discernment.

Were it not for my *connection* to the Guardians, I would feel certain there had been an error in choosing me. I wonder if any of those chosen before me were as ill adapted as I appear to be for these pursuits? When I wake in the morning I commit to being attentive and trying to understand the knowledge being shared with me. But, each day I find my mind wanders, and my skepticism causes doubt. I am incredulous about most of what the Wise Ones practice. I try to suspend my uncertainty, but I find it hard to believe one can actually *know* what the wind is saying or interpret the way bones fall. If I were to share what I am being taught here with the women of my home village, I could be certain of their response. They would advise a dunk in the cold ocean and a brisk tonic to cure my foolishness.

If these were the only duties expected of me, perhaps I would not be so bored or resistant. But, each day the Wise Ones take me to a place of darkness. We walk down a long hallway lit only by the lamps they carry. At the end of this corridor there is a series of alcoves tucked into stonewalls. They are raised off the ground to a height a little above my knee, and are about seven hands in depth. Actually, they have been made as comfortable as possible. In addition to a jug of water, there are bulky pillows and plush throws scattered in the space.

The Wise Ones lead me down this hall. They make certain I am comfortable and assure me they will return. Then they file back down the hallway, leaving me while the lights fade. It appears they believe I should take pleasure in the darkness. During the past few days they have told me ways to make the most of my time here. They instruct me to observe my breathing, making my breath out match my breath in. They have shown me how to sit comfortably with my feet tucked under my crossed legs and encouraged me to focus on *knowing* things beyond my normal apprehension. If this lasted for only a short time, perhaps I could tolerate it. But, I am alone in darkness for far too long. I can barely stand this, and if I could devise some method of escape, I would definitely employ it.

My only amusement during this time is to *focus* on the Guards. This particular diversion, I do enjoy. I'm almost certain I am creating some sort of disturbance among them by doing this, but this is a connection I can recognize and foster. Otherwise, I'm not certain with what it is I'm supposed to be connecting. They tell me it will come with time and practice. They express certainty that some day I will learn to *see* for the people of the Palace, the island and perhaps even beyond to the distant mainland. They say in this space I will come to *know* right action for me, for my Guardians and possibly even for the others that comprise this city. Once I have a *knowing*, I can bring it into reality by focusing my attention on it or change the direction of something I see by concentrating on another outcome.

I have tried this, and it does appear to work. The things I have focused on to bring into being have manifested. I have worked to visit the Queen, directed cool breezes on a day I thought too warm and, of course, asked for contact with the Guardians. All of these things have come to pass. I'm not certain they would not have happened without my attention, but it does make me question if what the Wise Ones are telling me might actually work.

*****

My life before arriving at Malia was largely free and unstructured. I am, therefore, unaccustomed to this type of focus on my activities. In the village I did have duties and chores, but they were woven into the fabric of my day so they seemed neither onerous nor demanding. Most days my father was at sea. On these days, I often walked to the village seeking the company of other women. When the tide was low, I would collect oysters, wading and diving in the shallows until my basket was full. Each day, women young and old would come together to share companionship while working. The tasks we completed were myriad. We mended small nets, bundled herbs, took peas out of their casings, or spun yarn from bowls filled with fiber at our feet. When a project was better done by more than one, we worked together. In addition to these tasks, everyone helped entertain and keep an eye on the children.

It was these women who brought my Mother to me. When I would laugh or cock my head in a certain way they would say, "You are so like your Mother." They told me how she made up silly songs, how she chose my Father and how everyone in the village understood she might know what they were thinking. It was clear these women had loved her. It was through them that I came to know her too. I learned what my Mother might have done, or what she might have thought. They told me repeatedly how proud my Mother was of me and how much she loved me. It seemed, according to my Mother, no other child had ever learned to clap, talk, walk, or climb quite as quickly as I. Through the women of my village I grew to know her.

Like me, many of the women opened oysters. I always shelled my oysters in the village so I did not have to carry heavy

22

shells back with me to the lodge. And, it gave me a chance to share the liquid and an oyster or two with one of the old ones. When Ritsa, stooped and frail, saw I was about to open my pile she would send me to fetch a bowl from her nearby cottage. The women of the village thought the water inside the oyster was one of the most valuable parts. I would wrap my hand in a sturdy cloth and slip the knife I carried into the hinge where the two shells met. A quick twist would separate the shells from one another and the liquid would run into Ritsa's bowl. After that, it was easy work to open the shell and cut the oyster inside away. A few of them always made their way into Ritsa's bowl while the rest went back in my basket for evening stew. I was not alone in this activity, as the younger women took responsibility to make sure all of the older ones were fed.

After half-day my father arrived home and I would meet him there. Together we would hang his nets and examine his catch. I was always amazed by the variety. Some fish were tiny, while others were longer than my arm. They were various hues from silver and gold to coral and copper.

Most evenings, we would create meals together. Depending on the type of fish, or just our mood, we cooked in different ways. Some of the fish we wrapped in wet leaves and placed in the embers of our fire. Occasionally, we turned them on a spit over a flame, but that was time-consuming, and my attention often wandered, leaving burned edges and, from time to time, burned fingers. My favorites were dishes we made in our clay pot. We would soak the pot in cool water and then place fish, my day's oysters, along with olives and hard peas, into the pot. We would cover it with a lid and then bank it in the coals of our late afternoon fire. In the morning, we uncovered the pot and found a delicious breakfast. Evenings with my father were spent singing, spinning, making nets, or telling stories. Although we were accomplishing tasks that needed to be done, it never felt like we were working.

In contrast, my time with the Wise Ones is always structured. We move from one activity to another, each of which is believed to have a purpose and a hoped-for outcome. There is singing, reading, divination, and, of course, darkness. It is hard to explain the quality of this darkness. It is not the darkness of an evening when the sky is full of stars. It is neither the darkness of a room where the embers of a fire glow, nor darkness where one can see a lamp in another space. This darkness is whole and complete. I could not see the walls of the alcove in which I had been left. I could not see anything in this darkness.

On my first day in darkness, I sat for what seemed to be an interminable time, and when I could stand it no longer, I decided I would find my way out. I thought it should be simple to follow the passageways back the way we had come. Uncrossing my stiff legs, I slid slowly to the edge of the alcove until I found the floor and began advancing through the darkness down the corridor. Placing my hand on the wall, I planned to use it as my guide back to the common rooms of the Wise Ones. I inched along carefully, feeling my way as I moved away from where they had left me.

I had little sense of distance as I moved determinedly on. Even with this disorientation, eventually I began to be concerned. I knew I was moving slowly, but I started to feel certain I had been walking far longer than it had taken to get to the alcoves. I decided I should go back and reversed my direction returning the way I had come. With each step I stretched my foot in front of me and explored the ground before I moved forward. Shortly after I turned around, I reached out my foot to find... nothing. There was only air in front of me. Extending my foot down as far as I could, I still only encountered blank space.

There had been no hole on my walk with the Wise Ones to the darkness. In my own journey from the alcoves, I had not before encountered any gap in the floor. I speculated the corridor had other passageways, and I must have taken one of them by mistake. Retracing my path was the only option I could think of to find my way back, so I decided I would move to the opposite wall. I tentatively began inching my way toward where I assumed the opposing wall would be. My estimate of the width of the hallway was five steps. I cautiously moved this distance. There was nothing. I paced off three more, and still there was no stone within my reach. A little gasp escaped me and it echoed, confirming what I feared, I was in a large open space, not a small hallway.

Panic coursed through me. I was lost in the dark. Being in the dark had unsettled me in the first place. Now, I was alone in darkness, far from where the Wise Ones had left me. I was disoriented and had no idea which way led back to the alcoves or toward the common rooms. I sunk into a small pile with my hands wrapped around my knees and started to cry. I realized I was cold, scared, and the situation I was in was entirely my fault. If I had not been so reckless and determined to protest being left, the Wise Ones would probably have come for me by now, and I would be in my chamber soaking in a warm bath.

In this place I lost all sense of time. I could not tell how long I had been sitting on the floor. I *pulsed* regular waves of panic, not knowing if I should try to find my way out or if it was hopeless. The only action I could think of to do was what the Wise Ones had told me to do in darkness. I started monitoring my breath, breathing in and out in equal amounts. This did calm me, so I kept focusing on my breath.

I can't say how long I did this. But, after a time, somewhere in the distance a light began to glimmer. I jumped to my feet, readying my excuses and apologies. The light drifted closer, but it did not look like the oil lamps of the Wise Ones. It was a shimmering oval that glowed a soft blue. As it drew near, I began to notice the light surrounded a form. Straining to see what the light held, I caught my breath. The figure in the light looked like me. I found myself wondering how I could be in two places at once.

No matter how unlikely it seemed, I was walking toward myself in the darkness. My mind reeled. I did not like the appearance of the woman moving toward me. She looked bitter, sorrowful, and harsh. From somewhere inside, I was aware she was walking toward me with the intent to merge with me. From the same intuitive source I *understood* she was not doing this to frighten me, but only because she was one of my potential destinies. I *knew* if she became one with me I would grow to be this woman. I found this terrifying. The idea that my future held this unhappy, disillusioned woman scared me more than the darkness. Only a few moments ago I would have found this difficult to believe, but my fear had redoubled at the appearance of this apparition. I wasn't certain what to do to keep her from *contacting* me, so I did the only thing I could think of. I closed my eyes, crouched on the floor and put my hands over my head. I stayed this way, and did not look up in case she was still there.

After a time, I began to hear noises but still would not raise my head. I wasn't certain if "I" would still be waiting, having gained the power of sound. But, then the *energy* overtook me, and I knew it was "*Them.*" I could make them out reflected in the light of their torches. A group of three Guards moved toward me with purpose and direction. They wore their customary garb of soft leathers, belted at the waist, their short swords strapped across their backs. I could see the one in front most clearly. Although I was not small, I estimated she was a head taller than I. Her dark hair was bound back, but despite her best efforts, it had escaped from its tie and curled around her face. She walked purposefully forward with powerful steps. As the group moved ahead, their lights cast shadows around a large open space confirming where I had gotten trapped in my escape. There was no hesitation in their advance. They had used my panic as a beacon.

"Young Queen." The one in the lead said in a tone that was a statement, not a question.

"Yes," I answered, my voice quavering. "Yes," I said again, trying to make my voice more forceful.

"We answer your *call*. May we escort you back?" she asked.

"Please," was all I could get my trembling voice to utter.

I was shocked when she scooped me up in her arms and began to carry me out of the darkness. Even in my diminished state, I could not help but take in her being. I could feel the warmth of her against me, and the heady scent of her floated up to me. Although I did not know her, I *knew* her.

"You could put me down," I said in a manner I was afraid was too familiar.

"With your permission, Young Queen, I would carry you," she replied.

I asked, "Is that necessary?"

Even though I could not see it, I could hear the smile in her voice. "We would hate to lose you again, Young Queen."

Sighing, I put my head on her shoulder, not really upset with being held by this woman.

In a very short time we were passing through the common rooms of the Wise Ones. Despite the queries of the women, the Guards did not stop. One of them who had not yet spoken said simply, "We are taking her to her chamber. You may check on her later."

We sped by them in a moment. The Guards retraced the path from the realm of the Wise Ones to my chamber. One of the three opened the door; one greeted the women of my chamber, explaining chivalrously that I had had a mishap, while the one who carried me deposited me gently on my bed.

It was then that I first met her eyes. Something akin to when I had first encountered Petra surged through me. In that moment, I knew why the Guards who had come for me at my father's lodge would not meet my eyes. A *connection* sprung easily between us. There was so much conveyed in her gaze. It held respect, loyalty, intensity, and passion. Within her eyes, the *energy* was so strong, it took my breath away. In that same moment, I was suddenly aware I was dirty, my hair a mess, and my clothing unkempt. She smiled at me briefly as if she understood. Then dropped her eyes to the floor.

"Young Queen," she spoke again. "We leave you so that you may recover yourself."

She took two steps backward, moved her fist across her chest to tap her shoulder, bowed slightly, and joined her companions at the door. In an instant, they were gone.

3

Standing on my balcony I can see the roof of "*Their*" shelter across the Court. It is a long, low building adjacent to an entrance to the Palace and spanning many measures of a square. There are two large rooms, each of which can house twenty women. The two old Warders have a room in the center, as does the Peer of the Guard. Her room, however, is private. In the larger rooms, ten cots line both sides of the walls and a chest is stationed at the foot of each bed. The Guards have a broad range of ages, from the Warders, who I believe might be as old as fifty, to several new Foundlings who I think are around fifteen.

It appears they do not notice their way of life is actually quite basic. They all arise at the same time, eat simple food, and do whatever their duties are for the day. These tasks vary from day-to-day, or at other times, from woman-to-woman. Sometimes they train in their Courtyard, the Warders bellowing directions and encouragement as they practice. On days too wet to exercise, I frequently see a group of them working on bows or staffs under the overhanging porch of their shelter. Often, a group will ride out. When they do, I watch them assemble. They gather in the Courtyard early in the morning and ready themselves for travel. I asked Reya what the purpose of their exploration is.

"It is their sacred duty," she responded simply.

Frequently, Reya appears surprised at how little I know of life in Malia. I know she has every intention of being a good mentor and is, in fact, an excellent teacher. But, Reya is steeped in the customs and traditions of the Palace and its women. She has little insight into how foreign this life is to me. She is kind and never gives the impression my questions are out of place. However, frequently she appears incredulous I have so little exposure to the most basic concepts of life here.

"They must know what is going on outside the Palace, if herds are gathering, if ships are entering or leaving the harbor, if friend or foe approaches, if fire is coming near, or if anything feels out of balance. They are alert for potential sources of danger. It is their job to observe and report what they see."

Pondering the information she had just shared with me, I asked, "To whom do they report?"

Again with a look of incredulity, Reya answered, "To the Peer of the Guard. She collects and synthesizes the information the Guardians gather and shares it with the Hearth Queen. It is the Queen's duty to know what is happening within the Palace. She must know if there is enough food and water, if there is sickness, if there is restlessness among the people, if a child has lost both of his or her parents, or anything else that might affect life in the Palace. It is the job of the Queen and her women to be familiar with all that transpires within the Palace and share that with the Peer of the Guard."

The task of being Hearth Queen was becoming more complex every moment. At first, I had been delighted at the prospect of being Queen. It appeared I would have unlimited contact with the Guards. I found Reya and the women of my chamber were willing to provide almost anything I asked. I had an amazing suite of rooms, a bath, and this balcony on which we sat. Although my balcony was not large, it had a roof that provided shade, and the breezes off the sea were a blessing. It had several comfortable chairs, two of which Reya and I occupied. Of course, one of the things I enjoyed most was my ability to observe the Court below.

Pausing in the open archway, Calida, one of the women of my chamber, politely interrupted. Directing her question to Reya she asked "I have water and wine from the stores and fish from the cooks. Shall I bring some?" It had taken me awhile to figure out exactly how many women I had in my chamber. They were always coming and going, doing things of importance that I would only later learn to appreciate. Finally, with help from Reya, I determined there were thirteen. I had learned most of their names, but even now I was missing a few. I had not even seen the Healer yet. She was at Knossos learning a special bone-setting technique from the healer there. Almost all the women of my chamber were close to my age. Despite that, I found them an exceptionally competent group with a broad range of skills.

Elayn knew about the keeping of animals and bees, while Lista could make anything grow. One wrote ballads that told of the adventures and exploits of the people of the Palace. Calida was learning from the Old Chronicler and knew most of the history of Malia. One of them was a midwife. Nyssa entertained us almost every night with her amusing, but extraordinary dances. Among them was also a mediator trained in resolving disputes. Alandra made some of the frescos that filled the Palace, while still another sang as sweetly as the dark-headed warbler that perched trilling on my balcony most mornings. One of them, Alega, was actually a Wise One, which I tried not to hold against her. She came every morning with her divining tools and forecast the day for the rest of the women. And, of course, there was Reya.

Saying these women were, in fact, "in my chamber" was inaccurate. The actual places where they stayed were down a long hallway which followed my sitting room. There door-after-door comprised what was called the "Spring Hall." I asked Alandra why it was named this.

She laughed and said, "The celebration of the Girl Child is in a few days. When we welcome her, you will see and understand."

Although the women of my chamber were very kind, they made it clear they were not servants. Each of them took turns bringing food and other necessities. But, after a few days for me to acclimate to Palace life, I was expected to take my turn with these duties as well. Calida explained whenever I had something that was required of me the women of my chamber would assist me. They would bring me food and drink, help me dress, bathe or do my hair. Whatever my needs were at these times, they would try to provide them and allow me to focus on the work I needed to accomplish. In return, when they had responsibilities, I would be asked to support them as well. Frequently, one or another of them was called away to use her skills. Accommodating the varied needs of these women, as well as my own, became part of the routine of living at Malia.

Gradually, from inference and conversation, I became aware these women were in my chamber because it was hoped, by the Queen, that I would learn to trust and value them. Over time I could discover their strengths, eccentrics, and styles. Because of their diversity, each of them touched a different area of the Palace. The women of my chamber were witness to the pattern of life within Malia. Just as the Guardians reported their findings to the Peer of the Guard, my women brought the knowledge they gathered to me and shared their insights and perspectives.

Calida's stare interrupted my musings and brought me back to the present. Trying not to be impatient, I inclined my head in acceptance of her offer of wine and food. Reya, however, looked at her appreciatively and asked, "We welcome your offer, Calida. May we help?"

Calida smiled at Reya, shook her head and disappeared through the doorway. Reya continued our conversation, not having lost her thoughts in the interval.

"Knowing about life in the Palace and the area which surrounds it are not the Queen's and the Peer of the Guard's only responsibilities. Both of them have duties in the spiritual life of the Palace as well."

"It is the Peer of the Guard's mission to guard her Queen and the sacred spaces of the Goddess. A Peer of the Guard's primary tool is herself. She utilizes all the resources she can to bring this tool into full use. She hones her skills, both physical and mental, so she will be able to respond effectively when needed. The Guardian's objective is to have no separation between her spirit, mind, emotions, and body. She cultivates one spirit, which shoots the arrow, crafts a staff, or wields her sword. To the Guardian, everything is a tool. She uses every experience for her spiritual growth. The Peer of the Guard is responsible for bringing this practice into actuality for the Guardians."

"The Queen's spiritual responsibilities fall in a different realm. She assures the celebrations for the seasons turning take place. The Queen uses the tools of the Wise Ones to work in the spirit realm."

She said as an aside to me, "This is why the Wise Ones share their skills with you."

31

Smiling, she continued, "The Queen tries to be in contact with the people of the Palace frequently. She gathers with them and moves among them. At other times, she simply *reaches out* to make sure they are in balance and *extends* gentle support. Because she has worked to *know* the people of the Palace, the Hearth Queen can discern an emergency. Many Queens can foresee patterns or use divination to anticipate the coming of difficulty. When this happens, she can align the people in hopes of manifesting a different outcome."

Reya held up both her hands and placed them back-to-back. As she did this, her fingers naturally curled into the shape of two crescents each of which faced a different direction. "This," she said, "is the symbol for the inward- and outward-facing Queens. Indicating her right hand, she said, "One Queen looks out to assure we are aware of whatever is outside the Palace." Gesturing at her left hand with a nod, she said, "One Queen looks in to make certain life in the Palace is functioning well. At Malia we call our outward-facing Queen the "Peer of the Guard" and the inward-facing Queen simply "Queen," but to be precise, both of them have the function of a Queen in Malia."

Dropping her hands, she reached down and with one of them lifted a small necklace. I had noticed it before, but this time she held it out for me to see. Her necklace looked like a tiny double-bladed axe. I had seen Reya and some of the other women in the Palace wearing this symbol. In fact, as I reflected on it, I had observed the image frequently throughout the Palace.

"This is a labrys," she said simply. "It is the symbol for the inward- and outward-facing Queens. Both the Queen's women and the Guardians receive a labyrs when they make their vows."

She slipped the necklace over her head, handed it to me, and paused. I knew she was giving me time to take in the information she had been sharing and also to help me understand the significance of the labrys. In a few moments she continued.

"The inward- and outward-facing Queens must make a *connection.* It is through this *bond* that the life of the Palace is protected and supported. They work as one to insure the welfare of the people. Often, after establishing a *bond,* a Peer of

32

the Guard and a Queen will choose each other as romantic partners. This is believed to strengthen their rapport, and it is also thought to be a sign of a blessing from the Mother."

Calida appeared again in the archway. She glanced at me in apology and then looked at Reya questioningly.

"Would your offer of assistance still be available," she inquired and then continued. "Lista and Elayn have just arrived exhausted, and we need more if we hope to feed us all."

"Certainly," Reya replied, excused herself, and left with Calida to assist in picking up more food.

This left me alone on the balcony with nothing to do except stare at the Guardians' Shelter. I *know* there are forty-three of them. I *know* because I can *hear* and count each one of them in my mind: there is the soft *touch* of Adesha, the insistent *call* of Drea, the quiet *contact* of Ianthe and the now-familiar *touch* of Karis who carried me out of the darkness. Unlike the names of the women in my chamber, I have certain knowledge of the forty-three names that comprise the women of the Guard. I can also *feel* the old Warders who instruct the Guards and direct their training. And, of course, I can *feel* Petra, a sweet, strong vibration that eclipses all the others.

At day's end they return home, to sit outside their shelter working on their weapons or leathers. They take pleasure in singing together, sharing stories or telling about the discoveries of their day. After these activities, they fall into bed exhausted, full with a sense of honorable purpose.

Sometimes in the night I *feel* them. When these feelings overtake me, I desire them all, from Maris, the oldest Warder to Tam, a cycle younger than I. Among them, there is a secret. I do not think their secret is actually frowned upon. It is simply a private connection not made known among others. I can *feel* it as hot pleasure that makes me damp between my thighs. So many emotions *fly* toward me during these times, it is difficult to sort their meanings. For some, this activity seems to be simply a release and a way to establish or maintain contact. The *sensations* of others carry longing and an expression of the physicality of love. Others *send* the simple act of pleasure shared among friends.

33

Life in my village had not prepared me for this. There were no women there like the Guardians. Something in the Guards awakened in me a fierce longing. If I dwell on the impressions from the Guard's Shelter long, my breathing changes and an urgency builds in me. Often when the *feelings* are about to overwhelm me, my hand finds its way into my own dampness. I savor their excitement and ride the waves of feeling pouring toward me. Although I cannot hear their cries, mine mingle with theirs as pleasure overtakes me.

I am not certain if this is an intrusion. Some nights I try to push the *feelings* away, but I do not know how to make them stop. I feel certain the Wise Ones would have techniques for dealing with this quandary. However, I can't imagine initiating a conversation about this with any of them. I picture their shocked expressions as I explain these *feelings* and my response. In addition to this challenge, I'm not certain I want to give up this pursuit. So far, it is one of my few sources of *contact* with the Guards, and for that reason alone I savor it.

One of my favorite times is when I stand on my balcony and observe the Guards below. Most of the time I choose to do this in silence and do not direct *energy* of any kind toward them. The first time I watched them in their Court they were practicing with swords. They were in four lines with eight or nine women in each. One of the Warders, later I learned her name was Hespar, was leading them in training.

She called, "Ready... parry, lunge, feint." And, other terms in what were to me a random order.

The Guardians moved in response to her instruction like dancers, each one mirroring the moves of the other women in the drill. I watched, filled with admiration at their adroitness and competence.

I had been watching for some time when Hespar called, "Turn."

Suddenly, the entire group turned toward where I stood on my balcony. I could make out Karis and one of the other Guardians who had rescued me from the darkness. I registered both surprise and pleasure. This I expressed in a *pulse* of delight and embarrassment. What happened next would have been funny if it had not been dangerous. Karis tripped on a forward movement and plowed into the woman in front of her. This woman in turn lost her balance and toppled over knocking down two women in the row ahead. Several others appeared disconcerted by this upsurge of emotion and simply stood frozen. Eventually, all of them looked up at me.

Hespar, whose back had been to me, stopped calling directions and turned to stare, open-mouthed. Despite this, she was the first to recover from the disruption.

"Help them up," she said waving toward the pile of Guards on the ground, trying to repress a smile. Several of them offered women their hands. With much fanfare and laughter, even flirtatious assistance with dusting off, the fallen women managed to get to their feet. Then Hespar again turned toward me.

"Young Queen," she called raising her sword, "we salute you." One by one the Guards each raised their swords and gazed at me.

After a few moments, Hespar called, "At rest." And all the swords went down.

She then continued, "Young Queen, may I suggest you might like to walk in the garden or view the new lambs in the northern fields? Actually, anything that will take you off that balcony." Her smile was broad, but her message was clear.

"Yes," I called back, in fact, happy to have been offered an escape. "I believe I am due at the Mysteries." Smiling back at her, I turned and retreated farther back into my chamber.

Stifled laughter floated toward me as I made my way inside. Although I said I had obligations elsewhere, I did not leave. I could not make myself go away from the pull of their *energy*. I stayed, watching, making certain I was silent on every front, until their drill ended and they left the Courtyard.

4

Each day I understand another facet of life at Malia. One evening a few days after I arrived, a woman I had not seen before appeared in my rooms. "Giada?" she spoke with a question in her voice.

I had not heard my name used often at the Palace, and was startled to hear it.

"Yes," I replied with trepidation. She looked like some form of a Wise One, and I was afraid she had come to fetch me for a special evening gathering of the Mysteries. Upon closer scrutiny, I realized she was not wearing the clothing of a Wise One. Although her tunic was white, it had subtle embroidery at the neck and hem. She was at least a head taller than I, and painfully thin. Despite the fact she seemed scrupulously clean, her thin dark hair hung lankly around her face. I found most people at the Palace appealing, but this woman was not attractive. She had a beaked nose and her skin was pallid. Her eyes darted around my chamber assessing what she saw and seeming not to approve.

Unaware of my suspicions, or perhaps too polite to acknowledge them, she continued, "I bring greetings from the Queen. These are a gift to you and the women of your chamber." She held out a bowl of delicious looking figs acknowledging the other women in the room with a nod. "If you are agreeable, the Queen would enjoy your company tomorrow," she said, looking at me expectantly.

I went from sullen dread to pleasant anticipation in a moment. Taking the figs, I replied in earnest, "I would be delighted."

"Then I will come for you tomorrow at half-day. I will be on time." She announced, giving me a significant look. She nodded again to the others in the room, and withdrew.

Nyssa sniffed and pulled her face into a scowl mimicking the departing woman. "I will be on time." She declared in a haughty tone. Alega gave Nyssa a disapproving look, but everyone else broke into amused laughter.

"Sweet Mother," I said trying to catch my breath, "who was that?"

"That was Keto." Calida replied. "She is on the Queen's Council, but almost everyone wishes she was not."

"Why?" I blurted.

Nyssa answered, "If there is a rule, any rule at all, Keto will know it and make everyone abide by it. If there is no rule, she will make one up and try to convince women to follow it."

Alega stared reprovingly at Nyssa. "You know that is not fair. Keto is very aware of her shortcomings." She then turned to me and explained. "Everyone knows Keto's story. She was born in a village not far from here. Her Mother became ill and did not feel she could care for her. The family did not have enough food or support to raise a young child. Keto was the youngest of the children in her family. When Keto was 6 her Mother surrendered her to the Palace."

"Keto judges her family harshly. She believes they were incompetent and lazy. When they brought her to the Palace, they kept all of the children who were old enough to work. Imagine how that would make one feel. On good days, Keto believes she was brought here for her own good. On bad days, Keto thinks there is something wrong with her and the Palace kept her on sufferance. She has tried to earn her place here by making herself indispensable."

There was a brief silence in the room, but Nyssa did not look in the least bit penitent. The questions which must have been simmering just under the surface of this interaction burst out simultaneously.

"I wonder what the Queen wants?" questioned Alandra.

"Why has she not called her before now?" Calida said perplexedly.

Nyssa contemplated while gazing at the ceiling, "What will you wear?"

Each one looked at the other as if her question were a *non sequitur* and then began to laugh. Nyssa jumped up and began rummaging in one of the chests that held my clothing, while Alandra and Calida continued to speculate among themselves.

The truth was, I wanted to see the Queen. I had questions I believed only she could answer. I wondered if, when she was newly chosen, she had felt as lacking in the skills required to be Hearth Queen as I did. I wasn't sure I would have the courage to ask her, but my doubts recurred frequently as I learned more about the responsibilities the position entailed. When I first met the Queen, she said she knew how it was to be in my position. I wondered just how similar our experiences were.

True to her word, Keto arrived punctually at my chamber at half-day. With Nyssa's help, I had chosen a soft blue blouse and a long, full golden brown skirt to wear. Although my clothing was comfortable, she assured me it was appropriate for the Queen's chamber. Keto led me down the flight of steps from my rooms, through a maze of halls, and up several more steps to the Queen's chamber. As before, the Queen sat at her wooden table surrounded by a pile of tablets. This was the second time I had found her alone. I anticipated people would always surround the Queen, but I was beginning to suspect she actually spent much of her time alone. She looked up warmly as we entered.

"Giada," she said, the warmth in her eyes carrying through to her voice. She then stood and hugged me. I felt my eyes mist with tears. Since my arrival, everyone had been kind to me, but no one had shown me physical affection. I missed the closeness of the women in my village, and the strong arms of my father. I was always embarrassed to cry in front of others, and felt this was an inauspicious way to start my first official visit with the Queen. So, I tried to suppress my emotions before I raised my eyes to her. I could never be sure what feelings were apparent to the women of the Palace. At times, I was sure they could see right into me, but if that were true, it was seldom acknowledged. In that moment, I could not tell if the Queen was aware how her touch had affected me.

Without acknowledging my emotions she began, "Giada, I hope you will sit Council with my women and me today."

I had come to accept that more than half the time I would not know what the people of Malia were talking about. Reya was trying to quickly impart as much information as she could to me, but there was so much I did not know. Things at the Palace were very different than in my village, I didn't even know what questions to ask. So, I simply nodded, hoping I was not getting myself into anything awkward by agreeing to her request.

"Good," she replied simply.

With Keto's help, the Queen began dragging soft chairs, pillows, and rugs from an alcove in the wall. She scattered these around the room in a somewhat random circle.

I did not know what to do to help, and the Queen had not indicated I should, so while she was busy with this task I studied her chamber. I assumed that, like my rooms, I was in just one of the spaces designated for the Queen and her women. The room was primarily stone. Similar to the realms of the Wise Ones, light wells lit the room from one side. Multiple coral colored columns with gray circular pillow-like tops separated the light well from the rest of the room. On one side of the space arches followed one another down the length of the room. Each of these openings contained an ornately decorated door which obscured whatever was beyond from view. Across the walls of the Queen's chamber, frescos of birds and sea creatures danced. While higher up on several walls, a border of interlocking spirals repeated the full distance of the room. Around each door, flowers climbed one after another, up one side of the frame, across the top, and then ran down the opposite side.

I had often been to Phaistos, the Palace closest to my village. My father told me I had been there first for my naming as a baby, and I had gone to that Palace most recently for the affirmation of my womanhood. The people of my village, traveled to Phaistos several times in a cycle for seasonal feasts and sacred days.

Both Phaistos and Malia had central Courts. Each of these enormous open spaces was large enough to hold all of the Palace's inhabitants in addition to the people who lived nearby. Apartments, balconies, temples, and walls surrounded these Courts on all sides. These were broken only occasionally by entrances and staircases both grand and functional. Each Court held several places designed for ritual. There were raised platforms and elevated porticos which could be used for both relaxing and ceremony. To me, the central Court of Phaistos had been magnificent, but I had never seen the interior of the Palace. I wondered if the inner rooms of that building were as beautiful as those of Malia.

Finished with her work, the Queen looked at me questioningly. "How would you be most comfortable?" she asked, gesturing at the accumulated assortment of seating. She, herself, walked to one of the chairs in the circle and sat.

I inferred she was asking me how I would like to sit, so I chose a pillow and rug near her on the floor and sat down.

"Have you met Keto?" she said, acknowledging the woman who had led me to her chamber as she joined us in the circle. "She knows of water."

Avoiding her question, I ventured a question of my own. "What does it mean... to know of water?"

The Queen smiled pleasantly at Keto in anticipation of her answer. Keto seemed ill at ease. She occasionally glanced up while speaking and when she did, it was the Queen at which she looked. "I monitor the wells and cisterns. I watch the tides and the moon to know when ships may safely leave the harbor. If there is a break in the water system in the Palace, I am the one people inform. And, when appropriate, I bring the exchanges of people at the wells and the docks back to the Council." She only glanced briefly at me during the last few words of her account.

I didn't know what to think about Keto. Her behavior was contradictory. She had seemed imperious and dour when she had come to my rooms. Now, in the presence of the Queen, she acted tentative. Her speech conveyed a sense of pride about her work while at the same time she appeared uncertain of herself. I was confused by her actions, but nodded to convey my understanding of what she had said.

It had not occurred to me there was someone who made sure there was water for my bath. I realized I had taken a lot for granted. It dawned on me there must be people everywhere who worked to keep the pal Palace ace operational.

The Queen looked kindly at Keto. She overlooked Keto's awkwardness and continued, "Keto is one of the women of my chamber. These women assemble today for Council."

40

True enough, almost before she finished her sentence women began appearing, chattering good-naturedly as they wandered into the Queen's chamber. Some exchanged information seriously, while others laughed and bantered. I was interested to notice the Queen was often included in these casual conversations. Gradually, women began taking seats around the makeshift circle. I was disappointed to note there was not a Guardian among them. Some of them lounged on the proffered rugs and pillows, while others set upright in chairs. Including the Queen and I, there were fifteen women in the circle.

When Reya had come with the Guards to find me, I had never seen anyone like her. I did not have words to adequately describe her, so I had identified her to myself only as a "Soft One." As these women took their seats, I recognized them as the Soft Ones in assembly. I also identified myself as one of them.

In an eerie unspoken accord, they fell silent and looked to the Queen, who moved to the edge of her seat and said, *"I call you to Council. I call the women who have sat on this Council before us to be with us and lend us their discernment. I call the Great Mother, the Sweet Girl-Child and the Ancient One to lend us their wisdom as we listen to each other and work for the good of Malia. I am Sacra, and I call you to Council."*

The woman to her left sat up straighter on her rug and spoke, *"I am Titaia and I answer the Call to Council."*

Moving to the next woman the declarations continued. *"I am Aoede and I answer the Call to Council."*

Each woman's acknowledgement of the Call to Council continued around the circle until it reached me. I was the only woman who had not yet spoken, and it was to me that all eyes turned. In that moment, I said a quiet thanks I had sat on the Queen's right and not her left. I sat mutely, I wishing someone had prepared me for this moment. I did not know, as I was not a member of the Queen's Council, if I was expected to answer the call as the others had. The anticipation of the women in the circle was palpable, and it made me uncomfortable. I looked to the Queen hoping she would prompt me. When she looked back, the response was not what I had expected.

41

I knew and enjoyed the *touch* of the Guards. Although they still made me uncomfortable, I was becoming familiar with the *feelings* the Wise Ones generated with their *contact*. I had felt before the *touch* of the Queen in my mind, but this was different. She was the Queen, but she was more than the Queen. Her presence vibrated as part of a matrix which also carried the *energy* of the others in the room. It was as if all the women of the Council were gazing back at me through her eyes. I was astonished by her ability to hold this power. With a flash of recognition, I became aware of the other beings she had called with us into Council and a feeling of warm acceptance spread over me. In that moment, the ancestors of this Council, the divinity she had invited, and the other women of the Circle were all part of me.

I knew what to say and, in fact, found myself saying, "*I am Giada and I answer the Call to Council.*"

After my acknowledgement of the Call to Council, one by one the women began speaking. I anticipated the energy of the circle would subside after I spoke, but surprisingly, it did not. I was still in *contact* with each of the women of the Council through the Queen. There was a strange silence in this room. My consciousness had always extended beyond myself. I often understood how people around me were feeling, had some knowledge of events which were to come, and even an awareness of what constituted right action in some situations. Although at times I found this uncomfortable, I had come to accept and even count on this facility.

Now, as I sat with the Queen and the Council, that sense was muted. I was surprised to find other types of *knowledge* replacing it. Though I had never been told the information, I *knew* each woman in the circle and had a vague idea of her responsibilities in the Palace. It was fascinating to discover that when a woman spoke, I could hear not only her words, but also her intention. This time the women's dialogue did not progress in an orderly manner around the circle as it had during the Call to Council. There was, instead, a random pattern to statements. However, as the exchanges progressed, I began to notice a flow in the way one woman's comments followed another's.

42

Damaris was the first to speak, "I believe there are currently no dangerous sicknesses in the Palace. There are only a few people in Malia unwell at this time."

She described persistent conditions affecting some inhabitants. One of the goldsmiths had an ongoing breathing problem which Damaris thought was related to the season. Aklinna, a Herder, was in pain from old-bones sickness.

"I am treating Thais, the beekeeper, with diktamos for head pain," she paused and focused on someone across the circle. "As we have agreed, I am letting you know we will need more of this herb soon."

Iole, the grower, responded, "We should be able to send it shortly. It has been gathered and is drying. The diktamos should be ready by the next waning moon. Will that be soon enough?"

Damaris looked into the air, calculating. "I believe so. We will make it last."

Nodding, Iole answered, "I will send it to you when it is ready." Already having the Council's attention, she continued. "The winter wheat was a good crop, but, due to this season's unremitting rain, it was harvested wet. It is drying. We hope to have it thrashed soon. We have discussed the possibility of rot, and watch for signs. Of course, if it becomes moldy, we will have to discard it." Iole paused, letting the meaning of her words settle on the women of the Council.

The women all simultaneously turned toward Aoede. Registering their concern, she replied, "We have sufficient grain in the stores to sustain a failed crop. By next spring we may be eating only vetch or barley, but we have enough to carry us through the seasons." Heads around the circle nodded in confirmation, and Iole continued. "The olive trees are in bloom, and I believe we can anticipate a plentiful yield. I know we will all be relieved, to find our stores full after last cycle's blight."

"Ah, that is as predicted," Khloe spoke from her chair across the room.

Inwardly I groaned as I recognized one of the Wise Ones. Although my usual antipathy for the Wise Ones remained, in this moment I could *understand* Khloe's meaning. This puzzled me, as I generally had limited ability to "*hear*" the Wise Ones because I blocked what I perceived to be their energetic invasiveness. However, as we sat together in Council, I could understand both her message and intention.

"The signs for this cycle's harvest were all auspicious," Khloe continued. "With the coming of the Young Queen, Malia has three Queens, which is always a good omen."

I noticed the other women of the Council all appeared to view her statement as relevant. Personally, I found her comments superfluous. Were it not for the fact that I could clearly *read* her intention, I would have suspected her of self-aggrandizement. While I pondered my lack of charity, several other women spoke. One member shared the state of the herds, and another told of the progress of musical compositions that were being prepared for the spring celebration.

A little more than half of the women had spoken when Akantha got to her feet from her rug on the floor.

"I bring with me today to the Council a new seal for approval. It is for Kyknos, the new grower. He would bring his grain to store and seal while awaiting trade on ships." As she said this, she began passing around a golden ring. I was sitting very near where Akantha had been in Council, so the ring came to me quickly. I saw it as she described it.

"As you will see," Akantha began, "it has the image of two identical beasts with lions' bodies and eagle's wings facing each other. It is somewhat like Amron's seal, but it is not the same. Amron's seal has a similar beast, but only one, and it is quite a bit larger. I do not think they will be easily confused."

To me, the ring was a wonder. I puzzled over how one could possibly make something so tiny and yet so intricate. I was dazzled not only by the artistry, but also by the metal itself. I had never held anything made of gold before. With a start, I realized the rest of the Council was waiting to see the ring, and I hurriedly handed it to the Queen.

The ring traveled around the circle while Akantha continued to explain other similar seals and how this one was different. When each member of the Council had viewed the seal, Akantha asked very formally, "May we then approve the blessing and dedication of this seal for Kyknos?"

She paused for several moments, watching as heads nodded and agreements were spoken. "I thank each of you for your affirmation. We will bless and dedicate Kyknos's seal during the celebration of spring." She sat down again, looking pleased.

The conversations of the Council continued with women sharing information about new frescos for the temple and renovations to the Palace. In the middle of an account of the resolution of a dispute between a goat herder and a cheese maker, a woman rushed into the room.

"I am Polona and I answer the Call to Council." This she said breathlessly as several women stood offering her their chairs. She accepted one and sat down with a sigh.

I expected the information about the goat herder to continue, but all eyes were still on Polona.

"It is a boy," she said. "Lavra is fine, as is the baby. It was a long, but not a difficult labor, both mother and child are resting comfortably."

A murmur of relief and pleasure circulated around the room. Crossing both of her arms over her breasts, the Queen spoke. *"It is with the blessing of the Mother that we add another child to our people. May he grow strong, sure of himself and knowing of his truth."*

The women of the Council chorused together, "May it be so."

Several of the women continued to focus on Polona. One brought her a drink from a table in the back of the room, while another excused herself to travel to the kitchen to bring her food. Damaris moved to a rug near Polona and began rubbing her hands and feet. I was surprised that while these activities were happening, the Council again began its work.

The women who had not yet spoken shared details about their sections of the Palace. Some of them simply stated they had nothing to report at this time. When all of the women of the Council had spoken, there was a pause, and I realized I was again the focus of attention.

The Queen looked at me kindly, still with the uncanny *incorporation* of the rest of the Council in her gaze. "Giada," she questioned, "could you speak to us of how it is with the women of your chamber?"

It had not occurred to me I was a part of anything that would be of interest to the Council. Someday, I assured myself, I would no longer be taken by surprise with the expectations of the people of Malia. I searched my mind hoping to find something pertinent to report. Finally, it came to me.

Tentatively, I began, "Kyma, the healer from my chamber, is at Knossos."

Several of the women nodded, encouraging me to continue. "She is learning a technique for bone-setting from the healer there. I understand it uses water to carry the weight of the body, which allows the bone to be set with greater ease."

The Queen kindly placed her hand on my shoulder and smiled. It made me optimistic my first report to the Council had been appropriate. Removing her hand, the Queen asked the circle, *"Are we at an end?"*

Her gaze traveled the room making eye contact with the women. A gentle strength radiated from each of them. It was clear they had influence, both with the Queen and within the Palace. It was also apparent they were aware of this power, and chose not to wield it in a way that conveyed dominance. The women agreed with voice and gesture the Council was indeed over. In a voice resonant with strength and kindness, the Queen spoke:

"For Malia, I thank you. May the Ancestors, the Mother, the Sweet Girl Child and the Old One hear our words and assist us in weaving a future for Malia that brings peace and prosperity. Our Council is at an end."

As she said these words, the *energy* in the room shifted. After spending more than an hour in a space filled with the *resonance* of the Queen and the women of the Council, the air seemed hollow. Sitting Council with the Queen's women reminded me of times I had been to a waterfall. When I first stand near the falls, I'm very aware of the sound it makes. After a few moments, my focus is no longer on the sound, and the noise fades into the background. It is only when I leave the falls that I become aware of the absence of its sound. The *energy* of Council had been like this to me. When the Queen first called the women to Council, the *power* had been palpable, however, as the meeting continued I had become accustomed to its force. Now, in its absence, I was once again aware of its strength.

As the Councilwomen began to leave, several of them came and extended a welcome to me. With less animation than they had on their arrival, the women exited the room in twos and threes. Conversations relating to the topics of the meeting, and some of a more personal nature, swirled around them and receded as they moved down the hall. Eventually, only the Queen, Keto, and I were left.

I could not tell what effect sitting Council had had on the Queen. She seemed smaller than she had only a moment ago. For the first time, I realized the Queen was actually a very small woman. Standing, she came only to my shoulder. I puzzled how such a tiny being held such *power*.

"Giada, Keto, would you care to share my meal? I find refreshment helps me center in myself after Council." This was the Queen's only comment on her condition.

I did notice Keto was particularly solicitous of the Queen as she asked, "May I bring you a plate?" Keto's eyes were full of unspoken questions as she addressed the Queen.

I wondered if Keto was in love with the Queen. It had been clear to me all of the women of the Council loved the Queen, but there was something beyond that in Keto's tone. I found this perplexing. But, I could not fathom Keto could be in love with the Queen. There were so many reasons why this did not make sense.

First and foremost there was Petra. Clearly, Sacra's affections were pledged elsewhere. But being honest with myself, I did have to admit Petra's relationship with Sacra did not change my fascination with her. So, perhaps that was not a good criterion on which to judge the nature of Keto's feelings.

But, what could there be between them? There was nothing about Keto I found desirable. She did not have the strength of the Guardians I found so appealing. I thought it perplexing a Soft One could be in love with the Queen. To me the Queen was a combination of many things, but definitely did not hold the energy of the Guards. Rista, one of the Grandmothers from my village, frequently said love did not come bidden and often did not make sense. If my suspicions were accurate, this was definitely a case in which this statement was true.

"Thank you, Keto," the Queen answered with kindness while steadily meeting her gaze. "I am fine."

And, with that, she walked toward the back of the room where food awaited. The Queen placed grapes and a honey cake on a dish and moved to the table at which she had been working when we came. Keto and I followed, serving ourselves, and then pulling out chairs around the table.

"Here," the Queen spoke as she gathered and stacked some of the tablets that cluttered the small table. "Let me make room."

Keto leapt to her assistance. She too stacked tablets, but hers had a regimented order which the Queen's lacked. When the table was clear, she brushed the tiny dried clay fragments which had fallen from the tablets into her hand and dumped them into the trash. Keto returned, checking to see if there was anything left undone. She nodded as if satisfied and motioned me toward the table where there was now space for the three of us.

Once settled, I watched as the Queen moved her hands over her food in a blessing and began to eat. We sat in silence for a few moments focused on our meal until the Queen asked, "Giada, how did you find Council?"

Caught with a bite halfway to my mouth, I was sure in that moment I must have looked like a young bird waiting to be fed. I tried to pull together my thoughts, bringing the most significant ones to the surface, while attempting to establish what I hoped would be a more suitable expression. Setting the food back down on my plate, I replied, "I learned I have taken a lot about the Palace for granted. How often do you sit Council?"

The Queen smiled at me and said, "We watch the moon. When it is three days past new, we sit, when it is three days past full, we sit again. It is at these times the *energy* for Council is believed to be best supported. It is my responsibility to *call* Council. When we convene, I *connect* with each of the women and assist in *linking* them to each other. Once we establish this bond, our communication and understanding are much clearer."

I suspected this was another one of the duties that accompanied being Queen. My familiar doubts about accomplishing these tasks surfaced. I thought this was the moment to ask my questions about what I considered my poorly adapted skills for performing the tasks of Hearth Queen. However, with Keto sitting with us, I could not bring myself to reveal my concerns. I decided instead to ask more about the Council.

"How did you learn the *connecting* skill you use with the women on your Council?"

"Do you know of Zakros?" Sacra asked.

I shook my head and replied, "Only that it is one of the Palaces."

"It is a walk of several days toward the sunset from here." She said these words and pointed. I was glad she had indicated the direction. For me, it was often confusing to know which direction was which after traversing the corridors of the Palace.

"When I was thirteen I was recognized by the Guards as a Hearth Queen. They brought me to Aellai, the Hearth Queen at Zakros, but I was not for Zakros. After I was recognized, Aellai had me sit with her Council. I cannot say I enjoyed it. My Mother was a Wise One on Aellai's Council and I felt awkward to perform this duty in front of her. Gradually, my self-consciousness faded and I began to understand the feeling of sitting Council. I found, for me, that feeling is like raindrops. Each raindrop falls distinct from the rest, but most often once they are on the ground they move until eventually they merge."

I had never thought of this explanation, but I knew what Sacra meant. I had felt the women of the Council both as the raindrops and the stream that contained them. Sacra was watching me and I could *feel* when she *knew* I had grasped the concept.

"For me," she explained, "it was not hard to *call* Council once I understood the women as individuals and also as a group.

49

Aellai made me *call* her Council and pushed me from one way of seeing to the other repeatedly.

I must have look panicked because Sacra smiled and went on. "Do not worry, child. Aellai was not always gentle in her ways of sharing knowledge. She doted on me once it was clear I was chosen, but I learned much from her which I have no desire to emulate."

Pausing, she moved her chair a little closer to the table. It was several cycles after I was "found" before I came to Malia and was recognized by the Guards and accepted by Adonia, the Hearth Queen here before me, as the Young Queen of Malia.

I realized I had totally stopped eating, and stuffed a bite into my mouth. Both Sacra and Keto shifted their eyes from me onto the honey cakes on their plate. It seemed they were giving me time to take in the information Sacra had shared.

I tried hard to think of some way to change the subject to what I hoped would be a safer topic. Finally I asked, "How many women are on the Council?"

"On the Council?" The Queen asked, glancing toward the ceiling and tallying with nods of her head. "Including me, there are fifteen. From now on you will be counted as one of the Council, which makes sixteen, and Reya is still considered a member even though she has moved to your Council."

It had not occurred to me, I too, had a Council. However, with consideration I realized it was true. Among the women of my chamber there were those with skills and contacts similar to what I had observed on the Queen's Council. Also, until this moment, it had not been apparent to me what Reya had given up in order to come to me. My gratefulness and appreciation for her increased as I took in this revelation. Following this line of thought and with a sinking feeling, I asked, "Should I be calling Council with the women of my chamber?"

"In time you will be expected to call Council for your chamber." The Queen responded, her tone implying she had some *awareness* of my apprehension. "There is no urgency in beginning. In order to *call* Council, you must be able to hold the *energy* of circle. Your work with the Wise Ones will show you

50

how to become proficient at this. Reya will be there to help until you become comfortable *holding* the circle."

"Toads!" I thought to myself. Up to that moment, I actually had no intention of paying any attention to the Wise Ones. I was optimistic one could actually carry out the duties of Hearth Queen without learning the skills of the Wise Ones. This revelation dashed my hopes. Until this moment I had not been able to see any practical application for their lessons. Now, it appeared I would have to concentrate on at least some of the exercises or Reya might be *calling* Council for me for cycles to come.

With another attempt at diversion, I asked, "Why are there fifteen women on the Council?"

"It is an arbitrary number," the Queen responded. "At times there are more, at times there are fewer. It depends on the needs of Malia, the people and the Council. A Council is made up of representatives from many aspects of the Palace lace. There are some positions that are always filled. There is consistently a healer, and, whenever one is available, there is a midwife."

"As you know there is someone on our Council for water," she said nodding at Keto in acknowledgement.

"As I sit for water, someone also sits Council for earth, air, and fire," Keto said joining the conversation. I noticed for the first time how she spoke. Most of the people in the Palace had a pleasant resonance to their voice. Keto, in contrast, had a nasal monotone quality to her speech which I found to be unpleasant.

"A Wise One always represents air on the Council. She can *commune* with the deities and divine direction when we lack insight. A grower who watches over the crops and a keeper who oversees the animals share earth on our Council. They work closely with the provisioner who stores and tallies our supplies. The fire Council member assures we always have a continuing source of fire. She makes certain our hearth fires are safe, and plans for the security of fires when the Earth Mother shakes."

Finishing her explanation, Keto gazed back at the Queen, clearly relishing this recitation of information she must have known by heart. I pondered if Keto would have been equally rapt if she and Sacra had been reviewing what she had eaten for breakfast or perhaps a list of supplies from the aforementioned provisioner. It was clear to me Keto was attempting and failing to keep her fascination with the Queen veiled.

The Queen, unaware or unwilling to acknowledge Keto's infatuation, continued, "At Malia we have a planner who takes care of the Palace building and its upkeep. Titaia is a mediator who works to resolve conflicts. Most Councils have a chronicler who stores tablets and knows the history of their Palace. When a Palace is fully functioning, there are often representatives from the arts. Akantha works with those who make the frescos and seals. There is also a musician and often a dancer who work on pieces for the seasonal festivals."

"It seems I have some of the same kind of women in my chamber," I replied after the Queen's enumeration of the positions on her Council.

"That is true," the Queen answered. "The women of your chamber hope you will choose them to be a part of your Council. Of course, you have no obligation to keep the women currently placed in your rooms. You may choose whomever you wish to be on your Council. If you find you cannot successfully work or *link* with a woman you may seek another, but I believe each one of them hopes you will choose her."

The Queen looked increasingly fatigued. Although her food was not finished she had stopped eating. She made the pretense of continuing to eat by occasionally pushing food around on her plate and nibbling small bites of honey cake. Keto, who was ever vigilant about the Queen, watched her intently.

"Sacra?" she asked. "May I bring you anything or call someone for you?"

"No," the Queen answered. "But, if you could walk Giada back to her chamber, I would be grateful."

Keto glanced at me and then back at the Queen. It was obvious she was disappointed and in a quandary. Clearly, this was not how she had hoped this exchange would end. At the same time, she was undoubtedly eager to do whatever the Queen asked of her. Keto's eyes shifted to her hands in her lap as she struggled.

In a few moments, Keto recovered herself and stood. She nodded to the Queen and said, "Of course." Keto's voice sounded restrained as if she were attempting composure. She extended her hand in my direction and then gestured toward the door. I too rose, and walked to the Queen's side.

"Sacra," I said, feeling self-conscious using her name for the first time. I placed my hand on her shoulder and with what I felt to be a burst of eloquence, I continued. "It was a privilege to sit Council with you and your women. Thank you for extending me this honor." The Queen looked up, her eyes full of appreciation.

"It was a pleasure to have you with us," she replied reaching up to touch the hand I had placed on her shoulder.

Keto stood watching. She appeared to be working at containing her impatience. Sensing this, I left the Queen's side and began moving with Keto toward the door. I allowed myself one final glance back in the Queen's direction and saw her unstacking the tablets which were piled at one end of the table. I was incredulous. It seemed Sacra intended to return to the work she had been doing when we came in.

I stepped through the door of the Queen's chamber with Keto following closely behind me. I was leaving with more questions about Sacra than I had when I had come. Keto did not speak at first while we transited several hallways and a set of steps. When she did speak, although her voice was kind, I sensed frustration lurking behind it.

"Giada, do you think the next time you are called to the Queen's chamber, you might be able to find your own way?"

I actually felt sympathetic toward her and so I could answer with unfeigned warmth, "Yes, Keto, I'm sure I will learn my way soon."

5

I returned to my chamber after what I had found to be another tedious morning with the Wise Ones. I discovered Alandra there diligently drawing in a tray of sand. I sat near her and watched her work. Even in this rudimentary medium, her art was exceptional. She was working on a design in which fern-like fronds danced in succession across the sand. I was caught up watching her creation and I didn't notice someone was in the doorway until Alandra smiled and spoke.

"Greetings, Fauntee." Looking self-conscious, Alandra dropped her eyes. It was clear to me from her actions, Alandra was infatuated with Fauntee.

I could not blame Alandra for her feelings. Fauntee was extraordinary. She was unusually tall, and her close-cut leathers were tied high on her side, showing long, powerful legs. She wore her thick dark hair in a style common to the Guards. It was shorter at the top which caused soft curls to fall around her face. The rest of her hair was long and very well kept. It was pulled from her face and tied at the back of her neck with a thin piece of leather. To me, she was not pretty, but she was quite striking. As she turned toward me, the muscles of her arms moved appealingly as she tapped her left shoulder and dipped her head in a salute of greeting.

"Young Queen," she spoke in a voice low and warm, "it would be my pleasure to escort you to practice." I grasped in that heartbeat she knew she was attractive and was not above using it to her advantage.

Although I wasn't sure exactly where she wanted me to go, to be honest I did not care. Other than being rescued, this was my first actual contact with any of the Guards. If she had been asking me to inspect goat pens I would have assented. I didn't know what "practice" was. I knew that if I asked Reya she would have told me in detail, but often I did not know what to ask. Reya's life, solely comprised of being part of a Palace, made it difficult for her to comprehend some of the things for which I had no frame of reference. I thought if I could only identify what

I needed to know, perhaps I would not be caught off guard as frequently. Regardless of my lack of understanding, I stood and began moving toward Fauntee.

"Umm, Young Queen, although it is lovely," she said, her gaze traveling suggestively over my clothes, "I believe it would be difficult to practice in what you are wearing."

I glanced down at the skirt and blouse I had on, looked up at Fauntee, and then over to Alandra in hopes of clarification. Alandra looked at my clothing, made a clucking sound and said to Fauntee, "Perhaps you could return in a little while, and we will find the Young Queen something more appropriate."

In one smooth motion, Fauntee nodded her head, touched her left shoulder with her fist and said, "Excellent. I will return shortly."

Once Fauntee was gone, Alandra began searching among the chests which held my clothing. "When we anticipated your arrival, we tried to foresee your needs."

Opening a second chest she said, "Ah, I think this is more suitable for practice."

She drew from the chest a set of soft, russet-colored leathers. "Reya guessed at your size. So far, her estimates have been accurate." She held out to me the leathers of the Guard.

"May I wear leathers like the Guard?" I asked.

"Of course," she answered, "We all wear them at times. For Guardians, this type of clothing is practical every day. The rest of us wear them when we have a need."

She walked toward me and offered me a piece of the clothing she carried. I took it from her and held it out in front of me at several different angles. Although I had seen the Guards wearing these clothes, how they worked was a mystery to me.

Alandra chuckled and said, "I will help you."

Even though I had not been at Malia long, I had lost my early self-consciousness. Clothing seemed optional in the Palace, and I was trying to adopt a more casual attitude. Calling on this new skill, I removed most of what I was wearing and laid the discarded clothes on a nearby chest.

"All right, hold this," Alandra said, handing me a piece from the shapeless pile of leather. With practiced movements she twisted, tied, and tucked, reached for another piece, and repeated the same actions until my outfit was complete. She pulled my hair back and secured it with a leather lace. When she was done, she stood back to admire her work. I could tell she was startled by my appearance.

"Do I look that strange?" I asked self-consciously.

When she answered, the tone of her voice conveyed awe. "No, Young Queen, you look amazing."

I gazed down at what I could see of my clothing. Being dissatisfied with my limited view, I walked quickly toward the bath in the next room. In the still water, I could see a pale reflection. Even I was shocked by the transformation. My breasts, held tightly by the leather, had taken on a fuller shape. My exposed legs accentuated the curve of my hips. The woman looking back at me from the water was a woman from Malia, and she was remarkable.

Reya and the women of my chamber had foreseen what I would require so fully that virtually everything I needed was on hand. I was filled with appreciation for their care. Walking back into the other room, I took both of Alandra's hands in mine and thanked her sincerely for her assistance.

"But, of course," she said with genuine warmth. "Would you not do the same for me?"

"Yes..." I began, but my reply was interrupted by the arrival of Fauntee.

Anticipating she might appreciate the new way I was attired, I looked up at her and asked, "Will this do?"

To my surprise, she met my eyes, gestured toward the door, and answered with clear approval, "Yes, Young Queen, it is perfect."

I was startled to see that she met my eyes. In that moment I felt a spark jump between us. I thought her extremely bold by Guardian standards and decided I would respond similarly.

I followed her direction and started toward the door. But, as I passed her, I intentionally walked within inches of her body, moving as close as I could to her without touching. I was so near I could smell her leathers and the sea salt scent that clung to her.

I did not look back, but casually headed out the door and began to descend the steps. Somewhere near the bottom of the stairway I realized I did not know where I was going. I paused, a little chagrined at needing her direction. Fauntee grinned, but did not comment on my predicament. She simply moved next to me, and we walked the rest of the way together.

To my delight, Fauntee led me to the same Court I had watched the Guards practice in from my balcony. Today, the Courtyard was full. There was a group of Guardians practicing with their swords toward the farthest wall. To the left, there was another cluster standing in a circle while two women moved together in what looked like a dance. The longer I watched, the more I suspected it was actually some form of defensive art. Fauntee and I walked toward a group in which there was a woman wielding a staff. I was surprised to see the women gathered around her. There were two Wise Ones, one of the cooks, Calida and Nyssa from my chamber, several women I did not know and three young Guardians, all of whom held staves. This was an odd assortment for what I supposed was the Court of the Guard. These women were, however, watching intently as the woman with the staff spoke.

The staff-wielding Guardian was short, coming only up to my shoulder, but she behaved as if she were taller than anyone else in the yard. Her thick hair stuck up in odd points where I suspected she had brushed it back, trying to keep it out of her way while she worked with her stick. Her frame was sturdy. She showed balance and skill as she moved her staff as punctuation for her words.

"If your staff breaks," she was saying, "it is not necessary to quit fighting. It is possible to go on with a shorter stick as long as your staff does not crack into a point. It is better to dispose of a sharp stick because it could be used against you."

Seeing Fauntee and me coming, she paused in her presentation.

"Drea," Fauntee said as we approached the instructor, "this is the Young Queen. She is here for practice."

I thought Fauntee's tone was abrupt and her gaze, as it met Drea's, carried an unspoken challenge. Drea ignored the provocation. Instead, she looked me up and down appraisingly as if I were a horse for which she was about to barter. She carried the pleasant smell of warm leather with her as she drew near. She made her assessment and quickly dropped her eyes. Taking a step back, she touched her right hand to her shoulder and asked, "Have you trained before?"

Fauntee stared at Drea as if her behavior toward me was disrespectful. Clearly making an effort to compensate for what she considered Drea's rudeness, Fauntee turned to me and said in a deferential tone, "Young Queen, I will wait while you practice." I could not help but watch as she turned and walked a short distance to a nearby wall. She casually leaned against it, bending one knee and resting her foot on the wall behind her. It became clear she intended to watch while I trained.

Reluctantly, I looked away from Fauntee and turned toward Drea, who was still staring at the ground. I found it difficult to carry on a conversation with someone who did not look at me. Setting aside my frustration, I replied, "I'm not sure what you mean, but if you are asking if I have ever used a stick like this before, the answer is no."

"Come over here," she said abruptly, and led me to a pile of staffs leaning against a low wall of the Court. She picked up a staff, held it near me, grunted and put it back. She tried several more until she found one which came level with my chin.

"Here," she said, thrusting the staff into my hand, "take this one and get in line with the others."

I was a little taken aback. Up to this point everyone at the Palace had treated me courteously. I was surprised one of the Guards was being so brusque. I wasn't sure how to respond. I did, however, take the stick she offered and walk toward the waiting group.

"Line up," Drea called gruffly to the group which had scattered and begun talking while she was working with me. "As I was saying," she continued addressing them as they came back together, "I know most of you are new to this, but everyone at Malia learns defensive techniques. It is important people know how to protect themselves. You may need to take care of yourself if a wild pig finds you in the woods, or if intruders discover you when you are alone." She faltered as if this explanation was a perfunctory part of her presentation which had come to an end. "Enough of this talk," she said, "pick up your staffs."

In a short time, I had learned to center my hands on my staff, that speed was more important than power in my strokes, and that the main point of this exercise was defense. I could strike as often as I wanted, but if hit once, I might go down. Drea emphasized several times that to turn one's back for more than a moment on anything attacking you was the height of stupidity.

I thought this activity was far more interesting than my morning with the Wise Ones. Not that I was particularly good at this either, but at least I was outside and moving. Another group of women with staffs began practicing across the Courtyard near Fauntee. They were clearly more advanced. Clacking and shouts erupted from that part of the Court as they worked on their exercises. Fauntee still held her pose leaning against the wall.

Drea moved us through a set of drills using our staffs. I did not actually exchange strikes with anyone, but I learned what it would be like when I did. As our training ended, I realized I was tired and out of breath. Drea instructed each of us to bring our staffs to her and she stored them in an enclosure against the wall.

I was the last to hand Drea my stick. Her gruffness melted away and a shy smile spread across her face as I approached. Again, she would not meet my eyes and shuffled her feet nervously in a noticeable reversal of her earlier directive behavior.

"How often will I practice?" I asked Drea even as I noticed Fauntee moving toward me.

I heard it before I felt it, a low rumble which sounded like thunder. Despite their similarity, I knew without doubt this noise had nothing to do with a storm. I watched as the women practicing at the far end of the Court stumbled, and then I felt the ground shift under my feet. I teetered momentarily before I could right myself.

Drea quickly lifted her head and looked directly into my eyes. With an internal shout she *pulsed* toward me, *"The Earth Mother shakes."*

This was quickly followed by another *call* not directed at me. *"Earth Guardians...action."* An echo of this *call* seemed to come from many sources, reverberating through the Palace. I was *hearing* the Guardians communicating an alert. My gaze was drawn to the far wall where the group of Guards had been practicing with their swords. The wall swayed and in a slow series, stone after stone began falling in a chilling cascade. At first, I was too startled to be afraid. However, as the scene unfolded a long-buried panic seized me. I saw my mother tumbling in the great wave that had carried her out to sea and from which she had never returned.

I flinched at the sound of another crash to my left. I did not have time to see what was happening because both Drea and Fauntee catapulted themselves toward me at the same instant. One moment I was standing gaping at the collapse of the far wall. The next, I could no longer see anything, and there was a throbbing pain in my shoulder. Although I could not see it, I could hear masonry thudding on the ground near me. The noise continued for a time and then gradually came to a stop with a final impressive thump.

As the noise diminished, Drea lifted herself partially off me, and I found I was staring into her eyes with the sky as a background. She raised herself onto her hands, and with the bottom half of her body pushed provocatively against mine, she looked down at me. It seemed she was unaware of the effect of her position. Regardless, I forgot the pain in my shoulder as her hips pressed against mine.

"Are you hurt, Young Queen?" she asked breathlessly and then suddenly, appeared to become aware she was lying on top of me. Now, seemingly self-conscious she rolled quickly to my side and into a squat.

I answered, also breathless, although I suspected for a totally different reason. "I fell on my shoulder, but I believe I'm fine."

Once Drea had moved, I could see Fauntee. When the two of them lunged toward me, Drea's dive connected with me first. Fauntee's entire front was covered with dust. I surmised when her leap missed, she landed in the dirt. She scowled at Drea while dusting herself off. The possibility of further interaction between them was cut short as both their heads abruptly lifted. They looked into the air like a dog catching a scent.

A heartbeat later I heard the *silent signal*. Like the previous one, the next two calls came from many sections of the Palace. *"Fire Guardians...action."* And a moment after, *"Water Guardians...action."*

Drea jumped to her feet saying, "Young Queen, are you truly unhurt?"

"Yes," I replied sincerely, rubbing my shoulder and sitting up. "I may be bruised, but on the whole I'm fine."

"Then, I am called away. If you will excuse me." As she said these words, she tapped her chest and then sprinted toward the opening nearest us in the Court.

Fauntee had primarily succeeded in getting the dust off the front of her leathers. With a charming smile that belied all that had just happened, she extended her hand to me where I sat on the ground. I took her hand, and she pulled me to my feet.

Once standing, I could see people everywhere. Smoke streamed from a window on an upper floor. Damaris, the healer from the Queen's chamber, was kneeling amidst wreckage from the far wall. Guardians were moving around the rubble with what appeared to be direction and purpose. Wise Ones, women of my chamber, and an abundance of others from the Palace ran and milled among the ruins. It seemed in this moment of crisis, everyone had an assignment and they all moved to do it with speed and skill.

I was astounded to realize that large stones surrounded the place where Drea, Fauntee and I had laid on the ground. Only at that moment did I realize how close we had been to being crushed. Drea and Fauntee had risked their lives to protect me. If a stone had fallen on Drea and me, she would have sustained the major injury while it was entirely possible I would have been unharmed.

I shivered as I fully realized what could have happened. Fauntee saw me tremble and immediately stepped to my side, putting her arm around my shoulder in a supportive embrace.

"Fauntee, I..." I began, but words failed me as I tried to express my appreciation.

"There is no need... It is what we are pledged to do," she said quietly into my hair.

"Fauntee?" With a sudden awareness of things beyond myself, I asked, "Am I keeping you from your duties?"

She smiled down at me appealingly and said, "Today, Young Queen, you are my duty."

I knew tonight I would carry the feeling of her breath on my skin into my chamber.

6

"What can I do?" I asked Reya as we sat together on the balcony of my rooms. "There must be something I can do to help put to rights what the Earth Mother has shaken loose."

"We all have duties in times of crisis," Reya responded. "You have not been here long enough to have a task."

"I want one," I answered earnestly.

"Excellent," Reya replied, "I know my work circle could use assistance."

"What does your circle do?" I queried.

"We take direction from the Water Guardians," she answered simply.

"What does that mean?" I asked, realizing by the way Reya paused and stared that she had been about to tell me. The longer I stayed at the Palace, the more I realized how much knowledge Reya had and how willing she was to share it. I was also learning to wait until she finished speaking rather than interrupting. I had just lapsed back into my questioning mode which had gotten me a fleeting look of exasperation. The expression quickly evaporated and she continued.

"The Water Guardians deal with issues which can be caused by water during or as a result of an emergency. Right now, my circle is examining the Palace and walking the hills looking for any signs of damage caused by water or to its systems. We also have women stationed on a rise near the sea to sound a warning if one of the waves that frequently follow a shake of the Earth Mother seems imminent. I have been working with a water circle since I was a child and was old enough to accompany my Mother. In Aellai's chamber at Zakros, my Mother knew of water."

"So, the Earth Guardians must deal with issues of earth, and the Fire Guardians' duty is to secure fires after a shake," I conjectured. "But, what do Air Guardians do?"

"Did you not *hear* them?" Reya asked looking at me curiously. "The Air Guardians facilitate communication. Air Guardians have a *signal* loud enough to be heard by almost

63

everyone in the Palace. Communication among the Guards is the responsibility of the Air Guardians. They operate a post where Guards can come to report progress or pass messages. It is the Guardians of Air who *pulse* signals to warn the others if needed."

"One member each from the Earth, Air, Fire, and Water Guardian's interacts with the woman from the Queen's chamber who works with the same element. These women act together to facilitate communication and develop priorities for the Palace with the Men's Assembly."

"Do the men of Malia have a Council like the Queen's?" I asked. Having had little contact with men since I had been at the Palace, I was wondering what part they played within Malia.

"I have promised to give Keto my evaluation of the state of water in the Spring Hall by sunset. May we walk while we talk?" Reya asked.

With a new sense of purpose, I agreed and we stood. I was surprised when we did not walk any farther than the bath in the next room. It took a moment for me to realize what water we were inspecting. There were two things connected to water in the bath. One was the bath and the other was the water supply. We walked toward a water tap near the wall.

"Reya?" a voice called from the other room.

"Here, Nyssa," Reya responded. Following the sound of Reya's voice, Nyssa, the dancer from my chamber, joined us near the bath.

As she entered the room, Nyssa peered at the bath and said. "I see this is fine."

"Ah," I said, "if the Earth Mother's shake had damaged the bath, it would be draining or empty."

"Right," responded Reya and with a grin she said, "and, we would certainly be hearing about it from the floors below."

Nyssa smiled, too, and joined us at the tap.

"Nyssa is also in the water circle. Together, it is our responsibility to complete the inspection of this hall." Reya pushed a slide which made water flow, and indeed, a small stream ran from the spout.

"It appears everything is working in the Young Queen's rooms," Nyssa said.

"Yes," Reya nodded, and the three of us walked through my chamber and out into the hallway.

Toward one end of the corridor which led from my rooms was the water source used by the women of the Spring Hall. We headed toward it together. Seeing this shared resource, I realized how extraordinary it was to have water in my rooms. No water flowed from this tap. It was clear something had been damaged during the shake.

"This is a problem," Nyssa observed.

"Yes," Reya answered. "We will have to alert the women of this Hall that Ieni will be in this area to repair the damage."

"Why will we need to let women know someone will be here to fix the tap?" I asked.

"Ieni is a man," Nyssa replied. "Men are not commonly in the Spring Hall."

"I see," I responded, acknowledging that, in fact, I had not seen any men in this area since I had been at Malia.

We moved down a stairway to another section of the Palace. Reya stepped through an arch to check another tap. When she rejoined us, she picked up the discussion. "There are sections of the Palace only women occupy. Generally, you will not find men here or in the places of the Guards nor the Wise Ones. Some parts of the Palace are dedicated solely to men. Unless there is an emergency, we would not enter the men's section without letting someone know. We all congregate in the Palace at large, but we also respect specifically designated spaces."

I opened a spout and watched the water flow as Reya continued, "You asked if the men have a Council like the Queen's. They do have an Assembly, but I do not want to give you the impression that it is like the Queen's Council. At Malia we recognize people do best when they have a challenge and something to which they can aspire. It is on this premise our men have constructed the King's Assembly."

Nyssa suddenly became very animated and when Reya paused, she jumped in. "The men have a leader whom they call King. On the longest day each cycle, those who would replace him challenge the reigning King. They identify their King in a sacred ceremony during which the men who would be King interact with a bull by "dancing." I had seen bull dances during the summer celebration at Phaistos. At that Palace too, one at a time men would run with the bull, vaulting over its back and through its horns. To me, it was truly like a dance. With fluid movements, men ran toward the bull, took hold of his horns and flipped head over heels, landing upright on the bulls back. The best bull dancers remained standing atop the bull while it cantered around the Courtyard.

Reya smiled at Nyssa and explained. "The equality between men and women in Malia is a foundation of our way of life. It is critical to the functioning of the Palace. A man who can dance with a bull is believed to demonstrate the skills necessary to maintain this balance. To move in synchronicity with a bull one must have strength of character, be willing to practice with dedication and the patience to work with an animal which cannot be dominated. The qualities developed by learning to dance with the bull are those believed to be needed by a King."

"Women dance with the bull first," Reya continued. "Nyssa hopes to dance with the bull at this summer's celebration." I could understand now why Nyssa was excited by our conversation and I was not surprised when she began again.

"Women dance with the bull first to assure he will not intentionally damage them or use his strength to control them. A bull which does not dance well with women is thought unworthy for choosing a King. Bulls that show dominance or aggression toward the women dancers are rejected. If a bull cannot be found which will dance with the women, it is considered an ill omen and the search for a King is postponed until the next holy day."

Forgetting our purpose, both Reya and I stood unmoving in the hallway as Nyssa elaborated.

"Once women sanction the bull, the men begin their dances. Some men train for many cycles to perfect their ability. The animal chooses whom he will accept as a dancer. A King is revealed in the man who works best with the bull. The men honor the bull in their rituals and celebrations. It is a sacred symbol of the strength, dedication, and collaboration of the men in our society."

I knew this activity was dangerous. At Phaistos, I had seen both men and women gored, trampled, and tossed into the air only to land broken and bleeding on the ground. My respect and concern for Nyssa vied for precedence. I opened my mouth to ask Nyssa if she would be safe. However, before I could begin I *knew* the answer. The information came unbidden. I had certain knowledge she would be unharmed. From this intuitive place, I could see Nyssa leaping from the back of a bull in triumph. In my vision, she was both pleased and proud of her success.

When this image faded, I realized Nyssa was looking at me as if anticipating the question I had been about to ask. Although the scene I had observed felt as if it had taken many breaths, in actuality, I suspected only a few heartbeats had passed. I searched for something to say which would indicate my insight. I finally settled on, "I *know* you will do well." I emphasized the "*know*" in my statement hoping to convey I had knowledge from a source beyond my usual awareness.

Reya looked at me intently, appearing to note my covert message, but Nyssa excitedly began again.

"Soon it will be spring holy day. All the men who will participate in this summer's bull dance will declare themselves at the celebration. I will name myself as a dancer then also. I hope you will give me your blessing after you are presented as Young Queen."

Although I had been nodding as I followed her explanation, my head froze, and I heard myself echoing, "Presented as Young Queen?"

"It is true," Reya said turning toward me. "Young Queens are introduced at Malia in the spring. You will be presented to the people of Malia as part of the spring celebration."

Many words came to mind when I heard this. But, most of them were words I had learned from fishmongers, in my village, and I feared they might not be considered appropriate for a Young Queen of Malia.

Seeing my consternation, Reya continued, "It is nothing you need to worry about or prepare for. You will simply stand on the stairs with the Queen during the ceremony. She will tell the people the Guards found you and have confirmed you as Young Queen."

"Nothing to worry about?" I repeated, still trying to take in this information. I had a mental picture of myself with the Queen in front of hundreds of people and my stomach lurched. Even the thought of simply being in a crowd of that size made me queasy.

Reya moved to my side and put her hand on my shoulder in a comforting gesture. "I am sorry if this comes as a surprise. The Queen will be there with you and I am sure will help..."

"The Queens always wear the most glorious clothing at celebrations." Nyssa interrupted.

Reya gave Nyssa the same look I got when I disturbed the flow of her conversation. Putting her irritation aside, Reya said, "I am growing concerned about reporting to Keto. Could we each take a different part of the Hall and then meet together when we are finished?"

Nyssa and I both agreed, and we divided up the remaining water sources. Reya described where those I had been allotted were, and we agreed to meet in my chamber when we were done. I moved mechanically from one tap to another, checking to see if they were functional, but my mind was not on what I was doing. It was instead on my part in the spring celebration.

I moved through my assignment, not paying particular attention to the people I passed or the work I was doing. At first, the familiar *tingle* sliding up my back startled me. But, I *knew* the feeling of her, so I was not surprised when I turned and saw Fauntee. She was as she had been when I had last seen her. Her long hair was maliciously styled. Her leathers were clean and closely fitted. It occurred to me she must pay particular attention to her appearance. I was delighted, but also a little nervous to find myself alone in this corridor with her. Though I had dreamt, even fantasized about this moment, now that it was happening, I didn't't know what to do.

"Greetings, Young Queen," she acknowledged me formally with a hint of boldness in her tone.

"Greetings, Fauntee. "I responded, all the while looking at the floor.

We stood in silence for a time.

"I *hear* you," she said simply. "I *know* what happens when you look at me. I even *know* what you think when you are away from me. I *know* what you wish for."

I wasn't sure what I felt. Her voice carried a whisper of the intrusion I sensed from the Wise Ones. However, before I could process these feelings, she lifted my chin, paused with a question in her eyes, waited a moment and then kissed me.

White-hot blinding light shot through my body and mind. It was as if a dam had broken and water that had been long held calmly in its confines poured from its cracks, flooding untouched places. I was hungry for her, greedy for the taste of her. But, I wasn't sure what I wanted her to do. And then suddenly I realized she *knew*. Images she *sent* surged through my mind and filled my body with a desire so intense I felt faint. My breath became ragged. And, without mindful awareness, I moved toward her kiss.

In a moment her hands caught my hips, pulling me toward her until we were pressed tightly together. She stepped toward me until my back was against the wall of the hallway. My body burned where it made contact with hers. All the while, she kissed me. Her tongue sought mine and enticed it toward hers. Her hands drew my hips firmly toward her, released them and then repeated the same motion. Desire flared in me as I responded to her movement.

This is it, I thought. This is what I have *sensed*. This is the secret they share, and now I...

Voices echoing down the hall brought me back. Fauntee took a step away from me, steadied me by leaning me against the wall, ran her fingers through her hair, and assumed an expression of casual conversation.

It was several of the Foundlings. "Fauntee," one of them called, "Hespar sent me. They are ready to ride out and await you."

Fauntee replied calmly, "Thank you, Tam. Please tell them I will join them shortly."

"I will," the girl replied importantly as she and the others headed back the way they had come.

"My Queen," Fauntee said formally with a slight bow, her closed hand moving to her shoulder in what I had come to know was their salute.

Her emphasis on "my" conveyed there was more in the words than their actual meaning.

"It seems I am called away."

I nodded, not knowing what to say.

"Until next time," she said smiling and traced the line of my chin lightly with her thumb. Then turning away, she followed the path the Foundlings had taken.

I stood leaning against the wall as my emotions swirled. My body was tingling, alive with unspent desire. There was a part of me that wanted to run after her and find any deserted place where we could be alone. At the same time, I remembered I had an obligation and that Reya and Nyssa would be waiting. I turned reluctantly toward my chamber. "Now," I thought to myself, "if I can only remember the way back to my rooms."

7

"The Hearth Queens of Knossos and Zakros are coming," Sacra said to me.

I was in her chamber and had found my way there on my own. Malia's rooms and corridors were a maze. When I arrived someone had to walk with me everywhere. Now, without help, I was able to find the places I commonly visited. Consequently, I could not be late for what I considered my daily ordeal with the Wise Ones or early to my training in the Guardians' Court. My one regret about loosing my escorts was I had forfeited my time with the Guards, who no longer came to take me to practice.

This new ability did leave me free to explore the Palace. Some of the autonomy I had in my village returned and I felt liberated. In truth, I wandered, at least in part, hoping I would encounter Fauntee or one of the other Guards. I tried putting one of the lessons the Wise Ones offered me to use. I would seek the *vibration* of a Guardian and follow it. Frequently, I believed the woman I was looking for was very close. It was the complicated construction of Malia that impeded me. Despite my best efforts, sometimes I could not locate a passage that would lead me to the woman for whom I was searching. I tried to convince myself this was frustrating only because I was unable to gage my accuracy. To be honest, I knew I was actually annoyed by my inability to make contact with one of the Guards.

There were times I was successful, but these encounters were usually not rewarding. When I found one of the Guards, she would salute and solicitously ask if I searched for her because I needed assistance. I suspected this question was a tactic to conceal she actually knew why I had been looking for her. Although I had long ago acknowledged that the Guardians could *hear* me, exchanges which drew attention to this unsettled me. I liked to think that unless I was directly contacting one of the Guards, my thoughts were my own. Clearly, this was not the case. After this daunting reminder of their skills, a stilted conversation involving a lot of stammering and foot shuffling on my part occurred. Despite this outcome, I found myself doing the same thing the next time I walked freely in the Palace. Well, I thought to myself, at least the Wise Ones would be pleased I was practicing.

When I wasn't pursuing Guardians, I sometimes tried to lose myself in the Palace and then find my way out. In these explorations I began to truly see the beauty of the Palace and its surroundings. I found a set of stairs that ended in an open rooftop. From this place I could see a verdant valley which gave way to a nearby range of mountains and a road that led to the not-too-distant sea. From here I could also observe just how large the Palace actually was. It reached out in every direction, sprawling and climbing as it crossed the valley and eventually merging into the surrounding town. It was difficult to believe this entire complex was the province of the Hearth Queen and that one-day I might be responsible for the Palace and its people. Sacra seemed to carry this duty with ease and grace. My familiar doubt reemerged as I considered if I would be able to follow her example.

As I considered Sacra's pronouncement about the visiting Queens, I watched her motion to the women in her chamber. Her signal for them to give us time alone was expressed as both a gesture and a silent *message*. In response, the women stood and quietly disappeared through the doors that led from the room.

Sulkily, I thought about how this visit from the Queens would disrupt my emerging routine. I was beginning to be at ease and have a sense of my days. At least, I thought, it might get me out of my time with the Wise Ones. Much to my dismay, this was the one activity I was expected to do every day. They felt in order to establish "a practice," one must focus daily on spiritual pursuits. So, early each day I wound my way to their subterranean space and tried to pay attention to what they shared with me. When the mysteries were over my schedule varied. One day was mine to spend as I chose. The next day I trained with Drea. I was beginning to develop some facility with my staff, and I drank in my time in the presence of the Guards. I spent every fourth afternoon with Sacra, and today was one of those days.

"Do the other Queens visit often?" I asked, spinning in my head a cozy interaction with tea and talk between Queens.

"No," Sacra replied, shattering my fantasy. "Thera, the Hearth Queen of Knossos, has never been here before, but I attended her presentation at Knossos eight cycles ago. Aellai, the Queen of Zakros, was here for the summer festival three cycles past. She has come periodically since attending my presentation many cycles ago. Presentations of a Queen do not happen often. Unless there is a serious reason for her absence, a Queen is honor-bound to attend."

I thought back to one of my conversations with Reya and felt certain she had told me there were four Palaces. So, a Queen must be missing. Looking for confirmation I asked, "Reya told me there are four Palaces. Will a Queen be absent?"

"You are correct," the Queen responded with her usual kindness. "The Hearth Queen of Phaistos sent a message saying she is with child and will deliver soon. Her midwife advised it would be unwise for her to travel, and regretfully, she concurred. She and her baby will come to meet you in the fall."

"Is it important she meet me?" I asked.

"Extremely," Sacra answered seriously. The Queens must know each other's *touch*.

Sacra seemed never to be still, and while she talked her attention was also on other things. I watched as her skirt swirled after her. The clothing Sacra wore was a blend of those worn by the wise ones and the usual dress of the Palace. It was not the ostentatious garb I envisioned for a Queen. It did not seem Sacra spent a lot of time on her appearance. She always looked attractive, but it appeared to be effortless. She cleared the remains of the lunch we had shared and started folding a pile of clothing. I, however, remained sitting in the chair I had been in during our lunch. Distracted by her inattention, I kept hoping she would stop and focus solely on our conversation. The Queen, however, appeared totally capable of doing more than one thing at a time and continued with her explanation.

"Do you know when I *reach* out to you?" She asked.

"Yes," I responded wondering why she asked.

"How do you know it is me, and not Reya?" As she spoke, the Queen moved toward one of the many chests which lined the wall. She paused scanning the assemblage, chose one and opened it. Rising, I felt like a puppy as I followed her.

"Well," I replied. "I *know* you."

"Exactly," she said as she deposited the stack of clothing she carried into the chest she had chosen, closed the lid and sat on it to face me.

Looking at me intently, the Queen continued, "It is best if you *know* each of the Hearth Queens. If raiders come from the sea or a great wave hits their part of the island, a Queen can *contact* the others to warn them or ask for assistance. I find it is easier to recognize someone's *energy* when I have met them... been in their presence. Do you also?"

I was caught off guard by Sacra's sudden focus and her question. "Umm...yes." I stammered. I do think it is easier to understand a *message* when I have met the person and know how she communicates."

"And so, I believe, do the other Hearth Queens." She agreed, and as quickly as her attention had been on me it was gone. Sacra stepped back and again examined the chests. She appeared to be cataloging contents, nodding her head while checking off an invisible list. Finally, she identified the chest she was looking for and opened it. She rifled among the contents, choosing from them a package tied in soft cloth.

Sacra held out the bundle to me and said, "Remember, when we talked about Adonia who was the Hearth Queen of Malia before me? She made the dress which I wore when I was presented to the people." She continued as if I had already seen what was in the package and knew what she was talking about. "I have made one for you. I hope it will..."

Her explanation halted as she took in my blank look.

"Please," she said, smiling and handing me the package, "open it."

I walked back to the table, sat down the bundle, and untied it. Layer after layer of multicolored, patterned fabric tumbled from the package along with a soft-laced bodice. Setting those aside, farther down in the parcel I found an elaborately

74

embroidered double apron and a wide cloth belt. As I gazed at these garments, I noticed they seemed to have a strange sheen. In fact, if I tipped my head to the side, they actually appeared to glow.

"Do they truly glow?" I blurted, again picking up the multicolored material and holding it out in front of me. What emerged was tier after tier of a magnificent, floor-length skirt.

The Queen looked at me with astonishment. "Can you truly see their radiance?"

I nodded, not fully understanding when she said, "You have far more ability than anyone suspects. These garments are made with intention. Incantations were chanted as the fiber was spun and woven. Invocations were sung as the fabric was sewn. In this clothing every stitch of embroidery and each knot carries a charm. The making of a Queen's ritual attire is, in itself, a sacred act. It is one of the magics of the Wise Ones. When a Hearth Queen's dress is, made, portions of the previous Queens clothing are incorporated..."

Her voice faded into the background as I stood frozen, the flounces of the skirt still clutched in my hands. I held magic. Not something which might be magic, but a true magic I could see and feel. In that moment, my perception unexpectedly altered. I could see Sacra, but I could also see other beings around her. She was encircled on every side by a group of vaporous women. I tried to focus on them, but they shifted, never becoming solid. They looked as other things do when you glimpse them through the currents above a fire.

There were too many of them to count. Each one was different and yet in some way, they were all similar. Every one had the same look of fierce gentleness. All of them wore the same dress, and yet, each of them was distinct. I could see generations of Hearth Queens standing alongside Sacra staring intently at me. I felt awe and wonder, apprehension and unease. For the first time, I understood myself to be part of a lineage of Hearth Queens spanning back farther than I could imagine. After a time, one of the Queens floated in front of Sacra. Although she was not appreciably different than the others, I still knew her to be ancient...the first Hearth Queen. She was from a time when the Hearth was only a fire her people gathered around. From this beginning, through the generations, the Queen's responsibility had remained the same. We were the inward looking Queens, honoring our pledge to safeguard our people.

This transparent figure superimposed herself over Sacra. As I watched, the features of the two Queens shifted and merged. I could still see Sacra through the mist of the older Queen, but the colors of their hair blended together into a deep ebony. I watched as the lines of Sacra's face altered, and she appeared to become taller. Almost before I could take in that image, another Queen stepped from Sacra's side and stood in front of her. Ever more quickly, one after another, the women moved forward, blended into the current Hearth Queen and disappeared. Watching this phenomenon, I understood Sacra had access to the wisdom of all the previous Queens of Malia. I also knew that, in time, this gift would be mine as well.

I could not tell if Sacra was aware of what was happening. She stood perfectly still, her expression did not change. I thought perhaps she was conscious of the encounter and choose not to move in order to facilitate it. I also considered it was possible this incident was happening out of time, and she simply stood frozen in that moment. The Wise Ones said magic happened outside the bounds of time and space. I wasn't sure what they meant, but regardless, I thought I might be experiencing it.

I backed away and dropped into one of the chairs surrounding the table. With that movement, the room surged back to normal.

Sacra blinked once and then asked, "Are you all right?"

"Umm, yes." I responded, not knowing if I actually spoke the truth. I wondered how I would begin to talk about this experience. I tried framing it in words, but nothing made any sense. Sacra did not say, "Oh, did you just see all the Hearth Queens since the beginning of time?" or some helpful other introduction to the topic. So, I sat, feeling awkward and overwhelmed.

I had always had an awareness of things outside the ordinary, but never before had I seen what seemed to be a gathering of departed spirits. I thought I should be comforted by the presence of the many Queens, but instead they scared me. Before I came to the Palace, when I was frightened my father would wrap me in his arms to comfort me. I thought about how much I would like his familiar touch right now and remembered him saying that if I sent for him, he would come to Malia.

"May my father come to the presentation?" I asked the Queen in what must have seemed like an extreme departure from our previous conversation.

The Queen blinked again and nodded. "Of course, your father would be welcome at your presentation. Is there anyone else you would like to invite?"

"I don't have any other family, and I think the other people from my village would find it difficult to be away from their homes and animals," I admitted.

Sacra looked at me thoughtfully. She walked to my side and gently put her hand on my shoulder. I could only stare at the ground, afraid that if I said anything I would cry.

After a short time she spoke. "I will go and arrange for a message to be sent to your father. It is only a few days until the spring celebration so we will have to be quick." I nodded, a lump still in my throat. All I could manage was a simple, "Thank you." The Queen's hand tightened on my shoulder and then she disappeared from the room.

*****

Aellai, the Hearth Queen of Zakros, was the first to arrive. She and her entourage spilled down the steps of the south entrance and into the Palace. There were many more of them than I had expected. Men, women, children, horses, and dogs all swarmed up the steps and into the central Court of the Palace. Standing on a balcony which faced the Court, I could not make out the Queen until I spotted a group of Guards. It had not occurred to me that, of course, the Queen would be traveling with some of her Guardians.

Trying to calculate the number of people streaming into the Courtyard, I wondered if Aellai had brought all of her Guards and half of the population of her Palace. I watched as what I thought was the last of her Guardians moved into the central Court, four of them bearing aloft a large square curtained box on horizontal poles. I was bewildered about the purpose of this contrivance. I watched as the four Guards carrying the box all simultaneously knelt to one knee. Another Guardian stepped forward, opened the curtains and extended her hand. Amid much grumbling, an ancient woman emerged.

It was not the Queen who caught my attention, it was the Guardian who offered her hand to the Queen who drew me. I felt a familiar surge like the one I had sensed when the Guards first came for me at my father's lodge. And, like the Guards who had discovered me, the woman paused in what she was doing and looked up in my direction. A swift current sprang between us. I knew this *feeling*. It was the same sensation I had when I first met Petra. I had little doubt I was looking at Zakros Peer of the Guard.

Aellai was aware of the interaction. She slapped her hand down into the upturned palm of the waiting Guardian.

"Thekia," Aellai thundered, in a space made to carry sound, the irritation in her voice rang clearly across the closed Courtyard. "I could have toppled on my head while you surveyed Malia's new Young Queen." Thekia's focus snapped back to Aellai, and her arm dipped from the weight of the old woman.

I stared at Thekia in fascination. I guessed her to be somewhere around thirty-five cycles old. I inferred she must be around thirty cycles younger then Aellai. Petra and Sacra were close in age. As a result, it had not occurred to me that a Hearth Queen and her Palace's Peer of the Guard could differ widely in age. But, here before me was proof.

I thought there was a vast difference between these two Peers of the Guard. Petra was solid, her *energy* underwritten by cycles of awareness, concern, and command. I felt I would be safe with her under any circumstances. The *connection* with Thekia was similar, but each woman was distinct. I felt in Thekia's *touch* naiveté coupled with strength and vitality. I found both of them appealing and decided it could take me days of contemplation to decide which one was more captivating. Now, I was almost certain the Peer of the Guard from Knossos would be traveling with their Hearth Queen. I wondered if I would have a similar response to her.

I puzzled over what made the *touch* of these Peers of the Guard so intense. Each of the Guardians had power, and yet I felt a concentration of strength in the Peers. They did not seem innately different than the other Guards and yet, there was something exceptional about their *contact*. I *sensed* each of these women was constantly in *touch* with all of the other Guardians in her Palace and now I suspected with the other Peers of the Guard as well. A steady *emanation* of information and details from multiple Guardians was consistently coming toward them. I wondered if the directed *signal* of multiple Guardians amplified the *energy* of the Peers and gave them the resonance which I found so fascinating. It struck me that their experience would be somewhat akin to constantly sitting Council. To me the *energy* of Council had been dynamic, and I felt different after having sat with that level of *contact*. I wondered if the Peers of the Guard had something akin to that quality of *awareness* all the time. I did not have long to consider this because Aellai began shouting.

"Sacra?" Aellai called, scanning the multiple openings in the central Court. I thought she was presumptuous to expect Sacra to be nearby when she arrived at Malia. There was a short pause during which Aellai spotted and targeted Adesha, one of Malia's Guards, and walked toward her.

"Where is Sacra?" she inquired. Although her request was stated as a demand, she *emanated* a charm which took the edge off the command. Her face brightened and she *focused* genuine interest in Adesha when she spoke. I noticed her request carried an undercurrent of a *resonance* which was quite compelling. Until this moment, nothing about Aellai suggested that I would like her. Now, though I believed her to be self-absorbed, I also thought she was charismatic. It was a fascinating combination. Aellai had all the charm and power of Sacra with none of her humility. I pondered how different it would be to serve a Hearth Queen rather than to be her colleague. I quickly thanked as many Goddesses as I could remember that I had been called to Malia and not to one of the other Palaces.

Adesha tapped her shoulder and inclined her head before responding, "Greetings Queen of Zakros. I believe she *knows* of your arrival and should be here shortly."

Appearing somewhat placated, Aellai focused her attention elsewhere. She turned toward the assemblage and, with her voice appreciably kinder, called. "Eidothea." A woman appearing to be Aellai's age limped from among the crowd.

"I am fatigued from the journey," Aellai pronounced. "When Sacra arrives and shows me where we will be staying, I will rest."

Observing the *connection* which leapt between them, I believed Eidothea to be one of Aellai's Council. I remembered Sacra's comments that, if I chose, the women now in my chamber could be with me for the rest of my life. I wondered how long these two women had been sitting Council together? Looking at both of them, I believed it was Eidothea who was more in need of rest. I suspected that, while Aellai had been carried to Malia, Eidothea had walked. Eidothea was clearly exhausted, but she nodded determinedly at the Queen. Aellai seemed thoughtless about Eidothea's condition but there was kindness in their interaction.

Before Aellai could give Eidothea further instruction, Sacra glided down the central steps and into the Courtyard. She appeared outwardly unruffled by the chaos of the assembled group. I deeply appreciated Sacra in this moment, especially in contrast to Aellai. My opinion of Aellai was again countered by the way she looked up at Sacra with undisguised pleasure. I remembered that Sacra had grown up in Zakros. Judging by her age, I assumed Aellai would have been Hearth Queen then.

"Sacra, my dear," she declared as she moved across the enclosure toward her, and in a moment they were in each other's arms. The embrace lasted so long that I became self-conscious watching it. Although they appeared not to care if they were observed, their *connection* carried an intimacy which caused me to feel awkward. In another pair of women, I might have suspected an encounter like this implied a sexual bond. In this case, even though their contact was familiar, it carried only the undercurrent of affection. It did, however, convey a profound affinity between these two women who had few equals. After a time, they stepped back, but their conversation was too quiet for me to hear. Eventually, Sacra took Aellai's hand, and they left the Courtyard traveling up the steps through which Sacra had entered.

In Aellai's absence, her people began the tedious work which accompanies travel. Guardians took chest after chest off donkeys. Some of the people in the square moved to assist them, and soon there was a large stack of belongings in the Courtyard. From what I overheard among the people of Zakros, I deduced some of these chests carried items for the spring ritual and gifts for Sacra. However, it appeared most of the chests were filled with Aellai's possessions. Although I had never witnessed Sacra in a similar situation, I suspected that no matter how tired she was, she would have been in the Courtyard assisting in the work rather than on her way to rest.

A few at a time, Malia's Guardians began appearing in the Courtyard and working alongside Zakros guards. Introductions and cheerful banter passed among them. Even between those who seemed never to have met before, there appeared to be a sense of recognition and camaraderie.

It took my breath away when Petra strode into the enclosure toward Thekia. The two women greeted each other warmly and clasped arms at the elbow. Clearly, they had met before and enjoyed each other's company. Not pausing long for pleasantries, both stepped forward and began assisting with Aellai's formidable pile.

Before even half of the chests were gone, news came that Thera, Knossos' Hearth Queen, had arrived. She had made her journey by sea and was being welcomed at the north gate. Malia's northern entrance faced the water, and it was only a short walk from there to the Palace. My vantage point in the central Court did not afford me a view of Thera's approach.

Although I would have never called Malia tranquil, the buzz which now filled the air throughout the Palace was intense. The arrival of the other Palaces Hearth Queens, preparations for the celebration, and the presentation of a new Queen all combined to bring Malia's residents to a level of excitement I had never experienced before. People were in movement everywhere. Women twittered, gossiping in good-natured anticipation as they moved from one activity to another. Boxes and chests sped by, their bulk blocking the heads of the persons carrying them. It amused me to imagine these objects were traveling by themselves.

The Palace was spacious, and I had never really felt it was crowded before. Now, however, *energy* pressed in on me from all fronts.

Despite the chaos, I was reluctant to leave my place. Sacra had sent word my father would arrive today. I guessed that his most likely entrance would be one that led into the central Court. So, I stationed myself on a balcony from which I could see the entire area. Although I was curious, and would normally have chosen to go to the northern gate to see Thera, right now I was anticipating a reunion with my father. Half-day had come and gone and afternoon trickled by as only time can when one is waiting. Reya had come to join me for a while, but she had been called away to other duties. After she was gone, I simply sat, my chin resting on my hand while I kept vigil.

I did not see him, but I heard his laugh. My father's laugh had always been hearty and infectious. With a flash of recognition, I leaped from my lookout and began running down steps and dashing through halls which led to the central Court. Breathless from my run, I charged into the mass of people congregated in the Court. I headed in the direction from which I had heard my father. The Court was even more crowded than I had thought from above. My movement was slow and frequently impeded by the people bustling by, full of purpose and excitement. I turned my head to listen, hoping to locate him, but I did not hear him again.

Suddenly, in a break in the crowd, I could see my father bantering good-naturedly with Ritsa. I could not believe Ritsa had made the journey. She must be nearly as old as Aellai. Looking beyond my father and Ritsa, I realized a handful of people from my village accompanied them. It was good to see the others, but I was overwhelmed with delight at seeing my father. I had not known how much I had missed him until he was there. Although I had not actually been at Malia long, so much had transpired I felt as if it had been several cycles since I had seen him. I push through the crowd, and ran the last few steps, launching myself toward him.

The impact of my collision with my father rocked him backward. Fortunately, he was a sturdy man and not easily knocked off balance. He recovered quickly, clasped me by the shoulders and held me out from him so he could look me over. After a moment's inspection, my father wrapped me in his arms and hugged me so tightly he picked me up off the ground. Eventually, he sat me down, but it seemed neither of us wanted to let go. We rocked gently back and forth for a time.

Finally, he again took me by the shoulders and held me away from him.

"You look different, so grown up. I'm not sure I would have recognized you if it were not for your…" He paused trying to find the right words. Smiling, he continued, "…attempt to knock me over."

I knew my father and understood his words were meant to tease. Normally, I would have replied in a similar manner, but at that moment I found myself holding back tears. I smiled at him, took his hand, and turned toward the others from the village.

Five of them had arrived with my father, Aspasia, the weaver, among them. I hoped this indicated the relationship I had hoped for between them was becoming a reality. I speculated her motivation for coming had been as much to be with my father as it had been to see my presentation. This made me smile. Along with Aspasia, there was Eudora who had been a friend since we were children, and Endre and his companion who sometimes fished with my father. And, of course there was Ritsa. Reluctantly releasing my father's hand, I put my arms around her. My pleasure at seeing Ritsa vied with my concern. It could not have been easy for a woman of her age to make this long a journey.

Putting my hand on her shoulder, I asked earnestly, "Ritsa, why have you come all this way?"

She smiled and pushed a lock of hair away from my face. "How often does one have the opportunity to see a new Queen presented?" she answered seriously and then continued. "And, it is even rarer to see a young girl you have known since she was born presented as a Young Queen."

I smiled at her acknowledgment of our connection. Before coming to Malia, my entire life had been spent in the company of the people of my village. Being away, I had come to realize how significant it was to be with those with whom one shared a history. Even now, if I were to simply say the name "Nilo" every one of these people would laugh as the image of a staggering, scruffy dog came to mind. Despite his appearance, Nilo was irresistibly charming and could win treats from even the most hardened curmudgeon. The bedraggled dog had become an icon in the village. His ability to wheedle delicacies from people caused us to use his name as a descriptor for anyone who exhibited similar behavior. Despite being surrounded by chaos, I grinned to myself and basked in the warm pleasure of having these villagers nearby.

I did not have long to dwell in this reverie because Titaia, the mediator from the Queen's chamber, made her way through the crowd to my side.

"Young Queen, this must be your father," she said smiling as she glanced back and forth between the two of us.

"Yes," I responded, "and these people are all from my village. They journeyed with my father for the presentation."

"Ah," Titaia replied, "it is good to have one's friends and family near for such an occasion. I have offered to escort your people while they are here."

Turning toward my father she asked, "Friend, may I take you and these other visitors to your lodgings?"

My father grinned his winning smile at Titaia and said, "It would be my pleasure to accompany you."

Titaia then turned to me. "Young Queen, your women await you in your chamber."

Wistfully, I told my father and the others I would see them again soon and turned toward my rooms. As I rounded the first flight of steps, I gazed through an opening into the central Court. I could see Titaia leading them to the eastern side of the Palace while she and my father carried on a lively conversation.

*****

Titaia was correct, the women of my chamber were indeed waiting. In fact, it was the first time I had seen them all assembled in one place. This alone told me it was an auspicious occasion.

The women of my chamber were never idle. Although I normally saw each of them every day, we only occasionally had free time to spend together. Elayn would tell me, as she rushed out the door, that she was off to deliver lambs from an ewe believed to be carrying triplets. I saw Lista after she had been up all night bringing in the spring grain harvest. Alega was frequently off to a discussion of predictions with the Wise Ones. Kyma, the healer, had returned from Knossos, and I was meeting her for the first time tonight. It was a wonder to see all of them together in one place.

They had scented my bath and put handfuls of colored flowers to float on its surface. Soft towels and perfumed oils waited on a bench nearby. I remembered Calida saying that when things were required of me, the women of my chamber would assist me. I wondered if this was one of those times.

"Young Queen," Reya said and the women around the room nodded acknowledging my arrival with a formal greeting.

"Tomorrow we will all be up before the sun," she continued, "so, we have come this evening to help you prepare for tomorrow's ceremony."

During the time I had been at Malia, my relationship with Reya had become friendly and casual. I grinned at her solemn speech, hoping it would lighten the mood. She smiled at me warmly, but her demeanor was unchanged. I understood she was trying to cue me that this was a serious moment.

Trying again, Reya spoke, "Young Queen, we would assist you with your preparations. We have made a bath for you which is meant to cleanse the spirit as well as the body." She gave me a short nod, indicating it was my turn to do something.

Well, I thought to myself, the first step in taking a bath is to remove one's clothing. Tentatively, I began unfastening my tunic. Reya nodded again, approving. Fluidly, Alandra stepped behind me and Elayn moved to my side. Alandra slipped my tunic from my shoulders, and Elayn gathered in the rest of my clothing as I removed it. Kyma stepped forward and gestured toward the bath. She offered me her hand and led me to the stairs, pausing to indicate I should descend alone. As I started down the steps, Nyssa began singing. Her strong, clear alto wove a melodic chant with a magical under-tone amidst the simple words.

> Today, change is coming.
> Tomorrow, we create anew.
> The wheel of the cycle turning.
> The same but ever new.

I understood the women of my chamber were weaving a magic and inviting me to step into it. As I descended into the bath, all of the women took up the song. It seemed to me the entire room reverberated with sound, like the singing of the Wise Ones. However, unlike the chanting of the Wise Ones, my body hummed in resonance with this tune. The water was cool where it touched me, and it seemed to vibrate along with the song. I floated among the petals and drank in the heady fragrance of the bath.

After a time, I submerged myself in the water. Being underwater had always been a place of comfort and fascination for me. I had been swimming in the ocean since I was a child. One of the few memories I had of my mother was of her taking me to the sea and setting me among the gentle waves. Water held no fear for me, and I could not remember a time when I was unable to maneuver effortlessly in it. Immersed in the sea, the sounds of the land world faded, and a wonder of dappled prisms danced over the sand. For me, this was an enchanted place full of wonder, mystery, and possibility.

Here in the Palace, my experience was no different. The muffled chanting pulsated through the water, and the images of the women surrounding the bath glimmered hazily from above. I felt the water and the women both holding me. There was no difference between the support of the water and the support of the women. My ability to depend on the women of my chamber was a natural part of the universe, like the ever-present buoyancy of water. Water could be trusted to sustain and the magic of these women carried the same feeling of strength. I wanted to stay, but my need for air pushed me to the surface.

The chant still spun around the room. Pushing wet hair out of my eyes, I stared at the women gathered around the bath. They gazed back at me, seeming to acknowledge the intentionality of the experience I had just had. Kyma stepped forward and offered me her hand. Reluctantly, I accepted it and slowly emerged. As I did, the chanting faded until, again, it was just Nyssa's voice. The song grew softer, diminished into a whisper and was gone.

Even though I had emerged from the bath, the powerful energy in the room did not diminish. Alega brought towels and wrapped my damp hair, while Lista helped me dry myself. When these tasks were complete, Alandra held out a soft, dark blue gown and helped me slip into it. She then led me to a stool near where Reya sat. Reya removed the towel from my head and began to brush my hair gently.

The room was quiet for a time while Reya stroked my hair. When it hung smoothly around my shoulders, Reya spoke. "Young Queen, we would weave for you a magic with our hopes and wishes for the new spring." With these words, she nodded toward Kyma, the healer, who began, "May you always be strong in body and mind."

While she spoke, Reya divided my hair into three strands and started to braid.

Alandra, the artist, spoke next. "May you always know beauty."

As these women stated their intentions, Reya folded another piece of hair into the braid. Each woman in the irregularly formed circle gave a blessing.

The chronicler, Calida, spoke after Alandra. Her wish was, "May you always know the relevance of your past to your future."

Pelagia, the woman who dealt with storage of grain and other materials, said, "May your blessings be too many to count." It was then that I realized each woman's wish was related to her area of expertise.

So it did not surprise me when Myrina, the mediator, wished, "May you always know your own truth and find ways to enact it."

The grower, Lista's blessing was, "May your life be filled with bounty," while Lalage, the midwife, said, "May you give birth to many things."

I wondered if these intentions were scripted. I would not have been surprised to learn that they had been repeated every cycle for each Queen on the threshold of the spring celebration.

When Alega, the Wise One, spoke, "May you always know the way of the Mother," I began to cry. Soft tears spilled down my cheeks and wet the fabric of my tunic. Despite my diligent efforts, I could not stop weeping. Reya continued to softly braid each wish into my hair, locking them in place and making them a part of me. Unable to meet their eyes any longer, I stared at my hands while the women continued.

Nyssa stood and actually pirouetted as she said, "May the dance of life come easily to you," and Elayn, the animal keeper, stroked the air as she spoke, "May the earth's creatures bring you joy."

Damia, the writer, wished, "May you always speak Her truth," and Iva, the builder, made me smile as she said, "May you always know what comes next."

Reya was the last to speak. She lifted a leather lace from her lap. With it, she tied the end of my braid, securing the wishes which had been shared. As she did so she said, "May She hold you in Her arms always."

There was a silence as each woman extended her hand to the woman next to her until the circle of women around me was complete. Inside the circle, I could feel a surge of energy travel from one woman to another until it connected them all. They stayed like this for a moment. Then Reya nodded, the women dropped their hands, and it was over.

The power which had filled the room grew fainter and casual conversations gradually began. I unceremoniously sniffed as my tears ended. Reya leaned forward and put her arms around me.

"Giada," she whispered, "will you join us on the balcony?"

Still unable to speak, I nodded in assent and made my way out of the room. Alega, Kyma, and Myrina joined us on the balcony bringing with them watered wine and soft cheese. We sat together, exchanging casual conversation which belied the depth of the experience we had just shared. As we watched, the sun went down over the top of the western mountain in brilliant hues of red, orange, and gold, ending the last day of winter.

Although no Guardian had been present in my chamber for these preparations, it could not be said that they were absent. Their *energy* hummed. It emanated strongly from their shelter across the Court, carrying with it an echo of the wishes and hopes of the women of my chamber. I wondered what the Guardians' intentions would have been if I could have heard them. I thought their wishes might have been similar to those of the women of my chamber, but I could not help but speculate about the ways they might have been different.

8

Brilliant, dazzling sunlight suddenly illuminated my sitting room. The first rays of the new spring sun rose over the mountain and streams of daylight flooded the space with bright warmth. My chamber's location in the western section of the Palace would lead one to presume that the eastern sunrise could not be seen. However, Malia was an architectural wonder. Its multistoried construction reminded me of the way children stack blocks. The Palace's upward direction was not constant. It was instead uneven, causing various rooms and hallways to stand out alone at the top of the structure. The Spring Hall was the highest part of the western Palace. Its placement allowed an unobstructed view of the mountains to the east and caught the rising sun.

This was particularly apparent today as the entire room burst into light. It became clear to me in an instant why this section of the Palace was called the Spring Hall. Those of us gathered to view this phenomenon quietly gazed at the vivid tones of the sunrise and a shaft of light which flooded my room. I watched in fascination as the light traveled gradually down the western wall of my chamber toward a fresco. The painting depicted a young girl around ten, holding the bud of a lily. With the exception of a scarf knotted around her neck, nothing about her clothing was distinctive. She was a Goddess we simply called "the Sweet Girl Child." Collectively, there was a sharp intake of breath as light touched the Virgin and she became vividly illuminated.

Sacra spoke, ending the silence. "We welcome you, Girl Child of spring. We honor and celebrate your renewal and rebirth."

In a surprisingly strong voice for such an aged woman, Aellai followed, "We welcome you, girl child of spring. Bless us with your gifts of growth and creation."

A tall, thin woman of about thirty, who I assumed must be Thera, the Hearth Queen from Knossos, said. "We welcome you, Girl Child of spring." Stepping back so several young girls now

90

stood between her and the fresco, she declared, "Bless and guard these girls and those like them who will grow to be the mothers of our future."

As the Hearth Queens spoke these words, the luminosity of the Sweet Girl Child shone, startling and intense. It held for a few moments longer, flashed softly, and then was gone.

*****

The evening before the illumination of the Girl Child fresco in my sitting room, the women of my chamber had warned me we would rise before dawn. In fact, they made certain I was up, dressed, and waiting in my sitting room when people began to arrive. I cannot say I accepted this gracefully, but instead grumbled about arising in darkness and the need to light lamps in order to see. My mood improved when Reya offered me the traditional spring holiday fare of honey cakes and quinces. I knew that while I was sleeping, she must have been up to fetch these from the kitchen. Gradually, all of the women of my chamber arrived in my room. Although they smiled and exchanged quiet greetings, I could tell by their demeanor that their purpose for coming was significant. Following their example, I, too, was hushed and circumspect.

Nyssa and Pelagia entered carrying the clothing Sacra had given me. Pelagia extended her hand to me saying, "Come, we will help you prepare."

The women of my chamber gathered, creating a circle with me at the center. Already in my undergarments, I stood accepting their offer of assistance. Truthfully, although I had spent some time studying the clothing Sacra had given me, I wasn't actually certain how the pieces all went together. I hoped the women of my chamber had more experience than I with these garments.

Nyssa held out the long, tiered skirt with its broad, multicolored, horizontal sections of fabric, and I stepped into it. Instead of adding to what I already wore, Pelagia asked me to remove my shift. Having observed the clothing of the Hearth Queen at the festivals of Phaistos, I was not surprised to discover the bodice she offered me was open, leaving my breasts bare. I found this top consisted of a short jacket with sleeves which stopped just above my elbows. The material of the sleeves curved down and under my breasts. Nyssa secured a series of laces on the front of the jacket. It held my breasts tightly and gave them an ampleness I had not anticipated.

A wide belt that tied in the back came next. The last piece of clothing was a double apron that hung just below the belt in both the front and the back. It was embroidered with elaborate diamond patterns. These intersected and repeated frequently giving the aprons an illusion of depth. Once my ensemble was complete Alandra asked me to sit. She produced brushes and several jars of paint and began embellishing my eyes, eyebrows, cheeks, lips and breasts. While she worked, Myrina brushed my hair. She pulled it back and tied it in a leather lace, just like when I practiced at the Guardians' Court. When their work was done both of these women stepped back and nodded approval. I could see in the reflection of the bath my eyes were darker and fuller, while my skin was robbed of the color it had acquired from many seasons of swimming in the sea.

As the women of my chamber worked to prepare me for the day, I could feel a change come over me. At times in my village, when I prepared for some special occasion, I would put on earrings and good clothes which had belonged to my mother. I knew the feeling of being myself, but different because of the change from my normal appearance. That feeling paled compared to what I was experiencing now.

I sensed I was merging with the other Queens I had seen becoming one with Sacra. I breathed in the air of their time, fresh and feral. Knowledge which a few moments ago I had not possessed came to me like recent memories. Love, fear, wisdom, compassion, understanding, and other sensations came to me so strongly and quickly, I could barely take them in. I was seeing through the eyes of generations of Hearth Queens. Their secrets and their strengths became a part of me. A few weeks ago I would have found this experience unnerving. I thought it might even have frightened me. However today, standing in the garb of a Hearth Queen, I felt comfortable and natural. For the first time,

I believed I might actually have been destined to be Hearth Queen of Malia.

I thought my transformation was complete, but I was mistaken. Reya moved forward from the circle, carrying with her a crown-like fluted hat. She asked me to kneel so she could place it on my head. Through the earlier Queen's eyes, I could see there had always been a woman in Reya's position. Until I had access to their knowledge, I had not understood that her function in relation to me was a sacred duty. To ride out with the Guard in search of a new Queen was an honor given to a woman trusted to hold the future of the Palace in her hands. It was her responsibility to train, tutor, and empower a new Queen. As I knelt in front of Reya, I saw her in a new way. Her patient friendship, wise council, and determined dedication to educate me about the role of a Queen took on new meaning. She had performed this responsibility with such grace, I had never realized she had been appointed to it.

Reya placed the hat on my head and offered me her hand. Her assistance allowed me to get up nimbly from the floor despite my long skirt. I conceded to myself that, although I had frequently worn a shift, I had little experience negotiating movement in clothing as intricate as the ceremonial attire of a Hearth Queen. Having successfully stood, I gazed at Reya. She took my hand and said warmly, "Come, Young Queen, we greet the spring."

I often felt Reya had access to my thoughts, but if she did, she never commented on them. I suspected like the Queen, Reya had training with the Wise Ones. It seemed that to be Queen, or like Reya, the trainer of a Queen, one must be multifaceted. This led me to consider the various areas in which I was being educated. I worked with the Wise Ones every day and, despite my antipathy for them, I was beginning to develop a moderate facility with their skills. My time with the Guards allowed me not only to expand my expertise, but also to watch how they interacted. Because I was with them for practice, I was learning about Guardian culture. Sitting Council with Sacra was teaching me about the organization of the Palace and exposing me to the diverse aspects of life at Malia. My instruction was structured so that I was learning about the workings of the Palace and the many people who comprised it.

As I contemplated this insight, the circle of women in my room began to disband. There was no formal ending; they simply started casual conversations and moved toward the sitting room. Reya picked up a lamp and gestured for me to follow. As I made my way into the next room, I could see the warm mauves and pinks that heralded the sunrise.

*****

Arising before dawn made the day seem long. It appeared everyone had something to do to prepare for the celebration except me. Damia, Nyssa, and several others were practicing music. Reya was sitting with the women of the Queen's Council and the other Hearth Queens. Lista had left to arrange flowers to decorate the portion of the central Court where the Queens and I would stand for my presentation. It was a large, raised dais under the western side of the Palace, a few steps above the rest of the space. Although most of the Courtyard was open to the sky, this section was tucked under a roof. The enclosure was supported by columns which allowed it to have one side open and gave access to the Court. I knew the people of not only this Palace, but also those who had come from Knossos and Zakros would fill the Courtyard only a short distance below. Reya told me that my father and the others from my village would be given spaces of honor near the dais.

I hoped to have time with my father while he was at Malia and I wondered if now might be a good time to visit him. Being bored and somewhat petulant I had considered lying down before the ceremony, but I did not think I dared take off my ritual clothing. Although I was fairly confident I now knew how the ensemble worked, I was unsure if I could put it back together without help. I was certain that if I rested, I would end up with my make-up smeared and my skirt rumpled. I knew my presentation would not be until after half-day so it would be a while before anyone came for me. This seemed to be a well-timed opportunity to visit my father and the others from my village without being missed.

I was uncertain where Titaia had taken my father and the villagers, but I thought I could ask people I encountered along the way until I found them. Not wishing to attract attention by traveling through the Palace in my ceremonial clothing, I removed my hat, and put on a long cloak which covered most of my attire. With these precautions taken, I moved down the stairs toward the central Court. This Court provided the main access to most sections of the Palace. In my explorations, I had anticipated passages would lead from one part of the building to another. However, I frequently found hallways ended without access to another place. This taught me that the best way to reach any destination was from the central Court. I decided to begin my search for my father there.

The atmosphere in the Court was much the same as it had been yesterday. People bustled, moving with intention. Even though it was quite a while until half-day, a crowd had begun to gather in the Courtyard. These early celebrants were milling expectantly, bantering and greeting friends, some of whom I suspected they only saw at holy days. Children squealed and dashed among the adults until they were shooed away. Many of those who called Malia home were becoming familiar to me, but I did not recognize these early arrivals. I moved into the Court and began scanning the crowd looking for someone I knew.

In confusion, I realized I recognized everyone. Each of the people in the Court wore a hazy halo and information about them came to me from some unbidden source. In consternation, I focused specifically on one man who was a short distance from me. Without conscious effort, a series of names that I knew were associated with him came to me. I continued to stare, unable to grasp what was happening. The man looked up questioningly and moved toward me.

"Child?" he queried, looking kindly but puzzled. "May I help you?"

"Do the names Cyril, Kairos, or Pello mean something to you?" I asked, ignoring his offer of assistance.

The man took a step back and, with a look of wariness, said, "My name is Pello. My father's name was Kairos and my grandfather's was Cyril. How is it you know these names?"

I did not respond, as I did not know the answer myself. I could no longer look directly at him while I searched for a reasonable response. So, I looked up and into the Court. The central Court was enveloped in a wavering light. In my distorted vision, I could see several images of the same section of wall. I found I could focus on each individual view and see it more clearly. In one cloudy impression, it seemed the wall was missing. In a heartbeat, it was lying in rubble on the ground and, in yet another, it was only partially built with the ladders being used to construct it still in place.

Shifting back and forth between these images made me dizzy. I remembered when Sacra handed me the clothing I was wearing I knew they were magic. I realized that coming to the Court while dressed in the magical attire of a Hearth Queen had been an error. I was wearing clothes specifically made to give the wearer access to knowledge beyond the normal scope of comprehension. I knew I needed to make my way back to my chamber as quickly as possible.

The ground moved under my feet and I was unable to judge the actual distance to the earth. I staggered as I moved certain anyone watching would think I had begun celebrating early with lots of unwatered wine. Looking up or asking for assistance seemed like equally bad ideas, as I imagined everyone and everything would be as fluid as the ground. Awkwardly, I placed one foot in front of another as I made my way toward what I hoped were the stairs to my rooms. Ultimately, I had only traveled a short distance when I misstepped and felt myself falling toward the stones of the Court.

I closed my eyes and resigned myself to the fact I would soon land unceremoniously on the ground of the central Court. I wasn't as concerned about being hurt as trying to determine how to deal with the insubstantial nature of my surroundings. I knew the source of my disorientation was my ritual clothes. I thought the only way to stop the effect would be to strip them off and proceed, nearly naked to my rooms. I did not think being nude would draw much attention, but I thought hurriedly undressing in the Court might. Having already given myself over to falling, I was surprised when my descent was stopped before I reached the ground. Strong arms encircled me and returned me to an upright position. My eyes flew open as I realized I was being held by one of the Guards.

Because she was so close to me, I could not actually see much of her. I knew she was taller than I and had the most beautiful hazel eyes I had ever seen. Her dark hair fell around her face accentuating high cheekbones and a mouth that looked eminently kissable.

I had spent a considerable amount of time watching the Guardians. Without any actual effort, I had committed their names to memory, and I knew this was Stava. With relief, I realized that when I looked at her, the spinning world stilled. I was drinking in the calm and savoring the essence of her when she spoke.

"I answer your call, Young Queen. How may I help?"

I thanked this morning's Sweet Girl Child that a Guardian had heard my distress and had come to assist me. Although I felt foolish, I was grateful. My thinking was so disordered I found it difficult to answer her question. Seeming untroubled by my lack of response, Stava kept her arms around me.

After a time she said, "Young Queen, I am going to release you. But, I will continue to hold your hands. Can you keep looking into my eyes?"

I nodded in acceptance. In truth, I was having no difficulty focusing on her. I acknowledged to myself that I was so captivated by her it would have taken a significant effort to make my attention go elsewhere. In her presence I felt suffused by a warm *energy*. It was as if Stava had transferred her calm assurance to me. We stood unmoving for a time. I could not actually judge how long we remained still, but eventually a peaceful feeling infused me. Stava seemed to know when I had reached a place of equanimity, and only then did she begin to speak.

"Young Queen," she asked, "were you going to your chamber?"

Diktynna's nets, but these women were polite, I thought to myself. If I had been the one asking this question it would have been something like, "I sensed you were about to run naked through the Court fleeing your inability to deal with the situation in which you found yourself due to your lack of foresight." But, Stava continued to patiently hold me both physically and energetically while I fumbled around for an answer.

At length, I found my voice. "Yes," I responded nodding, "My chamber."

Stava continued to focus on me and replied, "Then I will move to your side and, if I may, continue to hold you." It was clear to me she was able to assess a situation and envision remedies.

Under any circumstances continuing to hold me seemed like a good idea, so I nodded again. Smoothly, Stava let go of one of my hands. In a dance-like move, she shifted to my side and encircled my waist with one of her arms. I found our walk across the Courtyard fascinating. It was as if we moved within a sphere only she and I shared. Beyond the edges of this barrier I could see hazy stares of concern from other people, and the chaotic shifting of the Court. However, within the space Stava and I occupied, there was order. Calm permeated my universe, and I sensed it was the combination of her energy and mine which created the feeling. Strangely, even though only a few moments before I would have given anything to have my time in the Court end, now I wished it would continue indefinitely.

Once we began moving I realized I had not actually been far from the steps which led to my rooms. The stairs were wide enough that we were able to continue side-by-side until we reached my sitting room. As before, everyone else was away attending to their tasks. Stava led me through the room to a soft lounge and assisted me in taking a seat. The energy which encircled us seemed to expand until it encompassed the entire room. It then appeared to move beyond even those boundaries. Gradually, it faded, leaving me awed and embarrassed.

Stava made no motion to leave. She simply stood nearby with no seeming sense of urgency. Unlike before, she did not look directly at me. I had come to understand that most of the Guards did not meet my eye because they feared it might reveal too much. In this particular case, I was relieved Stava was not looking at me, for I feared I was the one who would give myself away. I was afraid that, with her mission accomplished, she would feel it was time to go, and I wanted her to stay. Even in my befuddled state, it occurred to me that conversation might encourage her to remain. I wanted to know more about the experience I just had. I knew that its effect on me had been intense, and I wondered if to her it had seemed the same.

"Stava?" I began haltingly.

"Yes, Young Queen," she answered.

"What just happened?" I queried, gazing up at her from my seat.

Stava looked uncomfortable, but began speaking. "Well, you were in the Courtyard, and I sensed you were in distress, so I offered you assistance."

Feeling more grounded every moment I was able to summons a look which I hope conveyed that was not what I was talking about. Belatedly, I realized it was wasted because she was not actually looking at me. I decided I would have to actually speak.

"I'm aware of that," I said. "What I want to know is what happened between us."

Stava looked uncomfortable. She shuffled her feet and appeared to be considering if she should answer my question. After a brief pause, she began to speak.

"Guardians share many methods for support, defense, and assistance. At times, the best strategy for dealing with a situation is to create an energetic container in which a person can reside for a time. It can be used to isolate someone who is hostile or to support an individual who is in distress. A person in distress is often comforted by having someone join her inside the energy."

"So, is that what you did with me in the Courtyard?" I replied tentatively sensing she was uncertain about providing this information.

"Yes," she admitted. "I am sorry I did not ask your permission, but I felt it was urgent. I have never seen a Queen unaccompanied wearing ceremonial dress. In the past, one of the Guards has always been called to escort the Queen if she moved among the people in ritual attire. When I saw you in the Court alone, I thought perhaps you were responding to an emergency."

"There was no emergency," I sighed. "I simply did not understand the ramifications of being in public dressed like this." I swept my hand down indicating the clothing I wore.

"I do not mean to be forward, Young Queen," Stava replied looking quickly at me, "may I stay with you until time for your presentation?"

I thought to myself, "This is perfect." Hoping to appear casual I asked, "Will you sit with me?"

Stava nodded, lifted the strap of her short sword over her head and placed it on the ground nearby. With a fluid grace she sat down near me on the lounge.

"Can you show me again?" I requested. "Can you do what you did in the Court?"

"But, you no longer seem to be in distress," Stava replied glancing quizzically at me.

"I'm not in any difficulty, but I would like to know what that experience feels like when I am not troubled," I explained.

"That is a measure for times of risk," Stava said seriously. "To use it now would be inappropriate."

"Well, then, what would be appropriate?" I coaxed.

Stava cocked her head to the side contemplating my request. After a few moments she closed her eyes and immediately I began to sense a shift in *energy*.

I felt her *reach* for me. Not physically, but with a subtle *energy* which extended out to *touch* my consciousness. My sense of it was akin to a friend knocking on a door. At first, I did not know how to respond to her *contact*. "Well, I reasoned, what does one do when there is a knock on the door?"

I answered myself, "one opens the door and invites the friend in." I wasn't exactly sure how one opened oneself, but I began to try to make space within me for her. Immediately, *warmth* surged through me and with it began a shared *connection*. Her *energy* reached out and I drew her in. I shifted to make a place for her moved toward her, and a *cycle* began between the two of us.

The feeling was intoxicating. I knew this was what I had been waiting for since the Guards first came to my father's lodge. I had always had some underlying idea of the possibility of this type of *contact*. In fact, part of my infatuation with the Guardians had been my hope of this kind of *connection*. Despite my desire to experience this type of *union,* I had not anticipated its powerful nature.

In my perception, the breath I drew in matched the air she breathed out. My heart was beating in synchronicity with hers. Most astounding of all to me was, I *knew* her. I saw her as a child in another Palace following the Guards with a stick stuck in her belt like a sword. I understood Stava's awareness that when she was older she would be acknowledged as a Guardian. I saw Sacra nodding in acceptance as Stava stood before her. I sensed her feeling of "coming home" as she stood before the Guardians' shelter at Malia.

I *knew* her in a way I had never known anyone before. What I drew into me was the essence of her. It was not that I knew only her thoughts, it was more than that. I could sense her spirit and understood what made her who she was. In that moment, I *knew* her to be brave, gentle, wise, and fierce. I thought some people might consider this type of *contact* an intrusion, but I reveled in it. In this moment, I was whole, complete, and truly alive.

Even in the midst of these revelations, I had no trouble finding my own thoughts. It occurred to me that if I could perceive her in this way, then it was likely she *knew* me also. A wave of self-consciousness spilled over me and I lost my grasp on the space I was holding open. In a few heartbeats, the energy fell apart and I was left breathless and empty.

Stava did not say anything. For the first time since we had entered my chamber, she leveled a searching look at me. But, I could not meet her gaze. I was afraid she had *seen* me. If she had access to me in the same way I had to her, I was anxious that she might know of my fears about being Hearth Queen, or sense my confusion about life at Malia, or most troubling of all, have perceived the depth of my desire for her.

I did want her. My longing was so deep and so strong it took my breath away. There was more to my wish for her than simple physicality. I wanted the energy we had shared to be a part of me. I wanted to carry her with me always.

When I did not meet her gaze, she reached out her hand and gently lifted my chin. With an echo of the energy we had shared before, she studied my face. I could not help but smile, but I was afraid to open myself again. She looked back at me with understanding. Her hand ran across my cheek, trailed down my neck, and came to rest on my shoulder. Without a word, she gently put her arms around me. We sat like that for a long while. After a time, she relaxed and I settled back against the lounge, one of her arms still encircling me. Sitting like this with her, everything seemed warm, soft and safe. I leaned my head on her shoulder and, despite my previous misgivings, fell gently to sleep.

9

Someone was gently calling my name. Deep in sleep, I did not respond. I was dreaming Stava and I were riding out together. We had just cleared the Palace and our horses were cantering while we laughed together pretending to race. The call came again, this time accompanied by a soft touch. I felt I was swimming out of deep water as I gradually came awake. With difficulty, I opened my eyes to see Reya and a small group of women gazing expectantly down at me.

Reya's voice, still gentle, was saying, "Young Queen, it is time for your presentation."

With a jolt, I realized I was still resting in Stava's arms. My eyes flew open in earnest. I wasn't sure why, but it embarrassed me to be found like this. My time with Stava had been platonic, but my feelings had been otherwise. I was concerned my sensual thoughts about her would be apparent to everyone. I knew Stava and I had done nothing about which I should feel self-conscious, but this did not negate my uncertainty. I wasn't sure if having a Guardian in one's rooms, especially lying in her arms, would be considered a form of misconduct. I searched the faces of the women who had come to accompany me to my presentation. The three women from my chamber, Reya, Alandra, and Myrina, stood patiently. From my sitting position, just beyond them I could make out the legs and belt of a Guard. Quickly checking the women's faces, I judged no one's expression held. My attention jumped next to Stava. Her face looked comfortable and composed.

How was it, I wondered, that I continued to get myself in positions where I felt uncomfortable? This was yet another in a litany of awkward moments I had experienced since being at Malia. My hope was to be calm and self possessed when I stood before the people of the Palace to be acknowledged as the future Hearth Queen. Instead, this experience had left me anxious. I wondered how I was going to proceed in a composed manner.

My attention returned from my predicament to my surroundings. Things in my chamber were proceeding normally.

Reya was retrieving my hat. The Guardian who I had not been able to see stepped forward. With some relief, I recognized Karis. I would not have been nearly as comfortable if it had been one of the other Guards who had come to escort me. But, Karis had already been with me when I was lost and had kept my dignity intact. I was hopeful she could do the same again.

I was not disappointed. Without comment, Karis offered me her hand and smiled graciously. "Young Queen," she said, "may I assist you in arising? It will be my pleasure to stand with you today during the ceremony."

I returned her smile and gave her my hand. As she pulled me up she glanced at Stava. I thought I saw her grin, but it was so fleeting I could not be certain it had actually happened. Stava came to her feet at almost the same moment and the two women simultaneously gave a brief nod.

Reya interrupted any exchange they might have had, saying, "Karis, Stava, may I ask you to step out of the chamber?" Karis," she continued, "we will meet you in the hall soon."

Both Guards acknowledged Reya's direction with a formal salute and left the room. I hoped Stava would look back, but she did not.

Once they were gone, Myrina and Alandra jumped into action. Myrina clicked her tongue. I thought now I would hear their disapproval. Instead she said, "Young Queen, I am afraid your hair is a mess. If you would sit I could arrange it again." As I moved to a chair, I could see Alandra once more unpacking her jars, and I knew she intended to recreate my makeup. "Well," I thought to myself, "if this was the worst consequence of today's exploits, I'm lucky."

It did not take long for Myrina and Alandra to finish their work. As before, Reya came forward and placed my hat on my head. "Come," was the only word she said. I stood and began to make my way toward the door, but Reya stopped me. She took me by the shoulders, saying, "You are Giada, destined to be Hearth Queen of Malia. You must release all doubt. Embrace and envision your future, for the people of the Palace will look to you for strength, refuge and reassurance. Uncertainty has no place now. Put aside your reservations, and take the next step on your journey."

As we left my chamber, I wondered if all new Hearth Queens got similar instruction before they were presented to the people. I was concerned that I alone required this specific guidance.

*****

Sacra's voice rang out, filling the central Court.

"Will those who would declare themselves dancers for the summer festival come forward?"

Although I had anticipated her presence in front of the people would be impressive, I had not foreseen the impact of her charisma. The huge crowd assembled in the Court hushed when she spoke. It appeared awe and respect vied for precedence among those present.

A few men and women stepped out of the crowd in response to her call. The men looked powerful. Sinuous arms met massive shoulders, while trim hips showed under strong chests. The girls too were strong, but carried this strength with a fluid grace. Nyssa stood in the midst of them poised and self-assured. The men's response to the Queen's request ranged from bravado to trepidation. On the other hand, the women all appeared confident and stood with a seeming sense of purpose in answer to the Queen's call.

"Alkestis," the Queen spoke turning toward the chronicler from her Council. "Record these names, for these shall be the ones who dance with the bulls this summer." Having given direction to the recorder, she turned to the assembled group.

Facing the women, she declared. "The task you undertake is no small responsibility. You will play a part in identifying the future King of Malia. Train carefully and well, for the journey on which you embark is indeed perilous. Be prepared to dance with daring, skill and diligence, for the charge you carry is vital to us all."

I had not anticipated Sacra's words or Nyssa's dedication would touch me, but I stood watching with a lump in my throat.

I remembered how excited Nyssa had been when she shared her intention to dance. I also recalled my *knowing* she would be fine. If it had not been for that, I would have worried about her choice to participate in the dance. However, because I *knew* she would be fine, I could watch this ceremony without foreboding.

When Sacra finished speaking, she stepped back and a man I had never seen stepped forward from the group assembled on the dais. I could not guess his age. He could have been anywhere between twenty-five and forty cycles. He was not tall, but clearly strong and confident. Although sparse, his clothing was impressive. His exposed skin shone with pungent oil which wafted toward me in his wake. The Queen smiled pleasantly at the man as they exchanged places. Although I had no one to confirm my suspicions, I felt certain this was the King.

The man moved to the edge of the steps, paused and considered the men who had stepped forward to announce their intentions. When he spoke his voice was surprisingly deep and resonant.

"Today you have made known your desire to join in the dance with the bulls at the summer celebration. Do not take this challenge lightly or simply as a test of skill," he proclaimed. "This is not only a competition. It is a request to be recognized as the chosen one of the Gods. For those who pursue this contest with false pretense there may be severe costs, for neither the bulls nor the Gods accept deception."

"Are you certain you wish to undertake this challenge?" He asked his question with a hint of intimidation in his tone.

One of the youngest men immediately stepped toward the King and proclaimed a forceful, "Yes." One-by-one each of the other men moved forward and similarly declared their intention to dance. The King smiled sardonically at the assembled group, issuing an unspoken challenge, and then resumed his place among those on the dais. I could not decide how I felt about him. Although he was personable which made me inclined to like him, he also projected an air of arrogance I found distasteful. I decided my opinion of him would have to wait until I had more information.

I was surprised when the next person to step forward was Akantha, the artisan from the Queen's Council, and with her, a frightened looking young man. Akantha spoke confidently as if she was accustomed to addressing large assemblies.

"People of Malia," she announced, "today Kyknos asks to dedicate his seal."

Sacra came forward again and joined them. Looking toward Kyknos, she said, "On this day, Kyknos asks us to bless his seal."

"This seal has been on view in the central Court for the last moon so each of you might see it." Akantha declared.

Without pause, Sacra continued, "today Kyknos asks that we consecrate his seal so that this blessing may bring prosperity and bountiful harvests. People of Malia, please join me in this blessing."

The crowd responded with jubilation. The dedication of a seal carried the acceptance of a person as a recognized member of a trade or craft. It conferred the sanction of the Palace and the people. It also confirmed that the person had been found skilled and honorable. Once a seal had been accepted, it virtually guaranteed the success of an enterprise. Akantha acknowledged the crowd with a slight bow and turned toward Kyknos. She handed him the ring bearing his seal. Although still clearly awkward, Kyknos took the ring with a bashful smile and left the dais as quickly as possible. Smiling at his back, Akantha followed him out into the Court.

A touch from Karis alerted me that my time for observation had come to an end. There was a rustling among some of those on the dais as three Hearth Queens and three Peers of the Guard stepped out to form a spacious semicircle, with each Guardian standing to the right of her Queen. Sacra and Petra were at the center with the other two sets of women on either side. Karis took my arm and led me forward. A bolt of anticipation shot through me, leaving in its wake both tension and excitement. I stood in front of the inward and outward facing Queens of three Palaces, my back to the people and the Court. Like the other Guards, Karis took her place on my right.

I felt Petra's gaze rest on me and with it came a *surge* of reassurance. The Guards echoed this support. My anxiety abated as I realized I was not alone, but was being assisted by the *energy* of the Guardians. I knew Thekia from watching her in the Court yesterday. In addition to the two Peers I recognized, a third stood beside Thera. She was an enormous woman who towered over everyone and was equally as dynamic as the other three. Not only was she tall, she was massive, but though her size was intimidating, her expression was gentle. My thoughts wandered off into speculation about how sensual it would feel to have her weight on me in a moment of passion. A *surge* coming from the Guardians brought me back, and I refocused my awareness on what was happening. Feeling much more at ease, I turned my attention to the Hearth Queens.

The three of them stood, each impressive in her way. Aellai was a tiny concentration of intensity, Thera was a powerful force in the full bloom of her mothering time, while to me, Sacra's beauty, awareness and intelligence eclipsed them all. Each of them gazed at me with attentiveness that bordered on being overwhelming.

After a brief pause, Aellai turned to Thekia and asked, "Is it she?"

I had heard Reya ask this question to the Guards when they found me at my father's lodge, and again Sacra had asked Petra the same question when I first came to the Palace. I knew this was my final confirmation by the Peers of the Guard as a Hearth Queen.

Thekia stepped forward, glanced at me, and spoke in a firm voice, "Yes, Aellai, it is she."

Aellai gazed at Thekia for a moment. I could see that despite Aellai's irritable temperament there was respect and affection between them. Aellai lifted her eyes from Thekia and nodded to Thera who in turn addressed her Peer of the Guard, "Dariah, is it she?"

The giant woman whom I now knew was called Dariah stepped forward and said, "Yes, Thera, it is she."

All eyes then turned toward Sacra. She smiled at Petra and asked, "Is it she?"

Petra returned her smile and answered, "Yes, Sacra, it is she."

Sacra acknowledged Petra's words and addressed me and, beyond me, the people assembled in the Court.

"You are confirmed by the Guards as the future Hearth Queen of Malia. The recognition of a new Queen does not happen often. When it does, we acknowledge and celebrate our good fortune. You bring the joy of spring to the Palace. You come to us as we celebrate the time of the Divine Girl Child, when lambs quicken in the womb, when grain sprouts in the fields, and the olives blossom on the terraces. Giada, you bloom in the heart of Malia, bringing life to the Palace and its people. You are the spring of Malia."

As Sacra finished speaking, she and Petra moved out of the semicircle of Guardians and Queens and toward me. I was surprised when the King joined them. "Each of us wishes to offer you a gift in recognition of your confirmation as the future Hearth Queen of Malia."

The King was the first to offer his present. His previous boldness diminished as he stood before me and his demeanor changed to one of respect and deference. He handed me a golden broach decorated with two twin bees facing each other. He did not say a word, only nodded, and then quickly stepped back.

Petra moved forward next. Her energy *surged* ahead to meet me as she approached. Although I had seen her occasionally in the Guardians' Court, this was the first time I had actually been in her presence since I met her in the Queen's chamber. The familiar feeling of understanding and sanctuary I felt in her presence flowed toward me, and I met her approach with unabashed admiration.

"Young Queen," Petra spoke, in a quiet voice not intended for the crowd to hear, "will you lower your head?"

I dropped my head in compliance with her request. She placed around my neck a leather cord on which hung a small golden labyris. Along with it came an overwhelming feeling of all being right in the world. Her *energy* made me believe I was in exactly the right place at precisely the right time. I was delighted to have something Petra had given me. In addition to being recognized as Hearth Queen, I believed I was being acknowledged as a resident of Malia. As I lifted my head, Petra placed her hands on my shoulders and looked directly at me. I caught my breath as her unspoken words communicated her hopes for me as the Young Queen. Petra did not turn her back to me, but took several steps away still holding my gaze.

Petra's enchantment was only broken when Sacra stepped forward. Warm affection flowed from her, and I could have no doubt she cared for me. When she reached me, she took both my hands and held them for a few moments, looking at each of them speculatively. After a time, she dropped my right hand. From a pocket concealed in her gown she withdrew a ring. She placed it on my middle finger saying, "This is your seal. Each Hearth Queen has a seal by which her stores and proclamations are recognized. From this day forward, you may mark your word and your belongings with this seal."

I wanted to look at the seal Sacra had given me. The ring itself was large, but the image was small and intricate. I did not have time to focus on what it represented. Sacra did not let go of my hand; instead she used it to turn me toward the Court. This was the first time since I had come forward that I actually faced the people. The crowd covered every available space in the central Court. People filled the Courtyard, sat on low walls, and perched on balconies. I caught my breath as I took in the full extent of the assemblage. In front, only a few feet away, I could see my father and the people from my village. For some reason, this unnerved me more than the multitude of strangers. Anxiety began to surface within me. Almost as soon as these feelings began, they were answered by the gentle *support* of Karis and the other Guardians. Buoyed by their encouragement, I faced the Court without apprehension.

Sacra seemed at ease. It was as if she drank in the essence of the people. She stood still and silent for a few moments and then began addressing the gathering. "People of Malia, I present to you Giada, your future Hearth Queen."

The crowd roared in response that was joyful and exultant. I looked out at the celebrants who seemed delighted to greet me as Young Queen. The same wavering light that had encompassed the Court earlier on my ill-fated attempt to find my father was still present. Panic surged within me. I feared being overwhelmed, as I had been earlier. This time I *reached* for the Guardians. They were there. Not only the four on the dais, but those within the crowd as well. The Guards from Malia, Knossos and Zakros all reached out with clarity and purpose. The *energy* of dozens of Guardians rushed forward in answer to my appeal. I felt like a bird lifted on the wind, and I looked into the crowd without fear.

It was as before. However, this time with the aid of the Guards, my focus was not distorted. I knew the people and understood their hopes and aspirations. This consciousness was both collective and individual. I remembered earlier in the Court I had been able to change my focus, shifting back and forth between different ways of viewing my surroundings. With a little effort, I found I could recreate this skill. I could center on one individual and see what she or he desired. I could also focus on the community and understand their wishes as a group. Suddenly, it became clear to me what Sacra had been doing in the moments when she stood before the people not speaking. I now understood one of the gifts of being Hearth Queen.

*****

Sacra and I walked together in the central Court, soaking in as much knowledge as we could about the hopes and desires of the people of Malia. I had no fear being among them. The Guards that accompanied us moderated both the physical press of the crowd and its psychic input. Drea, Hespar, and Maris joined Karis and Petra. The five of them walked with us while we moved among the people. The tenor of the crowd was jubilant. It was clear to me they viewed the arrival of a Young Queen as a renewal of sacred energy. I could also perceive they loved Sacra. There was respect, admiration and allegiance to her that circulated among those present.

The crowd was festive. There was dancing, feasting, wine and song among them. After a time, Sacra and I returned to the

111

dais where our food and wine were waiting. Father and the villagers were invited to join us. I sat with them enjoying their company and obvious pleasure. Stories of my village, my childhood and the exploits of other villagers were shared with the three Queens, their Peers of the Guard, Karis and even the King. I was surprised all of them actually appeared interested and entertained. As the festivities continued dusk began to fall, and small fires sprung up around the Court. Exuberance gave way to quieter, but no less genuine, celebration. Some of those with younger children began drifting home along with others who had long distances to travel in the morning.

It started as a whisper in the crowd, a small ripple of disturbance among some of the more discerning people in the Court. I watched as the heads of the three Queens on the dais lifted in response to the agitation. My attention immediately focused on the people, trying to perceive the cause of the disturbance. The Guardians' heads lifted only a moment later. The call came immediately. *"Guardians, alert."* I noted there was no specification of the type of Guardian being called. It was a call to them all.

There was an instantaneous response among those in the Court. People began to clear paths as Guardians sprung from their reveries, and a large group of men began to congregate around the King. Groups of Guards banded together and began leaving the central Court through the north exit. The men with the King formed lines and in an orderly procession moved through the same door.

I could only slightly distinguish the cause of the disturbance. It came to me through muddled impressions of concern and violation. The people who remained in the Court after the departure of the Guards and the King's men dissipated rapidly. Sacra took my hand and led me away from the Court as the first wave of understanding washed over me.

Sea Raiders were on shore approaching the Palace. Hazy flashes of boats, peculiar looking men, and groups of Guardians with weapons drawn presented themselves to me. With these images came an intense fear. My women, my precious Guardians, were standing in peril to keep the raiders from reaching the people of Malia. My knees grew weak and I was afraid I would sink to the floor. Even in their besieged state I felt them *reach* for me. Their strength was my strength, their courage my courage.

I gradually regained my equilibrium and began to return their *contact*. As they had supported me when I stood on the dais, I intended to sustain them as they faced the Sea Raiders. Sacra continued to lead me away from the Court toward the more enclosed regions of the Palace. Aellai and Thera followed closely behind us. As we moved forward, I recognize the halls that led to the Queen's chamber and knew it must be our destination.

As we got closer, increasing numbers of women joined us in the hallways. Keto appeared out of nowhere and dropped into step beside Sacra. Pelagia, Calida and Lalage from my chamber flowed silently in behind us carrying some of my ordinary clothing. When we reached the Queen's sitting room, many of the women from both our chambers and a flock of Wise Ones were already there. They were dragging chairs, rugs and pillows into a makeshift circle. Several of the Wise Ones were placing lamps and incense on a low table in the center of the room. As I pulled on my usual clothing, I recognized these activities were part of a plan.

One of the Wise Ones began to sing. I recognized the song as one we sang almost every day in the Mysteries. Although I had heard the words many times I had given little attention to their meaning. But, as the refrain lifted again and again among the voices of the women gathered in the Queen's room, I knew we had been preparing for just such an occasion. We were singing an incantation for the Guardians.

> *I am alive. I am awake.*
> *All that I need is mine to take.*
> *I have strength. I have power.*
> *I draw them to me in this hour.*
> *My sight is clear. My spirit bold.*
> *I draw to me the Goddess threefold.*

My usual misgivings about participating in the work of the Wise Ones were replaced with a profound gratitude for their training. I now understood it had been in preparation for a time like this, we had chanted day-after-day in the Mysteries. The melody and words did not require any attention, which left room for other perceptions. I knew the Guardians practiced every day until their reactions were incorporated into their bodies. I had not realized the Wise Ones, too, trained in their own way.

This song was followed by another, and yet another, all of which each woman in the room knew without conscious focus. The energy of these filled the chamber, swirled and soared away, leaving an almost palpable impression. When we had been singing for quite a while, there was a pause. One of the Wise Ones began to speak.

"I see Hespar and Ianthe." I was surprised to see her smile. "They have just toppled a giant raider and they are tying him to a tree with a bow string."

The chanting began again, but this time after each song the women paused. Sometimes there was silence, but often there was a bit of information about what was happening outside the Palace.

In one of these breaks, Titaia spoke, "Drea is furious. She cannot believe Sea Raiders have the audacity to attack Malia. One of the raiders keeps trying to strike her. Every time he swings she moves too quickly for him and is not there. He is beginning to tire. When he does, she intends to run and see if he will follow her. Adesha and Fauntee wait hidden near by with a fishnet. The three of them plan to capture him with it."

A round of chanting was interrupted by an audible gasp from Lista. "Pello is wounded."

With this pronouncement several women stood and prepared to leave the room. Among them were Kyma and Damaris the healers. Others rose to accompany them, offering their help to prepare for the wounded. For once, I did not mind the Wise Ones' singing. It seemed to have purpose, and I could feel the energy reaching out to those protecting the city. However, I wanted to go with the healers. I did not think I would be of any specific help with actual care, but I believed there must be other tasks which would need to be done. So I, too, rose. Sacra glanced at me, gave me an appraising look, and then nodded.

I could still feel the energy from the Queen's rooms as I departed. It *sparked* within me through the rest of the night. I could sense the Guardians, too. There was no fear coming from them. There was instead an insistent connection among them, and a reliance on the consistent training which allowed them to function as a unit. Kyma and Damaris appeared surprised to see me following, but once we reached the healing rooms they began to assign me tasks. I brought water, retrieved herbs from Iole's stores, and did other errands that freed them for more important work.

I was distracted by these activities, which I found a blessing. I also got occasional flashes of what was happening outside the Palace. The moon was full which made these images distinct. I noticed in these glimmers that the Guards never seemed to fight alone. They worked in groups of two, three, or more, accomplishing complex maneuvers which seemed to baffle and confuse the raiders. They fought back-to-back or in small circles which continually turned, so that no one ever became the sole focus of an attack.

Unlike the King's men, who fought with force and relied heavily on their weapons, the Guardians tricked and engaged in subterfuge to overcome their opponents. Many of them smiled and laughed while they whirled and evaded attacks. If one of them actually seemed to be in danger, several women would appear to confront and confound the invaders. Their methods appeared to be centered more on subduing and containing the raiders than actually damaging them.

Wounded did begin to appear, some of them limping in alone, while others were carried in by people from the Palace. The actual number of wounded was small, and I noticed more of the King's men were hurt than Guards. Kyma, Damaris and the other healers moved with skill and confidence to sew gashes, set broken bones, and put poultices on bruises. By dawn the incoming wounded stopped. Word drifted back to us that the Sea Raiders were no longer on the island. My *connection* with the Guards told me they were tired, but in good spirits. Many of them were still working to accomplish something, but I was not clear what they were doing.

Wiping her hands, Damaris came toward me. She looked tired and disheveled, as I'm sure I must have also.

"Thank you for your willingness to support us," she said. "Most of those who needed assistance have been sent home. There are only four who will require ongoing care. There are others coming to take over for us. It is time for you to go rest, too."

Suddenly, the full impact of my day came over me, and I realized I was exhausted. It had been more than a day since I had risen before dawn to watch the sun fill the windows of the Spring Hall. I felt no more disturbances coming from the people of the Palace or the Guardians. So, acknowledging Damaris kindness, I began my way back toward my chamber. I wound my way down the steps from the healing rooms and back into the bright sun of the central Court. The traces of last night's revelries were mostly gone. Only a few people moved about the Court, and they all seemed intent on accomplishing their morning duties.

I moved my hand to shade my eyes from the sun, and for the first time since last evening, I noticed the golden ring which now graced my finger. The ring was beautiful and fascinating. I had to focus intently to make out the image inscribed on it, four women with their arms upraised in a gesture of invocation. Each of them wore the ceremonial dress of a Hearth Queen. Interestingly, although their bodies were detailed, their heads were indistinct as if they could be any women. I knew these were the four Hearth Queens of the island. There were a variety of other representations, several plants, a tree, some fruit, and more I could not recognize. It was an amazing artistic accomplishment. I was proud to have it as my seal. My bed and bath called to me as I again began my journey back to my rooms. I found myself fervently hoping that being the acknowledged future Hearth Queen of Malia would not bring with it as many complications as there had been on my first day.

10

I was awakened by the silence. This morning the voices of the Guards did not come into my room from their Court below. On a normal day their shouts, laughter, and the clanging of their swords often woke me. I found it difficult to reconcile the contradictory feelings evoked by this way of being awakened. I was annoyed by their noise while at the same time delighted to have their sounds as the first thing I heard every day. Concerned, I reached out to *touch* them. Indiscriminately, I tried to connect with whomever I could. I was a bit overwhelmed as many impressions came to me at once.

Petra was standing on the prow of a ship grinning as if party to a good prank. Karis watched the shoreline intently while Maris was engaged in wrapping Ianthe's sprained wrist. None of them *emanated* any distress, so, despite the silence of the Court, all seemed well. What I felt instead of any disturbance was an animated prompting to join them on the beach.

Eager to find out why they were calling me, I bounded out of bed and began searching through my chests for something to wear. In my rush to get to the harbor, I was flinging clothes on the floor when Reya called from the door.

"Are you awake?"

"I have to get to the harbor," I replied excitedly slipping on a tunic and a soft skirt. I did not pause to acknowledge Reya, but began looking for my shoes. "Have you seen my sandals?"

Reya calmly crossed the room, moved aside a pile I had made while disgorging my trunks, and extracted a pair of sandals from beneath it.

Smiling, she brought them to me.

I pushed my foot into one shoe and began hopping toward the door while I tried to slip the strap of the other over my heel. Finally accomplishing the aim of my acrobatics, I hurriedly rushed out the door and began racing down the steps toward the central Court. I was surprised when I heard Reya call from behind me.

"Young Queen, would you mind moving with a little less haste?"

Slowing, I turned to see Reya moving toward me down the stairs. Impatiently, I paused to wait for her.

"I know where I'm going. I'll be fine," I panted, breathless from my rapid descent. Reya often joined me as I moved about the Palace. Most days, I was happy for her company, but right now I did not want to delay my progress waiting for her.

"I am not following you," she answered. "I am also called to the shore."

"Oh," I replied with disappointment while Reya descended the steps with far more decorum than I had just shown. I had been under the mistaken impression I was the only one being summoned by the Guards to the harbor. Sighing, I reevaluated the urgency of my journey as Reya joined me.

Actually, after my initial disillusionment, I was happy to have her with me. We walked companionably through the central Court and to the north gate toward the harbor, talking about the previous day. I shared with Reya my experiences in the healing rooms, and she told me what she had learned in the Queen's chamber after I had left with the healers. I was surprised to learn that women were still chanting.

"Someone will remain there monitoring and offering support to the Guardians until the danger is past and they have returned. When there is risk, the Wise Ones and women of the Queen's chamber sustain the Guards as they do their work. This job is equally important as those defending the Palace. The threat would be much greater if not reinforced by the efforts of these women." She explained, "At dawn, we began taking turns. Many of the Queen's women and the women from your chamber have gone to bed. Most of the Wise Ones remain. If the Guards do not return in a few hours, other women will go to relieve them."

"Does it always happen like this?" I asked, interested to understand how these women functioned in a time of crisis.

"Yes," Reya acknowledged, "we would never leave the Guardians alone without energetic support."

I was curious to know more about this exchange, but we had reached the shore where thirty or more women stood waiting. There were Guards from Zakros and Knossos as well as about half of the Guardians from Malia. Scattered among the Guards were local people and an occasional person from one of the other Palaces. All of them stared fixedly out to sea in anticipation. Sighting us, Hespar loped out of the group to meet us.

"Greetings, Young Queen. Greetings, Reya. It is good you have come. They are about to arrive. If you look," she said pointing, "you can see the sails."

In fact, I could see a ship. It was sailing quickly through the bright blue water toward us. Reya, the others and I stood in silence and watched its approach. It did not take long to make out the figures crewing the craft. There was movement everywhere aboard. I could see Adesha, Maris, Fauntee, and several other Guards from Knossos and Zakros pulling in the sails. A study in contrasts, Drea and Dariah stood side-by-side at the helm. Drea barely reached Dariah's shoulder, but I could not have said which one looked more commanding. I should not have been surprised to learn that these women could sail. A significant amount of Malia's activities were based on its relationship to the sea. However, it had not occurred to me until this moment that this, too, could be a skill of a Guardian.

Once the ship was close to the shoreline, Adesha dove over the gunnels and swam strongly toward us, towing behind her a sturdy rope. When she reached the beach she tied the rope to a post and the Guardians' vessel became one of many moored in the harbor. The ship looked strong and sea worthy, but it was different from the others berthed there. Its forward section sloped upward, making an arched curve which looked like the sprout of a young fern. The placement of its masts and the configuration of its rigging was also distinct. Although I was not certain, I suspected this ship had been won from the Sea Raiders.

The ship was still a moderate distance from land, so, calling and laughing, the Guards dove and jumped into the water. There was exhilaration and exuberance among them as they approached shore. They mischievously knocked into each other, slapped one another on the back, and wrestled playfully as they made their way toward the beach. I had seen the Guards riding and as they sparred at practice. I had watched them at rest outside their Shelter and found each of these experiences moved me both sensually and emotionally. However, I knew what I saw now would remain in my memory forever. They strode from the sea full of animation and pride, their damp clothing clinging suggestively to their solid frames. To me, each one of them was breathtaking, but the group of them together, celebrating their success, was truly moving.

As the Guards reached the surf they scanned the shore. Tam, the youngest of the Foundlings, was the first to see me.

"Young Queen!" she yelled, her voice filled with delight at having spotted me ahead of the others.

Immediately, a chorus of Guards all began calling to me at once.

"Giada." Several Guards shouted simultaneously. "Young Queen." More of them boomed above the surf. Much pointing and laughter accompanied their words and many of them gestured toward the ship.

Fauntee was one of the first out of the water. Closely followed by a collection of Guards, she approached me and saluted with mock civility.

"Young Queen," she declared grinning, "If you would be so good as to look upon the newest ship in our fleet...*The Giada*. It was taken on the day of your presentation and so, in your honor, we have named the ship after you." Fauntee turned and with a sweep of her hand indicated the vessel which the Guardians had sailed into the harbor.

Maris stood, her hair looking strangely uneven, on the prow of the ship. With this signal from Fauntee she unfurled a banner emblazoned with my seal. She held it in place over whatever had been there before. I could see the Guards were pleased and, although they were making this presentation with humor, there was an undercurrent of sincerity that accompanied the act. They all looked at me waiting for my response.

I didn't know how to react. My desire to convey that I was touched conflicted with my inclination to respond in the same playful manner in which Fauntee had addressed me. Eventually, lightheartedness won and I answered Fauntee in kind.

"It is indeed an awesome site," I replied, my voice and delivery mirroring that of hers.

"It leads me to wonder how such a grand vessel comes to be in the possession of the Guards," I continued.

"Ah," Fauntee responded still continuing with her mocking delivery. "That would be in 'The Telling."

"The Telling?" I answered, perplexed. "Can you explain to me, wise Guard, what is 'The Telling?'"

"To know of 'The Telling' you must join us in our celebration," she said, solicitously offering me her arm. We turned our backs on the azure sea and along with all of those present, set off toward the Palace.

*****

The section of roof that created an overhanging porch for the Guardians' Shelter was not large enough to accommodate all of those who had come with us from the harbor. It became even more crowded as people we passed on our way joined us, anticipating what was about to happen. Everyone began looking for places to sit or stand. Stava pushed buckets used for tooling leather into a corner, and Karis emerged from the Shelter carrying wooden chests she offered to people for seats. Temo, another of the Foundlings, placed logs in the fire pit, and coaxed the sleeping coals into a cheerful blaze.

The Guardians, all of whom occupied the innermost spaces under the overhang, were bedraggled. There were bruises on their cheekbones, bandaged legs were propped on boxes, and the hair on one side of Maris head was missing. With a vanity I would not have expected from the old warder, Maris kept smoothing down the remaining hair in the missing section. Her ministrations, however, had no effect and the sparse hair that remained continued to stick out at odd angles. All of the Guards were disheveled. Many of their tunics were torn and a few were even bloody. Despite this scruffy display, high-spirited *energy* and satisfaction swirled among them. Eventually, activity began to die down and a hush fell.

I watched as all eyes turned to Petra.

"Now is the time for 'The Telling,'" she announced. "Who will speak?"

Voices rang out simultaneously from many of the Guardians present.

"Peace," Petra shouted to be heard over the din. She nodded and acknowledged Alana, one of the Guards from Knossos.

All eyes turned to Alana as she began, "Aleksia, Cor and I were standing near the North Gate when we first spotted the Sea Raiders." Immediately hoots and laughter greeted her statement.

"All right, all right," she continued good-naturedly, raising her hands in a gesture of surrender. "Aleksia, Cor and I were, umm, talking with several women from Malia when we saw the raiders coming up the causeway. Cor is one of Knossos's Air Guards. She sent the alert." Many people glanced in the direction of a Guard I did not know, but assumed must be Cor. The woman nodded gravely.

Adesha spoke next. Looking around at the Guards from the other Palaces she offered an explanation. "I am the strongest swimmer and a Water Guardian. If an attack calls for a response by water, Temo, Charis, Nike and I form a water strategy. Our assessments led us to believe we could capture the invaders' ship."

"They had left only two of their people onboard," young Temo interrupted excitedly. "It was easy for us to swim to the ship. We tried not to make a sound as we swam, and we must have succeeded because we climbed aboard without anyone noticing. Once we were on board, we made noise in one of the holds to make it seem like something was wrong. The raiders raced into the stowage compartments, and then all we had to do was lock them in." Temo nodded expressively to the assembled group, clearly proud of her accomplishments.

"After that, the ship was ours," Adesha continued, good naturedly acknowledging Temo's young exuberance. "We were able to signal Petra that we had taken the ship."

Squaring her shoulders and standing up to her full height, Drea interjected, "All that was left for us to do was herd the Sea Raiders on shore back to the ship," she made this pronouncement as if the act was so simple it required little effort.

"Ari and I remained at the gate to make certain no invaders snuck into the Palace," Karis said wistfully. It was clear from her tone she had wished to be among the Guards on the beach. "Thanks to everyone's efforts, our post was uneventful."

Stava took up the telling next. "Maris and I were chasing one of the Sea Raiders when I tripped and fell. By the time I got up, he had caught Maris by the hair. I ran toward the two of them. The raider was poised to strike, and I was afraid I would arrive to late. But, Maris did not hesitate. In the limited space she had, she quickly swung her sword and hacked off a section of her hair. That freed her from the invader's grasp, and she had him on the ground in a moment."

Hoots and laughter greeted this account. The Guards and the others present began to chant, "Maris, Maris, Maris."

Eventually Maris stood, her uneven hair still sticking out at odd angles.

"I had not expected one of the Sea Raiders to help me with my barbering," Maris said gruffly, "but in my judgment, it is better to be missing a hank of hair rather than an arm." Chuckling and compliments came from the other women.

Nike, Ianthe and many of the Guards from the other Palaces took up the story. Each of them told the events of the evening from her perspective. Eventually, a cohesive narrative began to emerge. Water Guardians had secured the raiders' ship. The Guards from the three Palaces worked together and eventually tricked, trapped and corralled the invaders. Once they were caught, they were transported back to their ship and hauled on board. The Guards then put out to sea using the raiders' vessel. They sailed most of the night until they reached an island they had previously scouted. They left the invaders there and sailed back to Malia with their ship.

"It is a decent island," Hespar explained to those present. "If they look around they will find tools we left earlier. There is a good source of fresh water toward the interior. They will have to work hard, but I do not believe they will starve."

The wine bottle was beginning to circulate among the crowd and I noticed the drinking cups of the injured Guards were filled more often than others.

"It was a gift from Goddess that the Guards from Zakros and Knossos were with us last evening," Petra said, raising her glass and acknowledging the Guardians from the other Palaces." Our task would have been much more difficult without their help."

Thekia and Dariah, the Peers of the Guard from the other Palaces, nodded gravely at Petra in acknowledgement. The crowd briefly fell silent as everyone considered the possible consequences of an attack with less assistance. Eventually, conversations began again, but this time they were in quieter tones among small groups of people.

After a few moments Petra began to speak again, "We have had success today. With the help of the Guards from Knossos and Zakros, the Sea Raiders' vessel has become ours and has been named in honor of the new Young Queen." As she said these words, she gazed in my direction and I could sense the connection I felt with her *engage*. "The lives of sons have been spared, for although they be Sea Raiders, they too have mothers who would mourn them. We have cause for celebration."

A cheer went up among the Guards in acknowledgement of Petra's words and Ianthe began a bright tune on one of the Air Guard's pipes. Ari and Temo disappeared into the Shelter and both emerged with hand-held drums. In moments, they fell into cadence with Ianthe's tune. Guardians jumped from their seats and a circle of dancers began in the open Court. The same boxes that had been used for seating were now pushed against the walls as the circle grew. Even the Guardians whose feet were bandaged clapped to the beat.

I found it hard to believe these Guards had the stamina to have fought all evening, sailed all night, and still could dance this morning. But, dance they did, with movements as complex and as intricate as those of their weapons practice. Some of the Guardians made incredible leaps into the air while others moved in fluid ways reminiscent of waves in the ocean. The circle of dancers moved with serpentine curves among the people gathered for "The Telling." At rest, I found the *energy* of the assembled Guards to be intense, but the celebratory dance of the Guardians from three Palaces was almost overwhelming. They spiraled by me, one after another, and, as each of them passed, there was a flash of *contact*. I felt as breathless as if I too were dancing.

After the Guards had made several rounds of the Court they began pulling bystanders in to join the circle. I noticed Thekia, the Peer of the Guard from Zakros, reached for Reya and from nowhere Sacra emerged and fell into step beside Petra. I did not have long to wait before Karis offered me her hand and I was moving swiftly along with the others. The dance progressed with ever-increasing speed until I was breathless.

Just when I thought I would have to step out of the circle because I could no longer keep up, the music and dancing stopped abruptly. Shouts, clapping and laughter rang out from the panting throng. It appeared they had anticipated the sudden ending and had been building toward it. I found it hard to believe, but in a few moments Ianthe began another tune and a number of dancers formed a circle again. Karis looked at me questioningly, but I shook my head. My legs were trembling just from the efforts to keep up with the dancing I had already done.

There seemed to be no official end to "The Telling." In couples and small groups, people left the Court. Some of them moved back to their seats while others headed away, succumbing to rightful exhaustion.

Karis walked with me back to the porch and offered me a seat on one of the benches which regularly occupied a place in the enclosure. We sat together watching the remaining dancers without speaking. I studied her, hoping to feel her invitation to dance had been personal and might indicate an emerging bond between us. Her energy, however, remained clear, and I could *feel* no underlying significance in her actions. She had been asked to escort me to my presentation, and it seemed her invitation to dance had been an extension of that same assignment. I sighed quietly to myself wishing her intentions had been otherwise. She was a striking woman and it would have pleased me to notice any indication of personal interest. I felt none. It caused me to wonder how I might encourage her to be otherwise.

After a time she looked away from the dancers and spoke, "Young Queen, it has been a pleasure to dance with you, but other duties call me away. *The Giada* requires attention before she may safely rest in the harbor. Would you wish me to walk with you to your rooms?"

"No," I replied wistfully, "I think I will remain here and watch the dance."

"Then I will leave you unless you have need of anything else from me... some fruit or wine perhaps?"

"Thank you, Karis, I am fine." I answered. "And thank you for the dancing and supporting me at my presentation."

"It was my honor," she answered with sincerity, and with a charming salute, she left the Shelter.

I remained where she had left me and watched the dancers. The circle grew smaller over time. As I looked on, more people moved to the porch and sat with food and drink. I noticed Reya and Thekia were sitting together across the enclosure from me. I watched Reya, her eyes filled with affection, reach out and touch Thekia's cheek. After a time, they left the Shelter hand-in-hand.

My first reaction was surprise. It had not occurred to me Reya might have a sweetheart. It had seemed to me all her attention was focused on Malia and her work here. But, now I believed there might be more on her mind. If she and Thekia were involved, it seemed to me their relationship must be difficult. I remembered Reya's own words when she was explaining the Guardians to me, something like...

"A Guard is pledged for a lifetime to their Hearth Queen and the Guard. Nothing can supersede that commitment."

Thekia was Peer of the Guard of Zakros, and she would be promised to Aellai while Reya's obligations were here at Malia. In keeping their promises, they would very likely see each other infrequently. I wondered what future there would be in their relationship and if a time would come when they would be able to be together. I certainly hoped I would not become involved with a Guardian from another Palace for it was clear I was destined to remain at Malia.

I was deep in these thoughts when Nyssa spun onto a place beside me on the bench. She was somewhat breathless from the dance.

With a deep inhalation she grinned and began, "Did you know Karis is involved with Asteria?"

With a flash of comprehension, I understood Karis's polite, but cool reaction to my overtures. I gazed at Nyssa wondering if she had seen my interaction with Karis or if she had decided to share this information for some other reason.

Trying to appear unruffled I asked, "Who is Asteria?"

"She is a Wise One," Nyssa replied, her expression full of incredulity, "you must see her almost every day."

Well, I thought to myself, I didn't recognize her name, but I would certainly watch for her in the future.

"Have you seen Reya?" Nyssa asked, "I walked some of the races today and I wanted to tell her what I found."

"She left a little while ago with Thekia, the Peer of the Guard from Zakros."

Nyssa giggled and broke into a knowing smile. "That is no surprise."

"Are they too 'involved?'" I asked, speculating Nyssa could answer the questions I had been pondering.

"Oh, yes. They have been involved for years." She replied turning toward me on the bench.

"How do they manage when they are so often apart?" I wondered out loud.

Leaning toward me as if she was about to share a secret, Nyssa said, "They have not always been in different places. Reya and Thekia are both from Zakros."

I looked at her with skepticism, "then how did one of them end up at Malia and the other still at Zakros?"

"They had a disagreement." Nyssa almost whispered and continued, "Thekia was chosen to be Peer of the Guard at Zakros when she was very young."

"Aellai is..." Nyssa paused as if searching for the right thing to say. Finally she resumed. "Well, Aellai is not like Sacra."

"Yes, I saw her in the Court yesterday," I said, "watching her made me very glad to have Sacra as our Hearth Queen."

Nyssa nodded. "I have heard Reya told Thekia she should not accept the office of Peer of the Guard. Thekia is very gentle and Reya thought Aellai would take advantage of her. Thekia would not turn down the position of Peer because the other Guards had chosen her and she respected their wisdom. It is said Reya told Thekia the reason she was chosen to be Peer was that no one else wanted to deal with Aellai. After that the two of them did not speak for a long time."

"How do you know all this?" I asked with uncertainty.

"Well, Amara who is a cook at Zakros told Klotho who is the healer there. Klotho was called to Malia to help with healing..."

I raised my hand for her to stop.

But, she continued, "Well anyway, I heard it." Hardly taking a breath she went on, "and, not too long after that, Reya came to Malia for Sacra's presentation. She knew Sacra because their Mothers had been in Aellai's chamber. They shared having grown up under Aellai's rule. As we both just said, Sacra is a different kind of Hearth Queen than Aellai. Sacra asked Reya if she would consider being one of her Council. Reya believed her relationship with Thekia was over."

"Do you think she regrets her decision?" I asked.

Nyssa shrugged. She cocked her head listening as a new melody came from the other side of the Court. She smiled at me distractedly and bounced up from the bench. Without looking back, she ran across the Court and began the intricate pattern of the dance. This was so like Nyssa I couldn't be upset.

Our conversation left me wondering how Reya and Thekia had reconciled their earlier conflict. Did disappointment or distrust still linger between them? The commitments they made had been for a lifetime. Would there be a time when one or the other of them would be free?

I watched Nyssa and the other dancers full of exuberance. Unexpectedly I realized, it was well past half-day and I was hungry. Standing, I started to leave the Shelter. I had only taken a few steps when Fauntee blocked my way. I stepped to the side thinking to get out of her way. She made the same movement and I could not pass. I could *sense* agitation, and I was surprised when I looked at her to find she seemed upset. She stared at me intently for a time and I began to feel uncomfortable.

Eventually, I decided to speak. "Are you troubled?" I asked, meeting her gaze.

She did not answer, but snorted and turned away from me.

I waited for a while and when she still did not answer I asked again, "Is something the matter?"

"What do you think?" she replied irritably.

"Well, it seems as if something is the matter," I acknowledged. I found it strange she could be so distressed after the Guard's success with the Sea Raiders.

"Why did you dance with Karis?" she blurted, *waves* of resentment accompanying her statement.

"What?" I responded, confused by the energy that came along with her question.

"Why did you dance with Karis?" she repeated.

"Because she drew me into the circle," was all I could think to say.

Fauntee snorted again. "You know everyone will think you fancy her."

"Why will they think that?" I asked, wondering what Palace custom I had unwittingly invoked by agreeing to dance with Karis.

"It was bad enough you stood with her at your presentation, but to choose her to be your partner in the dance..." Fauntee's voice trailed off.

I was increasingly ill at ease with the conversation, and I did not know what to say. I had always enjoyed Fauntee's strong *contact* up till now but, to *feel* her *signal* in anger confused and frightened me.

Finally, I moved back in the other direction, wanting to leave. When I did, Fauntee jumped away and gave a grudging salute. She then turned and walked off.

Dariah, the giant Peer of the Guard from Knossos, intercepted Fauntee's anger. She walked toward me her gentle eyes full of concern.

"Young Queen?" she questioned, "Are you well?"

I was uncertain how to explain the situation, so I decided instead to ask for information about the meaning of dancing with someone.

"Well," she responded slowly as if contemplating how to answer, "the dance of the Guards raises *energy*. For many, this particular *energy* is, umm... has a physical component. At times, when women dance, the *energy* is conveyed from one woman to another. Often women choose to share this with someone for whom they have affection."

"Thank you, Dariah." I said, "that's very helpful. If you will excuse me I believe I will retire to my rooms now."

She nodded, tapped her shoulder in salute, and stepped aside to let me pass.

Every day at Malia I learned something new. With the information Dariah had given me, I could understand why Fauntee had been upset. Her behavior was still disconcerting, but at least I could comprehend what she thought had been happening. I found myself disappointed also. There had been no energy exchange with Karis. I wondered how it would have felt to dance with someone who facilitated that interaction. Next time there was a dance, I promised myself I would wait to accept a partner of my choosing.

11

Everything was the same and yet everything was different after my presentation. The other Hearth Queens and their Guardians returned to their respective Palaces within a few days. I still went to the Wise Ones every morning. Having seen how their training was used, I had gained greater respect for their work. Regardless, I continued to find them alternatively tedious and intrusive. To no avail, I searched for some form of divination to practice. I now believed to be effective as Hearth Queen, I would need to develop some facility with the skills of the Wise Ones.

I pondered how one might do this without becoming immersed in their world. Eventually, an idea occurred to me. Up to this point, I had considered the Wise Ones a monolithic group. I viewed each of them as interchangeable with one another. But, if Sacra and Reya had once been part of the Temple, then perhaps there was a Wise One or two with whom I could connect. I believed considering them as individuals had merit. If I could befriend a Wise One, I might be able to learn from her without enduring the posturing which seemed to routinely accompany the calling. Having made this decision, each day I watched. I decided that, to observe the Wise Ones outside the environment in which I normally interacted with them, might give me the most information. So I began my search. Every morning, when my time in the Mysteries was over, I followed a Wise One.

What I found was that, for many of them, most of their days were devoted to their work. Quite a few went down to the communal spaces occupied by the Wise Ones shortly after dawn and did not return until dusk. Some of them always seemed to be chanting and performing devotionals at various altars around the Palace. Periodically, they would clean these spaces, replace the flowers or symbols with which they were decorated, and rebuild them anew. I believed some Wise Ones were permanently devoted to a specific task or Goddess while others moved from place to place, hoping to understand the qualities of divergent deities.

There were shrines to different aspects of the Goddess scattered throughout Malia. There was one public altar to the Amazon Goddess tended by a Wise One. I understood the Guards had a private sanctuary they cared for themselves. Although I had never seen this site, I liked to speculate what it was like and where it might be. I reasoned it likely this space was also assigned to an Amazon. However, people often admired deities with a different appearance from their own. This made me wonder if the Guardian's sanctuary might be dedicated to a Goddess dissimilar to them. I very much wanted to see it and wondered if they would take me to it if I asked. There were also shrines to Gods dispersed around the Palace, and I assumed men also had private spaces for worship. If such spaces existed, I was unaware of their location and concluded they must be in the men's section of the Palace.

The Wise Ones tended a space for the Sweet Girl Child who I had seen alight in my rooms at the beginning of spring. Girls and mothers of girls were the most frequent visitors to this place. I watched the Wise One at this altar step back into a nearby alcove whenever someone approached. Most times, women would simply place an offering in this space and leave. However occasionally, they retreated quietly into the same spot the Wise One occupied.

I made up reasons to pass this opening when it was in use. After overhearing the conversations of those inside, I was briefly embarrassed about eavesdropping. I found young girls shared with the Wise One their fears and concerns about their emerging womanhood. The Mothers who came often expressed doubt or frustration about their girl children. The Wise One offered council and reassurance. She primarily listened, but when she spoke, she shared her perspective about this time in life. Growth and change brought challenges to a girl and those around her. She stated that learning to be independent, and deal with a maturing body and its sexuality, were normal parts of a young woman's early life. Although both mothers and daughters innately knew this, restating it appeared to comfort them and they left the Wise One with thanks and appreciation.

I was wistful when I watched the girls leave. In my early life, the elders of my village had offered support and direction. Although these women had been informative, even encouraging, there was no one trained to advise and celebrate young girls. The village women had been loving and supportive, but I wondered how my life might have been different had I had the encouragement and direction of a Wise One. As I pondered these thoughts, I realized I had found yet another way the Wise Ones' training could be useful.

I found Wise Ones were similarly stationed at other places of the Goddess in the Palace. The area of the Mother Goddess was a large sanctuary situated in luscious rooms. In one of the Mother Goddess's chambers, soft rugs covered the stone floors, and couches were scattered along the walls. Women came to this space, out of the bustle of Palace life, to rest, rejuvenate and be together when they were bleeding. Most women came into their power around the same time. So, elder Wise Ones whose bleeding days were at an end swirled among those resting, offering soothing tea, warm compresses and kindness.

In an adjoining room, women often talked among themselves and with a gaggle of Wise Ones. They solicited advice about birth, breast-feeding and raising children. Sometimes the issues brought to this Goddess required special expertise, so a healer was often present. Nearby, but removed enough to assure freedom from intrusion, were rooms for birthing. These too were comfortably appointed with space for whomever a woman wanted to be present at a birth. Family, friends, midwives, healers, Wise Ones, and special attendants for pregnant mothers were all commonly present at these times.

Some women requested singers, storytellers or musicians to be in attendance, while others preferred silence. In this space, women in labor were encouraged to be entertained or distracted as they chose. Those giving birth to other undertakings were welcomed into this space as well. Just like the birth of babies, women would gather those around them with whom they wished to share the beginning of an endeavor. The Mother Goddess' blessing and counsel were sought for projects about to be started, crops planted or creative activities begun.

The Old One held a place of honor just outside the south entrance to the central Court. She was the mountain that was centered behind her shrine, and shared her name, Dicta. Each day, most of the people of the Palace stopped to acknowledge her in some way. Guards paused to salute, women brought olive branches in homage to her, children stood on tiptoe to peer over the top of her altar and catch sight of the mountain beyond. This was supposed to bring good luck. By greeting her in this way, children sought to capture good fortune. I suspected many of the adults who stopped there actually had similar intentions but were simply more covert.

Dicta was believed to sustain Malia and give blessings to its people. Observances held in her honor helped maintain the social order of the Palace. One of these events was always held five days after the full moon. With Dicta at their back, Sacra and her Council would sit in an area which adjoined the Queen's chamber called "The Queen's Court" and listen to the people of Malia. The city's inhabitants came full of praises for the bounty of harvest or concerns about water shortages in summer. The breadth of what they shared encompassed the boundaries of human experience. Births, deaths, illnesses, disputes, declarations of love, even revelatory spiritual experiences, all came before the Hearth Queen and her Council.

The day after the Guardians' Telling, I was surprised to see Keto lurking in my chamber's doorway. Her scent of soap and fresh laundry drifted to me before I actually saw her. She appraised me briefly and then grudgingly began to speak, "Young Queen, I carry a message to you from the Queen."

I noticed her emphasis on "the." Although almost everyone in the Palace welcomed me, Keto remained distant. I was certain I could *touch* her and seek the cause of her reticence, but it did not seem necessary or even appropriate. I sensed her critical nature evaluated her own actions harshly. I believed her reserve had little to do with me personally, but was instead about my position as Young Queen. For someone in a Palace to hold the place of Young Queen meant the time of the elder Hearth Queen was coming to an end. Of all Sacra's Councilwomen, Keto was the most protective. I suspected she was not happy to see a "Young Queen" arrive at Malia.

Despite her prickliness, for some reason I did not understand, each time I interacted with her I felt compassion. I let this feeling overtake me as I turned to listen to her message.

Seeing she had my attention, she began, "tomorrow the Queen and her Council listen to the people of Malia. When the sun has moved over the roof of your chamber, she invites you and the women of your rooms to join her in the Queen's Court."

Keto did not wait for me to ask questions or acknowledge her message. She simply turned and began descending the steps before I could comment.

Even though she was gone, I smiled and spoke to the empty doorway, "Well, I guess I'll have to find someone else to enlighten me about what will happen tomorrow."

Which was exactly what I did. Later that evening when the women of my chamber returned to the Spring Hall, I sought out several of them and asked about the Queen's request. They explained that once a Young Queen was presented, her formal duties began. I would now be called upon to accompany the Queen whenever she performed official tasks. Listening to the people was an important responsibility for a Queen. Hearing the joys and concerns of Malia was a powerful tool. It is the duty of a Hearth Queens to know what was happening with the people of the Palace. Having a time when the inhabitants of Malia could share their thoughts with the Queen was an excellent way to gain insight into the heart of the community. Tomorrow was to be my first official function as a presented Young Queen. Myrina offered to send word to the women of my rooms asking them to meet in my chamber after half-day so we could walk together to the Queen's Court.

*****

The next morning led slowly toward half-day. I watched as the sun traveled over the roof of my chamber and moved

135

toward the mountains to the west. One-by- one the room filled with my women. I could tell by their demeanor that this was not a somber occasion. As we walked toward the Queen's Court, women laughed, chattered and told the news of their days. Kyma moved near me to share details of a mystery which was puzzling the healers.

A few days ago several people in the Palace began to behave strangely. Everyone who encountered them assumed they had drunk too much wine, but their behavior was more bizarre than someone who had been heavy handed with drink. A potter paced frantically and eventually smashed many perfect pots, all the while muttering she did not like the way they were talking to her. A grower had joyfully pulled all the immature figs from a tree and thrown each of them into the air so they might be free. A herder was hiding from his goats because he believed there was malice in their eyes and they were causing him to shake. Alandra, one of the women of my chamber, sat alone in a corner and rocked with her feet and legs twisted in odd contortions. Others tried to coax her out of this space to no avail. She just kept repeating, "It hurts, it hurts."

Damaris, Kyma and the other healers began looking for the cause of this strange outbreak. The malady did not function with the common movement of sickness. An ailment normally spread when people came in contact with someone else who was unwell. But, in this case, those who had regular interactions with the suffering were unaffected. At first it was difficult to get information from anyone whose behavior had been altered. However, over time the actions of these people returned to normal and, although they complained of pain and weakness, they were otherwise well. A band of healers began surveying those affected. They asked where they had been, what they had drunk, if they shared similar concerns, what food they had eaten, and with whom they had been in contact. After they had completed their inquiries they began to evaluate.

It took quite a while to compile the information gained from these conversations. Eventually, a commonality emerged. Each of the individuals who had exhibited variant behavior had eaten dark bread the day before they fell ill. In possession of this fact, a group of healers immediately headed to the kitchen. They questioned the cooks about the ingredients of the dark bread served two days before. They were informed the bread had been made with a combination of rye and wheat which was stored in the Palace's granaries.

Kyma ended her story when we arrived at the Queen's Court. This Court was much smaller than the central Court and had a series of steps which created seating. As we entered this space, Titaia greeted us and explained that the Queen and her women would sit with Dicta at their back on the right side of the Court. She invited us to sit on the left so that Dicta might be behind us also. Most of Sacra's women and the Queen herself had already arrived. Sacra sat in the seat closest to the ground and the open floor of the Court. The women of her chamber sat in threes and fours on higher steps. Reya motioned me into a space in the first row across the aisle from the Queen, and my women took seats mirroring Sacra's companions.

Other people milled about in the center of the Court, finding seats and greeting friends. When the commotion began to settle down, Sacra stood, gazed around the Court, and spoke, "People of Malia, we come here today to listen to your joys and concerns. Who would speak first?"

Unlike the Guardians who all began speaking at once when Petra had asked a similar question at the Telling, those in the Court hesitated at first. People shifted in their seats and looked around for who would begin. In one corner a group of young men pushed and coaxed a blushing man reluctantly to his feet.

The Queen turned toward him smiling, "Ieni it appears your friends would have you speak"

"Yes, I do have news," he replied sheepishly as he stood. "Lavra has acknowledged me as the father of her new boy child. He is a strong, healthy babe, and I am proud to be recognized as his father."

"Congratulations, Ieni," Sacra declared warmly in response. "It is indeed an honor to be acknowledged as a father."

Reya leaned toward me and whispered. "They say she not only acknowledged him, but they are a "'love match.'" There was no question she would name him when the time came. They will take a place together in a villa near the Palace soon."

My mind wandered from the continuing sounds of the people who filled the Court. I wondered why my mother had chosen my father and if they too might have been a "love match." Many women from the Palace and some of those from my village chose to remain in women's space to raise their young children. In the spaces of women there was a great deal of support from others for a child's parenting and care. It was as if a child had many mothers.

Making the decision to remain in women's space did not preclude naming a father. A woman could choose any man who agreed to serve as father to her children. One of the most important choices a woman could make was the selection and naming of a father. Frequently, this act had little to do with whom she bedded. Fathering and siring were seen as two separate skills and not every man was suitable for both. For most mothers, there was little sentimentality attached to naming a father. Fathers had regular access to their children and needed to be able to provide gentle support and guidance. For women who bore boy children, the father took an increasingly active role in a boy's life as he grew. Mothers who chose to remain in women's space relied on a boy child's father to inform him about men's traditions and their parts of the Palace. When the time came, and a boy, his mother and father all agreed, it was the father who took him to men's space as his primary lodging.

Sometimes an acknowledged father and the mother of a child would share their living space. It appeared to me this was more common in villages like the one I had come from than here in the Palace. Most living spaces in Malia were divided by gender, with only a few places a woman and a man could occupy together. However, adjoining the Palace were many homes and villas which encouraged mixed gender cohabitation and parenting.

As I had been musing about my mother and father and parenting in general, people continued to speak. A tanner reported on her new shed which she had equipped with innovative and, she felt, ingenious devices for plying her trade.

138

Several Guardians reported on potential items for barter they had encountered the last time they had ridden out. A few builders described the progress made on repairs to the walls which had fallen the last time the Earth Mother shook.

With some apparent uneasiness, Alkestis rose and began speaking, "there is dissension among the women of the archives."

There was a shift in the atmosphere among both my women and the Queen's. They paid closer attention to Alkestis words than they had to many of the previous speakers.

When Alkestis did not continue for a few moments, the Queen prompted, "Tell us about the unrest, Alkestis."

"As you are all aware," Alkestis began, "we have recently added rooms to the archives. Instead of creating ease as we had hoped, it has caused conflict. Calida was to create order among the records being moved to the new rooms. She set about this task and was making brisk progress when Enyo declared she saw another way for the space to be used. This probably would not have been a problem if Enyo had found a way to offer her suggestion constructively. Instead, she accused Calida of making the records inaccessible to others."

The Queen and the women of her Council looked concerned. I was personally surprised by this revelation. Calida was in my rooms every day, and I had heard nothing of this situation. This prompted me to turn to Reya.

"We must begin sitting Council with the women of my chamber," I whispered.

"Yes," she replied softly, "It is disturbing to learn Calida may be in need of support and we were not aware of it."

I nodded and returned my attention to the Court. From several rows behind the Queen, Titaia, the mediator from the Queen's Council, rose. She descended the steps and stood near the Queen. The two of them exchanged a meaningful look, and then Titaia turned toward Alkestis.

With sincere kindness she asked, "May I be of assistance?"

Alkestis pondered for a time and then nodded somberly.

The Queen watched Alkestis for a few moments, allowing her to make certain this addressed her issue. When it appeared she had nothing more to share and was comfortable the Queen spoke again.

"Alkestis, Titaia please come to us next moon and tell us of your progress."

Alkestis nodded again while Titaia said, "I will hope to bring you a report of improvement or resolution." With these words she climbed the steps back to her seat and sat again among the women of Sacra's Council.

The news continued with reports from the people of the Palace and beyond. They were at times edifying, poignant, and sad. As these accounts seemed to be coming to an end, Damaris moved from her seat behind the Queen to stand before us on the floor of the Court. She related the story Kyma had shared with me about those who had fallen ill. As part of her report, she drew from her pocket a handful of grain. She pored a portion of it into the Queen's hand and, walking the short distance between us, into mine also.

Seeming to take up the story where Kyma had been interrupted, she related that several healers and quite a few cooks had gone to inspect the granaries. Among those who went to examine the grain was a young woman named Calla. Calla had come from the pasturelands to the south to apprentice as a healer. She said that in her village when the winters were cool and there had been copious rain, the sheep would become crazed. They ran in circles, lay splayed on the ground kicking, or became timid and nervous. It was well known among the herders the cause for these behaviors was purple rye. Rye was normally a rich dark brown, but sometimes among the grain were also kernels of a deep purple. The herders believed that dampness made the rye turn purple. Those who consumed it occasionally, be they human or animal, became ill and behaved strangely until the effect wore off. If the purple rye was consumed repeatedly, it could cause more serious problems and even death. Damaris asked Calla if she could recognize purple rye, and Calla confirmed she could.

I had wandered through the stores which were behind my chamber on the first floor in the southeastern corner of the Palace. Even in the heat of the day, they were cool and dark, which made them an attractive place to explore. Eight of the largest vases I had ever seen occupied most of the space in this area. Each of these was twice my height. The vases had wide openings at the top, and then tapered gradually toward their base. All but one of these was in use and was sealed with wax into which had been pressed the seal of the grower to whom they belonged.

As Damaris continued, it was easy to picture this place. She reported the cooks identified the specific vases from which they had taken the grain to make the bread in question. Aminta, the cook who had collected the wheat and rye, had stood on a tall stool and ladled out some of the contents. She handed the grains to Calla who held them in the palm of her hand and stirred them with her finger. After a moment's search, she confirmed the rye contained some purple grains. Wanting to be certain the wheat was not also contaminated, Aminta retrieved some of its contents as well. Calla repeated her perusal of the grain and reported the wheat was unaffected.

Damaris had brought examples of the blighted rye with her to Court. Sacra and I now held samples in our hands. Ending her account, she looked with expectancy at the Queen. Sacra replicated the gesture Damaris had described, holding the grain in her palm and swirling it with her finger. I did the same. It was easy to see two distinct colors among the rye. Most of the kernels were a warm dark brown while others stood out with a rich purple color. It was clear the rye was tainted and would have to be destroyed. Although the decision was clear, there were ramifications of this choice. Reya leaned close to me and again began to whisper, this time in explanation.

"It is possible the rye arrived damaged. If that is true, then the grower who produced the crop brought bad grain to the Palace. The seals will have to be broken on all of that grower's goods in order to check for contamination. The Palace stores are a repository of grains, not only for Malia's consumption, but also for trade. Many of the stores at Malia are being held for ships. It is critical to the standing of the Palace among traders that we do not distribute unsatisfactory materials. If after inspection, it is found that no more of the grower's vases contain damaged grain, then it is possible the problem could be with the Palace storage itself. This means breaking more seals to check the quality of the materials. To break a seal without the grower present is a breach of Palace protocol and requires the action of the Queen."

After my presentation, my relationship with Reya had changed. Although she was still a valuable source of information, she no longer treated me like a child. It seemed we had now become equals and even more than that, friends.

I watched with anticipation for what would happen next. Everyone knew there were times when a Queen issued a declaration in the name of Dicta. A proclamation, made in the name of the mountain Goddess, was called, after her, an "edict." The act of standing before Dicta and making a pronouncement created an edict while the resulting decree, also drawn from her name, was a dictate. Because this situation might require multiple actions which superseded established Palace practice, it was likely Sacra would choose to issue just such a statement.

The Queen did not immediately move to take any action. Instead, she sat quietly with her raised hands folded, her chin leaning gently against them. It was clear she was considering the ramifications of making a declaration. After staying like this for several moments, she rose and turned to face the mountain. Her movement meant she also faced her Council. One by one she made eye contact with the women assembled on the steps. They all watched her intently. As their eyes met, each of them nodded. When it was clear there was consensus on the Council, still she did not speak. Finally, she raised her arms over her head with her palms turned toward the mountain. She stood like this for a time, connecting with Dicta and drinking in the power of the peak. She lowered her arms and turned. Briefly she looked at the assembled crowd, then raised her arms again and began to speak.

"People of Malia," she spoke in a distinctive voice I had never heard before, "I am called to speak with you today because the wellbeing of the people of the Palace is in jeopardy."

I unexpectedly realized she was not speaking for the Goddess, but <u>as</u> the Goddess. I had heard of the act of "drawing down," but had never actually seen it. I watched in wonder as Sacra continued.

"Because of this peril, seals must be broken on the vases among the Palace stores. Those which are found to contain tainted grain must be emptied and the grain destroyed. In my name, may this be so."

Her words were short and direct, but the impact of them was strong. Conversation buzzed among the assembled crowd as Sacra slumped back into her seat. When she finished speaking, she seemed to grow smaller and appeared somewhat dazed. Immediately, Keto and several other women from her Council were at her side, offering her water and support.

I felt a *pulse* from the Guards. It was similar, but different from the call they used for a crisis. It was simply a call to action. A group of Guardians milled about in conversation on the floor of the Queen's Court. They were already gathering, preparing to assist Aoede, Pelagia, and the others who worked in the stores, to carry out the edict. Gradually, their numbers grew as an increasing party of Guards answered the call.

I also noticed a group of young Wise Ones. Unlike most of those who had gathered in the Court, they made no movement toward leaving. Instead, they chattered among themselves while focused on watching the Guards. One of them in particular stared, the look in her eye betraying more than a casual interest. I could not tell if she watched anyone in particular, but I was pleased to find a Wise One who had interests outside the Mysteries, divination and darkness. There were so many Wise Ones at Malia I had to work to dredge up her name. With a start I realized this was Asteria, the woman Nyssa had told me was involved with Karis. Although young, I recognized her as one of the chant leaders. I decided she was the next Wise One I would follow.

*****

As I watched Asteria, I began to see a totally new picture of a Wise One. Although she was devoted to her duties, could divine by watching the flight of birds, and spent a large part of her day tending an altar to the Sweet Girl Child, there was more

143

to her than being a Wise One. In the evening, when her work in the Temple was done, she retreated to the space she shared with several other young women and emerged in clothing which did not at all resemble the robes of a Wise One.

Following her, I found one evening she joined a group in a large room used for dining during the day. It appeared on some nights this space became a gathering place for the young women of the Palace. Laughter rolled out the door and a few women brought watered wine which was shared among those who chose to partake. Guards, Wise Ones and representative members from all sections of the Palace gathered congenially in this space. In fact, I saw Nyssa and Elayn from my rooms enter arm-in-arm the first evening I followed Asteria there.

I wondered why no one ever mentioned this gathering to me? Would it not be considered seemly for a future Hearth Queen to be cavorting among those she would one day be called upon to care for? I decided to corner Nyssa and Elayn and finagle an invitation to join them one evening. For now, I made up my mind I would content myself with watching the interactions of those who had gathered in this space.

In my time at Malia I had learned its convoluted corridors and open light wells provided excellent venues for unnoticed observation. I searched for a place to monitor the erstwhile dining room and spotted an open landing on the level above the door. Scanning the hallway, I surmised the enclosed steps to the left of the entrance must allow access to the floor above. The Palace builders frequently took advantage of external light sources, and the opening on the upper level carried daylight down into what would have otherwise been a dark hallway. The stairway led to a landing and an open balcony, which overlooked the hall below. A curtain, used to block the sun in the heat of the day, separated the landing from the rest of the passage.

I dashed up the steps, ducked behind the curtain and positioned myself discretely on the balcony. From this perch I had an unobstructed view of the entrance to the room below. I was actually quite entertained in my hiding place. It allowed me to see a section of the interior of the space and some of the interactions happening inside. Some danced while others sang,

144

drummed and played instruments. In a corner I could barely see, several women played a game which used smooth river stones and players moved them from one pile to another in a strategy which escaped me. What surprised me the most were the young Wise Ones. I had pictured them much the same at night as they were in the day, their somber manner carrying over to a subdued and meditative evening. I could not have been more mistaken.

Wise Ones danced, sampled the weak wine, and coquettishly teased the Guardians and some of the others present. It did not surprise me in the least to find Guardians were willing participants in these flirtations, but, in an assumption I now realized was naive, I had not envisioned Wise Ones interested in liaisons. The evening wore on, and eventually I became bored with observing the interactions. I gathered my skirts preparing to descend the steps when Asteria came through the door with an impressive Guard. At first, I did not recognize the Guardian, but as they rounded the corner and turned toward the steps, I saw it was Karis.

Karis was leading Asteria by the hand and up the steps toward my hiding place. As they climbed the stairs, I could no longer see them. I could hear them giggling as they made their way to the landing on which I was standing. Although they were only a few feet away, the curtain I had positioned myself behind hid me from their view. Grabbing the edge of the drape, I stepped forward to greet them.

What I saw stopped me in mid-step. Karis had spread her cloak on the landing and Asteria appeared to be lying surprisingly comfortably on it. For a moment, I wondered how to deal with this situation. I had intended to announce my presence, maybe say a few teasing words and make my way down the steps, leaving them to their diversion. When I saw Karis lift the hem of Asteria's skirt, I realized I was too late to carry out my plan. Swiftly, I dropped the curtain and backed away from the opening.

Feeling very awkward, the only thing I could think to do was wait in silence. However, I found that among the three of us, I was the only one being silent. Waves of *feeling* wafted to me

145

from the aroused couple. Asteria's low moans carried easily to the other side of my curtain, and I could hear Karis' breath quicken with the sound. Totally at a loss about what to do, I sunk down on the floor of the balcony. I thought about covering my ears, but I knew that would not block out my *connection*. Eavesdropping both in actuality and with an inner *knowing* was not anything I would have intentionally orchestrated. Regardless of the fact I believed this should have been a private moment, I felt my own breath begin emulating Karis'. Although I schooled myself to do otherwise, I could not redirect my attention.

The sounds from the other side of the curtain signaled a quickening of their intimacy. Asteria whispered encouraging endearments between whimpers of pleasure. I could hear Karis' breathing coming in uneven gasps. The resonance of a shared cadence of movement carried clearly to my hiding place and in to my *awareness*. I had to put my hand over my mouth to stifle my own ragged breathing.

I pictured what might be happening on the floor of the landing. Karis could be lying next to Asteria, her forearm supporting Asteria's head. A rippling arm draped across Asteria's chest while a hand, hardened from practice, traced circles around her nipple. No, I thought to myself. Asteria lay with the cloak bundled under her head while Kariss tongue traced patterns lower and lower down her abdomen. No, I again changed my mind. Perhaps Asteria's fingers were stroking the damp bud between Kariss legs, eliciting the tingling *feelings* emanating from the other side of the curtain. Pictures flew by, each one more enticing and exciting than the one before.

Just when I felt certain if this continued a moment more I too would begin to moan loud enough to be heard, something began to change. Their lovemaking continued, moving to a crescendo of sound and movement. I assumed because they were wary of the possibility of being heard in the room below, the noise of their culmination was somewhat muffled. Regardless, their pleasure *pulsed* toward me bringing with it *waves* of shared feeling.

146

For a time, neither Asteria nor Karis moved or spoke. I was pleased because I did not know if I could stand more of the *connection* between the three of us. I was wet and winded. After several moments of silence, Karis began to murmur words of endearment to Asteria. Asteria replied with tender expressions of her own. It became clear to me they were truly in love.

I could hear rustling as the two of them untangled themselves and their clothing. A few moments later I made out the sound of footsteps on the stairs and, with a final intense *touch,* they were gone. That last *contact* made me wonder if they were aware I had been there all along. Somehow, I doubted it. If they had, I was certain they would not have proceeded with their tryst. I suspected Karis had felt my *touch* in the past when it strayed into the Guardians' Shelter. It would have been reasonable to assume me safely in my room engaged in familiar, but distant, observations. When I first found myself trapped on the balcony, I anticipated I would feel embarrassed the next time I encountered the two of them. However, now, because I had felt their *touch* and understood their hearts, I felt a closeness with them. I knew that this sense of *connection* was what I would experience the next time we met.

12

I awoke with a start. A tray clanged as it hit the floor of my chamber. Water from the bath in the adjoining room sluiced across the floor and cascaded off my balcony. Cracks and pops from the stressed building echoed loudly. In the dim light of morning I could barely see, but I jumped from my bed and automatically began the action which had been ingrained since my arrival at Malia... move to open space. If you judged the danger to be immediate, find a solid doorway and stand under its arch.

In my village when the Earth Mother shook, it was easy to run from any shelter into the open. There was no grand building like the Palace. Moving toward safety at Malia was a different matter. Its complicated passageways and multiple stairs not only slowed progress in exiting, but also were possible hazards. Collapsing corridors, disintegrating roofs and falling walls could all be major threats when the Earth Mother moved.

Soon after my arrival at the Palace, a trio of Earth Guardians had come. They walked me from my rooms to the nearest safe open space. In truth, I paid little attention to their training. I had been far more interested in simply watching them and listening to their voices than I had been in their directions. Consequently, I could only remember highlights of their instructions. Do not wait. Do not run. Do not go to the central Court. Always move downward.

I later learned the Earth Guardians met every person who stayed in the Palace and explained the quickest escape routes out of the building. It was obvious to me this was an onerous job, as I could not even estimate the number of people who visited and resided at Malia. Wishing I had paid better attention, I tried to stand. It was difficult to find my balance as I, and the building, swayed unsteadily. Eventually, I found my footing and simultaneously heard clearly the *call* of the Air Guardians as they *pulsed* a warning.

"Evacuate," was the only word in their message. I evaluated whether to stand in a doorway or move to open space.

As I pondered this question, the movement around me subsided. This lull in the Earth Mother's actions concretized my decision to flee the building and I moved toward the door. Before I got to the exit there was a sudden flurry of activity as Stava and Tam breathlessly dashed into my chamber.

"Young Queen," Stava gasped between breaths. Even in this crisis, both she and Tam still tapped their shoulders in acknowledgement.

"Come," she continued succinctly, holding out her hand.

Without thinking about my response, I grabbed the proffered hand. The three of us moved quickly into the hallway. As we became part of the throng assembled in the crowded passage, I could feel wisps of alarm and concern *waft* toward me. Women filled the hall. As they moved toward the stairs, the occupants of the Spring Hall clustered in small groups, and I noted an accounting was taking place.

I could hear Elayn asking those gathered near her, "Does anyone know where Kyma is?"

Pelagia answered immediately, "Yes, she is in the healing rooms."

"Then we are all accounted for," replied Elayn as the group quickened its movement toward the steps.

Around me I could hear the same question being asked repeatedly by small groups of women. In one group, when someone could not be found, a woman was sent to make certain she was not in her room, while the rest of the group continued down the hall. I was momentarily surprised to realize the group charged with accounting for my presence was the Guardians.

Everyone on the island was accustomed to the Earth Mother's movements, tremors had happened for as long as I could remember. The Grandmothers in my village reported these incidents had taken place since they were children. This level of repetition caused a certain amount of complacency. Most of the time, shakes were short, causing minor, if any, damage. However, sometimes the duration or magnitude of a shake was more powerful. Based on the level of activity thus far, I judged this event was substantial.

In confirmation, the earth rumbled again. The building rocked. I considered encouraging Stava and Tam to shelter in a doorway. Seemingly undaunted by the resurgence of activity, the groups of women from the Spring Hall continued calmly moving down the stairway toward safety. I saw a final flourish of a cloak as the last of them disappeared to the floor below. The compact construction of the passageway itself had slowed their departure. If I were to stand in the center of the stairs, and extend my arms out to either side, I could touch the walls of the enclosed steps. The stairway was barely large enough for two people to walk side-by-side, much less for a mass exodus. Despite this, the departure from the Spring Hall had been expeditious and efficient.

Stava, Tam and I were the last to begin our descent. I chided myself about my distractedness when the Guardians had instructed me. If I had been more aware, I thought it possible Stava and Tam would have met me on a lower floor and we would be well on our way to open space. I still clung to Stava's hand while Tam led the way toward the steps. Tam paused on the first stair and turned to make certain we were closely behind. Stava adroitly maneuvered me in front of her, and, in single file, the three of us began to descend toward safety.

The enclosed passageway made a muted rumble of warning. Abruptly, a wave of movement and sound surrounded us. Time shifted. In my altered perspective, blocks of stone began falling slowly. The roof of the stairway ahead of us gradually began to collapse. A tumbling cascade of stones steadily crept upward toward where we stood. I knew what was happening was actually taking place quickly, but I felt like I had an infinite amount of time to reach out and grab Tam's belt. As I jerked her backward toward me, time surged back to its normal pace.

My abrupt reversal of direction surprised Stava. She momentarily lost her balance as I shifted, jumping backward with Tam. However, in an instant, she righted herself and began pulling both of us upward. This time the movement of the stones actually did slow. One rock tumbled resolutely after another, creating a pile of rubble which blocked the passageway. Each

150

stone brought the crushing stack closer to us as we scrambled upward. In haste, we awkwardly backed up the stairs as quickly as possible. I had just started to believe we were going to make it back to the relative safety of the Spring Hall when three large stones precipitously gave way from the ceiling.

I was *aware* there was a problem before I actually knew what had happened. Stava and I were unharmed, but Tam had been caught under the last of the falling stones. The avalanche stopped abruptly. We warily waited a few heartbeats and then plummeted down the steps toward Tam. I had expected to *feel* a sharp surge of pain following closely after my knowledge of Tam's situation. To my surprise, this did not happen. There was only a slight *sense* of discomfort accompanied by a rising sense of panic.

"I am caught," Tam called even before we could reach her. "I cannot get my foot out."

Only a few steps remained of what had once been the stairway. It was now completely blocked by the accumulation of debris that had fallen. Tam was sprawled across several stairs, and her right leg disappeared eerily under the pile of stone.

"Are you hurt?" Stava questioned surveying the scene.

"I do not think so," Tam replied sounding astonished, "but I am trapped."

Stava and I made our way to where Tam was pinned. I crouched down beside her and took her hand. Despite what seemed to me to be a dire situation, she smiled shyly at me.

"I have always wondered what it would take to get you to hold my hand," she said grinning.

I was amazed she was able to joke in her situation. Had I been in a similar position, I was certain I would not have been able to find humor in the predicament. But, Tam continued to smile up at me while Stava surveyed the situation. Stava pushed tentatively on several rocks, shook her head and then squatted down near Tam and me.

"Can you move your foot?" she asked.

"A little," Tam responded.

"I can *feel* you are not in pain, but I can hardly take in how that could be possible," Stava said conveying a sense of awe.

151

"She's truly not in pain," I agreed, although I too could not understand how this could be true.

Two of the blocks that had pinned Tam's leg had fallen one next to another, leaving a small open space between them. At a precarious angle, a third stone was wedged between these two. Tam's foot was somewhere on the other side of the third rock. Despite Tam's bravado, I could *sense* her fear about being caught. I *reached* out to her with support and encouragement. Although this in no way changed her situation, her anxiety diminished.

A small cloud of dust drifted upward and the pile which held Tam's leg shifted slightly. I could *feel* that now she was in pain, but it was still very slight. Stava abruptly stood. She extended her hand and pulled me up to face her. I found it odd for the two of us to be conversing with Tam's prone body between us.

"I cannot move these stones. You must go to your balcony and sound an alert to the other Guards," she said to me seriously. "Be as clear as you can about Tam's situation. Tell them also where you are and to come get you."

There was a deep sense of urgency in both her speech and her manner. She *reached* out to me to convey how critical she considered the situation. In that *contact*, I was surprised to find an undercurrent of feelings for me. I realized with a shock, that Stava loved me. It was not the typical infatuation or adoration which I felt from many of the Guardians. It was a deep, genuine love. Although I *sensed* she was aware she had inadvertently shared her secret, she was far too preoccupied to convey any embarrassment.

"Go," she repeated. "Tell them to come quickly for the three of us"

I paused momentarily to look meaningfully into her eyes and then, without a moment's thought for disregarding the Earth Guardians' order not to move upward, I ran up the few remaining stairs to the Spring Hall. My balcony was off my sitting room and I dashed from the hall into that space. I did not make it far before in my haste I slipped in the water which streamed across the room from my bath. This slowed my pace and I made my way to the balcony with greater care.

With a force I had not used before, I faced the Guardians' Court and called the Guards. I *sent* words, feelings and images...Tam stuck under the stones, Stava's need for assistance and what I considered to be a plaintive picture of me on my balcony. There were several Guardians rushing across their Court. I watched as each of them paused and swiftly looked in my direction. Hespar covered her ears as if that would somehow block my *contact*. If I had not considered the circumstances to be so dire, I believe I would have found her actions amusing.

The response was immediate. As one of the Air Guardians, Drea, picked up my *signal*, she amplified it, making its reach broader and adding clarity. Reassurance at once *flowed* toward me from multiple sources. Despite the fact that I assumed the entire Palace must be in chaos, I could *sense* rescuing Tam, Stava and me became an immediate priority. I knew Drea was running for one of the builder's ladders. Charis sent conflicted images of her desire to assist and her immediate assignment to the high place near the sea to watch for one of the big waves which often accompanied shakes of this nature. Fauntee *pulsed* concern and vague words about fire. Most surprising of all to me was the swift response of Petra. She had immediately begun climbing precariously up the outer facade of the Palace.

Her climb began a long way from the Spring Hall and the balcony on which I stood. She balanced, taking careful steps on a low wall that adjoined the Queen's Court from which she leaped to a flat rooftop. Images of her progress *flashed* as she vaulted over gaps between structures and raced along supports on a narrow row of pillars, working her way closer to where the three of us were trapped. Her thoughts were a constant cadence of comfort and questions.

Her queries came to me as, "Are you all right?" She *projected* care and concern which *radiated* along with the inquiry.

I was instantly lost in the *contact* between Petra and me. Her *touch* took away my anxiety and I calmly replied, "Yes." Reassurance *flowed* from her again.

"I will be with you in a moment," she *sent*.

I battled with myself to focus on what I believed to be the true intent of her statement. I liked the feeling of those words. "I will be with you." Petra had been lost to me since my infatuation with her at my first meeting with Sacra. Other than my presentation and "The Telling," I had barely seen her. Petra had been closed to me. She was a vague presence tingling at the corner of my consciousness. I sensed she was aware of my fascination and held herself at a distance both in terms of *communication* and actual contact. Knowing this was probably wise did not diminish my indignation or irritation at being unable to *reach* her. However, with just this single *touch,* my exasperation melted. She was coming for me. Among all of the conflicting priorities which must exist at this time, I was paramount. I savored this notion with satisfaction.

Petra's undaunted progress toward the balcony made me wonder if she had transited this route before. There must have been a time when Sacra had been a resident of the Spring Hall and I speculated about possible trysts that might have led Petra to this spot. As I considered this possibility, Petra dropped with a flourish onto my balcony. The distance from the rooftop to the floor was significant, and she dipped on one knee to recover her balance. Then she was immediately at my side, and I was again overwhelmed by her presence. The severity of the situation around us dimmed and I was lost in the sensation of her.

She took me by the shoulders and looked deeply into my eyes. I could not breathe, and I conjured her making declarations of unending love for me, awakened by the peril of the situation in which she found me.

"Are you in fact undamaged?" she asked, continuing to stare at me intently.

"Yes," I gasped, leaning toward her thinking she would take me in her arms.

"Excellent," she replied, pushing me gently back upright. "They will be with you shortly to take you to safety." And with that, she was gone.

Reeling from the abruptness of her departure, I almost lost my balance. I now understood the true urgency that had caused her precipitous climb up several stories was Tam. Abashed at being a much lower priority than I had imagined, there was nothing for me to do but peer over the edge of the balcony in anticipation of rescue.

Once Petra was gone I was increasingly aware of the continual pattern of *interaction* that swirled around me. I knew the Wise Ones would have instructed me to *focus* on one source at a time in order not to be overwhelmed by the chaotic intensity. Following this advice, I tried to sort out the sensations coming toward me from all directions. Sacra's *signal* was clear, ringing out distinctly among the others. I could *discern* she was unharmed and *sending* a calm rhythm of reassurance to the scared and scattered people of Malia. I had more difficulty sorting out the Guards. Water Guardians were calculating ways to soak areas that were smoldering. A number of Guards were at the bottom of the steps which held Tam. They stood on top of the pile of stones and carefully removed rocks from the base of the mound that held her. They passed these from hand-to-hand down and away from the rubble.

I had been so focused on the divergent energies which *wafted* toward me, I was startled when the top of Maris' head came into view. Her hair was still uneven from her encounter with the Sea Raiders. It gave her an impish look as she swung a leg over the balcony. I had anticipated being rescued by younger Guards, but the old warder did have a knowing charm about her. As if in answer to my hopes, in the next moment Adesha appeared.

The two Guards shared with me their plan for our descent. They had gotten a ladder from Drea, but even with it the path to the ground was not direct. Using the ladder, we would go down from my balcony to the flat roof of the second floor that jutted out below my chamber. Bringing the ladder with us, from there we would travel across several rooftops until we reached a section which would take us directly into the Guardians' Court. I must have looked skeptical for, in tandem, they both assured me this should not be difficult. Adesha would precede me down the ladder and Maris would follow. Setting aside my doubts, I determined to take part in the plan with as much confidence as I could muster.

The ladder leaned dauntingly against the outer wall of my balcony. Adesha climbed nimbly over the edge and stepped down a few rungs. I did not believe there was a graceful way to descend a ladder. So, setting aside any modesty I felt, I tucked my skirt into its belt. Unlike the agile movements Adesha had made a moment before, I awkwardly boosted myself up to the wide ledge of the balcony with the ladder behind me. I sat on the edge and tried to determine how to get my feet to go in the opposite direction. I understood in theory how ladders worked. However, now I was faced with using one, I could not figure out how to begin.

It took a few moments, but Maris eventually comprehended my dilemma and offered me instructions. "It will probably work well if you stand and balance on the ledge of your balcony. I will stand in front of you and you can put your hands on my shoulders for stability. When you step backward, Adesha will be there to guide your feet on to the rungs. Many people find it best not to look down."

Although I now understood what was needed, I was still reluctant. Finally, mustering my courage, I took Maris's hand and stood, placing my feet on the rim of the balcony. It was easy to shift my grasp to her shoulders. All that remained was to step backward. Determinedly, I moved one foot back into the air. As Maris had assured me, Adesha gently took my heel and placed it on the first step of the ladder. I lifted my other foot, and she repeated the process.

Now that I was actually on the ladder, it did not seem nearly as daunting. I stepped down one more rung without coaching. Then tried yet another. Adesha did not change her position with my descent. Her arms, which firmly grasped the sides of the ladder, surrounded me and I slid along the length of her body as I moved. This brought an all-new aspect to the climb. If I had realized escaping from my balcony would mean I would be wedged between the ladder and Adesha, I believe I would have complied more readily. I felt Adesha *reach* for me with both assurance and a tantalizing undertone.

The act of climbing down the ladder took on a much more pleasurable dimension. When Adesha moved down a rung, of necessity she pressed against my back and glided enticingly downward. When it was my turn to move, I repeated the process in reverse. I began to wonder how many steps the ladder had and hoped there were many. I could hear a snort from Maris as she scrambled on to the top of the ladder and began to follow us. I believed the energy Adesha and I were emitting was undoubtedly palpable.

Eventually, with a mixture of regret and relief, I stepped onto one of the large flat rooftops of the western wing of the Palace. Although we were still several stories in the air, the large level expanse did not disturb me. I had found my way onto Malia's roofs before. From there I had observed the sky and watched blazing coral sunsets with the Wise Ones. Adesha and I waited for Maris to reach us and then, taking the ladder, began our trek across the expanse. There was a gap between the section of the building we had climbed to and the next. Without even a pause, Adesha sprang across the opening. Although the distance between the buildings was not far, I stopped to evaluate my willingness to make the jump. Standing by me on the roof, Maris motioned forward and nodded encouragingly. In my time in the village, I had often bounced from one seaside outcropping to another. I had even leaped from small cliffs into the ocean without hesitation.

This was no different, I told myself. If I pictured this jump as simply moving from one sea ledge to another, I knew what to do. I took three steps backward and ran. Following Maris' advice, I did not look down. For a moment, I soared through the air stories above the ground. Then Adesha's arms were around me and the comforting surface of another flat roof was under my feet. Maris leaped nimbly over the opening and joined us. She pointed out the section of roof that would lead us directly into the Guardians' Court, and we continued our journey toward solid ground.

Our flight brought us close to the edge of a roof which faced the central Court. From this vantage point I could see a significant portion of the Palace. Smoke snaked from several windows off the Court and an acrid stench rose toward us where we stood. We watched as a line of people passed buckets toward the fire. A Guard and one of the goldsmiths were moving toward the healing rooms supporting a limping woman. Most surprising of all was a change in the Queen's Court. Instead of its orderly construction, there was now only a jumbled pile of stones. Debris filled the steps upon which we had sat only a few days before. A wall was missing, creating an unobstructed view of the mountains beyond. I found this new view disconcerting. The wall, which had defined one of the outer borders of Malia, was gone.

The progress Adesha, Maris and I had been making was stalled by this unsettling scene. Adesha stood shaking her head while Maris reached out and took my hand. I was not certain if she was supporting me or I her as we both adjusted to the new shape of the Palace. We were all startled out of our dazed states by a distant rumble. The roof underneath our feet shifted and bucked. I staggered in an attempt to keep my balance.

This time, I *felt* genuine pain from Tam. The sensation was so strong I was briefly nauseous. Often small movements that came after a shake could cause more damage to already compromised buildings. There was no way to know if the roof we were standing on was stable. Without prompting, I began to move quickly toward the edge of the roof Maris had indicated as our destination. The two Guards were at my side. When we reached the edge, Maris positioned the ladder for our descent. This time I did not hesitate. When Adesha stepped down a few rungs I was quick to follow. The flirtation of the previous trip was lost in our desire to rapidly get to the ground.

When we reached the bottom I found myself grateful to simply be standing on comparatively solid ground. Maris began dusting off her leathers, and Adesha tipped her head as if listening. I concentrated and could also *hear* the communication among the Guards full of multiple priorities and actions.

In a moment Adesha said, "Young Queen, there is much which requires attention. Maris will take you away from this Court to a place which will be safer."

She smiled, dropping her eyes, seemingly shy now that she had delivered me securely to the Court. It seemed the Guards were always responsive and attentive to me in any crisis. At these times, they met my eyes and I could feel their connection to me. However, when the problem to which they had responded was resolved, they disappeared with amazing speed. I confess, I longed for languid days which included no imminent calamity and a Guardian or two to keep me company.

As if she had heard me, Adesha gazed quickly in my direction. Suddenly self-conscious, I was the one who looked down first. My eyes were drawn upward, again following the motion of Adesha's fist as it moved to tap her shoulder and, with that and a smile, she was gone. Maris took my hand, thankfully choosing not to reveal any awareness she might have of my thoughts. She led me out of the Court and into the open space which was our ultimate destination.

As Maris and I moved out of the Palace and into the surrounding area, I *heard* Stava. She *reported* Tam's release and condition. She *sent* images of Tam standing on one foot while the other was held in the air at an awkward angle. Although enough stone had been removed to free Tam, Stava communicated clearly that the stairway to my chamber was still filled with debris. I noticed how easy it was to hear her *signal*. It occurred to me that Stava sending me to my balcony to alert the Guards had been a ruse. She had only been attempting to get me out of possible danger without argument. Stava had been well able to make herself heard, she simply wanted me to be in what she considered the safest place possible. I sighed, thinking how easily I had let myself assume she actually needed my help. I had come to know many things about Malia's Guardians, but it was clear to me I still had a lot to learn.

"The Wise Ones believe it is a sign," Sacra said as I sat with her and Reya in the Queen's quarters.

I quietly puffed out air in derision. I thought to myself, "The Wise Ones believe everything is an omen."

Sacra looked at me quizzically and continued, "In this case, I believe they are right," she said, responding to my unspoken allegation.

I pondered when I would remember Sacra could *hear* me. Being reminded of this, I attempted to realign my thoughts to be more charitable and focused again on the conversation.

Sacra looked earnestly at both Reya and me. Wistfully she admitted, "I have not bled since the celebration of the dead nine moons ago. I have been waiting for confirmation it was time to publicly acknowledge this change. I sat in darkness yesterday." Sacra paused, drawing in a long breath before continuing, "It became clear to me then, I can no longer delay making this announcement."

I understood Sacra was saying she no longer bled, but I knew there was more to her statement. I wasn't sure what underlay her confession, but she had certainly captured my attention. Reya, however, seemed to understand Sacra's meaning. She reached out and took her hand. Both of them looked pensive, but Reya also *emitted* an undertone of respect and admiration as she said, "It is the greatest of blessings to have an Elder Queen. A Queen moving to the Fall Hall has always signaled a time of wisdom and strength to the people of Malia." As Reya made this observation, her eyes never left Sacra's.

Sacra sighed, still looking introspective. "I know you are right," she said trying to brighten. "I am certain it will cheer the people of the Palace to have an Elder Queen. Especially after the destruction, they too will see it as a good sign."

This was the first I had heard Sacra speak about the condition of the Palace. The damage from the last shake of the Earth Mother had been extensive. Walls were down all over Malia, many water systems were no longer functioning and several roofs lay on the floor of the rooms they were intended to shield. I was amazed at the people's resilience. The residents of Malia viewed restoring the Palace as a sacred duty. Within hours of the shake, they were putting things back in order and making plans to rebuild damaged sections of the Palace.

These repairs would, however, take time. I had not been able to stay in my rooms since the Earth Mother's movements. In fact, I was prohibited from re-entering my chamber even to pack my belongings. Iva, the builder from my chamber, told me the stairs were unstable and the risk too great to allow them to be used. Being unable to get into the Spring Hall, I was obliged to recite a list of things I considered necessary to Keto so she could have them moved to my new room. I was discouraged by her disapproving reaction to my requests. It appeared she did not look favorably on my need for even the simplest of things. Despite Keto's judgments, the chests I requested appeared later that day in my temporary quarters. I later learned they had followed the same path Maris, Adesha and I had used to escape my rooms. This realization, and a series of suppositions about what it must have taken to remove the chests, led me to understand Keto's objections.

My current space was much smaller than my old rooms had been, and my women could not congregate comfortably in them. The residents of the Spring Hall were scattered about the Palace. I missed the effortless contact I had had simply by proximity to the women of my Chamber. Although light wells adjoined these new rooms, I missed the bright morning light of my old quarters. I was particularly disappointed not to have access to my bath. But, I reminded myself to be grateful. Many of the residents of Malia and its outlying villas were living in much more uncomfortable situations.

"When will you move?" questioned Reya still holding the Queen's hand.

"I have been trying to decide," the Queen answered thoughtfully. "The most appropriate time would be as part of the celebration of the Old One later this cycle. But, I think that is too long a wait. Giada's rooms are uninhabitable, while both the Summer and Fall Halls are undamaged. Although it may seem

161

oddly placed, I think it will have to be in a few weeks as part of the celebration of pleasure and fertility. I know I should be pleased, but in truth, I find this bittersweet."

"All times of transition hold both joy and sorrow," Reya responded with wisdom. Sacra looked at her proudly as all elders do when someone younger repeats a truth they have learned from them and internalized as their own.

Although I felt Sacra was primarily speaking to Reya, I interrupted as I finally understood the meaning of the conversation. "Are you saying you intend to move out of the Summer Hall?"

"Yes, child." Sacra agreed. "I believe it is time for you and your women to move to the Summer Hall. The shake may have precipitated this decision, but it was immanent regardless."

I was taken aback. I assumed the Summer Hall was the permanent home of the Hearth Queen. To me, the Summer Hall and its adjoining Queen's Court were linked inextricably with Sacra and the women of her Council. I believed when it was repaired, I would move back into the Spring Hall. I was looking forward to being in the place I had come to consider my own. The idea of moving did not appeal to me.

"Why would you do that?" I stammered. As the words escaped my lips, I believed I sounded petulant. I had not intended them to be so, but only to assure Sacra the change was unnecessary.

"Giada," Sacra responded with kindness, "I am sorry. We too often assume you already know of Malia's customs."

I wondered to myself where Sacra found the patience to consistently interact with me so gently. "Let me make tea," she offered. "It seems this conversation may be longer than I anticipated," she removed her hand, patting Reya's as she stood. "Perhaps Reya will explain?" Sacra said, looking questioningly at her. Reya nodded and then looked to me.

"At Malia we follow the cycles of the seasons. I know you understand this. The entire island celebrates the changing of time," Reya began. Her look carried a question despite the fact that her words had been delivered as a statement. I nodded acknowledging my understanding.

162

"In the Palace, women follow these cycles. We watch the cycles of the moon and sun and try to attune our lives to be in harmony with them. Their movement through the sky is the basis for our celebrations and circles. We also recognize the cycle of a woman's life when she moves from one phase to another. We embrace children as they are born with the blood of their mothers. We honor girls as their blood welcomes them to womanhood. We celebrate the blood given by women to open their wombs to pleasure and fertility. Mothers bring forth new life with blood and courage. When the Old One holds our blood and gives us wisdom we honor this also. When finally, the blood of our body is stilled, we give ourselves back to the Mother Goddess with gratitude and wonder."

Finding Keto had left water warming, Sacra made tea quickly. She turned to face us, with three cups of tea on a tray. She passed a cup to Reya and one to me. I could smell the pungent scent of dittany accompanied by something I did not recognize. Resuming her seat, Sacra blew on her tea to cool it and nodded for Reya to continue.

"Sacra is choosing to acknowledge the Old One has claimed her. Her cycles have stilled, and she no longer follows the rhythms of the moon with her blood. When a Queen acknowledges being claimed by the Old One she moves from the Summer Hall to the Fall Hall."

I was glad to have my tea. It allowed me to gaze into the cup while I explored my feelings. Although I had come to love the Spring Hall, I knew there was more to my objections to Sacra's move. I strove for a deeper understanding of my concern. My familiar doubts about being Hearth Queen surfaced. Sacra's move to the Fall Hall was to me a harbinger of things to come. Although nothing had been said, I felt this brought me a step closer to my time as Hearth Queen. I was not ready to give over my place as "Young Queen" and take on the duties of so serious a position.

Eclipsing even my doubt was my unwillingness to be without Sacra. She was a touchstone for me. It was true that she listened to the people, but she also listened to me. I never found her counsel to be intrusive. She seemed to be able to provide insight without judgment or expectation. I feared it would take me an eternity of observation and integration before I perfected these skills. My ability to conjure generosity and patience was largely modeled after Sacra's interaction with the people and her Council.

The comforting sound of Sacra's voice overrode my concerns. "I will still be Hearth Queen. I am only moving to the Fall Hall, Giada," she said, answering again my unspoken words. "You will never be without me, or the other Hearth Queens. I know you felt us with you before, when you wore your ceremonial clothing."

I nodded, but dropped my eyes as they filled with tears. Sacra reached out and gently lifted my chin.

"I, too, will be among the Ancestor Queens one day. Whenever you wish my counsel or the wisdom of the other ancient Queens, you need only call to us. With or without the dress, we always stand at your side. We will never leave you, Giada. Through time and trouble, through struggle and joy, we will always be with you. You will never be alone."

Her hand stroked my face where she had held it, and I knew she spoke the truth.

13

And so the change began. There was much determined effort, as the Fall Hall was made ready for habitation. Although the space was used periodically, it had been a time since anyone had lived there. Simultaneously, a cautious recovery of the contents of the Spring Hall was undertaken. Not only were my belongings retrieved, but also the myriad other things which comprised the effects and paraphernalia from the other rooms of the hallway. Workers had begun shoring up the walls of the fallen stairway, creating an even narrower passage. This made it even harder to carry things down the steps. Consequently, most of the residents' possessions were hauled across rooftops and lowered to the ground as part of their move to a new location.

The normal routines of the Palace were interrupted. I was surprised to find that all but the most necessary labors had been suspended as the people of Malia worked together to rebuild and facilitate the move of its Hearth Queen. Several of the Wise Ones carried stones. Some of the women on the Queen's Council hauled lumber. Artists restored frescos. Builders worked from sunup well past sundown, when it became too dark to see. As before, I worked with the water circle, checking the Palace's supply. We inspected and reported on the taps throughout the building and beyond. This time, we walked trails into the mountains toward Malia's water sources. When we found places where the water's course had shifted, we memorized landmarks and reported these to the Water Guardians.

The water circle congregated each day in the central Court to share its progress. We reviewed the sections of the water system which had been surveyed and made plans for those that remained. Leaving from this gathering, it surprised me one day to see Petra climbing down a ladder from the scaffolding above. I was caught off guard by this unexpected encounter and found myself confused about how to greet her.

Petra, on the other hand, moved toward me both physically and energetically. She turned toward me smiling. I felt the familiar *connection* spring up between us as well as the buoyancy contact with her brought me.

"Young Queen," she said casually tapping her shoulder and then looking down began to dust off her leathers while she spoke. Then glancing back up to were she had been working she dropped her head and in a conspiratorial tone she confided, "I am often pleased when everyone in the Palace is called to work and I am asked to take up a hammer. Do you know that I come from the villages too?"

I shook my head in surprise and she continued. "My father is a shipbuilder and I learned the trade from him. If I had not been called to the Guard, I would probably be a builder today. Now, instead of me working with him on the ships, he works with my five brothers." She sighed wistfully.

"My other duties do not allow me much time to use that skill. Sometimes I do miss it. Occasionally, I get to fashion a bow..."

Her talk trailed off as if she had caught herself revealing more than she intended. Before our exchange could continue, a shout from where Petra had been working interrupted our conversation. She looked up and waved to the others in acknowledgement.

"It seems my expertise is needed." She smiled, still gazing up in the direction of the scaffold and looking pleased. She turned again toward me and looked down. I realized in that moment how tall she truly was. "If you will pardon me, Young Queen?" Petra asked tapping her shoulder but not actually waiting for a reply.

She was gone. Climbing the ladder to rejoin the group, leaving behind only the scent of her sun-warmed skin and her leathers. I realized this was the longest conversation I had ever had with Petra and I hadn't said anything. Chiding myself for not speaking, I allowed myself the indulgence of watching her work. When I thought I was becoming conspicuous, I tried to look as if I had just remembered some thing important and scuttled away to resume my water circle tasks.

I was amazed and proud of the efficiency and skills shown in response to this emergency. As I watched Sacra I began to understand the role of a Hearth Queen in this process. Sacra was everywhere, seeking information which made this relentless effort possible. Did workers have enough food? Was there childcare for those whose skills were needed? Did the Healers have what was needed to address the requirements of the injured? Were enough provisions being delivered to the Guardians who kept watch for a great wave which often followed shakes of the Earth Mother? Her attention was unfailing, and her presence ubiquitous.

I knew, in the midst of this confusion, she also gathered her belongings, packed her chests and dealt with her emotions about declaring herself an Elder Queen. A few days after our conversation in her rooms, Sacra sent word asking my women and me to join her in what remained of the Queen's Court. Cleaning the rubble from this space had taken precedence. Although it was not completely restored, at least the Court could now be used. I *knew* by both deduction and intuition that Sacra intended to announce her intentions to move.

Reya helped me send word to the women of the former Spring Hall who were now scattered about the Palace. When the time arrived to meet with Sacra, we walked together toward the gathering. As Reya and I passed through the central Court, Alandra, Lalage and Elayn fell into step with us. From an opening on the other side, Calida called a greeting. When we entered the Queen's Court the rest of the women from my rooms were there. I was surprised to find that I held a fierce affection for each of them. I had not realized how much I truly missed these women.

In the Spring Hall, I had become accustomed to interacting with the women of my rooms without effort. I had not seen them as a group since the destruction of our Hall. I wanted to hug each of them and tell them how glad I was they were safe. In this moment I realized I could no longer delay sitting Council with these women.

Without hesitation I turned to Reya and said, "Three days after the next new moon I will sit Council with my women."

Reya looked at me with a combination of surprise and pleasure. One corner of her mouth twitched upward in amusement. It was only then I realized I had spoken without question or hesitation, like a Hearth Queen.

"Of course, Giada," Reya replied. She continued talking as we made our way into the Queen's Court and took seats. "There are several customs which traditionally take place before a Queen sits Council for the first time."

I looked at her quizzically, inviting her to continue.

"You must consider if you wish the women who were chosen for you to continue as your sworn Council. When a Hearth Queen sits Council for the first time each of the women who will comprise the group makes a pledge. They are asked to hold their position on the Queen's Council as their primary commitment. They must give precedence to the Queen's requests above any other obligations. If the Queen asks for a Wise One to leave the darkness, or a Healer to leave a birth, she must come. Unless the Queen has agreed to her absence, any woman on her Council must answer her call. Even I would be bound to honor the Queen's call if she were to call me."

I wasn't sure how I felt about this, and I must have conveyed my confusion in my unspoken reaction because Reya affectionately patted my shoulder.

"Come, Giada," Reya said. "I have been with you for several moons and you have not felt my absence when I have gone to the Queen, have you?"

I snorted in response. As I tried to re-orient my attitude, I noticed the rest of the women from my rooms and the Queen's Council had arrived.

Reya lowered her voice as women began taking seats around us. "There are many things to reflect upon in deciding whom you wish to have on your Council. Each woman has her own way of dealing with situations. Considering if her responses will be useful to you is essential. Hopefully, over the time you have been here, you have observed these women. It is important you can *hear* each of them clearly and that they provide information in a way which is easy for you to understand. With me as the exception, the women who have been with you in your rooms are all young. If you choose them for your Council, they may be with you for a lifetime."

I was cataloging the information Reya was offering in order to use it later to evaluate my choices. But, her last statement caught my attention.

"What if I make a bad choice?" I questioned.

"If you find a connection is not working you may release a woman from her pledge," Reya answered. "This does not happen frequently so your choices must be made with care. It is uncommon, but a woman on your Council may ask to be released from her promise. Poor health is the most common motivation for this request, although occasionally it can be for other reasons."

I nodded in understanding. From the corner of my eye I saw Sacra approaching the middle of the small Court. Reya stopped speaking and both of us watched the Hearth Queen as she made her way to the center. At this moment, I found her to be outstandingly beautiful. She wore her ceremonial robes, and a dried garland of summer foliage encircled her head.

On our island, there was not much rain in summer. During the hot moons the flowers were sparse and the color of the land was golden. The circlet Sacra wore was woven with grasses in the muted colors of summer interspersed with its rare flowers. If I had been in Sacra's place, I would have been exhausted. But, Sacra seemed to radiate a vitality which touched those around her. I realized that, aside from having a force all her own, Sacra was being energetically sustained by her Guardians, her Council, and the Wise Ones. Watching her now I understood for the first time that to be Hearth Queen, one must not only be able to extend oneself to the people, but one must also be able to internalize support from those who offered it.

Reya leaned to me. This time she spoke in a whisper.

"Once you have decided who you wish to have on your Council, you must ask each of them if they are willing to serve. It is a deep commitment, and some women may need to examine if they will be able to extend this promise to you," she sighed and continued, "I have never regretted long accepting Sacra's invitation to serve on her Council." I wondered about Reya's regrets. I remembered what Nyssa had shared with me about Reya and Thekia's after The Telling. To be pledged to a Queen and to find oneself loving someone at a distance I thought would cause conflict.

A hush fell over the Court and I took Reya's hand. Sacra stood before the women of the two Councils, hers that had served her for so long, and mine which I was about to form. She took a deep breath and addressed the gathering.

"The Old One calls me," Sacra proclaimed. "I feel her presence within me more strongly every day. I must move to a place where I will be in harmony both within and without." Having made this declaration, she removed the summer garland from her head. Keto stepped forward and offered her a different one.

This circlet was filled with the colors of fall. It too was dried, but contained the silver-green of olive, the red-gold of grape along with the riotous colors of rain-drenched autumn flowers. Sacra placed the fall garland on her head.

"The Summer Hall will not be empty," she announced to the group. "Giada and the women of her Council will come to their new home as I leave it. To have an Elder Queen and a Young Queen both at Malia signals a time of change."

As she said these words, Sacra moved toward me. She held out her hand to indicate I was to join her. I had not known I would have any part in this announcement. I wondered for the hundredth time if I would ever know all the traditions of Malia, but I rose to join her with more alacrity than I might have in the past. As I stood in front of her, Sacra placed the summer circlet on my head. Then gently kissed my cheek. She smiled fleetingly to the assembly, turned, and was gone.

*****

I found Sacra's announcement of being claimed by the Crone anticlimactic. I had anticipated something much more complicated to mark this transition, but a brief announcement of her change in status was all it entailed. Over the next few weeks the Palace prepared for this shift. Sacra's chests were packed, her belongings gathered, and, on the celebration of pleasure and fertility, she and her Council moved into the Fall Hall. As Sacra's

170

possessions and women disappeared from the Summer Hall, mine began to materialize. I had spent part of the last several days filling baskets and crates with the contents of my temporary quarters. Near half-day I decided I would take several of these to the Summer Hall myself. My motivation was in part to share in the work of moving, but even more I wanted to examine my new rooms unaccompanied.

Keto had challenged me to learn my way to the Summer Hall. Consequently, it was one of the first routes in the Palace I had memorized. Despite the fact that I had walked exactly the same course many times, this trip was different because I was not going to meet Sacra. In the past, I associated my walks to the Summer Hall with Sacra's nurturance and direction. This time there would be no one there to greet me. I would be alone in this place which had become so familiar and now was so changed.

I trudged up the steps and surveyed the nearly empty space. The Council room, which was now to be mine, still held seats and pillows, but Sacra's table and tablets were gone. The sitting room of the Summer Hall was well illuminated by light wells on one side. However, this light was diffuse and very different from that of the Spring Hall. In the morning and the evening the light in my previous rooms had been direct and intense. In comparison to the Summer Hall, it had been almost stark in its simplicity. In the Spring Hall, high ceilings complemented clean walls which were adorned only by an occasional simple fresco. The curtains that surrounded the bed and even the walls were white. The room was beautiful in its austerity.

This room of the Summer Hall was a study in contrasts. Almost every surface contained some sort of decoration. Large coral columns with grey pillow-like extensions at the top divided the light wells from the larger area of the space. There was a series of ornately decorated doors along one wall. Blue dolphins jumped in frescos interspersed with water birds. Flowers and spirals adorned the doorframes. I found this chamber almost overwhelming because of the intense beauty of its pervasive decorations.

Although I had been in Sacra's Council room many times, I had never been past it into the rest of her suite. I was confident one of the multiple doorways along the far wall would lead to additional rooms, but I was uncertain how to determine which opening to investigate. I tried pushing on several doors before I remembered Petra had come out of one of them the first day I met with Sacra. A gentle push opened it and revealed the chamber beyond.

This space was surprisingly different from the Council room. The ceiling was low and the ambiance was one of comfort and warmth. The scent of flowers accompanied by the fresh smell of the ocean wafted toward me from the large, open doorway to my right. Comfortable chairs and cushions occupied the left corner of the room. Centered on the wall directly in front of me was a magnificent bed covered with a luxurious, wine-colored spread. I knew this color was rare. It required crushing hundreds of shells to create a dye which yielded this shade. Setting down my basket, I crossed the room and ran my hand over the coverlet. I half believed its color might make it somehow feel different to the touch. Other than a lingering *impression* of Sacra it was, however, unremarkable. The room felt warm and intentionally constructed to be a safe refuge from the duties of a Hearth Queen.

An enticingly sweet fragrance drew me through the large open doorway at the far end of the room. It led me out on to a glorious rooftop terrace. This space was every bit as large as the room from which I had come. Flowers spilled down walls and many outstandingly beautiful pots held an amazing variety of sweet-smelling blossoms. Canopies tied to tall posts were draped in various places creating pockets of shade, and under each of these were a variety of choices upon which one could sit or lounge. In the center of the space, water gurgled as it fell comfortingly into a small pool. But, it was the view that made me catch my breath. The sea stretched before me, its azure intensity lined by a golden strip of beach. If I listened, I could just hear the waves as they found their way to shore. Without thinking, I found myself moving to a bench, engrossed in the sights and sounds before me.

I was uncertain how long I had been sitting, held by this scene, before I was startled into consciousness by a sound behind me. I turned to watch a small group of people carrying several of my chests into the room. This company included several artisans, a beekeeper, a waterwright and Fauntee. Setting down the chests, several of the movers immediately began to use them as seats. They joked with one another about which chest was heavier and who had handled the exertion with the greatest ease. Not wanting to get into another situation where I was caught with others unaware of my presence, I stood and made my way to the doorway.

Panos, the beekeeper, saw me first and jumped with a start. Following her gaze, all heads turned in my direction. They seemed embarrassed about having been overheard. Ultimately the group recovered and all but Fauntee nodded in acknowledgement. Fauntee, her eyes on the floor, lifted her fist to her shoulder in the Guardian salute.

Eleni, the waterwright, was the first to recover. "Young Queen, you surprised us," she acknowledged.

"It was not my intention to startle," I replied, also feeling awkward. Fumbling for something to say, I continued, "I have never been in this bedchamber or garden before. The view from the terrace is amazing."

The movers all looked to Eleni, seeming to have declared her the *de facto* communicator. She stared back at them, as if pleading for assistance. There was an uncomfortable pause as she searched for words.

"Umm, yes," she answered, "it is extraordinary," she paused and looked at the others. They looked back at her, none of them coming to her aid.

Apparently at a loss, she continued, "well, ah, unless you have further need of us, we will carry on with our other tasks."

"Of course," I agreed, glad this uncomfortable exchange was coming to an end. As an after-thought I added, "Thank you for moving my chests."

This broke the silence of the others and they all joined in letting me know that no thanks were needed. With these acknowledgments, all of them except Fauntee stood, nodded again and made their way toward the door.

With a lack of her usual bravado, Fauntee looked at her feet and shifted uncomfortably. She blurted self-consciously to the exiting group, "I will meet you later."

There was a brief pause and some furtive smiles as the movers reached the door. Eleni called back over her shoulder, "We will not wait for you if you find yourself delayed." And with that, they were gone.

I was a little disconcerted at being alone with Fauntee. Our last exchange had been the uneasy interaction at the dance after "The Telling." Fauntee seemed nervous, but despite this, she started to speak.

"Young Queen," she began, the *energy* which ran beneath her words was a whirling miasma of contradictions. Not meeting my eyes, she reached out and gently took my hand. "I believe I should apologize."

I did not know what to say so I simply stared at my hand in hers as Fauntee continued awkwardly.

"I am afraid I behaved badly," she stammered. "I sometimes forget you have not long been at the Palace and may not understand the significance of your actions. Dariah told me you asked her the meaning of the dance." Ending her declaration, she stole a look at me without raising her head.

Her behavior confused me. Normally, my ability to *read* a Guardian allowed me to breach most communication barriers. However, I could not at present make sense of Fauntee. My *contact* with her seemed to have layers of meaning. I could sense possessiveness, resentment, and true contrition. It was hard to reconcile these conflicting emotions. I could also *feel* in her a deep sensual hunger.

My reaction was also conflicted. I was aware her statement contained no true apology. Regardless, I felt sympathy and was pleased she wanted to explain herself. There was a part of me that believed I should graciously accept her superficial apology and leave. However, there was another piece of me which responded to her desire. I was sorting out these reactions when suddenly Fauntee reached out and wrapped me in her arms. My need to unravel my feelings fled with her touch.

Her lips were on mine. Her hands slid down my back and grasped my hips. Desire flared fully in me as she lifted me briefly off my feet, took two steps and dropped me gently onto the nearby bed. Without a moment's hesitation, she was beside me untying the sash which held my tunic together. My breathing changed as her tongue found its way through my lips. Her hand traveled down the side of my body, her forearm grazing my nipple. Fingers traced their way past my waist and across the flat of my belly. The *contact* between us began to fall into the familiar cycle I had felt before. I lost myself in the *feelings,* both physical and profoundly intimate.

I could not believe the noise when I heard it. I stifled a groan. It escaped unexpectedly full of the multiple meanings of the moment. Before I could open my eyes, Fauntee was standing and in an instant she was out the door and onto the terrace. I had managed to sit on the edge of the bed, wrap my tunic around me, and I was tying its belt when Sacra entered. She gazed at me knowingly, a bright fire alight in her eyes. Setting down the empty wooden box she was carrying, she immediately walked to the terrace. Briefly, she disappeared from my view but returned quickly to the room.

"She is gone," Sacra said sounding annoyed.

I thought of Petra's climb to the Spring Hall balcony and wondered if there was a similar route down from the terrace. Sacra stood for a moment looking intently at me. Then she seemed to put aside her irritation and came to sit beside me.

"There is nothing wrong with what you do," Sacra said, her exasperation melting away into concern. "It is only with whom you choose to do it that concerns me."

"I would advise you to be careful," the Queen continued. "There is, of course, an affinity between any Queen, young or old, and the Guardians." As she said this, a smile flickered around the edges of her eyes, and I wondered if she, too, felt the insistent desire. "To share passion with another is a gift of the Mother. However, to exchange favors, even to be indiscriminately flirtatious with the Guards is unwise."

On some level, I had been virtually certain Sacra would be distressed with my actions. I did not understand why I felt this way, but I was relieved when she approached the situation with clarification rather than judgment. Eventually, I was brave enough to raise my head and look at her. Sacra put her hand on my knee and continued.

"The Guardians must work closely together and maintain a bond of trust. To engage in behaviors which may cause jealousy distracts them and can reduce their effectiveness. In the end, it is the Queen who suffers if the Guards are not in harmony. They watch over and protect not only the Queen, but also the entire Palace. If they become preoccupied or competitive, we are all at risk. Sleep with someone else," Sacra suggested.

She may as well have said, "Sleep with a goat," for all the interest I had in bedding anyone but a Guardian. It was not only the physical contact and release I was seeking. I wanted the *connection* with them. I hungered for the cycle Stava had shown me and this seemed the easiest route to establish it.

"Giada, you know what the Guardians promise when they are sworn. These Guards are sworn to me. Should any of them come to love you, the conflict could be difficult. Your choices and behavior will greatly affect their responses to you."

Although I understood the rationale behind Sacra's words, for the first time since I realized she was involved with Petra I was resentful of her. Sacra had continual access to her Guards. They surrounded her with an ongoing stream of support and contact. Without access to them I would feel alone and neglected. I wondered if she had ever felt this way and could understand my disquiet.

As always, Sacra seemed to *hear* what I was thinking. "In time, your own Guards will come to you. When you discover them you will have different choices to make."

This time I was exasperated by her access to my thoughts. I was uncertain how to respond. I did not think I could promise her I would no longer interact with "her" Guards provocatively. My longing for them was a force which seemed to emanate from some source beyond reason. If I excised this part of me, I was

176

afraid there would be nothing left. I would be a hollow shell devoid of any animation. Although Sacra had reacted to her discovery with equanimity, I was angry.

Since I did not know how to respond it seemed best to simply leave. I stood, gave my belt one final tug, and moved toward the door. Sacra stood, too. From the corner of my eye I could see her crossing the room to where she had set down her box. With her back to me she spoke in a voice I was not certain I was intended to hear.

Sighing, she said, "It is not always easy, Giada. It is not easy."

I was half way down the steps before I remembered I had left my baskets, still full, on the table.

14

On my initial tour of the Summer Hall it had not occurred to me my rooms would no longer overlook the Guardians' Court. As my first few days in this space passed, it became clear to me how much I missed my opportunities to observe the Guards. I had not realized how often I had arranged my days so I could sit on my balcony and watch them. In the morning, I surveyed the Guards as they prepared to ride out. In the evening, I studied them as they assembled to share the events of their day. Given Sacra's direction, I thought perhaps it was better I did not have this luxury, but it had been one of my favorite diversions. Because I could no longer actually observe the Court, I instead *reached out* to access them and savor the feelings this contact engendered.

I counseled myself to be content with my regular practice in the Guardians' Court. As with virtually everyone in the Palace, it was still part of my routine to work with the Guards every few days. In my time in training I had begun to gain some facility with my staff. I still studied with the novices, but I frequently felt my expertise was beginning to surpass some of the others in my group.

Drea confirmed this suspicion. She stopped me one day as I walked across the Court to select a staff.

"Young Queen," she said as she moved forward, abruptly blocking my way to the staves. As a second thought, she tapped her shoulder in greeting. For some reason Drea's challenging manner always amused me. Because I could *hear* the underlying feelings which accompanied her behavior, I knew she was actually as soft as thistledown. I smiled at her warmly which only seemed to unnerve her.

Drea stammered as she continued. "Err, Young Queen," she began, "if you would walk with me, you will train with Ianthe today."

I must have looked surprised because Drea quickly *extended* her contact and expanded on her announcement. "In the future, your training with me will be every other time you come to this Court. Ianthe hopes to teach you to shoot."

I coughed into my hand trying to suppress a laugh. I could tell from Drea's response she believed my reaction to her pronouncement implied I would miss her, which, truth to be told, was accurate. She did not wait for any further answer from me, but began purposefully making her way toward an opening in the outer wall of the Court. Drea did not look back to see if I was behind her, so, with only a momentary hesitation, I followed her out beyond the confines of the Guardians' space.

I trailed Drea across the outer edges of the Palace to a place where a group of people was in various stages of working with and learning about the bow. Some of them watched intently as Ari coached them on how to string a bow. I smiled, observing several of them struggle to bend their resilient bows down to capture their strings. Ari modeled her statements by adroitly wrapping one leg around the shaft of a bow and nimbly bringing its string up to slide into the notch designed for that. Not far away, another set of trainees released flights of arrows across a range toward a low sand bank. Drea scanned the gathering, targeted Ianthe by the sand and moved toward her with purpose.

"Ianthe," she shouted as she got close enough to be heard.

Ianthe turned looking for the source of the shout. Her eyes smiled as she saw Drea coming in her direction. I was surprised, given Drea's brusqueness and bravado, that the other Guardians seemed to respect her. Drea's heart was that of an Amazon even though the body she inhabited was a head or two shorter than the rest of the Guards. Her bravery and dedication must have allowed them to accept her.

As Drea reached Ianthe's side she finally looked to see if I was following. She impatiently motioned for me to join them even though I was only a short distance away. I surveyed the two women as I approached. Ianthe and Drea were at opposite ends of the Guardian spectrum. Drea's thick dark hair escaped its ties in random spikes. Her body was compact and yet distinctly powerful. What she lacked in stature she made up in spirit. She appeared to be focused on her mission to deliver me

179

to the range and mildly aggravated at having her day interrupted with this errand.

Ianthe in comparison was tall and even-tempered. I had seen her before, but under the open sky, I could not help but notice her eyes were the bright blue of the sea near shore. There was no denying she was striking. My eyes traced the sinuous muscles of her arms across her strong shoulders to the soft warm brown of her hair. She exuded a powerful charisma, but was self-effacing and seemed largely unaware of her compelling impact. Remembering Sacra's advice, I tried to shift my thoughts away from how it would feel to have her arms wrapped around me to focusing on the bow she held in her hand.

Once I reached the two of them Drea inquired briskly, "Will you make certain she is returned to the Palace?" she asked jerking her head in my direction.

This time Ianthe smiled fully and assured her she would walk with me back to the Palace when practice was over. Drea turned toward me and I felt a brief surge of true *connection*. I remembered how, without any hesitation, she had risked her life during the previous shake to insure my safety. In that moment I, too, could overlook her shortcomings. She abruptly severed the connection, tapped her shoulder, turned on her heel, and was gone.

Ianthe shook her head at Drea's departing back. Then, without a word about their interaction, she turned toward me and asked, "Will you walk with me?" She led me a short distance away from the rest of the group. "Young Queen," she said turning toward Dicta, "tell me what is the farthest thing you see."

I gazed across the valley toward the hazy peaks in the distance. "I can see the mountains," I replied.

"Good," Ianthe answered. "Tell me more about them."

"Well," I continued, "I can see trees on the closer low hills, but they fade on the larger peaks in the distance. The farther ones are almost blue today."

"Excellent," Ianthe said grinning. "I have found this exercise to be one of the most useful in judging a persons suitability for shooting. In the past, I have worked diligently trying to hone the skills of a would-be archer only to find they could not even see the target."

I laughed good-naturedly in response. I could not help but warm to her quiet charisma. I found it interesting how similar and yet how distinct each Guardian was. They ranged in age, body type, personality and even *energy*. However, there was something about each of them that was the same. They seemed to be able to see beyond what lay in front of them off to some distant point. I wasn't sure if what they saw was a possible future or simply a different view of the world. It gave them an ethereal and, at the same time, earthy quality. With a start, I realized Ianthe was speaking to me. I was uncertain what I had missed while pondering the intricacies of Guardians. I picked up her words midsentence.

"...the tree at the edge of the shooting bank," Ianthe was saying. "Lift your finger and point at it."

Even though I had missed the beginning of her directions, I understood she was asking me to point at a tree about thirty paces away. I raised my hand and leveled my finger in the direction she had indicated.

"Now pick a spot, like a leaf or a burl, and point directly at it," Ianthe instructed. I selected a brown leaf among the green and focused on it.

I nodded and said, "There is a leaf that is a different color about half way up the tree. Is that a good marker?"

"Yes," Ianthe responded. "Close one eye. Is your finger still pointing at the leaf?"

Incredulously I answered, "No, it's aiming at the trunk of the tree. How is that possible?"

"Keep your finger where it was and close the other eye," she continued. "Is your finger on the leaf now?"

"Yes," I replied giving a little leap of excitement over my success.

"We each have an eye which is true," Ianthe explained. "It is important to know which that is because if one shoots with the other eye the target will always be elusive."

I felt I had already learned a lot about getting an arrow to its mark, and I had yet to touch a bow. Ianthe led me back to where a group of bows leaned against a low branch. She selected one and gave it to me.

"Here," she smiled handing me the bow. I was briefly lost in her eyes, but my consciousness came sharply back into focus as the smooth, cool wood of the bow came to rest in my hand. "Since your right eye is true, hold the string in your right hand. Now, pull the string back to your ear."

I gripped the wood with my left hand, the string with my right, and tried to pull it back. I made it only a short distance before the string snapped back with a forceful thwack. Ianthe laughed good-naturedly.

"If you had been able to pull that bow..." she began and then interrupted herself again with laughter. "Dariah, the Peer of the Guard from Knossos, left it here when she came for your presentation. We have all tried to use it, but none of us can. Let me get you a more suitable one." I could see her teasing held no malice. It was instead a way to include me in the camaraderie of those who had tried and failed at the same endeavor.

This time the bow she selected was smaller, and I easily brought the string to my ear. "Ah," she said exchanging the bow I was holding for another. "I think perhaps that one is too light. Try this one."

It was more difficult to pull the third bow, but the exertion felt somehow in balance. Ianthe watched me intently as I drew back the string.

"I think this one will be good," she declared, confirming my own assessment.

Ianthe and I moved toward the remains of the group that had been shooting. Many of them had gone back to their other duties, but a few dedicated archers remained. From a collection of supplies, Ianthe selected a quiver and a handful of arrows. These she offered me with a certain amount of solemnity. I could not discern if she actually saw this as a serious occasion or if she was playfully making this presentation. She plucked an arrow from among the others and held it out for me to examine.

"Look," Ianthe directed as she held out an arrow for my inspection. The shaft was about as long as my arm. It was made of two pieces of wood fitted together and bound with a fine piece of sinew. The way the sections were placed created a small notch at the end. A tiny Sinewy string held three sets of feathers in place near the gap.

"Keep watching." Ianthe continued as she picked up a nearby bow. She fitted an arrow on the string and sent it flying impressively to a small scrap of fabric attached to the sand bank beyond. She repeated this several times. Each time the arrow was within a finger's width of the one next to it. I watched, fascinated by her skill.

Pausing, she turned toward me and explained, "When you draw the bow, you give it power. When you release the string, that power moves to the arrow. You and the bow give the arrow the gift of flight." Not only did Ianthe's words convey her message, but a direct stream of *contact* carried the meaning also.

I wished everyone who had been providing me information had as clear a *signal* as Ianthe. Had that been true, I believed I would have learned much more quickly. But, upon reflection, I realized the Wise Ones did exactly that. However in their case it made me uncomfortable. I chided myself about being impressed by the Guards' connection and irritated by the Wise Ones.

"Now, you try," Ianthe directed. "Slot the gap in the arrow into the string, pull it, sight the bank, and release the arrow."

I followed her instructions. However, my first arrow fell to the ground only a few steps from where I stood. It distressed me my initial attempt had been so poor. I was even more embarrassed Ianthe was there to witness it. I had half believed archery would come naturally to me and my arrow would be true. From there, I hoped Ianthe would be impressed with my innate ability and we would shoot side-by-side, each complementing the other's skill. Clearly, that was not going to happen.

I shook my head, sighing.

"Do not be disappointed," Ianthe counseled. "Almost everyone begins the same way."

"Hold your elbow up, away from your body and try again." As she spoke, she touched me gently and lifted my arm to an almost horizontal angle. I tried to repeat her words, "Pull, sight, release," but they echoed as only an undercurrent. My attention was captured by the heady touch of her hand.

My second attempt made it a few paces farther. This time I was so disheartened I could not even look up. I stared at the ground and then suddenly felt Ianthe's arms around me.

"Slot your arrow," she coached "Raise your bow." As she said these words her arm moved forward with mine. "Pull the string." Her hand closed over mine "Release," she directed.

This time the arrow flew swiftly to its mark. Ianthe did not immediately remove her arms. We both watched in anticipation. The arrow flew quickly and pinned the scrap of cloth even closer to the bank. The pleasure of making the arrow fly and her touch comingled within me. I leaned back toward her. However, in a heartbeat she was gone. I could *sense* her embrace had been only a well-practiced teaching technique. I sighed, wishing it had been otherwise.

"Excellent," she said. "Now you do it."

With Ianthe watching and instructing, I pulled arrows from the quiver on my back and loosed flight after flight. Eventually, all on my own, I was making them land in the bank. I realized with delight I had succeeded in learning the basic technique.

As I practiced, a woman shooting nearby repeatedly distracted me. She shot multiple times in quick succession, then mumbled to herself while pacing impatiently waiting for, "Gather your arrows," to be called. When the range was clear she practically ran to the bank to retrieve her shots. Her pacing began again after she returned and waited for the "loose arrows" to be heard.

As I continued to practice, I watched her from the corner of my eye. She was dressed oddly. Part of her clothing seemed to be the leathers of a Guard, but they hung on her loosely. The Guardians' typical attire was fitted and allowed for the optimum range of motion. I could not imagine she could move well in her oversized garment. Not only was her outfit strange, but also so was her *energy*. It carried some of the awareness of the Guards, but that was a construct which overlay insecurity and a strong current of self-importance.

184

She was not a Guardian. The innate sense I had for identifying the Guards did not register her among them. Nevertheless, her shooting was excellent. Each time she released a volley of arrows they would strike her target all within a hair's breadth of each other. After each round of shooting, she would look around at the Guards present to see if any of them were watching. As most frequently they were not, she would huff moodily and begin pacing again. I found myself uncomfortable with both her demeanor and the *energy* she emitted.

I continued to shoot for a while longer. After a time, Ianthe extended her hand indicating I should turn over the bow I had been using. She loosened the string saying, "Next time, I will teach you how to unstring a bow yourself." We stowed our equipment and together began to walk back toward the Palace.

I could not help thinking about the disquieting *energy* of the woman shooting near me.

"Ianthe," I questioned, "who was the woman..." I paused unable to think of a charitable description. Finally I settled on, "Umm, the excellent archer?"

"Ah, you must mean Malaina. She truly is one of the best archers at Malia," Ianthe replied.

"She is not a Guardian," I proclaimed simply.

Ianthe looked uncomfortable, but said, "That is true. I am glad to hear you confirm it. I think she believes if she can show herself expert in the skills of a Guard, we will accept her as one of us. I know several Guardians have explained to her we are not the ones who acknowledge a Foundling."

"Has she been taken to Sacra?" I asked, thinking perhaps my perception was colored by the fact she was *not for me,* but that possibly another Queen might recognize her.

"No," Ianthe replied. "She does not seem to want to be presented. I believe she knows in her heart she is not one of us. This, however, does not stop her aspirations."

"How odd," I answered. "Why would someone persist in trying to be acknowledged as a Guard when it is clear they are not?"

We had reached the opening in the Palace wall which led into the Guardians' Court. Ianthe glanced at me questioningly and then indicated a nearby bench with a dip of her head.

I nodded, understanding her unspoken inquiry, and we walked together to sit in the shade of the wall.

"It is not that uncommon," Ianthe confided. "There are many who wish to be Guards who do not have the call."

I swiveled in my seat and stared at her in surprise. Ianthe continued candidly, "It seems many women are attracted to the life of the Guards. They wish to be a part of our sisterhood. They envy our strength and freedom. I cannot say I blame them, for were I not a Guardian myself, I too would be trying to become one."

"But, they don't have the *energetic*," I said skeptically.

"You and I know that is true. However, some women hope being a Guard is a skill which can be learned... not a thing to which one is born," Ianthe said in agreement.

"But, Malaina's *energy* does not extend out into the world," I stated as if that were obvious to everyone.

Ianthe looked at me quizzically and nodded, encouraging me to continue.

I paused struggling to convey concepts I had never spoken before. "Well," I said, trying to formulate an explanation, "I am uncertain how others identify the movement of *energy*, but I primarily experience it as a force which moves in or out. Those whose *energy* moves outward know their world by pushing their awareness into it. They understand the things and people around them by making contact with them externally."

"On the other hand," I explained, "when I want to *know* something I draw the person or situation into me. I evaluate them from an internal place. I think each of these ways of perception has limitations and pitfalls, but both also have strengths. Those with outward energy sometimes do not see what is right in front of them. However, they often have an awareness of danger or things happening at a distance even into the future. I added for clarity, "To me, the energy of a Guardian extends outward."

Ianthe was clearly contemplating my statements, so I continued, "The other Hearth Queens and I have energy which moves inward. The Queens are sensitive to even the minutest fluctuations in people and events. From this place of internal awareness, repeating patterns are clear and the needs of people are apparent. Obviously, there are concerns with this type of discernment. If one pulls in illness or disturbance, it can be unsettling and hard to put aside."

Ianthe nodded excitedly. "Yes," she said, "I have always known this, but I had not framed it in words. It is like when we share pleasure..." Her words trailed off, and a flush crept up her neck from under her leathers.

For some reason, her reference did not make me uncomfortable or even aroused. I paused to congratulate myself, thinking perhaps I was making progress on realigning my reaction to the Guards.

"You are right," I replied, feeling pleased with myself. The energy of the Guardians and the Hearth Queens moves in synchrony. When a Guard's energy extends outward, a Queen can catch it and pull it to her. Not only is the energy of each perceptible by the other, but together they create balance. For me, the *touch* of a Guard can clear residual feelings left by internalizing something troubling."

"Is it the same for you?" I questioned.

Ianthe did not answer but instead *reached* for me. I could sense in her a hunger for the *contact* I was describing. Her *touch* was not intrusive and included an inquiry seeking my consent. I found I also craved this type of communication and welcomed her overture. The familiar feeling I had experienced with Stava on the day of my presentation and even Fauntee during our abortive encounters sprung to life. I quickly began taking in the *energy* she pushed toward me. As I drew Ianthe inward, her *energy* filled me. To me, it was as if my usual awareness was gently pushed out of its normal confines, creating a flood of *current* which spilled from me toward her. Our energy cycled as a circuit of contact was completed between us.

This time I found I could choose not to experience this *contact* in sexual terms. I was aware it held a sensual component. However, I became conscious there was another path I could follow which did not lead toward bedding her as the ultimate outcome. I could feel Ianthe's *touch* clearing the haze from my consciousness. She carried away residual unrest I had not even realized I held. My disquiet melted as her energy converged with mine. As my awareness moved toward her, I realized I too had a similar ability. I could find where she was not in balance and help encourage stability. Within me, her worries and distress had no meaning and melted away. I felt certain her experience of my uneasiness was similar.

It was true this experience was intimate. A part of me wanted to abandon the ethereal quality of this encounter. I thought about how it would feel to reach out, take her hands and put them on my breasts. I could feel her energy shift in response. I refocused on creating balance and the erotic spike dissipated. It stabilized into the form it had previously taken. I began to feel revitalized and centered. Ianthe took a deep slow breath and I knew she too felt balanced and refreshed. Gradually, the link between us diminished, leaving behind a feeling of contentment and wholeness.

I wasn't sure what to do now that Ianthe and I simply sat on the bench facing each other. I felt a deep intimacy and connection with her, but, at the same time, I felt awkward about what to do. While I was pondering this, Ianthe gently reached out and touched my cheek. It was an uncomplicated gesture of appreciation and affection.

"I am truly blessed," was all she said. Then rose tapped her shoulder and walked through the gate into the Guardians' Court.

*****

I could not decide if I wanted to see Fauntee or not. A part of me was constantly looking for her and yet I was apprehensive about our next encounter. My indecision had yet to be tested, as I had not seen her since my visit to the Summer Hall. Because I no longer had a view of the Guardians' Court, I could not see if she was following her daily routine or if her behavior had merited some consequence.

I contemplated sneaking up the fallen staircase of the Spring Hall to surreptitiously peer from my old balcony into the Court below. I had even gone so far as to concoct an excuse that I believed something of mine was still there. However, several things stopped me from executing this plan. First, I would have to ignore the current prohibition regarding the use of the stairs. Setting that aside, it seemed likely that if I encountered someone working on the restoration, they would offer to help me with my search. I wasn't sure I could keep up a pretense in the face of what would then prove to be a diligent investigation. Also, depending on whom I might meet, it was likely they would know the true reason for my outing, which meant my fabricated motive would simply embarrass me.

If I were to follow Sacra's advice, it might be best to limit my contact with the Guardians. I wondered how this would be possible as the pulse of *communication* and *connection* with them was still my constant companion. To me, it would be like trying to ignore a pebble in a sandal. One could continue to walk, but with each step there would be a reminder. No matter how insistent one was on ignoring the pebble, its presence would continue to make itself known.

I did have many other things that I could be doing. My promise to convene my first Council was on my mind. In truth, I had spent many hours contemplating the women who had been originally chosen for me. I had even pondered this question in "darkness," which proved to be the first time I found it useful. I surprised myself by wishing I had established some competence in divination. In this particular case, I thought it might be helpful in making decisions. Given that had not happened, I simply began to consider my feelings toward the women who had been in my rooms.

I would, of course, ask Reya to be on my Council. She was a mainstay in my ability to function. She counseled me without ever suggesting my inexperience or willfulness was unacceptable. In honesty, I cared for her deeply and trusted her to have my best interests at heart.

Each of the other women had redeeming qualities. Nyssa had won me from the beginning with her playful spirit, mixed with her incongruous bravery. I remembered the fierce affection I had felt for Calida, Alandra, Lalage and Elayn when I had encountered them in the Queen's Court after we were separated. I knew by this feeling they should be a part of my Council.

I had watched Kyma in the healing rooms after the shake, and I understood her well when she told me about the illness caused by wheat. I knew our communication was excellent. Lista was dedicated and knowledgeable in her craft of growing. I had witnessed her commitment and ability to make order out of chaos during the last harvest. Not only was it imperative to have someone on my Council who understood crops, a woman who could organize people and respond to hectic situations was invaluable.

I remembered Myrina's nonjudgmental manner when she found me disheveled in Stava's arms. This I thought was a quality I would definitely need. Iva's blessing before my presentation, "May you always know what comes next," was a phrase that had remained with me. Pelagia had been efficient in her response to the wheat crisis and Damia had impressed me with her clear ability to impart meaning through lyrics and story.

The only woman of whom I was uncertain was Alega. She was the only Wise One who had been among my women. I found I had difficulty *connecting* with her. For me to *find* and *understand* the rest of the women I was considering for my Council was easy. Alega, however, was an enigma. When I *searched* for her, I could only find vague impressions of her *energy*. I knew some of the women believed her daily forecasts useful, but I primarily found them tedious. I also believed her priorities were not as a member of my rooms. Although all of these women were busy and worked hard, they seemed to value spending time in the Spring Hall. In contrast, Alega's main focus seemed to be the work of a Wise One.

However, I doubted my ability to judge Alega without prejudice. I was concerned my disinclination toward all things connected to the Wise Ones was coloring my assessment. Setting that aside and evaluating her on her own merit eluded me. After some consideration, I decided I would need a Wise One on my Council. To me, Alega was palatable and she had an established relationship with the other women who had been in my rooms.

Having made my decisions, I began to seek out the women I had chosen. I found Iva working industriously in the central Court. In a clear voice she was calling out instructions to the builders who worked on repairs to the Palace. I moved to her side as she paused to scrutinize a small structural drawing.

"Iva, do you have a few moments to talk?" I asked.

She looked surprised to see me in this space, but smiled warmly. Shouting a few more instructions to the assembled builders, she came to stand beside me by the central Court's broad staircase.

"Actually, Giada," she said sighing, "you could not have come at a better time. I am definitely in need of respite. If I had to explain one more time to Jase how to align the column he is working on, I think I would have pushed him from the scaffolding."

"Well," I replied laughing, "I'm glad I could save someone's life with so little effort today." Now that the moment to speak had actually arrived, I found myself feeling awkward. Although I had spent an inordinate amount of time contemplating who would make the best members of my Council, I had not actually thought about what to say to them. Asking a woman to make a commitment that would, in all probability, affect the rest of her life, was serious. I looked at my hands trying to frame my request.

"Iva," I began, "it is time for me to convene my own Council. As I have come to know you, I have developed a deep respect for you and your work. I believe we will work well together, and I would like to ask you to be a part of my Council. There is no need to answer me now. Take as much time as..."

I did not even complete my sentence before Iva interrupted.

"Yes," she stated simply and then, pausing for only a moment, continued, "I hoped you would ask me to sit Council with you."

191

She looked off into the distance as if she was able to see something not apparent to me. "There are only a few things I know without doubt. I am not a Wise One," she said as an aside. "But, I want to be with you in your work as Queen. I know jointly we hold a vision for the future and together we will assure Malia's continuance and strength. My understanding of this is not based in reason. It came over me like a wave the first time I saw you on the day you arrived. I knew then, Giada, you and I will create a future for Malia."

I had envisioned many possible outcomes in reply to my question. I had anticipated requests for time to consider, cheerful acceptance and even polite refusal. This poignant answer from Iva, however, took me by surprise. She looked at me meaningfully, her eyes full of excitement. I understood she was waiting for an acknowledgement.

In this moment I knew what it was to be Queen. Although I had no direct knowledge of the premonition expressed in Iva's words, I knew the accuracy of her vision. This, I thought, is a part of what makes a successful Hearth Queen. Having the ability to know the truth when it is spoken even though one has no personal knowledge of the fact.

I moved closer to Iva and took her hand. "Iva," I said, "I understand and believe you. In the future, I will look to you when I am uncertain." She sighed in apparent relief and patted my hand where it rested on hers.

"I am with you, Giada," Iva responded, "together we will care for Malia."

I realized she had taken a risk in being direct with me about her foresight. She could have simply accepted my invitation without revealing any information about her knowledge. I felt honored by her trust. This, I thought, was an auspicious beginning to my Council.

With one exception the other invitations to serve on my Council were uneventful. Women's responses ranged from delight to solemn acceptance, and only Alega asked for time to consider my request. In a few days she returned with her answer. She was respectful but declined, stating her resolve to be fully committed to her work as a Wise One. As I had considered this possibility, her reply did not surprise me.

This left me with an important decision to make. I had reasoned before, I would need a Wise One among the women on my Council. However, I did not know any of them well. I thought perhaps Asteria, the young Wise One I had followed, might be someone in whom I would find an ally. However, I was concerned she did not take her responsibilities seriously. I shook my head at my own thoughts. I had questioned Alega as a member of my Council as I felt she took her role as a Wise One too earnestly, and now I doubted Asteria's participation because she might not be dedicated enough.

Regardless of my reservations, I decided I would ask Asteria, as the only other Wise One whom I already knew. This, I thought, would not be difficult as I saw her with the Wise Ones every day.

15

Even though I had been at Malia for some time, I had yet to fully explore the Palace. I now knew well the route from the Spring to the Summer Hall. An escort was no longer sent for me when I went to practice in the Guardians' Court. And, although a reason for voluntarily traveling there escaped me, I had learned the path downward into the realm of the Wise Ones. When I asked Alandra to be on my Council, I mentioned I had never seen where the artists worked. She did not respond immediately, but turned her head to the side and gazed upward with her eyes unfocused. I could tell she was searching her memory.

"I believe you are correct," she acknowledged with some surprise. "We must remedy this. Can you come with me tomorrow?"

The next day Alandra and I met in the central Court. The comfortable warmth of the spring morning carried with it a salty breeze from the sea. She greeted me cheerfully, and we walked together companionably toward the southern entrance to the square. I always enjoyed Alandra's company and was looking forward to spending time with her. Although I believed she did not always share a connection to common reality, the passion she held for her art redeemed her occasional inattention. She was clearly excited about sharing the parts of the Palace she frequented with me. Always animated whenever she spoke about her craft, today she was buoyant as she led me toward a series of rooms on the edge of the central Court.

"These are only some of the workshops," she said earnestly as we moved toward an opening in the Court wall." A number of the crafting spaces are outside the Palace. Tanning, dying and some of the jewelry making are all activities which do not lend themselves to working in areas near where people reside."

I looked at her in puzzlement.

"Vapors and... the smell." Pinching her nose she said, "I will take you to see those places on a day when there is a good wind." She smiled, amused at her own humor.

"Our workshops are at the southern end of the Palace where they catch the best sun." She continued as we walked along a short hall into one of these well-lit spaces. An acrid odor assailed me from down the corridor. It made me wonder how bad the other smells must be if this one was acceptable.

A couple of young women and an ancient one squatted together on the ground. In front of each of them was a large mound of shapeless clay. I had seen the young ones at "The Telling," but I did not recall the old potter. As we entered she was saying...

"...brought with you clay you have found and, hopefully, cleaned correctly. Today we will be testing your clay to see if it will..." They all glanced at us as we crossed the threshold. The old woman looked briefly exasperated, but quickly regained her composure. "These are my apprentice potters," she said gazing up at me from her position on the floor and pointing in the direction of the others. The young women nodded in greeting, but quickly returned their gaze to the aged potter.

"We have no wish to interrupt your lessons," Alandra replied. The old woman glanced back at her as if to say, "You already have." There was, however, no need for her to speak as her look expressed the entire context of her message.

Alandra looked at me and rolled her eyes. With a tilt of her head she gestured toward the door indicating we should leave. As we made our way down the hall she whispered, "That was Adelfa, one of the master potters. The young apprentices consider it a privilege to take instruction from her because she knows the secrets of the symbols."

I thought about the many clay things I had seen at Malia, from tiny items which could be held in one's hand to enormous vases taller than most people. I had noticed almost all of them carried some kind of design." Do you mean the markings on the pottery?" I inquired of Alandra.

"Yes," she replied, "although they may appear abstract, each of the images carries a meaning. None of the work is random."

"That's interesting," I answered. I decided to inspect the symbols more closely. I did not know if I would be able to interpret the messages hidden in the images, but I thought it would be interesting to try. As we talked, we moved down the hall toward another door. In this room a young woman and a pleasant looking middle-aged one sat facing each other behind identical tall benches. Both of their faces were new to me.

They each looked up as we entered. The older woman got to her feet saying. "Welcome, Young Queen, to this place of beauty and inspiration." Gesturing toward the other woman she said, "This is Zosime." The younger woman rose awkwardly to acknowledge the introduction. When she stood, I could see one of her legs was bent and did not support her well.

She caught her breath and her balance at the same time. "Welcome, Young Queen," she answered, repeating the words she had just heard without appearing to assign any meaning to them.

"And this is Nileas," Alandra said indicating the older woman with obvious pleasure. "She is an accomplished metal worker. I believe she and Zosime made your seal ring."

My attention went to the gold ring I had worn every day since my presentation. Without thinking, I raised my hand to glance at it. At once, Zosime reached out and took my wrist. It seemed that to her, my hand was only a conveyance for the jewelry it bore. I was surprised by her action, but did not pull away. With her touch came *awareness*. Her mind did not flow along ordinary channels. It was not void, but fragmented in an unusual way. I glanced at Alandra who returned my look with a *pulse* of acknowledgement.

"Ah, yes, the seal ring of the new Young Queen," Zosime breathed as she gazed at their work. Despite the fact that she and Nileas had just greeted me as such, she appeared unaware I was the "Young Queen" for whom the ring was made. A moment later she seemed to notice she still held my wrist, and her eyes slowly followed my arm upward to gaze at my face. Only then did she seem to become fully aware of me, and she suddenly dropped my hand.

"Zosime is one of the most talented apprentices among the metal workers," Alandra said, her statement conveying more meaning than the words carried.

196

"That's excellent," I replied. Genuinely touched by what I perceived to be the girl's isolation, I *reached* toward her in an attempt to access the complicated shifting of her mind. Her response was to drop back down on her stool with a look of incredulity. I could tell she *heard* me and was strongly affected by the *contact*.

At once, a torrent of lucid nonverbal *communication* came pouring from her. Things Zosime had held in check because of an inability to convey them came streaming toward me. Despite her awkwardness, I recognized she was extremely intelligent. Her communication seemed to be limited by an inability to order her thinking. The realization that I could follow it without the need for her to translate thoughts into words appeared to be a relief. Suddenly, an almost overwhelming outpouring of pictures and feelings came flowing toward me. As much as it irritated me to admit it, the Wise Ones had warned me about the possibility of this happening. They had even shared a technique for dealing with this type of unintentional concentrated *contact*.

Most of the time, I opened my perception to take in as much information as I comfortably could. However, some people's method of *communication* was too intense and almost anyone under stress could convey details more stridently than they intended. The Wise Ones thought that this type of *contact* verged on rudeness and that one should limit access to anyone committing this indiscretion. They made me repeatedly practice pulling my consciousness into a tight channel which restricted excessive external input. Their belief was that everyone should be able to do this instantaneously, but in particular a future Hearth Queen needed to be expert at this technique.

I had no sense that Zosime intended to be disrespectful. Nevertheless, her *contact* was too forceful. Almost without thinking I narrowed my *focus* as I had done so many times in the Wise Ones' exercises. In response to the change in my energy, Zosime's countenance fell. Her shoulders dropped and her entire body appeared to sink in on itself. Although I did not widen my *connection*, I *sent* back reassurance and acceptance. Zosime immediately responded by modifying her *contact* to a more acceptable level, and I began to understand what she was trying to tell me.

She was lonely. Although the people of the Palace were kind, she was unable to communicate easily with most of them. The possibility of understanding and connection had excited her, and created the storm of *contact*.

I reached out and touched her shoulder." I am Giada. Will you come to me soon for tea?"

Zosime brightened. She started to *stream* again, but caught herself and simply nodded. Her hand reached up and covered mine where it rested on her shoulder.

"Good," I replied although Zosime had actually said nothing. "I will send word to you soon." I patted her hand and slipped mine off her shoulder.

All of this happened in no more than a few heartbeats. If someone without the ability to *read* another had been watching, they would not have observed anything between Zosime's introduction and my invitation to tea. Almost all of our *communication* had been on an internal level. Despite this, I felt like I knew her better than some others with whom I had regular contact. I was looking forward to seeing her again.

This time I was the one who indicated it was time for us to go. Nileas smiled *extending* support and approval for my interaction with Zosime. I suspected she, too, understood Zosime's complicated *contact*. As Alandra and I stepped back out into the hall, I realigned my focus. It occurred to me I had just behaved like a Hearth Queen. Hearth Queens moved among the people seeking areas where there was disquiet or imbalance and took steps to correct them. I had *sensed* Zosime's discomfort and was already contemplating how to address it. I still had doubts about my ability to serve as Hearth Queen. However, this realization made me wonder if it was true I had some intrinsic ability to function in this role.

I continued with Alandra toward what I learned was her workspace. It was all color and light. Splashes of paint dotted the floor and randomly decorated the walls. I could not decide if Alandra and the other painters were careless or if they had tried

198

various hues in a variety of places to see how they interacted with the light. I decided both were likely.

The excitement she had shown earlier bubbled to the surface again. She began speaking so quickly that I caught up with her halfway through a sentence, "...is where we mix pigment." She said indicating a table set away from the sun near the door where we had entered. It was littered with a selection of bowls stained with assorted colors. "To get brown we burn and crush clay," Alandra explained, and with a grin she continued. "We get black from the residue left from lamps. People often think it strange when I wander around the Palace looking for dirty lamps to clean"

Walking toward another corner of the room, she picked up a clay tablet. It was like the ones used for writing, however, this one was decorated with the colorful image of an octopus. "We practice before we begin work on anything which will be displayed." Alandra continued, "When we are actually painting, we have only as long as it takes for the plaster to dry to complete the work. So, we need to have everything ready and an idea of what we hope to portray before we begin."

"I had to practice for a long time before I was proficient enough to start..."

The remainder of Alandra's sentence was lost to me as I tried to focus on a muted thread of *contact*. I held up my hand toward her, hoping silence would help me concentrate. Immediately, she became still. I could make out distress, but beyond that the *signal* still eluded me. In contrast to a few moments before when I had pulled my awareness into a tight channel, this time I opened my consciousness seeking the source of the *communication*.

Straining, I tried to understand the faint *sensation*. Alandra stood watching as I tried to follow the weak *signal* to its source. Finally, I heard Malaina, the would-be Guardian I had seen when I practiced with the bow.

I could just make out her message. *"Guardians alert."*

At first I wondered why Malaina would be calling the Guards, but in no more than a heartbeat her signal was caught and amplified by several others. I could feel Drea, Ianthe, and

199

other Air Guardians catch and augment her communication. Within moments I felt Sacra's *awareness* touch Malaina and the message burst into clarity. Images *flooded* my senses.

Malaina and the Foundling Temo, riding with supplies for the Guards who kept watch a distance from the Palace. There was the smell of Sea Raiders. Then I saw an image of Temo's feet kicking as she was forced face down across the front of a Raider's horse. Finally, I saw the raiders backs and the horses faded into the hills.

The images were rough and sputtered through my consciousness. However, they conveyed the *message... Sea Raiders had carried off Temo.*

Five *calls* came at once. Sacra, several Air Guardians, Petra and I all simultaneously called *"Guardians Alert."* I could *feel* the information spreading among the rest of the Guards. The response to the situation began immediately.

Suddenly, I was aware of Alandra's workshop where bright paint flecks mingled with others that danced before my eyes. I had extended my consciousness far beyond its normal bounds and found myself disoriented. Alandra reached my side within a heartbeat. She extended energy in support while at the same time producing a stool and slipping it under me. Fleetingly, I thought how comforting it was in this crisis to be with a woman who was to be part of my Council. Then I closed my eyes and put my head in my hands.

*****

"What were you thinking?" Petra asked, her disbelief and concern floating palpably along with her question.

Temo stood nearby staring at her feet. She shifted her weight from side to side but did not answer.

"Child," Sacra said, her voice serious but soothing, "we are not interested in disciplining you. Your experience with the Sea Raiders has been punishment enough. We simply want to know how it happened you rode out without a partner."

"Malaina was with me," Temo muttered timidly glancing up at the others.

Sacra and I sat on rough boxes under the overhanging porch that adjoined the Guardians' Shelter and opened onto their Court. Petra and Maris stood close by while Hespar paced in exasperation not far away.

"We are aware Malaina was with you, but she is not a Guardian," Petra replied.

"What is the first rule for a Guard leaving the Palace?" Hespar barked, pausing midstride and turning toward the porch. She raised her voice partly in anger and also so it would carry to where the group was assembled

"Never leave the Palace without another Guardian," Temo answered by rote, gently kicking the dirt at her feet.

"Then what were you thinking?" Hespar asked repeating Petra's original question in a much more intimidating tone.

"Malaina wishes to be one of the Guards," Temo responded hopefully.

Hespar snorted, turned and strode several steps back into the Court.

"Is there no one with whom you have trained?" Sacra asked, her voice sounding kind but conveying her incredulity.

"I train most often with Tam," Temo responded looking optimistically at the Queen. "She cannot ride out now because of her injury."

Hespar walked to the edge of the porch enclosure again. In almost a whisper she said, "And, could you think of no one else who would ride with you? You know any of us would have gone. Toads, I would have gone," she declared and then stomped back out into the Court.

Petra and Sacra looked at each other and then at Hespar. I sensed they thought her interactions were not helping. After a few moments Petra moved to an empty box and sat. She motioned to Temo and patted the place beside her. "Come, sit," she requested, and Temo reluctantly joined her. Maris followed and stood behind the two of them.

"Do you know why Hespar is upset?" Petra questioned. Temo did not answer, but shook her head.

"Hespar is disturbed because things could have turned out very differently." Maris said joining the conversation. "We could still be searching for you or in mourning." For the first time Temo looked truly remorseful.

Petra began again, "We all know Malaina wishes to be counted among the Guard. We also know she is not one of us. Wanting to be one of the Guard and being one are two very different things."

For the first time Temo looked directly at Petra. "But, Malaina shoots better than any of us. Her stick work is perfect and she is excellent with a sword."

"Being good at the skills of a Guardian does not make one a Guardian," Petra said seriously. After a long pause she asked, "Can you tell us what happened?" Her question made it clear to me she intended to try another approach.

"Well," Temo began, "Malaina and I were taking provisions to the Guards on watch. We were passing out of the low hills and onto the beach when suddenly three Sea Raiders were riding hard toward us. I did not see them coming. I think Malaina must have because she had been beside me, and then, suddenly, she was gone. One of them rode fast and got in front of me, and then two others were on either side of my mount. They boxed me in. The one on my right pushed me hard. I tumbled onto the horse of the man on the other side and he grabbed me." Temo paused in her story, her whole body trembling.

When Temo began her account, Hespar had come in from the Court and taken a seat beside her. As Temo paused, Hespar put her arm around the Foundling's shoulder and, in a voice so soft it belied her earlier anger, she said, "It is all right, Temo. You are safe." The three older Guardians surrounded her. Their reassurance was palpable.

After a time Maris asked, "Where was Malaina when this was happening?"

"I do not know," Temo responded, her look clearly conveying her disappointment and confusion.

Hespar quizzed. "If Malaina had been the one the raiders were trying to capture, where would you have been?"

Temo rallied, "I would have been at her side. If they had taken her, I would have chased them and fought. If they got far into the distance, and I felt I would not have accidently hit

Malaina, I would have shot at them. And, I would have raised the alert."

"That is right," Petra acknowledged. "That is what a Guardian would do. But, Malaina is not a Guard. When you needed her, she was not there. She could not make herself act. It may not be in her nature to risk herself for another."

Temo looked taken aback. "It had not occurred to me she might not be able to take action."

"A Guardian has a special nature," Petra continued. "She will risk her own life in the face of danger. Although it is possible for any of us to be momentarily stunned into inaction, when we recover we move toward, rather than away from, a threat."

I could see understanding beginning to dawn on Temo's face. It was Maris who picked up the exchange. "When you rode out with Malaina you put us all at risk. Malaina could not act as your partner. The raiders then had an advantage. She does not train with us, nor does she have the natural inclination to act as a Guard. She could not *communicate* with you, and it was mostly luck she sent a signal that the Queens and some of the Guards could hear. If you had not escaped, all of the Guards would have ridden out in search of you."

Sacra leaned forward toward Temo. "You know it is I who recognizes the Guards?" She inquired and then continued, "I see no trace of that energy in Malaina. A donkey may wish to be a rabbit, but that will not make it so. It is true anyone may learn the skills of the Guards, but being a Guardian is something to which one is born. It cannot be ignored when it is inconvenient. It is a truth which cannot be denied. You and your sister Guardians are part of a web of awareness and power. In the past, wherever women have gathered there have been Guardians. And in the future, Guards too will stand to protect and honor women. Do not devalue your heritage by allowing another with a different destiny to claim yours as their own." Hespar rose again and made her way into the Court. This time I was fairly certain the emotion which took her there was not anger.

Although showers were rare in Malia in late spring, the morning had dawned full of mist and with the smell of rain.

While the Guardians and the Queen had been speaking, portions of the sky had begun to clear. As the conversation ended, a beam of sunlight broke through a gap in the clouds. Though most of the Guardians' Court and the Palace remained shaded, a bright shaft of light suddenly hit the overhang. Tubs of water always sat on the porch ready for leatherworking. The ray of light was caught in these and bathed the three Guardians in a breathtaking, wavering reflected radiance.

The young Foundling Temo was gazing up at Petra, admiration filling her face. Next to her, Petra sat with her arm around the younger woman. Behind them Maris stood, one hand on Petra's shoulder and the other on Temo's. The three of them together reminded me of images I had seen of Maiden, Mother and Crone Goddesses, but those icons did not seem sufficient to describe them.

Temo held the same innocence and wonder as the Maiden, but on her, the effect was different. She held more resolve and vigilance than the Maiden and, although the purity was clearly the same, she carried it with a boldness of spirit the Maiden lacked.

One would never call Petra a mother figure. Even though she emanated the same quality of a woman ripe with sensuality and promise, her energy radiated a sense of purpose and a feral awareness that the Mother could never possess. Though any child, or woman for that matter, would feel safe and cherished in her arms, it would not be the comforting embrace of the Mother. She was clearly a woman in the prime of life, a loyal and yet untamed companion to the Queen.

Maris was like a Crone, and not like one at the same time. Her sage wisdom and patience had been honed through decades of service and observation. She understood her strengths and had come to terms with her weaknesses. When one asked her to share her knowledge she was immediately forthcoming, but she did not require that others adopt her methods. She had learned to communicate well while understanding the value of silence.

The sun shifted, glinted briefly off the three identical labryses around the women's necks, and then disappeared back into the clouds. Maris stepped out into the Court toward Hespar.

Petra and Temo both stood, and the moment was gone. I knew, however, this revelation would not leave me. I had glimpsed the Foundling, the Companion and the Sage, the powerful symbols of the lifecycle of the Guardians. Having been taught to honor the patterns of a woman's life, I now understood this included more possibilities than I had ever envisioned.

16

"How did Temo get away from the Sea Raiders?" Reya asked, her voice conveying bewilderment.

She and I were unpacking large baskets of clothes, linens and cosmetics which had come from the Spring Hall a short time ago. The precarious condition of the damaged sections of the Palace made the pace of moving slow. Consequently, there was plenty of time to unpack, but often no convenient place for things to go.

"It was her horse," I answered distractedly. Instead of listening to Reya, I was examining an ivory comb. Sacra had given it to me on my first day in the Summer Hall. It had beautiful, intricately carved markings along its top. After Alandra's revelation about symbols, I gazed at them wondering if they, too, had meaning. To me, this gift was a token, an acknowledgement of the change in my status to that of a Summer Queen. I was grateful the people of Malia did not consider me "The Queen" However, since my move to the Summer Hall, I felt there had been a change in my interactions with Sacra.

I thought Sacra no longer considered me a "girl child" Perhaps my intention to call my own Council and my move to the Summer Hall had coalesced to change her thinking. I had several responses to this transition. A part of me cherished Sacra's nurturance and was reluctant for that to diminish. However, I was proud to have attained a new status. I was almost certain I would not like any responsibilities which came along with this change, but I hoped the benefits would offset any difficulties.

Earlier today a diligent group of movers had carried a large chest into my rooms. They waited patiently for me to tell them where to put it, but it took me quite awhile to decide where the chest should go. I chided myself, thinking if I could not determine the location for an item of furniture, how could I possibly make choices that might affect all of Malia? Forcing myself to make a decision, I asked the movers to put the chest near the doorway to the long hall which led to my water room.

This, I now determined, would be an excellent place for my new comb, and I carried it to the chest.

"Her horse?" Reya repeated bringing me back to our conversation with both words and a slight *nudge* to assure I was listening. "What did her horse have to do with her escape?"

Putting down the comb, I leaned on the chest determined to give Reya my full attention. "Temo says her horse, Clio, will not stay tied. When the raiders took Temo, they made off with Clio, too. She did her usual trick of nibbling on her tie until she was loose. Tam and Temo have been spending hours in the paddock teaching their horses to come when they whistle. With diligence, and bribes of figs, they have taught their mares to respond to their call."

"Would not the Sea Raiders have heard her whistle?" Reya questioned as she bent nearly double to retrieve a skirt from the bottom of a basket.

"The Guards always teach their horses to come to a sound in nature. Clio is trained to respond to a kite's call. It must not have seemed out of place to the raiders. When Temo realized her horse was loose, she whistled for her, and Clio came. Once Clio got to Temo, she expected a treat and began to nuzzle Temo thinking she must have one hidden in her pocket. Whatever raiders make their ropes out of is something Clio liked. The horse nibbled enough of the rope Temo had been tied with for her to break free. Temo escaped with nothing worse than a few bruises from where Clio had eaten her bonds."

Reya shook her head and offered me the corner of a coverlet to fold. "Temo has the luck of the Mother. We are certainly blessed she was returned to us unharmed. Women stolen by Sea Raiders seldom come back. Reya's narrative was choppy, punctuated by shakes and snaps as we smoothed the cover into a tidy bundle." Before you came, Aigle, the potter, was captured. When she refused to eat or drink the raiders threw her overboard. She was lucky, a ship picked her up and brought her home.

I sucked in my breath appalled at their cruelty, but my curiosity got the better of me and I asked, "How long was she in the water?"

"Several days," Reya said almost in a whisper. Finding her voice, she continued, "Aigle has never been the same since they took her. She does not often talk about her experience but when she does, her words are filled with warning. Of course, she did not know their language, but from what she *understood* she believes they want our land. They take women because they intend to settle here, have as many children as possible and be Kings in their own right."

Suddenly, I thought I was going to be sick. Holding up my hand, I motioned for Reya to stop. The Sea Raiders wanted Malia and they wanted to breed our women like goats. This information was so foreign I was having difficulty integrating it. Did they not know a King was not simply pronounced, but chosen by the bull? How could they force a woman to bear a child she did not choose? And, most difficult of all to understand, how could they think Malia could belong to them? My mind reeled as I tried to assimilate the values of this convoluted culture.

Reya was immediately at my side. Her *support* reached me even sooner.

"I am so sorry Giada, I did not realize..." Reya mumbled, putting her arm around me.

"Do they not know the Mother? Are they not Her children?" I asked, not really expecting an answer.

"All people are Her children, but some of them act like orphans," was Reya's reply.

*****

A babble of noise and excitement drifted up to me in the Summer Hall. It was unseasonably warm, and the heat had driven me to my rooms to await the milder temperatures of evening. Although it was still too warm for comfort, the assumption something must be happening drew me from my languor. I pulled on the lightest shift I could find and opened the door to my Council Room.

One-by-one the women who would constitute my Council had moved to the Summer Hall from temporary quarters scattered throughout the Palace. Unlike the Spring Hall, in this new space their rooms were a floor below and connected to the Council Room by a long stair. This placement gave my rooms an illusion of privacy and a view in every direction. However, like in the Spring Hall, the Council Room of my quarters had become a place to congregate.

Consequently, finding Lalage, Pelagia and Damia in the adjoining room did not surprise me. Lalage was standing on tiptoe peering out one of the openings that faced the central Court. She was calling back reports on her observations to the other two women. Pelagia and Damia were attempting in their own way to deal with the heat. They had fashioned a large palm frond into a fan and were taking turns creating a breeze for each other. Damia was discussing ways they could mount the palm and pull it with a rope instead of holding it themselves. Their inventiveness made me smile, and I acknowledged to myself the good choices I had made for my Council. I was learning to rely on these women and was glad they were close at hand.

However, before I could even greet them, Tam bounded awkwardly into the room. She was a study in contradictions. She was full of exuberance, but her injured leg kept her from expressing it in her usual way. Regardless, she was almost bouncing as she announced, "A new Foundling has come." After blurting out her message she realized she had forgotten to salute. With a look of chagrin, she tapped her shoulder. She continued, barely able to contain her excitement.

"Thekia brought her from Zakros which means that Aellai must not have *known* her. She is about to be presented to the Queen to see if she will be acknowledged. They do not want to do this in an open Court and as your chamber is the largest, they have sent me to ask if they may use it."

"Of course," I replied without thinking.

"Then we will all arrive soon," Tam called over her shoulder as she skipped as quickly as her leg would allow toward the stairs.

Turning to Pelagia and Damia, I asked, "Who will come?"

Damia began ticking off people on her fingers. "Of course, all of the Guards and the Queen's women. And, there is always a

Wise One or two who feel "called" to attend an acknowledgment," she said the last part with a sigh, and I wondered if I might have an ally in my disinclination for the Wise Ones.

Hearing that Thekia was at Malia, my thoughts moved to Reya, wondering if she would be pleased to find this errand had brought Thekia here.

Lalage turned from the window and the four of us began dragging chairs and cushions from the storage alcove. Karis and Charis were the first Guardians to arrive. They tapped their shoulders and offered help. More people followed and the space filled quickly. A buzz of excitement and anticipation moved through the room. I was surprised at the level of animation among the Guards. They stood in small groups engaged in serious discussion. I could only catch snatches of their conversations.

"Thekia says she has been to the other three…" Adesha was saying to Ianthe and Ari.

"What will happen if the Queen does not acknowledge her?" Tam was asking Stava.

Before Stava could reply, Petra and Sacra entered the room and a hush fell. I felt the familiar *surge* of connection and yearning as Petra acknowledged me with a nod and a tap on her shoulder. The two women crossed the room and chose seats next to each other. I suspected their nearness was not based on their connection, but because of their relative positions on this occasion. They settled themselves without the usual banter. The others in attendance began to perch on chairs and cushions while a number of Guardians chose to lean provocatively against the wall. I felt the arresting appeal of these women wash over me. Seeing the Guards together like this still took my breath away. Being one of the last to enter, Reya spotted me from across the room and came to stand by my side.

Sacra and Petra had only been sitting for a moment when Drea and Thekia entered the room accompanied by the woman I assumed must be the Foundling. From where I stood, I could see only the three women's backs as they came into the room. Even from that position, I could tell the Foundling was not what I had anticipated. She towered over Drea and was even a bit taller than Thekia. Her shoulders were exceptionally broad and her hips narrow. However, what I would have normally found attractive on her looked awkward. Her walk was lumbering and lacked the fluidity I had come to associate with the movements of the Guards.

Most surprising of all to me was her age. I had anticipated a woman close in age to Temo or Tam. However, from what I could see, she appeared to be at least as old as I, if not a bit older. I wondered how it was possible a Guard could not have been found until she was nearly grown. The Foundling was not dressed like a Guardian. She was in clothes similar to those worn by the people in my village. They were plain and functional for the work of the fields or the sea.

The two Guards and the Foundling crossed the room and stood in front of Petra and Sacra. Thekia cleared her throat, nodded to Petra and addressed her comments to Sacra. "I bring you greeting, Sacra, from Aellai. She sends a message that this Foundling is not hers. She also wishes you to know that Alkes..." As Thekia spoke the Foundling's name, she nodded in her direction and then continued formally. "...has also been taken to Thera, Hearth Queen of Knossos and Talitha, the Hearth Queen of Phaistos, who do not recognize her as one of their Guardians. However, they do agree she is a Guard."

A murmur rose from the assembled group. I was glad Reya had come to be with me, and I leaned toward her adding my voice to the whispers.

I asked softly, "Does that mean if Sacra does not acknowledge her she will not be accepted as a Guardian?"

Reya lifted her shoulders to convey her uncertainty, but before she could respond, Sacra was on her feet walking toward the Foundling. The waiting women all seemed to collectively hold their breath as Sacra closed the distance to the tall, awkward woman. Alkes stood, her shoulders hunched, looking dully down at the floor. Sacra reached out and with great gentleness lifted the Foundling's chin. Several heartbeats passed as she stared into Alkes eyes. She moved her hand to the Foundling's shoulder saying, "She is not mine." I did not think

Alkes could have appeared more downtrodden, but with Sacra's words, her shoulders sank even more.

What before had been a mumble was now an uproar. Among the clamor I could hear someone asking, "How can that be?" Another said, "But, the other Queens said she was a Guard." Sacra only hesitated a moment before putting up her hand to quiet the group. I felt her *reach* for me before her eyes found me in the crowd. She gestured for me to join her and the Foundling. Although I knew at some point I would have Guards of my own, it had not occurred to me the time might be now. With a great deal of skepticism, I crossed the room.

I was not even half way to Sacra when Alkes' head jerked up and she abruptly turned toward me. Her eyes met mine, and a sensation like being hit by a vast ocean wave overtook me. For a moment, I reeled as the *energy* of the connection pushed me backward. There was no doubt I *knew* this woman. I thought I had *known* the Guardians of Malia, but this link was far beyond the tie I had with Sacra's Guards. In that instant, I understood Alkes was mine. But, I was also aware that I didn't like her.

Before I could formulate a response to my feelings, Alkes took two giant steps toward me and dropped to one knee. I looked at Sacra not knowing what to do.

"Is she yours?" Sacra asked. I didn't know what to say. There was no doubt this Foundling was mine, but I didn't want her. Her body seemed to be put together wrong. Each body part on its own was fine, but taken as a whole she was ungainly. I stared at Sacra with what must have been a look of incredulity. Was I supposed to acknowledge this woman who I found unpleasant?

Sacra's gaze never wavered. She simply nodded as if in response to my unspoken question and asked again, "Is she yours?"

"Umm, yes," I stammered, "I think she is mine."

Alkes raised her head, her eyes full of tears and admiration. It was clear whatever antipathy I felt for her was not reciprocated. In fact, just the opposite seemed to be true. She was enraptured.

"Oh, no," I mumbled to myself under my breath. I could not believe this was happening. I had, of course, anticipated the day I would have Guards of my own. In my dreams they would have Stava's smile, Drea's courage, and Petra's wisdom. They would be nimble, striking and courageous. Their bodies glistening as they practiced.... I realized that right here, in front of everyone, my fantasies were leaking out. I could never tell how much of my thoughts were conveyed to others, and I blushed wondering if I had been transparent.

Seeming to want a more definitive statement from me, Sacra asked again, "Is this woman your Guardian?"

"Yes," I stated simply, trying to keep hesitance out of my voice.

Sacra, with Petra close behind her, crossed to where Alkes knelt. Petra offered her hand and Alkes stood, her agility belying her earlier awkwardness. Sacra's simple words echoed those Reya had asked the Guards in my father's yard the day I was found. "Is it she?"

For a time Alkes did not answer. She still gazed at me, her eyes full of wonder. Finally, in a voice which thankfully I did not find grating, she replied, "Yes, this is _my_ Queen." All the while she continued to beam down at me from her great height.

An insistent _pulse_ from Petra drew Alkes' attention away from me. Although always regal in her bearing, Petra appeared to grow taller as she _pushed_ her energy forward. Her gaze trained intently on Alkes, she asked, "Do you wish to pledge yourself as a Guardian to Giada, the future Hearth Queen of Malia?"

"Yes," Alkes answered simply, keeping her eyes fixed attentively on Petra.

"Do you understand this is a pledge you make for a lifetime?" Petra asked.

"I will gladly pledge my life as a Guardian for Giada," Alkes spoke these words with a nod in my direction.

All right, I thought to myself, perhaps she may have some redeeming qualities.

"Then we will take your pledge and your oath now," Petra continued, asking, "Where are you from?"

"Chania," Alkes said.

"Then, Alkes of Chania, do you pledge your life to Giada, the future Hearth Queen of Malia, and commit to be her Guardian?"

Alkes looked blankly at Petra. Again, I felt my irritation with her rise to the surface. With a look of consternation, Petra deliberately nodded her head to give Alkes an indication of what the answer to her question might be.

Picking up on Petra's prompting, Alkes blurted, "Yes"

"Then repeat after me. I pledge myself to the service of Giada, the future Hearth Queen of Malia, and her Guardians." Alkes again looked uncertain. Petra moved her hand in a "come on" gesture, indicating she should say the words she had just heard.

As Alkes began her reply, Guardians from all sections of the room began to move toward Petra and Alkes. Systematically, they arranged themselves in a crescent several rows deep behind Alkes facing Petra. When Alkes stopped speaking, Petra nodded and responded. "Then Alkes of Chania we hear your pledge, and from this day forward, we will count you among the Guardians. The oath we take states our intentions. We will speak it now together." With these words, the entire group of Guardians began in unison.

"I pledge myself to the service of the Goddess and her women." As they paused waiting for Alkes to respond, I could feel the energy of the assembled Guards *surge* through the room. Again, I thought I had *known* their energy, but I had been mistaken. I had *known* the Guards in play. I had known them in action, but I had never *known* their sacredness. I was aware there was a temple space in which they congregated. A bit indelicately I had speculated on what might transpire there, but I had not anticipated the solemn power of their spirit. I listened in awe as they continued.

"I vow to keep my body sound and able, for it is my primary tool and a reflection of my sacred connection to the Goddess. I vow to hone my skills, both physical and mental, so I will be able to respond effectively when needed."

After each sentence they paused, waiting for Alkes to repeat the words they had spoken. At first, she replied tentatively, but as the recitation continued, she gained confidence. Her responses became stronger and more certain.

"I vow to act with honor and integrity, being truthful and principled so I will be considered trustworthy." The Guards continued, "I vow to be vigilant, alert for and anticipating potential sources of danger. I vow to use my intuitive skills to perceive conflict as or before it occurs."

The intensity of the call and response of their oath was almost palpable. Although I had seen these principles in action, I had not been aware there was a statement that articulated them. I stood in awe as the conduct I had seen enacted was named in their declaration.

"I vow to be ready to take action should any threats or acts of hostility be committed in my presence. I vow to be a shield from even the naive or benign when they create disturbance. I vow to be courageous, acting with a boldness of spirit. I vow to keep appropriate silences, being judicious and discreet in communicating information. I vow to act in ways which foster self-respect and dignity both for myself and others. I vow to create safe space for women to meet, honor and celebrate."

I could see the oath was having an effect on Alkes. After she repeated the first few stanzas, she raised her head. Within a few more lines her shoulders straightened. In a way, Alkes reminded me of myself. There was a part of me which always *knew* the energies of a Hearth Queen. Although, I had possessed this knowledge, it was not until arriving at Malia that I found there was a framework in which it functioned. I thought perhaps Alkes might have been in a similar position. The instinctual "born to Guardian" in her had understood what the oath described, but until hearing it, she had no firm construct within which it functioned. I sighed wishing there was an oath for Hearth Queens. If there had been, perhaps I could have carried out my duties better. Instead, I felt I had been learning them in a rather hit-or-miss manner. Even as my thoughts spun, the Guardians continued.

"I vow to respect and honor my sister Guardians. I vow to listen to the Earth, finding ways to protect Her and all her children. I understand and accept the charge to protect and safeguard women. It is my inviolate duty to guard the sacred spaces of the Goddess, her women and her Priestesses. This is my spiritual path. It is to this I am called. To these things and to Her service, do I consecrate myself."

The energy *swirled* as these statements came to an end. It reached out to *enfold* each Guardian and then the rest of us in the room. It extended farther to *surround* Malia. Beyond that the energy *pulsed* to encircle the island. It seemed to be ubiquitous as it increased, building a bridge to the mainland, the world and touching the universe. The spiraling energy connected with everything, even the part of the whole which was the room in which we stood. Having completed this circuit, the energy grounded itself, leaving a lingering spark in those present.

Alkes glowed. In fact, as I looked around, all of the Guardians appeared luminous. I wondered if this was a byproduct of their work. To me, their spiritual practice seemed tangible. It was so unlike the ethereal wanderings of the Wise Ones. In this moment, I wished I were a Guardian.

I felt Sacra's *touch* alight on me and I knew she was indicating I was supposed to do something. I stared at her blankly. "Greet her," she whispered.

Ugh, I thought to myself, but I *pulsed* toward Alkes. She turned toward me. Her energy was much more balanced. I reached out my hand and we touched for the first time. Her hand in mine felt like a dead fish. There was no doubt about it,q I found her distasteful. Despite this, I tried to formulate what I hoped would be appropriate words of welcome.

"Alkes of Chania, I accept your pledge," I said, hoping that would do. Then I quickly dropped her hand and stepped back.

Guardians took my place. Casually, two and three at a time they warmly welcomed her. They greeted her with a traditional salute, patted her on the back and made offers of friendship. I watched Alkes brighten. She looked more comfortable every moment. Gradually, the room began to clear. When only a few people were left, Alkes turned toward me expectantly. She was clearly waiting for instructions. *Toads*, I thought to myself, I had no idea what to do with her. I searched the room hoping someone would give me direction.

Sacra had paused near the stairs listening to Elayn who was telling a story. Turning toward Alkes, I offered, "There is fruit and tea on the table in the corner. Please help yourself." Appearing to take my suggestion as an order, she moved diligently toward the proffered food. I practically ran to where Elayn and Sacra stood. Elayn was finishing her story. Sacra smiled, clearly amused at the anecdote. They both turned and were about to descend the stairs.

"Wait," I called to Sacra a bit breathlessly. Still smiling, she turned in my direction. What do I do with her?" I blurted, pointing toward where Alkes stood.

"With your Guardian?" Sacra questioned. "What do you want her to do?"

"I don't know," I replied with a rising sense of panic. I envisioned Alkes standing in my Council Room day-after-day staring at me with that look of admiration and responding to my every suggestion with dog-like devotion. Or even worse, lying on a palate just outside my door, keeping watch over my comings and goings.

Sacra nodded at me and turned back to Elayn. "Elayn, would you tell Aoede I will meet her in the granary in a little while?"

"Of course," Elayn replied and then looking at me, continued sincerely. "Congratulations on finding your first Guardian. I am sure there will be many more to come." She nodded to Sacra and disappeared down the steps.

Taking my arm, Sacra asked, "May we sit on your terrace? I have always found it a pleasant place to escape the heat." With a deep sense of relief, I crossed the room with Sacra heading toward my personal chamber. As we neared Alkes, Sacra called to her.

"After you have eaten, go to the central Court. Ask anyone you see to show you the way to the Guardians' Shelter. There will be Guards there. Tell them you need clothes, and they will help you."

Alkes hastily dropped the food she was eating and immediately leaped to follow Sacra's instructions. Alkes turned toward the door repeating, "They will help you." I marveled at the ease with which Sacra directed the Foundling. I doubted I would ever learn to be as clear, casual, and kind. Together we made our way through my chamber and out onto the terrace.

Sacra was right. The breeze from the sea was cool and the islands of shade on the terrace were inviting. She walked toward a bench like she must have done a thousand times and I wondered if she missed the Summer Hall. If she did, I suspected no one would ever hear of it. Sacra had been claimed by the Crone and had accepted this change of status. She sat and patted the seat beside her. In my befuddled state, I wished I could put my head in her lap. I decided instead I would take her hand. We sat quietly together for a few moments before I began to blurt out my feelings and questions.

"Why is she so old?" I asked breaking the silence.

Sacra squeezed my hand saying, "What would have happened if she had been taken to the Queens before you were found?"

Suddenly, I realized why Alkes had not been identified before. I began softly, my words picking up speed and volume as I spoke. "If Alkes had been taken to the Queens before, none of them would have *known* her. She had to wait for me to be here to acknowledge her. I wonder if she's been waiting long?"

"I do not think she has been waiting. She probably only started to feel the call after you were presented. It took her awhile to make her way here. She has been to every Queen on the island," Sacra said smiling.

I tried to smile back, wondering if I should confess I found Alkes distasteful. Instead, I decided to pursue a more pressing question.

"Seriously," I began, "what do I do with her? I don't even know where to start. What are my responsibilities?"

"Every Queen interacts with her Guardians differently," Sacra acknowledged. "You will have to decide how you wish to work with yours. I gave this a lot of thought before I developed my own practices."

Sacra took her hand from mine and reached across to a nearby stand. She retrieved two fans, offering me one. I took it and began insistently fanning myself. Sacra's conversation became occasionally punctuated by the swish of feathers. Aellai always keeps at least one Guard within the sound of her voice. She believes part of their duty is to serve her. Personally, I do not find that useful. I prefer my Guardians to be bonded as a group rather than focused on me. Their reliance on one another is essential. When a response is required, I do not want them looking to me for direction. I want them looking toward each other."

Stating what seemed to me to be obvious, I said, "I don't have anyone else for Alkes to bond with." I was fervently hoping that did not mean she would have to bond with me.

"Would you like to consign her to Petra to be housed and trained with my Guards?" Sacra asked.

"Could I?" I replied, hearing the relief in my voice.

"It is likely," Sacra replied. "You will have to ask Petra. I cannot speak for her, but it is not uncommon to have the Guards of a future Queen fostered among those of her predecessor. However, you will need to have some type of regular contact with Alkes."

I wrinkled my nose. Sacra turned her head to the side, inviting me to speak.

"Umm," I began, "I don't think I like her."

Sacra laughed. Not a giggle, but an outright chortle. She was clearly attempting to control her response but not succeeding. "I am sorry, Giada," she said trying to stifle further laughter. "It seems ironic you find a Guardian of your own, and she is the only Guardian I have ever heard you say you do not like."

I flounced, turning away toward the sea, and did not respond.

"There is a lesson in everything," Sacra counseled. "There must be a purpose behind why she has been called to Guardian for you."

I could not fathom a reason why a Guard I did not like had been given to me. Sacra reached out and put her hand on my shoulder. "More will come, Giada," she whispered. "In time, more will come."

17

The slower pace of my orientation had now come to an end. It was not that my routine had changed. I still spent mornings with the Wise Ones, and then practiced in the Guardians' Court or visited Sacra. In addition to this, I now needed to find Petra and ask her if Alkes could be fostered among her Guards, convene my first Council, and invite Asteria to be part of it.

I decided my most pressing duty was to get Alkes placed with Sacra's Guardians. On Alke's first night, I had put her in a guest room and told her I would return the next day. I still had no idea how to direct Alkes and hoped Petra was willing to assume this responsibility. For the first time since I had been at Malia, I had a specific reason to interact with Petra. I found my reaction mixed, containing both hopes and fears. I was delighted about the prospect of having a private exchange with Petra. On the other hand, I also felt self-conscious about being alone with her. Regardless of my convoluted emotions, having a conversation with her was still my first priority.

The truth was, I didn't know where to look for her. She and I moved in very different spheres within the Palace. Since I wasn't sure where to find her, I decided to try the Guardians' Shelter first. Although I had been under the overhanging porch of the Shelter several times, I had never been inside. I found having a legitimate errand to take me there titillating. The arousing *emanations* that crept from the Shelter into my awareness were becoming woven into my fantasies. I savored my first look at the source of these alluring visions.

I selected my clothing with care. Overlooking my more comfortable attire, I chose instead something I hoped would be provocative. I piled my hair atop my head and even put on some of the eye makeup popular with many of the women of Malia. I regretted I did not have a bath like the one in the Spring Hall in which to judge my efforts. With a sigh, I gave a final pat to my hair and set off on my search for Petra.

I bounded down the stairs from my Council Room into the central Court. I knew I would still need to travel several intricate passages in order to reach the Guardians' Shelter. My journey took me down a number of long hallways and past the altar of the Sweet Girl Child. I was just moving toward its door when Asteria stepped out. I stopped just short of running into her. With exasperated acceptance and a nod to my training with the Wise Ones, I acknowledged this as an omen.

Asteria and I both began apologizing at the same time. "Oh, Young Queen, pardon me," she said. "I was not expecting..."

"Asteria, I'm sorry..." We simultaneously started giggling at our similar response. It was good to feel this easy, kindred laughter between us. I could tell, however, she was about to take up whatever errand had called her from the altar, so I quickly continued.

"Asteria, I'm wondering if you have a moment to talk?" I asked, taking advantage of the synchronicity of this meeting, but finding myself somewhat self-conscious, remembering the incident in the stairwell. Uncertainty about whether she and Karis had been aware of my presence made me uncomfortable, and I felt a blush begin to creep up my cheek.

Asteria, however, proceeded as if nothing had happened. "Perhaps we could sit in here," she said, drawing back a curtain that covered the opening to the alcove beside the altar. I nodded and entered, ducking under her upraised arm. Although I had practiced my conversation with Petra while dressing, I had not prepared to ask Asteria to be on my Council. Quickly, I tried to organize what to say while she closed the curtain and motioned me to a comfortable cushion. Asteria moved effortlessly to a nearby pillow, her ease revealing her familiarity with this space.

She looked at me intensely for a few moments and then said simply, "Yes"

My expression must have conveyed my bewilderment.

"I mean, yes, I will be on your Council," she continued clarifying her previous statement.

"But...," I began, "how did..."

"Khloe told me several of the Wise Women had reported the likelihood you would ask me to be a part of your Council. Apparently, there have been signs revealing your intention."

I liked the way she said this. It was a simple statement, not made theatrically or with feigned omnipotence like some of the other Wise Ones would have done. She was only stating a fact known to her. Although I found this particular exchange somewhat unnerving, the more I interacted with Asteria, the better I liked her. I was glad I had not rehearsed what to say. Anticipation of our conversation might have made me follow a script rather than allowing myself to respond authentically.

"Good," I replied casually. "Three days after the next new moon we will sit Council." I searched for something more to say. I wanted to establish a rapport with her. Unfortunately, all I could think of were questions about the Guards and the evening gatherings I knew she frequented.

Asteria sat patiently, her head turned slightly to the side, waiting for me to gather my thoughts. When it became clear I was struggling, she began again, "Perhaps you would like to go with me some evening to one of the young women's gatherings...?"

My eyes opened wider and I looked at her with incredulity. During my time at Malia I had become certain many of the women in the Palace could intercept the thoughts or feelings of others. I had begun an inventory of those I believed might be particularly gifted in this. Now Asteria would definitely go toward the top of that list. Attending an evening gathering was something I had wanted to do since I first knew they existed. I had woven complex scenarios of my first visit there. I saw Guards assembled around me laughing at my witty banter or being asked by any number of Guardians to dance or sing with them. With a jolt, I realized Asteria was staring at me. I was fairly certain I had just been sharing my daydreams with her. Asteria, however, looked unperturbed and was again waiting patiently for a reply.

"Yes," I stammered, "I would like that very much."

"Excellent," she responded "The gatherings happen a few days before the new and full moon and half way in between each.

We will meet tomorrow night as the new moon draws near. Would you like to go with me?"

I considered trying to give the impression my schedule was complicated, but thought better of it and simply answered, "I would like that."

"It is settled then," she said, "I will come for you tomorrow." With these words she rose, opened the curtain, and stood aside so I could pass. I smiled at her warmly, thinking I had just had a conversation with a force of nature. Her self-assurance and poise were enviable. She appeared to be no older than I, but her ability to be at ease belied her youth. I hoped one day I, too, would have her self-assurance. She smiled back at me, and I found myself wishing all of my interactions today would be as easy as this one.

Standing alone in the hall again, for a moment I felt adrift. Gradually, I re-oriented myself to what had brought me to the hallway in the first place. Petra... I was searching for Petra and had been on my way to the Guardians' Shelter. Taking a deep breath, I began again toward the Guardians' Court. The Court seemed brilliant to me after the relative darkness of the internal halls. Once my eyes became accustomed to the light, I could see the Guardians' Shelter looming enticingly across the Courtyard. I considered turning back to start again another day. But, instead, I gathered my courage, dashed through the sunlight, and through the open door of the Shelter.

There was no one there to greet me. In fact, there was no one there at all. I stood hesitantly on the threshold, not knowing what to do. Eventually, my curiosity pushed me forward. Directly in front of me were two small rooms. To both my left and right were spacious quarters where rows of beds lined the walls. I suspected one of these smaller spaces was Petra's. A glance in each of these confirmed they were unoccupied. Examining these smaller spaces occurred to me, but I wanted to see one of the larger rooms. I went into the quarters on the left.

The smell was what I noticed first, a succulently pungent blend of horse, leather and woman. I breathed it in wishing there was a way to carry it with me. I wanted to see everything in the room at once. I moved forward, running my fingers over one thing after another. Was this Ianthe's blanket? Did Drea drop an arrow here near her bed? Had Karis left a pair of her leathers on a hook on the wall? The items which cluttered this space gave off the *energy* of their owners, and I wanted to sort these out to confirm my impressions.

I was almost certain I had determined which cot was Stava's. Being in contact with an object sometimes enhanced my perception, and I decided to lie down on the bed. I put my head on the pillow and stretched out on the cot. Contemplating the roof above me, I tried to see it through the eyes of whoever rested there at night. My consciousness swirled as I sank deeper into the lingering sensations held in this place. I could *feel* impressions of pride in a job well done, concern about mastering a sword stance, and even a deep hunger for the touch of another woman. My awareness meandered among the feelings that lingered there.

After a time, I sank down into the bed. It held me as though it were a cocoon from which I could emerge as an entirely new being. I breathed in the essence of Guardian. Each time I thought I had captured the spirit of what it was to be a Guard, a new layer of understanding revealed itself to me. Lying in this space, I could grasp a hint of their perception.

Through an open window I could see an ordinary tree. At first, I saw it as I always did, but as I gazed at it, my awareness shifted. It was no longer simply a tree. It was instead, a collection of leaves. When lifted by a slight breeze, they moved in synchronicity. However, each leaf had a character of its own and maintained individuality. If I directed my awareness to a leaf near the top of the tree, I could connect with it and observe my surroundings through its consciousness. From the perception of the leaf, I could see far out into the sea and land which surrounded Malia. When I had just begun to take in this phenomenon, the leaves shifted back into being one tree. Did Guardians inherently have the ability to perceive things in more than one way, or was it something they learned? I was awestruck by this insight and remained in this space for quite some time shifting between these two ways of seeing.

It was their laughter I heard first. Jumping up, I brushed off my skirt attempting to appear casual. I tried to find a neutral expression which would not convey my covert explorations, when a group of Guards burst into the room. At first, they did not notice I was standing at the far end of their quarters, but within a heartbeat they became aware of me. Their reactions were mixed. I could *sense* one was in readiness to secure the space, several *reached out* to find who I was with a force which pushed hard against me, and yet another formed the beginning of an alert to other Guards. These reactions faded into echoes as each of them realized it was me who stood in their Shelter.

"Young Queen," Adesha said self-consciously, taking her hand off the hilt of her sword. "It is a surprise for us to find you here." As she spoke she looked around, acknowledging the rest of the small group. All nodded in awkward agreement.

Ianthe seemed to be the first to fully recover, and with her usual courtesy asked, "May we help you?"

"Petra," I stammered, my head still swimming with the intensity of my recently altered perception, "I'm looking for Petra."

"She is helping the bull dancers prepare for the summer celebration," Ianthe replied, "May I take you to her?" Her words carried a *pulse* of reassurance.

"Yes, I would appreciate that," I answered attempting to *shield* my discomfort.

I did not know if I had breached any conventions by simply wandering about in their Shelter, and I was embarrassed to have been caught. Even more disquieting was the realization that, in order to leave this space, I would have to pass through a double line of Guardians. Ianthe stood at the far end of the group. Adesha and Charis stood in front of a section of cots on the left, while Karis and Nike stood similarly aligned on the right. The space between the two sets of Guardians was quite small, and yet no one moved. One by one, as clarity about my situation became obvious, grins appeared on the Guards' faces. My emotions vacillated between intimidation and arousal. I stood unmoving until Adesha, with a courtly motion of her hand and a nod of her head, indicated they were waiting for me to pass.

With extreme bravado, I began moving forward. The two rows of Guards sprung to attention, their hands at their sides, their chests extended even further than they had a moment before. "Sweet Mother," I muttered, sucking in my breath and trying to make myself as small as possible. Having started toward them, I could not make myself stop.

With all the daring I could muster, I walked toward the first set of Guardians. As I advanced, they drew back enough to let me pass without touching. I came within a finger's breadth of the women on each side of me. Trying desperately not to make contact with either of them, I inched my way sideways between Adesha and Karis. My entire being tingled, and I could *feel* their energy reach out to me. Their bodies, however, remained at attention as I squeezed past. In their *touch,* I sensed that, if they perceived any real sign of discomfort, they would have moved quickly to let me by. I was exasperated to be so transparent, and knew they were aware that a part of me was exhilarated by their tantalizing closeness.

Heat rose within me. I knew my face was on fire, as were several other parts of my anatomy. Charis and Nike did not have quite as much self-confidence as Adesha and Karis, and I was grateful their *energy* was not as intense. With regret and relief, I made my way past them to stand in front of Ianthe. She reached out her hand as if nothing unusual had just happened. She could not, however, disguise the laughter in her eyes.

"Young Queen," Ianthe said smiling, "if you are through dallying, I will take you to Petra."

I found I could not speak and simply took her proffered hand. Walking with Ianthe into the Court, I realized my first visit to the Guardians' Shelter had not been a disappointment. It had been, in fact, every bit as exciting as I had anticipated.

*****

Petra was standing atop a pile of stones in the center of a circular enclosure. I watched her turn first one direction and then another as she followed the movements of a large bull and shouted instructions to nearby women. Ianthe had brought me

227

to an area a short distance outside the southern entrance to the Palace. While we were walking, she explained that this was where bull dancers practiced.

"Why is Petra here?" I asked trying to connect Petra's role as Peer of the Guard with the bull dancers.

"She was one of Malia's finest dancers before she accepted her position as Peer of the Guard." Ianthe replied, seeming to imply I should have known this.

My impression of Petra shifted. "Do you mean she chose to give up bull dancing in order to be Peer of the Guard?"

"No," Ianthe answered, "not in order to *be* Peer of the Guard, but because she *was* Peer of the Guard. She could have continued if she had chosen, but most Peers find their duties encompassing. They try to eliminate distractions. To train for the dance, one must practice every day and risk being hurt. Petra loved the dance, but she loves the Guard more"

"How did Petra become Peer of the Guard?" I asked, trying to fathom what would make her give up something she loved.

Ianthe gave me one of those looks I had become familiar with in my time at Malia. I could tell she was taken aback by my lack of knowledge of the basic organization of the Palace.

Still looking incredulous Ianthe replied, "We chose her. The Guardians chose her." My look conveyed my bewilderment so she continued. "When a Queen moves to the Winter Hall, her Guards may choose to retire or recommit to the new Hearth Queen. Often a Peer who has served with an Elder Queen will relinquish her position when that Queen cedes her responsibilities. When Adonia, who was Queen before Sacra, moved to the Winter Hall, the Guard who had stood as Peer with her gave up her post. The Guardians chose Petra to replace her."

"How is the Peer of the Guard chosen?" I asked, curious about the internal workings of the Guards.

"When a Peer of the Guard decides to relinquish her position she announces it to the Guardians." Ianthe explained. "Once she has made her declaration, the Guards are charged with determining who we believe will serve best as Peer. A few days before the old Peer of the Guard is slated to leave, we gather. We sit in silence until we feel called to rise and stand behind the woman we think will serve best as Peer of the Guard."

"How long does a decision take?" I asked visualizing a process which might require days.

"It varies," Ianthe answered. "When Petra was chosen the decision was made quickly"

"What happens if there is no agreement?" I inquired.

Ianthe gazed upward as if remembering, "We all sit and look to ourselves to see who we believe will serve best as Peer. When Petra was chosen, a handful of women went to stand with Maris. Because we were not in agreement, we returned to our seats. We had not been sitting long when Maris rose and took up a position behind Petra. The women who had originally stood with Maris, one-by-one joined her, until in the end, we all stood with Petra. We stand behind her still."

Ianthe and I had shared all this while watching the bull dancers performing their daring acrobatics. There were varying degrees of skill among those who practiced, while some Guards seemed to simply be spotters. Across the ring, I could make out Nyssa as she sprang forward to grab the horns of an enormous bull and hurl herself onto its back. My stomach lurched, as she briefly floated in the air. Once on the bull, she did not vault off, but stood atop the animal as it moved around the enclosure. I did not realize I was holding my breath until she jumped off and bounded over to greet me.

"Young Queen," she panted wiping her forehead. "How delightful you have come to see us practice."

I did not have the heart to tell her that had not been my intention. But, with unfeigned sincerity, I was able to answer, "You are amazing, Nyssa. I saw the bull dances many times at Phaistos, the Palace near where I grew up, but I never knew any of the dancers. Watching someone you know perform is inspiring."

Ianthe nodded politely to Nyssa and moved away from our conversation toward Petra.

"It is only a few weeks to the summer festival and all of us who are dancing must be ready," Nyssa informed me. "We practice every spare moment."

I tried to focus on Nyssa as she was talking, but my attention strayed to Ianthe as she approached Petra and motioned toward where I stood. Petra nodded, gave a final comment to the young girl practicing, and walked toward me.

I could feel Petra's eyes on me. In some corner of my mind, I was aware Nyssa was still talking. However, her words were only a droning sound as Petra and Ianthe drew near. The two Guards paused politely and waited until Nyssa stopped speaking. I could see her staring expectantly at me, waiting for a response.

Toads, I thought to myself, wishing I had been listening. It seemed I would have to answer her in front of Petra and Ianthe when I had no idea what she had been saying. The Guardians now also looked at me in anticipation.

I scanned my possible responses and finally decided on what I hoped would be an acceptable reply. "I will truly look forward to seeing your dance on Solstice." Apparently, this was not too much of a *non sequitur* because Nyssa smiled and began kicking the dirt under her feet.

Petra leaped in. Tapping her shoulder, she said warmly, "Young Queen, I understand you are looking for me."

This was not at all what I had envisioned for my meeting with Petra. I had pictured us alone in some cool shaded place, with Petra's intense blue eyes focusing on me with understanding and appreciation. Instead, I was standing in the sun, dusty and hot from my walk to the bullring with Ianthe and Nyssa watching.

For a short time I faltered, but my need to divest myself of Alkes overrode my disappointment. Summoning my courage, I began, "Petra, Sacra advised me a Guardian of a Young Queen may be fostered among the Guards of an Elder Queen. If you agree, I would like to place Alkes in your care." Petra nodded. I hoped she would pick up the conversation, but she simply waited.

Glancing self-consciously at Ianthe and Nyssa, I forced myself to continue. "Would you be willing to have Alkes placed among your Guardians?"

"Yes, Young Queen," Petra said with sincerity. "It would be a privilege to train your first Guardian." As she said this, she reached across and took my hand with both of hers. The world around me began to spin. I looked into her eyes and for a moment, everything else faded into the background. There was only the two of us standing together in the warm sun with the smell of spring on the air. Then one of the bull dancers yelled. Petra's attention quickly shifted from me to the enclosure. She dropped my hand, turned and began walking toward the dancers calling instructions and encouragement as she went. Nyssa followed her at a trot, and even Ianthe was drawn toward the excitement.

It was over. I found myself standing alone. My anticipation of my first conversation with Petra had been unfounded. Although her brief touch was enough to leave my heart racing, I had not found the experience particularly satisfying. As I began to trudge back toward the Palace, an echo of my exchange with Ianthe came back to me. "When a Queen moves to the Winter Hall, her Guards may choose to retire or recommit to the new Hearth Queen." Someday, Sacra would move to the Winter Hall. When she did, I wondered how many of her Guards would choose to become mine. Sacra had said one day I would have Guards of my own, but it had not occurred to me that in the future her Guardians might be mine. I harbored a secret desire that Petra would be among them.

*****

Although the night outside was dark as the new moon approached, the room into which Asteria led me was ablaze with light and full of laughter. She had come early to my rooms to help me pick clothes and arrange the long tendrils of hair which now flowed down my back. I was both excited and nervous about being part of the young women's gathering for the first time. When I finished dressing, Asteria took my hand. We walked together through the twisting passages of the Palace until we reached the room where the women congregated.

She paused at the entrance and looked at me. "Are you ready?" she asked.

"I'm not sure," I answered. "But, I think we'd better go in anyway." Asteria smiled, and together we stepped forward into the brilliant room. There was a momentary lull of conversation and activity as we entered. I wondered if this happened every time Asteria arrived, or if it was solely my presence which caught everyone's attention. I did not have to speculate long. In the space of a breath, the room sprung to life again.

My gaze wandered, taking in the scene. The erstwhile dining hall made a fine location for this gathering. The room was large. In the center, tables and the necessities of a dining area remained. Like many of the spaces at Malia, the left side of the room was open to the central Court. Pillars along that section of the hall created alcoves where women congregated in small groups. Many clustered around several boards where small stones were being repeatedly moved from one indentation in the board to another. The moves were accompanied with much commentary from onlookers. To the right of the door was a table loaded with food and drink. At the far end of the room, musicians were getting out their instruments.

A mixture of women from the Palace were present. Artisans and Wise Ones mingled. Growers came together with cooks, sharing information about crops and provisions. Several of the women I had seen practicing for the bull dancing socialized conspiratorially at one of the tables and, of course, there were Guards everywhere. An *awareness* of their nearness murmured in my consciousness. I found their accessibility in this setting both intimidating and stimulating.

I knew better than to walk toward the games. These diversions required knowledge of strategies I had yet to master. Food, however, was something I understood. I nodded to Asteria in the direction of the refreshments. She smiled in acknowledgment and still, hand-in-hand, we crossed the room toward the tables filled with refreshments.

Unlike many of my previous encounters at Malia, this time my fantasies began to match my experience. Guards soon surrounded Asteria and me. Drea was first to stride confidently across the room to welcome us. Adesha and Karis quickly followed her. They, in turn, expressed their pleasure at seeing the two of us. Tam, her limp now barely noticeable, left one of the game boards and crossed the room also. Asteria wasted no time in beginning to flirt with all of them in succession. Karis stepped forward into the circle of Guards, shook her head smiling, and led Asteria away in the direction of the music which had begun from the back of the room.

My visions and reality now diverged. The witty banter I had imagined escaped me. I stood staring at the remaining Guardians, searching desperately for something to say. My thoughts ranged among multiple topics, trying to find a subject I hoped would be interesting. The silence was becoming awkward when Temo saved me. She joined us, courteously holding out two drinks and offering me my choice of watered wine or mint tea. Already somewhat at a loss, and fearing wine would only make it worse, I chose the tea.

It seemed Drea could not stand silence long, and soon she began to expound on a sling technique she had taught Tam and how Tam had excelled under her tutelage. Adesha sighed, rolled her eyes, and punched Drea lightly on the shoulder. With mock annoyance she said. "Drea," and shifted her eyes toward me. It was clear she was indicating to Drea that talking about training was not a topic for this time and place.

"Urr, of course," Drea answered and began again, choosing a more inclusive topic by commenting on what an exceptionally warm day it was for the season. Talk then moved along easily. Although I found I was not the clever conversationalist I had hoped to be, occasionally I joined in the exchange. Engrossed in the dialogue, I did not see Stava until she stood beside me. She waited politely for a lull in the conversation before turning to me with a smile.

"I wonder if you might like to dance?" she asked.

The truth was I very much wanted to dance with her, but I was uncertain what dancing entailed in this environment. I remembered what Dariah had said after "The Telling" about how choosing a partner signified more than the simple desire to dance. Although, truthfully, I did not mind making a statement

233

by dancing with Stava, I thought, observation might be the better part of wisdom at this time.

I reached out my hand to her and replied, hoping my voice conveyed my interest. "I am afraid I am unfamiliar with the dances. Would you be willing to escort me to the floor and watch with me?"

She took my hand and graciously answered, "I would delightedly escort you anywhere, Young Queen." Pleasant tingles ran up my arm from her touch, and I could feel an easy *connection* spring up between us.

The musicians had moved to a central position and dancers were snaking hand-in-hand around them. Stava and I stood to one side and watched. After a time she leaned toward me and said quietly, "Actually, Young Queen, it is really quite simple. May I show you?"

If, at that moment, Stava had said it was quite simple to fly, I'm fairly certain I would have agreed to try. I looked up at her and smiled in agreement. Instead of taking my hand like the others who were dancing, her strong arm reached around my waist. She pulled me snugly next to her hip so that we both faced the other dancers.

She began to explain, "This dance has six steps," slowly, she walked through the pattern, waiting each time until I replicated the movement. Gradually, we began moving more quickly until eventually we were following the cadence of the music. After we had done this successfully several times, Stava slipped her hand from around my waist, took my hand, and moved us into the line of dancers.

It was exhilarating. Although this dance was slow, its rhythmic pulse was enticing. I lost myself in the ambient *hum* of pleasure from the Guards, my own connectedness to them and the music. Stava and I drifted together for several more dances until she led me away from the floor.

"Young Queen," she said, without the vaguest indication of breathlessness, "I am afraid I must leave you now. It is my night to keep watch." She bent to brush my cheek with her lips. "I suspect I will not be cold because my memory of this evening will warm me." With these words she tapped her shoulder and was gone. I suddenly found myself breathless, and it was not the dancing which was to blame.

In a haze of pleasant feeling, I wandered back toward Asteria. I wondered if Karis, too, was on evening watch as she was no longer at Asteria's side.

Asteria smiled at my approach and quipped, "You seem to be floating."

"It's true," I confided. "Stava is so enticing. I wish I were free to do more than just dance with her."

"What?" Asteria questioned with a look of confusion. "Have you made a pledge to someone else?"

I laughed thinking how unlikely that situation was. "No," I responded, quelling my laughter. "The Queen has advised me it is unwise to get involved with any of the Guards."

Asteria looked at me in astonishment. "That is ridiculous," she answered. "Both you and the Guards are at liberty to be involved with anyone you choose. No one at Malia may enjoin you from any liaison."

"But, the Queen..." I began.

Asteria put up her hand to stop me. "All of us here at Malia are free to make our own choices. Any opinion the Queen gives you should be considered advisory."

I was about to ask Asteria for more clarity when Karis reappeared. Karis grinned at me, but held out her hand for Asteria. Asteria shrugged in my direction, took Karis's hand, and together they skipped toward the music. This dance was totally different. The dancers were still in a line, but they raced and jumped through a complex series of movements. I decided to learn this intricate dance so I could surprise Stava at the next gathering. As the line of dancers twisted around the hall, I leaned against a pillar counting their steps and mentally rehearsing the complicated pattern.

Fauntee came from out of nowhere. With one quick movement she turned me away from the dance. Sliding me back into the darkness of one of the alcoves, she pushed me against the column. Her actions startled me, and I was temporarily frozen. At first, she did not say anything, but moved her head down my bare shoulder taking in a long breath. It took me a moment to realize she was inhaling my scent. I found this disturbing.

She lifted her head and met my eyes. There was a wildness in them I had never seen before. With a guttural sound that seemed to emanate from somewhere outside her, she whispered, "Tell me you are mine."

I stuttered, feeling more uncomfortable every moment. " I, umm... I don't...," I began.

Suddenly, Karis and Asteria were there. Karis calmly placed a hand on the other Guard's shoulder. Asteria pulled me away from the pillar.

"It is time to go," Asteria said, leveling her gaze at Fauntee, her voice cold.

Fauntee glared back at her and shook Karis' hand from her shoulder. Without a word or a backward glance, she stalked off into the central Court.

Still holding my hand, Asteria said, "Perhaps we should actually go. May Karis and I walk you to your rooms?" Even though her words were calm, I could *feel* the underlying concern they carried.

Although the experience with Fauntee had been brief, I had found it unnerving. The whole incident confused me, and I more than welcomed Asteria and Karis' companionship. Asteria never let go of my hand while Karis took up a position on my other side. Together, the three of us began walking back toward my chamber. My mind whirled as I tried to understand Fauntee's words and actions. Honestly, I was attracted to her, but in a visceral way which defied explanation or common sense. The more I interacted with her, the more confused and wary I became.

Without prompting, Karis began to speak, "Fauntee is damaged. When she was young, Sea Raiders overwhelmed her entire village. Her people were traders and the raiders followed one of their boats to the village seeking treasure. Fauntee heard them coming and hid, but she saw. Guards found her sitting alone among the dead repeating, 'I hide,' over and over."

"The Guards took her into their shelter and, in time, Sacra knew her to be her Guardian. She is a fierce fighter who appears self-assured, but under that, one wonders if she is still the Guardian child who did not defend her parents or home."

I shook my head, trying to force the vivid images that this story evoked from my consciousness. I could *feel* Asteria reach for me with support. Karis reassuringly put her arm around my shoulder, and the pictures abated. Sensing I had regained my composure, Karis continued.

"Fauntee seeks to have mastery over herself and her environment. Whenever she finds either to be out of her control, she moves toward whatever she believes will restore her security. You, Young Queen, will at some time have responsibility for the entire Palace. It does not surprise me that Fauntee finds this irresistible."

I took several deep breaths trying to forestall tears. Up to this moment, I thought all Guardians to be above reproach. Certainly, I was aware some of them had flaws. Drea was full of self-importance. Tam was unconscionably flirtatious. I even believed Thekia should have stood up to Aellai, but primarily, I had considered their imperfections to be minor. Confronted with the blatant fallacy of my beliefs, I now needed to reconsider my assumptions. It appeared there were some Guards who might not have my best interests at heart at all times.

Asteria, Karis and I had walked to my rooms while we talked. With kind words and promises to meet again soon, the two of them left me at the steps which led to my chamber. Their comfort and reassurance followed me as I ascended. I could not say if I was despondent for Fauntee or for myself. I only knew I was glad for the consolation of my bed and the oblivion of sleep.

*****

For the first time, the outer chamber of my rooms was filled with my Council. I felt a sense of wonder and anticipation as I observed these thirteen women. Several sat perched on pillows and chairs among the bright decorations of the room, chattering in eager expectation. Alandra was showing Iva a new seal she had made. I suspected Lalage had recently attended a birth because she reclined, eyes closed, on a nearby cushion.

Calida, Kyma, and Damia paused in their conversation and looked up as Reya and I came in. The rest watched Nyssa as she animatedly demonstrated acrobatics in the far corner of the room.

As we entered, Reya called to the women with Nyssa, and they quickly scampered toward the rest of the group. There were rustlings as everyone became comfortable, but eventually all eyes turned toward me. Reya and I had prepared for this moment, and I was ready with words of welcome.

Taking a deep breath, and summoning what I hoped would be appropriate *energy* to carry my speech, I began, *"Sisters, we are called here today by the moon who waxes into her third day. On this day, the women of Malia sit Council. This Council comes together today for the first time. It is our intention to meet like this countless times in the future. It is my honor to confirm that each of you has consented to be a part of this Council."*

There was a brief silence as the women in the room surveyed each other. Gradually, murmurs progressed into accolades as members of the newly formed Council began acknowledging and congratulating each other. But, within moments, the celebration faded and the women fell silent, looking attentively in my direction. With Reya's assistance, I had practiced for this moment. I had even employed some of my time in darkness to work on the skill which was my responsibility in convening this Council. I *opened* myself and began to *connect* with the women in the room.

Finding Reya in this way was simple. We had practiced this together as the new moon approached, and I *reached out* to her with confidence. Previously, if anyone had told me the next woman I would establish a connection with would be a Wise One, I would have scoffed. However, my recent interaction and emerging friendship with Asteria made her easy to *find* and *touch*.

I was surprised when these two women became a channel for the rest of the Council. It was through Asteria that I established a *link* with Alandra, Calida, Damia, and Kyma. Reya brought with her Elayn, Iva, Lalage, Pelagia, Lista and Myrina.

Even in the intensity of this moment, I wondered how Reya and Asteria had the ability to establish *connections* with so many of the women of the Council. I was filled with gratitude and wonder at their skill. The only woman remaining was Nyssa. It was easy to *draw* her exuberant sweetness into the circle. My *bond* with the Council was now complete and the group was *connected*.

At first, I found this disorienting. In the past, I had tried to restrict taking those around me into my consciousness. Now, my natural inclination to *pull* others' awareness toward me became a tool for joining my Council. I wondered if many women shared this ability, or if this was a skill unique to a Hearth Queen. Although I had practiced the words with Reya, it was almost instinctual that the strangely familiar words I had heard in Sacra's "Call to Council" sprung obediently to my lips.

"*I call you to Council. I call the women who have sat Council before us to be with us and lend us their discernment. I call the Great Mother, the Sweet Girl Child, and the Ancient One to lend us their wisdom as we listen to each other and work for the good of Malia. I am Giada, and I call you to Council.*"

I looked to my left at Lista. Through her eyes I could see a reflection of the other women of the Council and also a group of olive trees which occupied her thoughts. Without prompting she began, "*I am Lista and I answer the Call to Council.*"

As I had looked to Lista, she in turn shifted to her left toward Elayn, who took up the invocation. "*I am Elayn and I answer the Call to Council.*" As each woman named herself into the circle, the *energy* of the Council built until it seemed to have a vitality of its own. I had stepped into a place where I *knew* each of the women in the Circle and had muted, but tangible access to their thoughts and concerns.

After all of the women had spoken, there was a brief silence. Seeming almost regretful, Alandra cleared her throat and began to speak. "It is common custom for the women of a Queen's Council to hold similar seals. If this Council wishes to observe this custom, I would be honored to create a seal for us."

No one spoke immediately, but several women nodded in agreement. I was aware that, for some of this Council, possessing a seal seemed a much more definitive statement than the act of sitting together in this space. I surprised myself when my wish to extend acceptance and reassurance to these women transformed itself in to a *pulse* that reverberated gently throughout the room. Several sets of eyes turned briefly toward me before a lively conversation about the design of a seal began.

I watched with admiration and awe the first action of my Council. Although I maintained the *link* that facilitated communication among these women, there was no need for me to participate actively. This allowed me to study faces with heightened perspective. Calida was animatedly reporting on the history of previous seals of different Queens' Councils. Although appearing attentive, I perceived Kyma was clearly bored and did not give a fig what the seal looked like. Damia was engaged in the discussion, but only from the perspective of creating an account of this Council's first meeting. My knowledge of the underlying motivations of the women in the Circle occupied me as I became accustomed to my new awareness.

Without warning, I felt the room shift. At first, I thought it was one of the small shakes that often occurred on the island. I gripped the sides of my chair and started to rise, knowing even a minor movement often signaled the beginning of a larger event. With even a tiny shift, we had all been trained to move to open ground. I looked to the other women expecting to see them preparing to leave.

No one moved. They continued their discussion as if nothing had happened. I stared at Pelagia who was speaking. As I did, her image faded into a misty version of her actual appearance. I could see the cushion on which she sat through the haze she had become. Startled, I looked at Kyma who sat next to her. Kyma seemed perfectly normal. One-by-one I scrutinized the women. Among them, only Asteria, Kyma, Iva and Nyssa were not swathed in mist. I turned to Reya to ask if this was a common experience in Council and found she too wore the same indistinct exterior. I was shocked into silence.

Reya stared at me in concern. I dropped my head into my hands and rubbed my eyes wondering if perhaps I had eaten purple rye. When I looked up again, everyone had returned to normal. The discussion continued with friendly suggestions and ideas. Only Reya seemed aware of my distress.

Eventually the Council members' conversation slowed. Reya had advised me what to do when this happened. "In your head, sing one verse of a song you know well. If no one is speaking by the time you finish, the Council may be closed."

The fully embodied Reya put her hand on my arm, and I felt a *surge* of power and strength flow through me. She also *pulsed* toward me the words for ending the Council. I found I was reluctant to scan the room, fearing the same disconcerting images would occur again. Ultimately, I took a deep breath, picked the perkiest song I could think of to use as my guide, and glanced at the women. They were all solid, pleased with the outcome of their discussion and ready to move forward.

The song in my head ended without further comment from anyone. I summoned a much more confident voice than I felt and asked, *"Are we at an end?"* The women nodded and a few affirmed vocally that they considered the Council to be over. With Reya's *support* still surrounding me, I said the final words of my first Council.

"For Malia, I thank you. May the Ancestors, the Mother, the Sweet Girl Child and the Old One hear our words and assist us in weaving a future for Malia that brings peace and prosperity. Our Council is at an end."

I sensed the energy shift. When Sacra's Council had drawn to a close, I had felt a similar change. Like before, I was aware of a hollow sensation which replaced the power the Council had produced. At the time, I had wondered how Sacra felt at the end of her Council. I still did not have an answer to that question, but personally, I was exhausted.

18

The morning of the summer celebration dawned with the scent of the sea carried on the breeze. Nyssa had been right. The time until this celebration had indeed been short. There was the usual bustle that preceded a festival at Malia. The air also carried a constant *hum* from the men's quarters. This seemed unusual. Generally, I was only aware of muted *contact* from that part of the Palace. Perhaps the upcoming dance of the King created a palpable energy of anticipation.

Reya had explained that I was to join the Queen on the dais in the central Court to watch the dance. I had become aware there were occasions at which the Queen's presence was required and, by extension, mine also. These events were a combination of festival, spiritual observance, and affairs-of-state. The ceremonial dress of a Hearth Queen signaled the importance of the occasion. I rummaged among my chests and found the magical gown Sacra had given me. Carrying it with me, I moved toward the commotion I heard next door.

The sounds from my outer chamber indicated my rooms were in chaos. When I opened the door of my personal space, I found women dashing about in cheerful preparation. I watched quietly for a moment. I had come to love these women and this place. My doubts about my abilities to function successfully as Hearth Queen were gradually abating as my responsibilities became clear. I was still uncertain how useful the skills of a Wise One were, and I rankled at the continued demand that I spend a significant part of every day attempting to develop them. Setting that one component aside, I acknowledged my first Council had been a success, and I was pleased with the women who comprised it. I was progressing steadily with my training among the Guards. My expertise with my stick and bow had advanced until I was fairly certain I would be introduced to an additional practice soon.

I had explored Malia and learned from the Healers and Midwives. The grain storage and kitchen spaces were familiar to me from the earlier investigation of the purple rye. Through my service on the water circle I learned about the water systems of the Palace. The Wise Ones had taught me to read and make the marks which conveyed meaning. I had grown to know the Guards, the enigmatic women who had drawn me to Malia in the first place. Sacra had infused me with information at a pace which occasionally overwhelmed and amazed me. This all led me to feel pleasure and gratitude at the now-familiar scene.

It looked as though many of the women present were attempting to support Nyssa who showed no signs of needing assistance. I believed their ministrations were actually aimed at assuaging their own concerns about her role in the upcoming bull dance, rather than truly assisting her with preparations. A general murmur of excitement moved through the room, and the questions which circled among the women all seemed to have a similar theme. "Will the bull dance with the women?" "Will a new King be chosen?" "Will the old King remain?"

There even seemed to be friendly rivalry as women discussed their favorite competitors and guessed at possible outcomes. I was surprised many of them knew so much about the intrigues of the men's quarters. Nyssa stood in the midst of the turmoil, apparently unaffected. She *radiated* an aura of poise and confidence. Unlike the complex costume of a Hearth Queen, her clothing consisted of only two very simple, but beautiful, garments. She wore an unadorned golden halter made to support her small breasts and a short kilt of the same material. The women of my rooms fussed about her, braiding her hair and offering amulets prepared to insure her safety. She accepted these with grace, tucking them into her clothing with nods of appreciation. As I entered the room, she met my eyes. It was clear she hoped my appearance would create a diversion.

Indeed it did. Seeing me emerge with my ceremonial dress over my arm almost everyone's attention turned from Nyssa to me and they immediately began assisting me to prepare for the celebration. I had become used to, and even began to enjoy, the nurturance of these women. They flitted about finding pins for my hair, makeup and even under-things appropriate for my ritual attire. In a short time, I was transformed into the image of a future Queen of Malia.

I had not anticipated the arrival of the Guards, but suddenly, seemingly from out of nowhere, Adesha, Tam and Charis emerged. My consciousness shifted with their appearance. I had forgotten this would happen when I donned the Hearth Queen's gown. Everything in the room began to glow subtly and I was now aware of things which had previously been obscured.

Because I was looking directly at the Guards, as this happened the first thing I *sensed* was Tam's satisfaction. As I observed her with my heightened senses, I was aware this was the first official function at which she had a role. She accompanied Adesha and Charis to learn the responsibilities of a ceremonial Guardian. Her pride and honor at being chosen for this position were obvious.

I looked away from the Guards and in my altered vision the women in the room swirled. They became more than themselves and more themselves at the same time. They were each distinct individuals, but they were also a myriad of other women who had moved within this same room attending to the needs of a Dancer and a Queen.

Even the room itself pulsed and changed. Frescos appeared and vanished just as quickly. Walls became visible and then melted away into other forms. Just as my head was starting to spin from the constant transformations, Adesha stepped purposefully into my line of vision. As she did, my perception cleared. I was familiar with this feeling, it was the same as Stava's intervention on my imprudent journey through the central Court. In a heartbeat, I could feel Charis *connect* with Adesha encapsulating the random observations generated by the Hearth Queen's magic and giving them focus. A little belatedly, but strong and solid, Tam *energetically* took up her place beside them.

"Young Queen," Adesha said holding my gaze with determination, "we come to escort you to the celebration." I sensed that this encounter also had happened repeatedly over the cycles. A cadre of Guards had come, like this, for their Queen, their *energy* sparking the final phase of her transformation. I held out my hand to Adesha. As my fingers moved, I was aware of the misty presence of other Queens who had performed this act before. Countless Queens took the hand of innumerable Guardians and they walked together toward the summer dances.

*****

The central Court was filled with people and activity, even more crowded than it had been for the spring celebration. Bull dancing marked an important occasion. This day could see the influence of a King coming to an end or continuing. People were pushed back to the edges of the walls by a large circular enclosure that had been erected in the center of the Courtyard. For a moment the assembled throng seemed overwhelming, but even as I made this observation I *felt* Adesha, Charis and Tam energetically surge forward to meet the demands of this new setting.

In the enclosure Nyssa, along with several other women, confronted a majestic bull that took my breath away. Even with the focused support of attentive Guardians, I was awed. The animal stood well above my head. Its matching crescent horns extended even farther, making it seem colossal. The creature was entirely black, its sleek coat glistening in the morning sun. The women in the enclosure with it, however, appeared unaffected. They moved with and around the bull with self-assurance and skill. They gently interacted with the animal with clear admiration, but no apparent sense of distress.

Nyssa and the other women took their time. They seemed unconcerned that a crowd watched them, their entire focus on the bull. The animal was uneasy in these surroundings. He snorted and scuffed the ground in agitation. The women still appeared unaffected. They moved together cautiously toward the huge animal, making crooning sounds and comforting gestures. As she walked to stand in front of the bull, I recognized Eleni, the waterwright who had helped move my things to the Summer Hall. She stroked the bull's black head and whispered to him. The bull eventually settled into a placid state. Eleni seemed to have woven a magic which quieted the bull. Finally, the massive creature stood steadily in place. Within a heartbeat,

245

two of the women on the ground tossed the youngest among them on to the bull's back, and the dance began. I was so concerned for the dancers that I wanted to look away, but the scene was compelling.

The first dancer barely touched the animal. Her two hands landed briefly on his back before she vaulted onto the dirt on the other side. Almost before she hit the ground, another took her place. The second woman lingered longer atop the bull, leaning on her hands. Her body rocked from side-to-side before she flung one leg over the animal's back. Suddenly she was in motion, spinning atop her perch. One leg and then another flew repeatedly to either side of the bull before she too dropped to the Court's floor. Several women followed her and each successive dancer made moves that were more complicated. As the last bull dancer dove off the animal's back, she flipped in the air before landing solidly on the ground.

Before I could catch my breath, Eleni turned her back on the bull and knelt. She cupped her open hands, and Nyssa bounded toward her. Eleni rose, flinging Nyssa into the air and tossing the dancer onto the bull. Suddenly, Nyssa was aloft. She soared through the air, grabbing the bull's horns. These she used for a series of complicated movements turning and spinning between the pointed tips. Finally, she landed on the bull's back and, standing steadily, flung her arms into the air. With only a moment's pause, she leaped forward, her hands landing briefly on the animal's back. Then she jumped to the ground with a high, twisting flip. Her sense of triumph and pride *came to me* strongly, even through the assembled crowd. The scene before me was so much like my vision of this event, it brought a surprisingly certain sense of confidence in my ability to *know* the future.

Eleni walked from in front of the bull toward the dais. She paused on her way to touch Nyssa on the shoulder and nod, acknowledging her success. Eleni bounced up the steps and stood before those of us assembled on the platform. She approached the King, to whom she simply nodded. Thus confirming the bull had been approved for the dance of the King's.

The atmosphere suddenly changed significantly. A bellow from an official brought a group of men striding into the ring, one of whom I recognized as the King. Several men waved to the crowd, but even more of them focused on the bull, assessing its temperament and condition. They assembled into a circle with the official and I saw movement. At first, I could not tell the purpose of these actions, but when they stepped back, I could see they all clutched small stones. One of them showed the official his stone with a sense of triumph. The official briefly compared his stone and another competitor's, but it became clear his selection was the largest and signaled he was to go first. With no further ceremony, the dance for the Kingship began.

A group of four Guardians stepped into the ring. Two stood at the bull's front and two at his back. I believed their charge was two-fold. They were to assure the animal was handled with care and also to serve as spotters for the competitors. When they reached their position, they turned in my direction. I could clearly see Drea and Adesha at the animal's rear. I also caught sight of Ianthe who stood on the far side of the bull. The closest Guard had her back to me. When she turned to the official to indicate their readiness I realized the fourth woman was Stava.

My heart leaped. In the same way I had *known* Nyssa would not be harmed by her interaction with the bull, I *knew* Stava was at risk. I was anguished to realize her potential danger. I wondered how I might interrupt and have her removed from the dance. If I had any influence as the Young Queen, this should be within my power. However, as I stood to walk into the Court, the *energy* around me *surged*. Adesha, Charis and Tam were aware of my intention to walk into the dancing. It was clear they believed this would put me in jeopardy. I had never before been constrained by the Guardians and I did not like what I felt as control over my actions. Before I could evaluate further, three Guards had stepped from behind my seat to my side.

"Young Queen," Adesha said, "it would be unwise for you to enter the Court at this time. How may we assist you?"

At the prospect of explaining why I was about to face down a bull, my courage failed and I sunk back into my seat. I could not find words to express my *knowing*. Adesha did not press me further, she and the others simply resumed their previous position. I was angry, but for now I thought I would have to content myself with trying to protect Stava energetically.

The first man's interaction with the bull was in such conspicuous contrast to the women before him that I wondered if he had been training at all. He ran rapidly, straight toward the animal and tried to leap toward its horns. Instead of allowing the man to do as he had done with the women, the bull caught the man mid-dash and flipped him high into the air. The would-be King spun once above the creature's head and then fell hard toward the Court floor. Drea caught him perfunctorily, with obvious distain, she helped him stand and walked him out of the enclosure.

The next candidate was the exact opposite of the first. He moved slowly toward the bull, never directly meeting its eye. Although I could not hear what he said, I could see that as he approached, he spoke gently to the animal. Once he got close enough, he reached out and scratched the bull's forelock. The creature butted him gently, and the man moved forward. My agitation eclipsed my curiosity, and I could not watch any more.

I closed my eyes. The Wise Ones had tried to teach me several protection incantations, and I struggled to recall one I might use to safeguard Stava. Finally remembering, I mumbled the words. Despite the invocation, I still had a strong sense of impending disaster. I kept my eyes shut and had only the crowd's responses to inform me of what was happening. There were gasps, shouts and even a few silences. Finally, a huge accolade arose from those assembled. I surmised the current dancer's performance was over, and he had been successful. I looked up to see this potential King acknowledging the crowd's recognition, but as another participant walked toward the enclosure, again, I could not look.

Most of the dancers followed without incident and I started to doubt the accuracy of my foreboding. I wondered how I could have been correct in one situation and wrong in another.

Suddenly, a collective gasp alerted me something was wrong. My eyes flew open, and I saw one of the competitors running from the bull. The creature chased him with speed and determination before catching him from behind. The bull lowered his head and, with his snout, lifted the man and flung him far above the ground. The would-be King landed a few steps in front of the animal which then ran forward trampling him. The pure power of the creature was now channeled into rage. I tried to envision what had happened to upset the previously cooperative bull.

Before I could get an impression of what had caused this transformation, the Guardians were in action. Adesha was first to get to the confrontation. She ran diagonally toward the angry animal waving her hands to distract him. Her diversion was successful, and the bull abandoned its previous target to chase her. I was amazed at how fast the huge animal was. When he began following Adesha, Ianthe and Drea sprung into motion. They sprinted toward the bloody, fallen man, scooped him from the ground and carried him to safety. Stava was only a heartbeat behind Adesha. She dashed diagonally between Adesha and the animal. The bull interrupted his charge just long enough for Adesha to vault over the rails of the enclosure. Having lost its target, the bull turned toward Stava, who ran toward the other side of the arena.

Having deposited the fallen competitor, Drea and Ianthe sprinted back to the ring. Adesha ran a few steps along its boundary then jumped into the enclosure and back into action. I thought the Guard's movements were more like a dance than anything else I had seen that day. The four women dove and spun near the bull's hoofs. They wove around the animal, synchronistically dashing before him, each creating a shield for the others in an amazing display of skill and daring. Drea, often more courageous than wise, ran so close to the bull that she had no place to retreat. The crowd gasped, but she coolly rolled between the animal's legs and sprung up on the other side to make another pass. The bull was beginning to tire. His charges were becoming shorter, and his rage was losing momentum.

Everyone had jumped to their feet to seek a better view, and I lost sight of the Guard's movements in the ring. I could hear the bull's snorts accompanied by the racing feet of women, but, despite my diligent efforts, I could not see the Guardians. The crowd gasped again. I could not see what had happened, but I heard the call of the Air Guardians.

"Guardians alert."

Swiftly, Adesha, Charis and Tam left the dais and moved through the crowd. Fear froze me in place. I *knew* it. I *knew* it every time anything happened to one of the Guards and this time I knew it was Stava.

Despite the press of the crowd, I *opened* my awareness. The Guard's energy seemed confused. The normally ordered communication channels of the Air Guardians *hummed* with conflicting messages. *The bull had escaped from the enclosure. Stava was hurt and Drea was down. No, Drea was up and apparently unharmed. The bull had been restrained. Stava was being carried back to the Guardians' Shelter.*

This was the incident that I had anticipated. It had caused me to contemplate facing down a bull to remove Stava from the enclosure. A small break in the crowd allowed me to see Stava being carried out of the ring toward the Guardians' Shelter.

Not knowing how badly Stava was hurt was unbearable. Without considering the consequences, I tried to think of a plan to get from the dais to the Guardians' Shelter. The Wise Ones had spent days trying to teach me to "shield," a complex system that blocked one's energy from the scrutiny of others. They seemed convinced a Queen would need to be able to protect herself from any possible intrusive actions. Although I was certain this was not the intent of their instruction, I thought I could now use this skill to get to Stava.

I drew all of my energy inward and began to back slowly off the dais. To my amazement, my shielding worked! Being focused on the activities in the Court, no one noticed my stealthy retreat. I moved slowly backward until I reached the hallway which adjoined the dais, and made a rapid dash toward the Guardians' Shelter. Only a few steps into my exit, I felt the now-familiar disorientation that my ritual clothing caused.

Determinedly, I stripped them off and left them on a bench outside the altar to the Sweet Girl Child.

Although nudity was not unusual in the Palace, I thought my shield would be easier to maintain with my body covered. To my left I saw a series of hooks that held cloaks for women's use when they visited the shrine. I grabbed a deep blue cloak and with a swirl, threw it over my shoulders, tying the laces as I continued toward the Guardians' Shelter.

I flew through the now-familiar maze of corridors and columns until I reached the Guardians' Court. There was no one on the Shelter's overhanging porch or in the Courtyard. I charged across the distance and into the darkness of the Guardians' space.

"Stava!" "Are you hurt?" I asked breathlessly before my eyes became accustomed to the dim light. I rushed into one of the large side rooms of the Shelter toward what I had previously decided was her cot.

I could just make her out, lying on the bed. My stomach lurched as I anticipated all of the ways she could have been hurt by the bull. To my surprise, she propped herself up on her elbows, and smiled at me roguishly.

"I only twisted my ankle. It feels better already." She said gazing down at her injured foot. I thought a lot of this response was bravado, but before I could reply she began again. "I am comforted to know you will come if I am injured," she admitted. Her eyes twinkled, conveying far more than her words alone. Quelling the emotions which accompanied her statement, she continued, "Maris will never allow a Guard to remain with the bull if she thinks a woman might be damaged in a way which would cause more injury. Despite my assurances that I was not badly hurt, she would not let me stay. She sent me to recuperate, and then let everyone else go back to the Court." She said these last words with a sigh.

"I think it's worse than you are admitting," I accused. "I could *feel* it when it happened."

"Could you now?" she smiled tantalizingly.

"Yes, I could." I replied. "The people on the dais must think I am quite the fool... rushing away with no warning."

"Can you feel me now?" she asked sending a *surge* of warm pleasure along with her words.

I wanted her. I did not care what consequences might come, I craved her. I stepped closer and I could feel what my closeness did to her. I could feel the heat flame in her. I *heard* her call me closer yet, even though no words were spoken.

With only the cloak from the Sweet Girl Child's altar covering me, my breasts were bare. I knelt beside her cot. I reached out and took her hand, placing it over one of my exposed breasts. We moaned simultaneously. This was no playful excitement. This was the full passion of a Hearth Queen for one of her own. I called her forth. I drew her strength into me, setting the cycle of energy that was in some ways more compelling to me than the physical experience. She was no victim of my desire. Her energy rose to connect with mine. She came forward to meet me, her power strong, sure and directed.

Dropping her hand from my breast, Stava reached for me and pulled me to her on the bed. I lifted my cloak, rested one knee next to her and swung my other knee over her, sitting astride her hips. She reached up, with both hands this time, and teased my nipples until they came erect.

I leaned down over her. My kiss hot, deep and fervent. My tongue found hers, and pulled it toward my mouth until it slipped between my lips. I cannot tell how long this kiss lasted, for to me that moment was forever. Although I was intent on continuing as we were, one of her hands left my breast, and she gently pushed me upright. There was a brief struggle with the fabric of my cloak. Eventually, her fingers found their way into the dampness beneath.

I had not been prepared for the intensity of her touch. Forgetting where we were, my head rocked back and I moaned urgently. Stava's hips rocked under mine and a rhythm began between us. This was all there was in the world. It was the world. The heartbeat of the universe rolled back and forth between us. I wanted to find the same place of excitement in her, to explore, to touch, to lick, but I could tell that pleasing me ignited her desire. Her passion rose along with mine, the energetic cycle linking us surged. I could no longer tell which

252

energy was hers and which was mine. I was lost, drowning in the waves of power and desire that flowed between us. I had not thought the *energy* between us could intensify, but with a swell it overtook my whole body. The *link* between us pulled her with me and we soared into ecstasy.

In my euphoric state I did not hear the words, but I did recognize shouting. Fauntee was in the doorway rushing toward us. I was dazed as Stava wrapped her arms around me, rolled me over the side of her cot and laid me gently on the floor. That same momentum carried her up and off the ground, onto her feet. She was fumbling among her belongings reaching for her sword. Fauntee was yelling, at Stava, at me. She was white with rage. Suddenly, I noticed Fauntee's sword was in her hand, and she was swinging it toward Stava. Stava was unsteady on her feet. Her injured ankle could not hold the weight of her body, but she parried the blow that Fauntee leveled at her.

I was so stunned I could not understand what was going on. However, reality soon dawned on me. They were not playing. They were fighting. They were fighting… over me. Fauntee's blows were raining down on Stava who, although at a distinct disadvantage, was managing to evade Fauntee's assault.

"*Stop!*" I *pushed* a strong inward signal toward both of them.

When that seemed to have no effect, I yelled in full voice and, with a determined mental touch, "*Stop now!*"

But, again they ignored me.

Guards began pouring in the door. The first ones in tried to grab Fauntee. She intercepted them, hitting Ianthe with the flat of her sword and sending her sprawling. Fauntee then lunged forward, again trying for Stava, and this time her slash connected. Blood seeped from Stava's arm, and the blow knocked her to the floor. Guards were everywhere now. Their training served them well as the group worked together with precise movements to stop Fauntee. Tam rolled under Fauntee's feet knocking her off balance. Charis grabbed Fauntee's sword as she fell. Three more Guardians pinned her to the ground and held her there in spite of her struggles.

Although I had been primarily cut off from her for several moons, I felt a strong *surge* of contact from Petra. Her *touch* held a question tempered by concern and incredulity. I was confused and frightened by what was happening. Without thinking, I *relayed* images to her of what had just occurred between Fauntee and Stava.

Blazing hot anger hit me like a blow. I had been trying to get up from the floor, but the strength of this fury knocked me back to the ground. I lost track of everything else as waves of rage engulfed me. I *was* the anger, pain and disappointment. There was no space between these feelings and me. However, gradually I was able to differentiate again between these overpowering emotions and myself. I identified Keto and several other women from Sacra's Council as the source. Some of the Wise Ones were furious that I had been so willful as to disrupt the peace of Malia. But, most devastating of all, I realized the disappointment came from Sacra.

19

I stood and waited for Sacra in the Fall Hall. In contrast to the turmoil of my emotions, the day outside was still. I could see through the columns that stood outside Sacra's rooms. No breeze lifted the leaves of any tree within sight. It seemed the whole of Malia, even the wind, was dispirited in response to the events of the day before.

The rest of yesterday had been awful. Without ceremony or permission, Karis scooped me up from the floor of the Guards' Shelter. Accompanied by several other Guards, she carried me back to my rooms. No one said anything. They did not accuse. They did not judge. They simply took me to my room, sat me on the beautiful bed, tapped their shoulders and were gone. For the first time since I had seen them at my fathers' lodge, they were truly not present in my mind. There was no underlying hum of contact from the Guards, or from anyone else in the Palace. I was frighteningly alone and could not discern whether this silence was deliberate or a consequence of my distress.

None of the women of my chamber were present. There was no one to ask for Council. There wasn't anyone to speak to at all. I threw myself down on the bed and cried. I did not need anyone else to berate me, that I could do on my own. How could I have been so willful? Why had I not heeded Sacra's warning about creating divisiveness among the Guards?

Along with these recriminations came concerns for which I had no answers. Was Stava all right? How badly was she injured? What would happen to Fauntee now? Each time another question emerged, a fresh torrent of tears followed. I don't know how long I sat like this. Eventually, I walked onto the terrace which adjoined my rooms. There I stayed, staring out at the distant sea, until long past sunset.

In the morning, my chamber was still hushed. Reya entered quietly and sat on the bed holding my hand without speaking for a long time. I began to sob. She moved closer to me and put her arm around my shoulder. I still could not *hear* very well. I believed she was sympathetic rather than angry, but without my normal perception I could not be certain.

Finally, she spoke. "Sacra wishes you to come to the Fall Hall."

So, I now stood in Sacra's sparse rooms waiting. Reya had walked with me to the door, smiled briefly, and was gone. When I entered the room Sacra was not there. I fidgeted while waiting, picking up first one of her possessions and then another, trying to distract myself. I was setting down one of her bracelets when she entered. She looked at me with such a mixture of emotions I could not discern how she felt about the previous day's events. I glanced at her, believing my mortification must be palpable. Sacra did not speak, and I did not know how to begin.

We stood like this, Sacra gazing intently at me while I looked mostly at the floor until she finally spoke.

"You must go. Take Alkes and go." Her tone was not angry, but exceptionally firm.

"What did you say?" I asked, thinking I must have misunderstood.

"You must go," she repeated. "It is not safe for you here. Maris and Hespar will guide you and Alkes into the mountains. There are people there who will welcome you. You must leave now... today."

When the impact of her statement hit me, I felt like I had been punched. Nausea overwhelmed me as I tried to think of some way to stay this command.

"Sacra," I began, "I..."

"Stop," she directed, putting up her hand and indicating with both voice and gesture that she was not willing to hear my reply.

Sacra continued her *contact* so strong it reached me even in my befuddled state. "You will *know* when to return. Do not attempt to come back until you *know* for a certain it is time. You must come to a decision if this is the life you want. If it is, when you return, you will be Hearth Queen. If you choose to come back, send Alkes to Malia, and people will come for you."

"Do you understand what I have said?" she asked, her *energy* so intense it bored through me like sunlight through mist. "Answer only yes or no," she directed.

"Yes... I think so," I replied and took a breath to continue.

"Then you must go now," she interrupted, pointing toward the door.

I continued to stare at her. My protests caught in my throat, and wracking sobs overtook me. For one brief moment, she looked at me with compassion. Then she turned her back and left the room.

Emotions overwhelmed me and I collapsed on the floor of the Fall Hall. Was this my punishment for disregarding her guidance? Was there any way for me to redeem myself? I rocked back and forth where I sat, unable to rise. It was Maris who eventually came for me. She sat beside me and gently put her arms around me and held me. I cried onto her shoulder, my tears staining her leathers. We sat like this, not speaking, until finally my gulping breaths abated.

"Are you ready?" she asked.

I looked at her quizzically and she continued, "Alkes and Hespar are waiting by the southern gate. Reya has packed the things you will need. We must leave now." There was urgency in her voice which did not seem to correlate with the current circumstance.

"Now?" was all I could choke out.

"Yes, Young Queen," Maris said evenly. "We must leave immediately."

I felt tears sting my eyes again, but I rose and followed Maris slowly out of the Fall Hall.

*****

It was the first time I had ever been in a place where I could not hear the sea. During our three-day journey, the four of us rode and walked, getting progressively higher with every step. The chill of the mountains seeped into my bones and my soul as we moved onward. I paid little attention to the land we traversed and asked no questions about where we were going. I walked, only watching where to put my feet so I would not stumble. The three Guards were solicitous, stopping when they thought I was tired, feeding me when I should have been hungry, and cutting soft fur branches for my bed at night.

But, I did not care. I could not find my way back from the dark place I had sunk into when we left Malia. Food was of little interest to me. Instead of sleeping, I lay silently for hours staring into the night sky. In truth, I could feel little of anything. The *knowledge* and *contact* which had buoyed and informed me only came in whispers now. The three Guards who accompanied me seemed miles away. Their concern washed around me like a leaf in a swift stream.

When we eventually reached our destination, I had no interest in the place of my exile. Several women escorted me with kindness to a small hut and arranged my modest belongings. They clucked over me like hens and bundled me into a soft down pallet which lay on the floor. I don't know how long I stayed like this. Women came and went. They brought me broth and stayed with me until I drank it. In time, I realized Alkes sat outside the door of my shelter almost every moment. This was what finally roused me. Alkes, who I could barely tolerate when I first encountered her at Malia, watched me ceaselessly. She crouched outside my door, monitoring who came into my space during the day and laying across the threshold at night. She inquired for my needs with caring, but without invasion.

Ultimately, it was concern for her which stirred me. Alkes was gaunt. Her previously hearty frame had dwindled until she looked like someone who had been taken by a fever. In time, I noticed her tender *call*. Several times a day she would *reach* for me. Never pushing and in no way demanding, she tried to establish *contact*. Eventually, I began to *hear* her. Quietly in the beginning, but with increasing focus over time, Alkes pulled me from my despair.

The first time I actually sent a *pulse* of communication back, she jumped to her feet and unceremoniously stuck her head into my hut.

"Young Queen," she said, her voice full of incredulity, her face filled with wonder. "You have come back."

I smiled at her faintly, and she jumped back away from the door. Through the narrow opening of my hut I could see her scuffing and cavorting. In time, I realized she was dancing. I laughed out loud which only sent her into fresh paroxysms of joy.

Day by day I recovered. Each morning I was a bit stronger and more myself. I could *hear* again. The *hum* from the people around me was different, but distinguishable. I *caught* a reoccurring theme of concern about the despondent stranger who languished in the village. Eventually, I realized it was me they worried about. Along with my apprehension about Alkes, this knowledge helped drive me from my melancholy and back into interacting with those around me.

My appetite returned along with my curiosity. After what seemed like an eternity of gloomy shadows, I ventured outside the small enclosure which had sheltered me in so many ways. Alkes lept to her feet. Her hand crossed her chest, and she tapped her shoulder just as if we were still in the Palace. Everywhere I went she followed like a faithful puppy. After her loyal vigil, I could not be angry with her despite her ubiquitous presence.

Once outside the shelter, I realized I was in the mountains. Previously, the peaks and valleys of these hills had always loomed as a distant presence, but I had never actually been among them. Now, I found myself surrounded in every direction by towering summits.

The view I had before was reversed. I could see the land below and beyond the sea, as if both were children's toys. The mountains loomed around me, giving me a sense of awe and mystery. Their face changed moment-to-moment. In the morning, mist often obscured the peaks from view. As the day wore on, this haze melted into smoky tendrils that hugged the tops of trees and lay delicately along the valleys. Some days these hilltops appeared as gray pinnacles, their presence ominous and portentous. At other times they soared above, full with hues of green and gold until they merged with the blue of the sky.

I was surprised to find the mountains were not as smooth as they appeared from a distance. They were instead cluttered with outcroppings and strewn with boulders. As I looked more closely, I realized some of the things I had taken for stones were moving. I thought about asking Alkes, my ever-present companion, what they were, but decided I could answer my own question by simply moving closer. When I did, I recognized they were sheep.

Sheep surrounded the small village on every side. Up and down each nearby slope and even into the valleys beyond, they grazed. Over time, I came to know these animals were at the center of most of the community's activities. They were watched, protected, utilized and treasured. Sheep were shorn. The wool was spun, woven and bartered. The resulting cloth was exchanged for both necessities and trinkets at the Palace and among trading vessels. Their meat provided a primary food source as well as another item for exchange with Malia and the ships.

The people of this encampment explained to me sheep required vigilance. They could fall victim to any hungry predator and had only a few instinctive behaviors upon which they could rely when confronted by danger. Their major reaction to a hazard was to huddle together and turn their backs to the threat. This created one mass with seemingly no beginning or end, and, in truth, it did seem to befuddle some predators.

I learned to participate in the patient observation of these animals from the men and women of the village. I enjoyed the unexpected peace and beauty I found in this activity. There was the amazing softness of young lambs when their conscientious mothers allowed me a touch. I laughed out loud to see the hilarious moments when these same small creatures began to practice jumping. At first, they would leap straight up into the air, only to land exactly where they had started with seeming amazement at their achievement. Sheep in movement resembled a river flowing. Even their bleating became part of the background of this place, their noise replacing the familiar sound of the sea.

As time went by, I came to a kind of tranquility and was finally able to ponder the questions I had held at bay for so long. When had Hespar and Maris left? What had my Council thought when suddenly I was gone without even a good-bye? These questions led me to more difficult ones for which I also had no answers. What had happened to Fauntee after her attack on Stava? Was Stava badly hurt? Ultimately, it occurred to me that Alkes might know some of the answers. I did not have far to go to find her. She was leaning against a nearby tree, in conversation with a villager. Alkes never traveled far from my side and frequently glanced in my direction. Watching them, I had little doubt their exchange was about sheep.

Indeed, Alkes did have some of the answers I sought. Maris and Hespar had left two days after we arrived. They thought it best not to disturb me with notice of their departure. Alkes did not know what, if anything, had happened to Fauntee. However, she did report that Stava had been only slightly injured. Despite my curiosity, I could not bring myself to ask other questions. I was comforted by the information Alkes had shared. I set aside my anxiety and tried to resume the soothing life I had cultivated among these mountain people.

The village itself comprised not more than several handfuls of huts, each of which held only a few inhabitants. The people themselves were unassuming and kind. I suspected if I had come to this place directly from my village I would not have found these mountain people unsophisticated. But, after my time at Malia, they seemed simple, their pursuits and activities confined to what seemed to me insignificant projects in which I had little interest.

The inhabitants of the community treated me, and by extension Alkes, like visiting dignitaries. No assurances from me could convince them that in this setting I held no particular standing. Despite my protests I found food was often delivered to my door, my clothes were regularly spirited away and returned clean, and I was not required to participate in any of the routine tasks of the village.

Conversely, they did look to me for other things. When someone was badly injured or seriously ill, they sent for me. Both men and women from the encampment came to me in search of guidance and solace. Unexpectedly, they petitioned me for healthy children, increased flocks and even love spells. Although I consistently repeated that I had no extraordinary talents or abilities, their perception of my capabilities did not alter.

Alkes, on the other hand, fit easily into the life of the community. Interacting with her in the Palace I had found her dull and obtuse. Conversely, the villagers viewed her with admiration. In this environment she was thought clever and adept. The Guardians had found her in a similar village and Alkes brought skills and expertise new to these people. Primary among them was the introduction of a donkey into the flocks. Donkeys and sheep had similar predators, but unlike the defenseless sheep, the donkey would bray and kick to defend itself. Consequently, the donkey protected the sheep and brayed out warnings of impending attack. Alkes also shared that a lamb wrapped in warn cloth soon after it was born could ward off the shaking sickness that took so many of these young creatures. Her knowledge created a demand for her skills among the villagers, and gradually she began to spend some time away from my side.

Despite the warmth of these simple people, I found that mountains are cold. I longed for conversation which extended beyond weather, children and sheep. Even sitting in darkness with the Wise Ones began to seem preferable to the tedium of mountain life. However, my desire to return to Malia did not bring any change. Life in the village continued as it had been. The end of summer came, signaling time for the harvest celebration and preparations for winter. The seasons turned with no contact and no reason for any hope of returning to the Palace. It was not until the first scent of spring was in the air that it happened.

20

Suddenly the space which had been silent for so long was filled with *communication* and disruption. The Air Guardians' alert rang out clearly even on the isolated mountain that had been my home now for several seasons. Alkes heard it too and ran quickly from a nearby field to my side. I clutched her hand, as she and I both felt the impact of the destruction.

There were the boats of Sea Raiders. There was fire. The Palace was ablaze. It burned in so many places it was impossible to fight. People streamed out of every exit... Following what we had been taught, in a crisis, move to open ground. There was the smell of the raiders as they sprung from hiding. All was chaos.

One and two at a time, the voices began to still.

Titaia, the mediator from the Queen's Council...gone.

Thais, the beekeeper...gone.

Temo, the Foundling...gone.

From my sweet Stava there was a burst of regret. Carried with it was the smell of smoke, the clang of swords and a surge of devotion. And then suddenly, that too was gone.

I could see the color drain from Alkes' face. She was my only constant during this unprecedented *knowing* of distant disaster. The messages of the Guards *swirled* around us, bringing only anguish. *Gone, gone, gone.* The people of my heart were being destroyed. Malia, the home of my spirit, was being razed. The truth was too brutal, the devastation too intense. I sunk to my knees, unable to bear the weight of the tragedy.

Suddenly, we were not alone. A translucent figure stood before me. She wore the ceremonial clothing of a Hearth Queen. I could never say for certain if it was Sacra or if it was one or all of the Queens of Malia. I jumped to my feet and moved toward her.

"Come home. It is safe now," was the only message. Then the figure wavered, faded and all was silence again. Alkes and I stood, abandoned and shaken on a distant mountain, far from Malia.

*****

"There is no other option," I almost yelled at Alkes. We had been going over the same ground since the appearance of the Hearth Queen earlier that day.

"I will not go without you," Alkes said resolutely crossing her arms over her chest and setting her jaw. Her stubborn refusal made me remember what I had thought of her when I first saw her at Malia. Over our time together in the mountains I had come to view her differently. But, now, she seemed to be the same dimwitted, obstinate dolt I had taken her for at first, and I was on the verge of losing my temper.

Finally I gathered enough composure to try and reason with her.

"Alkes," I began, "the last thing Sacra said to me was, 'When you know it is time to return, send Alkes to Malia." I could not tell if my words were having any effect, so I continued, "You must go. It is what Sacra instructed."

"I will not leave you," she replied, but her tone had changed slightly, revealing a hint of doubt.

"Alkes," I said more calmly and placed a hand on her shoulder, "the Queens have come to me. Did you see them?"

"No," she replied peevishly, apparently disheartened at her inability to share my perceptions.

"They told me to come home." I waited, taking a deep breath, hoping the weight of this statement would sink past her resistance. "And I won't be alone," I continued. "I'll be here with the people on the mountain. Isn't there someone you could designate to watch over me?"

"Watch over you..." Alkes repeated, her voice trailing off toward the end. She had the most annoying habit of repeating the last few words of sentences.

"Well, I guess Elan might do," she replied rubbing the back of her head. She then began a litany of all the acts of bravery and brilliance Elan had completed in the time we had been there. It was clear to me that Alkes had more than a passing interest in Elan. I was willing to listen to Alkes praises if they ended in a decision for her to return to Malia.

I waited none too patiently while her recitation continued. When Alkes paused to take a breath, I jumped in. "See," I interrupted. "Who could be better to look after me while you are gone?" Arguing with Alkes was like fighting when one person has a sword and the other has none. Fortunately in this instance, I was the one with the weapon.

"Hum," she replied after some thought, "I suppose I could trust Elan to make sure you are all right."

"Excellent," I answered, pushing on while I still had the advantage. "Then you must leave as soon as possible. Do you think you would be ready to go tomorrow?"

"Tomorrow?" she echoed, "no, I can go today." She said rising, the scent of sheep wafting from her.

At that precise moment I could have kissed her, but I thought that would only lead to more confusion.

"Really, Alkes? That's wonderful, simply wonderful. Can I help you pack?" I said jumping up and starting for her hut.

As she had promised, Alkes was ready to go soon after half-day. I walked with her along the path until it became clear she would make better time alone. When I turned back toward the village, she reached for me awkwardly and drew me toward her. Quietly, she whispered, "You must come to no harm, Giada. That is what Petra told me before we left. You must come to no harm." She repeated the words as if she had been instructed to memorize them. With this admission, she released me and began quickly making her way down the mountainside.

*****

There was nothing to do after she left but wait. I counted the days. It took us eight days to walk and ride from Malia to this settlement. Alkes would be traveling this distance on foot. I anticipated it might take her as long as a half-moon to reach the Palace and then a bit longer to return. I watched the moon grow bigger in the sky each night. I studied her as she shrank away to a tiny sliver and then returned again in the shape of a Guardian's bow. When the moon grew towards full once more, I watched for Alkes every day. I sat for hours on an outcropping that faced the path across the mountain below. The villagers believed I was watching sheep. I did not tell them otherwise.

I had been waiting all morning when one of the villagers came to me. He asked if I could help his young daughter who had been stung several times by bees. I rose reluctantly from my perch and followed him back to the encampment. The cure was not hard. I had scraped the stings with a sharp stone to remove the stingers, applied a poultice to her injuries and recommended dittany tea when I *heard* Alkes *call. She was on the mountain. She was nearly here.*

I jumped from the ground beside the girl's pallet and ran down the path toward where I believed she would arrive. Once I reached the edge of the small plateau where the village was nestled, I could see her. She was walking with great purpose toward the encampment. She was not alone. I could not make out whom she had brought with her. Squinting into the sun, I was only able to see the outline of a tall lean figure that came up the hill, easily keeping pace with Alkes.

I *sent* Alkes welcome, delight and pride. It was true. I was proud of her. After her initial reticence, she had taken on her duties with the determination characteristic of her single-mindedness. I waited impatiently until finally, I could stand it no more, and then plummeted down the path toward the two women.

It was Keto who met my eye as I climbed the last rise that separated me from the two of them. Keto, cheeks flushed from the climb, but the rest of her was pallid as an albino goat. She stopped abruptly in her ascent and Alkes almost ran into her. She stared at me, her *signal* silenced, her face inscrutable. After a time, she held out her hand.

I walked toward Keto with trepidation, well aware I had never been one of her favorites. She took my hand, dropped her head onto my shoulder and sobbed. I held her gently while she silently cried. The only indication I had of her tears was the spreading dampness on my tunic. As I looked over Keto's shoulder, Alkes caught my gaze. She shook her head and tenderly *sent* only one word... "*Sacra*."

When Keto's tears abated, she raised her head. With surprising reverence in her eyes, she croaked through a ragged breath, "I greet you, Giada, Hearth Queen of Malia."

*****

"It is in ruin?" I said as I sat with Keto and Alkes outside the hut which had become my home.

"I don't understand," I blurted. "What do you mean, it's in ruin?"

"It is in ruin..." Alkes repeated after me. My pleasure at her return faded as I was reminded of her annoying behaviors.

"There is very little left," Alkes replied as simply as if she were reporting the events of her day. My irritation with her obtuseness began to surface.

Keto looked up from the tea on which she was blowing and offered, "She means the Palace has been destroyed. Only a few things are salvageable."

Although I heard her words, I could not imagine Malia was gone. It was so immense. There were rooms, corridors, hallways, and Courts... workshops, granaries, and terraces. How could they all be gone? In the eerie way the women of Malia had of answering unspoken questions, Keto continued.

"The raiders set fires," her voice was flat. She reported the information with no emotion.

I could not bring myself to ask the other looming question. Where were the people? What had happened to the residents of Malia? For a moment, Keto looked up at me knowingly, and then her eyes fell back down to gaze vacantly at her cup.

"Some people remain," Alkes said, surprising me with her perceptive answer. "But, they are not at Malia."

"Then where are they?" I blurted, not being able to fathom the inhabitants of Malia abandoning the Palace. They had restored it after fire before. Within days of the earthquake, reconstruction was underway. I knew the people of Malia had been rebuilding the Palace for generations. Why would they abandon it now?

"Malia is no longer safe," Keto again answered my unspoken question. "When the raiders retreated, they abandoned several people who had been taken from the island as slaves. Each of them agrees. The Sea Raiders want our land and our women. They say the raiders plan to return again and again until we can no longer hold them off. It seems the raiders have done this many times and in many places before Malia. They create 'kingdoms' of their own that they rule with cruelty."

Anger and despair rose in me in equal measure. I had been taught all people were children of the Mother. It seemed impossible to reconcile this belief with the actions of these barbarians. How could we abandon Malia to them? I wished a plague to strike the Sea Raiders down or a great wave to carry them off.

For what I believed was the first time in our acquaintance, Keto looked at me with compassion and continued, "The Queen's Councils, what remains of both yours and Sacra's, have met. The Wise Ones have asked the sky and sea for omens, and the Guards have spent days devising defenses. Ultimately, they all have come to the same conclusion: we must move away from the sea to a place protected from the Raider's pillaging and from which we can see them coming."

I shook my head with disbelief and then lowered it into my hands. Alkes came to sit next to me. I knew it was her intention to be of comfort, but I was beyond consolation. After a time, she began to explain.

"The Guards have identified a location they believe will be secure. It is high in the mountains but still has a view of the sea. The people of the Palace are gathering what remains of their belongings and journeying there to build a new home. They wait for you, Giada."

Part of me was surprised by this declaration, but another piece of me already knew the truth of her statement. Despite the foolhardiness of beginning a trip at sunset, I was ready to leap up this moment and start a journey to them. In this instant, I knew myself to be Hearth Queen. It had been, and still was, my destiny to be Queen of Malia in whatever form it existed. These were my people and this was the work I was born to do. It did not matter if we were housed in a Palace or on a hillside, the people of Malia were still my responsibility. I had begun to plan our departure when suddenly I remembered Sacra had sent me away. I believed my impulsive behavior had put women at risk. Suddenly, I wasn't sure if the people of Malia would accept me.

"Will they consent to have me as Hearth Queen?" I blurted.

Both Keto and Alkes looked at me blankly. If the situation had not been so dire, I could have been amused by their confusion. When I tried to shield my thoughts, I was unsuccessful, but now, when I desperately wanted an answer, they were bewildered.

"Sacra sent me to the mountains because I created a disruption among the Guards," I clarified.

Keto actually laughed out loud. "Child," she said, "have you thought all along you were sent away because of your dalliance with a Guard?" She rocked backward on the log on which she sat and chortled to herself again.

With difficulty, Keto restrained her cackling and continued, "Despite warnings about the inherent problems, Hearth Queens have been bedding Guards for longer than anyone can remember. It is the stuff of which alliances are made and rogues are recognized."

"But, she seemed so angry," I countered.

"If she had not behaved as if she were angry, would you have listened to her and stayed in the mountains?" Keto questioned.

I pondered my response. The truth was, if I had not thought Sacra had been furious, I would have convinced Alkes to take me back long ago.

Without waiting for my answer, Keto continued, "Sacra sent you here so you would survive. The Wise Ones and even Sacra herself knew the Palace was at risk. We could not endanger you, Giada. You are the future of Malia."

21

The new mountaintop settlement of Malia did not look much different from the village of the sheep people. Huts which looked amazingly similar to those of the encampment from which I had just come were in various stages of completion on a small section of flat terrain high above the sea. Fires burned brightly around the village and people sat together enjoying their warmth.

What most distinguished these two communities was the new settlement's incongruous assortment of items which dotted the landscape. A giant vase which towered well above my head stood next to the most rudimentary of cooking spits. In another section, a beautiful frieze of the Sweet Girl Child hung precipitously on a ramshackle shelter. In the distance, I could see one of the magnificent bulls used for the dance of the King was tethered.

The people ran to greet us. At the Palace, I could not have begun to count the number of inhabitants. If I had put down a stone for every time I filled the fingers of both my hands, I know there would have been a huge pile before I was done. Now the people were few. I suspected it would be some time before I ascertained exactly how many of them there were.

The survivors' condition varied greatly. Some were injured. Kyma and Damaris, Healers from my Council and Sacra's, moved quickly around a makeshift infirmary. At first sight of them, I began to cry. I had feared that there would be no one to deal with medical concerns in the new village. If this were true, I feared for all of us and our ability to deal with sickness or injury. Knowing two experienced Healers remained was the beginning of hope.

Some of the people were physically unharmed, but spent their time staring off into the distance at nothing in particular. I recognized this malady because it mirrored my own previous melancholy. Many survivors had lost people of deep significance to them. They had mothers, siblings, partners, husbands or children who had all vanished with the violent attack by the Sea

Raiders. Some of them reported they repeatedly saw pictures of the carnage or heard the screams of their loved ones. I walked among them often, listening and providing what comfort I could.

A number of the villagers focused solely on work. They toiled from the moment they rose until exhaustion eventually overtook them. There was, of course, an abundance of things that needed to be done. Consequently, the diversion they used to escape confronting their issues was in plentiful supply.

A third group moved rapidly through many emotions. One day one of them would be angry, the next day the same person would be overwhelmingly sad. One survivor would act as if we would be returning to the Palace at any time, while yet another would spend almost all of the time at a makeshift altar petitioning various divinities.

Among these damaged people were Sacra's Guardians. Karis and Ianthe, Drea and Tam all remained. As a group, they looked worn and despondent. These surviving Guards had redoubled their vigilance. Two of them sat watch from sunrise to sunset, the other two throughout the night. With the arrival of Alkies there was now someone else to take a shift and she rotated in bringing reliance and reassurance. From the heights of the new village, a large expanse of land could be seen and, at a distance, the sea. Sitting so close that their shoulders almost touched, a pair of them could be found at all times staring down into the valley below.

Despite this encompassing duty, they were not idle. Drea and Tam made arrows by the handful. Tam carved and bound them while Drea spent her time fletching these projectiles with speed and skill. Drea counted their creations repeatedly, each time adding one or two more to her stockpile. Tam appeared to have lost all volition and simply took direction from whatever Guard was near.

In the evening when she should have been sleeping, Drea was most often sitting with Karis and Ianthe as they stoked blazing fires and placed in them the rudimentary beginnings of the traditional short sword of the Guards. Ianthe practiced with her bow until her fingers bled. Her shots were true, but she seemed never satisfied with her skill.

271

I sat with them many nights, listening to their loud silence and the things they could not say. Their nearness brought me comfort, and I believed my presence consoled them also. One-by-one, each of these women came to me and offered me her pledge as my Guardian.

Of them all, Karis seemed to be the most herself, and one night shortly after my arrival, I understood why. Asteria came to the fireside. I was so delighted to see her, I squealed like a child and almost knocked her over with my welcome. She was equally delighted to see me. We rocked in each other's embrace until we became aware the Guards were grinning at us. Asteria managed to look at them reproachfully and for a moment, everything was like it had been at the Palace.

My joy at seeing Asteria was boundless and with her came more wonderful news. I learned there were survivors who had not yet arrived at our hilltop sanctuary. They were still collecting anything salvageable from the Palace and foraging for other items we would need. She told me that other women from my Council and Sacra's were coming. Iva, the builder from my Council, was in the valley supervising the selection of timbers for our new dwellings. Sweet, brave Nyssa had been here, but had gone with Alkestis, the chronicler, to the ruins to unearth what they could of the library. Iole, the grower, and Khloe, one of the Wise Ones, were gathering herbs and seeds. With her report, I began to believe we had the people needed for a sustainable village.

I saw the first glimmer of hope among the Guardians when Thekia, the Peer of the Guard from Zakros, climbed the hill into the camp. Six other Guardians and a group of stragglers accompanied her. She revealed with sorrow that Aellai was gone and raiders occupied Zakros. A foraging party from Malia had found Thekia and her followers. They had told her of our encampment and she had led her group here. I believe Drea slept for the first time that night. Many of the other Guards' strange behaviors dwindled with the coming of these reinforcements. A few days after Thekia's arrival, I knew the Guardians were gathering. After a short time, Thekia came to find me.

She found me visiting with the injured, bringing them items newly retrieved from the Palace. She tapped her shoulder in greeting and in her unassuming manner, she asked to speak with me. One of the limitations of this new village was that I had no private space. Thekia saw me searching for a secluded place in which we could have a conversation.

She smiled knowingly and offered, "Perhaps we could walk."

I was glad of both her offer and her company. We had not gone far when she announced, "The Guardians have appointed me Peer of the Guard. I wanted you to be the first to know."

My life in the past few days had been as variable as a spring breeze. There was no consistency. I had been filled with both overwhelming joy and sorrow. I thought of how Thekia had responded to my *call* when we had first encountered each other in the central Court at Malia. For the first time since I had left the Palace, my desire surfaced, and I felt longing rise in my body. I could sense the recognizable pull of the *contact* I had come to know as the first *connection* with a Guard. I smiled at the knowledge, but put it away for another day. There would be time, I reminded myself as I glanced up at Thekia. I could tell she *knew*.

"We will work together well," I said in reply to her announcement, and I was aware she understood my statement might have more than one meaning. She did not retreat, but took my hand and placed it over her arm. Together, we walked back into the village.

The behavior of the Guards changed. In a few days I heard some of them laugh. What had *come* from them up to this point had been an indistinguishable mumble. Now, however, it emerged again into the strong *connection* I had previously known. I began to believe Thekia and I could create a sustainable community here in the mountains above the ruins of the Palace.

*****

It was time for the Remembrance. I was anxious about the ceremony. There were too many dead, too much loss. I was uncertain if I could be a part of the experience without breaking down, much less convening it. Subtly, people had asked when the remembrance for the dead would occur and I knew they were prompting me to schedule the rite. Despite my misgivings, as the moon grew toward full, I knew it was time.

The people assembled in a space that was becoming the central Court of the village. It lacked any of the splendor of the central Court at Malia, but it was an open space, capable of holding a group and a sizeable fire. The women who remained from my Council and Sacra's began a circle on my right while the Guardians circled to my left. The villagers completed the circle. The Guardians had already laid a large bonfire and at a nod from Thekia, Ianthe set a bright flaming arrow into its center. As the fire leapt into flame, I stepped forward.

Taking a deep breath I began, "There is no way to explain loss. The actions of the Crone are often unfathomable, but she too is a part of the cycle. Without her there can be no rebirth, no renewal, no return. For the ones who leave us, it is not difficult. It is those of us that remain here that mourn. With the smoke of this fire let us send our loved ones into the arms of the Mother. With each branch we burn let us release our sorrow, state our remembrances, and claim our memories."

With no hesitation Asteria came towards the fire and said, "I bring cypress the wood of divining, blessings and protection for the Wise Ones whose wisdom will be missed." As she spoke these words, she laid a supple branch on the growing flames. Many people came from around the circle speaking names and placing branches of their own. Thekia moved toward the fire slowly and leaned her offering against the pyre. "Reya," she murmured and gazed into the fire unmoving. I could see her shoulders shaking and I knew she was crying. I too had brought a branch for Reya so I stepped to Thekia's side and placed mine next to hers. I reached for her hand and we stood together feeling the heat of the fire. In time, we returned together to our places in the circle, but we were not the last to step away from the tribute to the Wise Ones.

While we waited Thekia had calmed and again she moved toward the fire to state her remembrance. "The branch I place is of strong, hard working oak for the Guardians lost." Moving back into the circle she closed her hand and tapped her shoulder in the Guardian's salute. Tam laid her branch for Hespar and Maris. I was surprised to see Iole's tears as she placed a bough for Fauntee. With great tenderness I walked again toward the fire and reached into the flames. I whispered Stava's name as I released my offering. I could not hold back my tears. There were so many gone. So many of my strong, beautiful Guardians who I would no longer see at practice, at play or at work. My tears turned into sobs. I could not move away from the fireside. This was the time for crying I counseled myself. When Drea spoke Petra's name there seemed to be no one in the circle whose eyes were dry or who did not carry an offering. So many people came forward with remembrances that many of them had to wait before placing their branches.

"I bring dittany for the Queens." Nyssa said simply as she placed a sprig of the herb on the fire. Spray after spray of dittany was piled on to the fire as people brought forward their remembrances. Those from Zakros spoke Aellai's name and the people of Malia invoked Sacra. The smoke became thick and pungent. Dancing among the smoke and flames I could see a shape. In the midst of the rising clouds a face faded and reemerged finally coalescing into form. I caught my breath as Sacra's figure emerged. We had called her and Sacra had come one last time.

The smoke formed her gown and some of the wood of the fire the Guardians had laid seemed to become her arms. Watching with amazement, I saw her presence turning to look at those of us in the circle. Gradually, her gaze moved to me. Her eyes were fire. They blazed with strength and intensity. I gazed at her with longing. For a moment we stared at each other and then the fire leaped from her eyes. I could feel it as it filled my heart and with it came so many emotions. In that moment I knew her, as I never had in life. With a final spark, the legacy of the Queens jumped from her. It hit me so hard that my knees buckled and I crumpled on the ground in front of the fire. This was her last bequest. A thing she could not pass to me in life because she had sent me away to safety, but as I drew in my next breath I knew I held a Queen's power.

*****

The new village began to fall into a semblance of order. Food was being prepared and there was enough for everyone. The Guardians had explored the mountain and its surroundings and had made well-reasoned plans for our security. Those who had been wounded were healing and beginning to resume their duties.

There was enough. Among the inhabitants there were sufficient skills that we did not lack long for anything. We had builders, growers, Wise Ones, and even artists to make beautiful things. Without the confines of the temple, the Wise Ones were forced into the life of the community. They proved to be most useful in many areas of village life. News came that a cave had been found nearby, and so spending time in darkness could start again. With a certain amount of chagrin, I admitted to myself I was looking forward to taking advantage of this discovery.

My life attained a cadence. As I had previously, I practiced with the Guards. I chanted with the Wise Ones. But, now, I spent time making sure I understood the community's needs. I anticipated problems and communicated regularly with Thekia. In this there was little effort. Our relationship was satisfying and together we achieved balance in this new space.

As days passed, the population of our village grew. People found their way to us, and those who had gone to gather supplies and forage returned. Among those who came back to our new mountain home was Iva, the builder from my Council. She came with timber and plans. The skills she had used at the Palace easily transferred to creating structures suitable for our new homes. She set about this task with determination and vision. The buildings were not as large or elaborate as those of the Palace, but they looked welcoming and secure in this environment.

She had been back for a time before I actually saw her. I had seen the evidence of her work. The makeshift infirmary was being replaced with a more suitable structure and there was an open sided shed going up where the Guards kept watch. I concluded she was working hard and decided I would find her instead of waiting for her to look for me.

I was not surprised to discover her, as I had before, shouting instructions to villagers who were at work erecting an altar. Her face filled with delight when she saw me.

"Giada," she called and left what she was doing to greet me.

"I'm so glad you're here," I said as we drew near each other. We hugged for a long moment and then stood awkwardly, not knowing what to say next.

When we did speak we both started together. "Giada," she said just as I uttered, "Iva." We both laughed which broke the tension. She called to the workers letting them know she would be back soon, and we wandered through the village. She excitedly showed me places where she thought the land would be suitable for different buildings. I watched her with wonder. Among all the people, she seemed unaffected by these new circumstances. She paused in her descriptions and looked at me in confusion.

"Are you not excited about creating our new home?" she asked in bewilderment.

"Iva," I answered, "Malia is lost. This place is only a pale refection."

"No, Giada," she replied in all seriousness. "*This* is Malia. Remember, I told you that from the moment I saw you, I knew you and I held the future of Malia. This *is* that Malia," she paused turning toward me and blocking my path."

"This is Malia," she repeated, waiting for her words to register. "Malia is not a Palace. Malia is not a place. It is the people. It is the ideals of our culture. It is where individuals live in harmony with each other and nature. It is where the Mother, the Sweet Girl Child, and the Ancient One lend their magic and show their power. No one can burn this down. No one can still its message. You and I, Giada, we make the future of Malia, and it will not be forgotten. Malia will live in us, in our children and their children. Our tales will travel with our progeny. There will be a story of a time when women were strong and men were kind. It will live in our bones. And, when we return, we will find each other again and recreate whatever we can of this truth. This knowledge will reappear to open our hearts and show a way for people to live. Giada, this *is* Malia."

Her words were like the sun breaking through the clouds after days of haze. The despair that had haunted me from the time Alkes and I had first stood in the village of the sheep people lifted. Iva had told me long ago she and I held the future of Malia, but I had not understood her words. I breathed in the air of this mountain in a different way. Our way of life would survive. It would be transformed from what it had been in the Palace, but it would not die. It would never die.

I felt my heart open, and I looked at Iva with wonder. "This is Malia," I repeated for the first time, but I knew I would say it over and over in my days as Hearth Queen. The Queens after me would repeat it as well, for there would always be Hearth Queens and the Guardians would recognize them. And, the Queens would recognize the Guardians. The cycle would not stop. Into every place and in every time we would be born, bringing with us knowledge and power that neither raiders, nor disaster, could quell.

*****

I sat alone on a hillside which overlooked the remains of the Palace and beyond it, the sea. If I listened closely I could just hear its rhythm. It was the sound of my childhood, the sound of the Palace. But, a new resonance had taken its place. The stillness of the mountain echoed in synchronicity with my heartbeat. I breathed it in along with the crisp mountain air. For a few moments, I had stolen away from my duties, even slipping away from Keto. In a fascinating turn of events, Keto was now devoted to me. I knew she did not love me as she had Sacra, but her consideration and fondness filled my days. She did all within her power to expedite my responsibilities.

Behind me the people of Malia built their new life. Necessities were being supplied and even a few pleasures were beginning to find their way to us. The Guards had brought a new Foundling and, indeed, I knew her to be one of them. She had made her pledge to me, and Thekia had taken her oath. I knew in time more would come. I could *hear* the buzz of purpose and order that came from their new shelter. Their dedication and constancy still filled my heart with wonder.

I heard a noise and turned to see Asteria moving toward me. When she came within a comfortable distance for speaking she asked, "May I disturb you?"

"You are not a disturbance," I replied. I could tell from her behavior she had something to share with me. My friendship with Asteria had continued to grow in this new setting, and I relied on her for Council and insight.

"I have something for you," she said, holding out a box. "I have been waiting until it was the right time. I felt this token should hold promise, not grief. I know our sorrow will never truly be over, but I see in you now the hope of tomorrow."

With these words she handed me the box and nodded to indicate I should open it. I lifted its lid slowly, with both curiosity and care. Inside were the scraps of a Hearth Queen's ceremonial clothes. They were tattered; the edges scorched, but there was enough fabric to begin the skirt of a dress.

"Asteria," I began, but so many emotions overtook me I had to sort them out before I could speak.

"Where did..." I began but I realized that was not what I wanted to know, and I started again. "How did you find this and manage to bring it here?" was the question I was finally able to formulate.

She took a deep breath, looked at me earnestly, and began, "Everyone was running from the Palace. I was among them. I tripped and fell. The press was so strong I feared I would not be able to regain my footing, but suddenly there was a *command* so strong that the people around me parted. Sacra stepped into the opening and pulled me to my feet."

"This is what she said: 'I knew I would find you somewhere. I did not, however, expect it to be here on the ground.'"

"I was surprised at her humor during such a dire time, but in a moment she became serious."

"You must take this," she directed, holding out this box to me. "Promise me you will give it to Giada. She will know what to do with its contents."

"But," I started to protest. I was about to tell her I was sure she would be able to deliver it herself. I felt certain she had no need to entrust it to me, but she stopped me.

"Child," she said, "I know you will be with Giada again, just as I know I will not. Pledge to me you will give her the box and this message."

I looked at Sacra, but tears blurred my vision. "Pledge to me," she repeated.

"Yes," I said, "I will."

"Tell her I have always loved her," Sacra said fighting back tears herself. "Tell her I will keep my promise. She will never be alone."

I was too amazed to speak. Asteria came and sat beside me. Her story told, she was now also silent. I reached into the box and hesitantly laid my hand on the frayed fabric. A whisper of the ancient Hearth Queens floated toward me. Among them, I recognized Sacra.

After a time she said, "I have never understood the significance of what was in the box. Why would a collection of scorched fabric be of such importance?"

"It is a piece of the ceremonial dress of a Hearth Queen," I replied. "Sacra made my ritual clothes herself. She incorporated pieces of her dress into it and also some from the gown of Adonia who was Hearth Queen before her. She did not know how long this custom had been observed, but each Hearth Queen's dress included pieces of the Queen's garments before her. This is part of one of those dresses." As I said this, I held out the fabric to Asteria. She touched it reverently and then said, "Come then, we must begin."

I looked at her without comprehension. "We must make you a dress," she said simply.

She and I stood. Arm-in-arm, we walked together toward Malia.